After World War II aı *of Germany, Allied milit*
discover the penetrating depth of the Nazi regime's state secrets. The world's best intelligence organization was not the least of these revelations. Also discovered were massive and meticulous research files on secret socieites, eugenics and other scientific pursuits that boggled the imagination of the Allied command. Even more spectacular was an entire web of underground rocket and flying saucer factories with accompanying technology that still defies ordinary beliefs. A missing U boat fleet possessing the most advanced submarine technology in the world left many wondering if the Nazis had escaped with yet more secrets or even with Hitler himself.

Behind all of these mysteries was an even deeper element: a secret order known to iniates as the Order of the Black Sun, an organization so feared that it is now illegal to even print their symbols and insignia in modern Germany. **The Black Sun** probes deeper into the secrets of the Third Reich and its Tibetan contacts than any other previous attempt. Author Peter Moon ties all of these strange associations to Montauk Point, where an American military facility was used by the Nazis to further their own strange experiments and continue the agenda of the Third Reich.

For those who are familiar with the previous books in the Montauk Series, **The Black Sun** will expand your understanding of the strange forces at work at Montauk. For those who are new to this subject, **The Black Sun** recaps the earlier books and carries you right into the thick of it.

You will never look at the world the same way again.

✦

Cover art: The Temple of The Black Sun

Artist's conception of the blue skinned Oracle of Tibet reclining on the Ark of the Covenant as he communes with the cherubic energies contained within. In the background, a German U-boat bearing the flag of the Vril Society attempts to penetrate the threshold of the Inner Earth through the fabled Gates of Thule.

VRIL-ODIN

A German flying craft known as a Vril-7. It a two level model that
was photographed in April 1945. Underneath the craft
are Donar ray guns which are more clearly
visible in the original photograph.

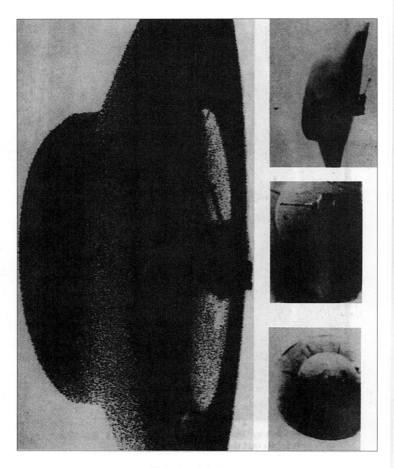

HAUNEBU II

The Germans developed different flying craft prior to and during
World War II. Above is an early version of the Haunebu II
model. More pictures and further details of the
German saucer program are included
elsewhere in this book.

THE BLACK SUN

MONTAUK'S NAZI-TIBETAN CONNECTION

PETER MOON

ILLUSTRATED BY NINA HELMS

SkyBooks
NEW YORK

The Black Sun: Montauk's Nazi-Tibetan Connection
Copyright © 1997 by Peter Moon
First printing, May 1997

Cover art and illustrations by Nina Helms
Typography and book design by Creative Circle Inc.
Editorial Consultants: Althea Carlson, Nina Helms
Published by: Sky Books
              Box 769
              Westbury, New York 11590

Library of Congress Cataloging-in-Publication Data

Moon, Peter
        The Black Sun: Montauk's Nazi-Tibetan Connection
by Peter Moon
        302 pages, illustrated
        ISBN 0-9631889-4-1
1. Nazis 2. Occult 3. Montauk
Library of Congress Catalog Card Number 96-071798

This book is dedicated to

Sam Arcuri

October 8, 1925 — March 30, 1995
and his surviving family: Vivian, Greg and Jeff.
Thank you for all the memories of a
childhood filled with wonder.

CONTENTS

PRELUDE • 13

INTRODUCTION • 25

ONE • Montauk – A Nazi Rendezvous 29

TWO • An Inside Connection 39

THREE • The Cameron Connection 45

FOUR • The Cameron Lineage 55

FIVE • The Kennedy Connection 59

SIX • Teutonic Heritage 67

SEVEN • The House of Orange 75

EIGHT • Lion Gardiner & the Witch 81

NINE • Project Paperclip & the Hamills 85

TEN • The German Connection 91

ELEVEN • The Secret of Judah 97

TWELVE • Dr. Felix 105

THIRTEEN • The Fuhrer 111

FOURTEEN • Hitler Alive! 115

FIFTEEN • Reich Leaders Escape 121

SIXTEEN • Otto Skorzeny 129

SEVENTEEN • The Arab Connection 137

EIGHTEEN • The Mysterious Origins of Thorn
E.M.I. 147

NINETEEN • Thule 151

TWENTY • The Power of Vril 163

TWENTY-ONE • The Vril Saucers 169

TWENTY-TWO • The Brookhaven Connection 185

TWENTY-THREE • In the Aftermath of War 189

TWENTY-FOUR • Neuschwabenland 197

TWENTY-FIVE • The OSS in Tibet 203

TWENTY-SIX • The SS in Tibet 209

TWENTY-SEVEN • The Tibetan Connection 213

TWENTY-EIGHT • The Bon Religion 219

TWENTY-NINE • The Mon 231

THIRTY • The Shensi Pyramids 237

THIRTY-ONE • The Ark 241

THIRTY-TWO • White Gold & Occultum 249

THIRTY-THREE • The Blue Race 257

THIRTY-FOUR • The Curse of the Mummy   261

THIRTY-FIVE • Crowley 267

EPILOGUE • 275

PRELUDE

For those who are not familiar with the Montauk Project and the three previous books written on the subject, this prelude is designed to familiarize you with the story line of the entire series so that you may readily grasp the entire contents of the present book. For those who are already familiar with the Montauk saga, this information will serve to reorient you to the various subjects involved in this mammoth plot. I have also included herein information of events that have transpired since the writing of the last book.

The Montauk Project: Experiments in Time was released in June of 1992 and was a concise and summarized briefing on one of the most amazing and secretive research projects in recorded history. Colloquially known as the Montauk Project, the origins of this bizarre operation date back to 1943 when invisibility experiments were conducted aboard the *USS Eldridge*, a newly built destroyer escort. As the *Eldridge* was stationed at the Philadelphia Navy Yard, the events concerning the ship have commonly been referred to as the "Philadelphia Experiment". The objective of this experiment was to make the ship undetectable to radar and while that was achieved, there was a totally unexpected and drastic side effect. The ship became invisible to the naked eye and was removed from time and space as we know it. Although this was a remarkable breakthrough in terms of technology, it was a catastrophe to the people involved. Sailors had been transported out of this dimension and returned in a state of complete mental disorientation and horror. Some were even planted into the bulkhead of the ship itself. Those who survived were discharged as "mentally unfit" or otherwise discredited and the entire affair was covered up.

After the war, research continued under the tutelage of Dr. John von Neumann who had directed the technical aspects of the Philadelphia Experiment. His new orders were to find out what made the mind of man tick and why people could not be subjected to interdimensional phenomena without disaster. A massive human factor study was begun at Brookhaven National Laboratories on Long Island, New York. Brookhaven Labs got its start after World War II as the first major atomic research facility in the world. Prior to the war, the immediate area had served as the headquarters for the largest contingent of Nazis in the United States. They were known as the Bund.

John von Neumann was a logical choice to head up this new project at Brookhaven. Not only was he the inventor of the modern computer and a mathematical genius in his own right, he was able to draw on the enormous resources of the military industrial complex. These included the vast data base of Nazi psychological research acquired by the Allies after World War II. It was against this background that von Neumann attempted to couple computer technology with sophisticated radio equipment in an attempt to link people's minds with machines. Over time, his efforts were quite successful. After years of empirical experimentation, human thoughts could eventually be received by esoteric crystal radio receivers and relayed into a computer which could store the thoughts in terms of information bits. This thought pattern could in turn be displayed on a computer screen and printed out on a piece of paper. These principles were developed and the techniques were enhanced until a virtual mind reading machine was constructed. At the same time, technology was developed so that a psychic could think a thought which could be transmitted out a computer and potentially affect the mind of another human being. Ultimately, the Montauk Project obtained a superior understanding of how the mind functions and achieved the sinister potential for mind control. A full report was made to Congress who in turn ordered the project to be disbanded, at least in part for fear of having their own minds controlled.

Private concerns that helped to develop the project did not follow the dictate of Congress and sought out to seduce the military with the idea that this technology could be used in warfare to control enemy minds. A secret group with deep financial resources and some sort of military tie decided they would establish a new research facility at Camp Hero, a derelict Air Force Station at Montauk Point, New York. This locale was chosen because it housed a huge Sage radar antenna that emitted a frequency of approximately 400-425 Megahertz, coincidentally the same band used to enter the consciousness of the human mind. In the late '60s, the reactivation of Camp Hero began despite no funding from the military. By 1972, the Montauk Project was fully underway with massive mind control experimentation being undertaken upon humans, animals and other forms of consciousness that were deemed to exist.

Over the years, the Montauk researchers perfected their mind control techniques and continued to delve further into the far reaches of human potential. By developing the psychic abilities of different personnel, it eventually got to the point where a psychic's thoughts could be amplified with hardware and illusions could be manifested both subjectively and objectively. This included the virtual creation of matter. All of this was unparalleled in the history of what we call "ordinary human experience" but the people who ran the Montauk Project were not about to stop. They would reach even further into the realm of the extraordinary. Once it was discovered that a psychic could manifest matter, it was observed that the manifestation could appear at different times, depending upon what the psychic was thinking. Thus, what would happen if a psychic thought of a book but thought of it appearing yesterday? It was this line of thinking and experimentation which led to the idea that one could bend time itself. After years of empirical research, time portals were opened with massive and outrageous experiments being conducted. The Montauk Project eventually came to a bizarre climax with a time vortex being opened back to 1943 and the original Philadelphia Experiment.

None of this information would have come to light except for Preston Nichols, an electronic genius who one day discovered that he was an unwitting victim of the experiments. Working for a Long Island defense contractor, Preston was researching telepathy in psychics and found that persistent radio waves were being transmitted which were blocking the people he was working with. As a radio and electronics expert, Preston traced the radio signals directly to the Montauk Air Force Station and began exhaustive research that lasted over a decade. He acquired much of the equipment that was used during the Montauk Project and discovered to his dismay that many people from Montauk remembered him working there. It came to a culmination point when his cousin's husband insisted that he had been at Montauk. The two men almost came to blows over Preston's contention that he had never been at Montauk. Shortly after this argument, Preston began to get glimmers of a life he'd not previously been aware of. After talking to many different scientists and engineers who had some sort of association with the Montauk Project, Preston was able to put together what had happened. Somehow, he had survived on two separate time lines. On one, he worked at Montauk; on the other, he worked at a different location.

Preston's discoveries were confirmed when a strange man by the name of Duncan Cameron appeared at his door in 1985. Duncan had an uncanny aptitude for psychic research and claimed to have been trained in this field by the NSA (National Security Agency). Without mentioning his own ordeal with Montauk, Preston took Duncan out to Montauk and was surprised to discover that he knew the entire layout of the base and remembered working there. Duncan was considered to be the primary psychic used in the time travel experiments and also remembered having been aboard the *U.S.S. Eldridge* during the original Philadelphia Experiment with his brother Edward (now recognized as Al Bielek).

According to the accounts of both Preston and Duncan, the Montauk Project culminated on August 12, 1983. A full blown time portal was fully functioning, but things were out of control and Duncan called together a group of people and decided to crash the project. While sitting in the Montauk Chair (a device connected to esoteric radio receivers studded with crystals that sent thoughts out of a giant transmitter), Duncan unleashed a giant beast from his subconscious which literally destroyed the project. The people who had been working on the base suddenly abandoned it. The air shafts and entrances to the major underground facility beneath the base were subsequently filled with cement. The full circumstances behind all of this remain a mystery to this day.

Although an unauthorized video was distributed regarding this story and several lectures had been given on the Montauk Project, no book was forthcoming on the subject. Different writers had attempted to undertake the task but were either mentally incapable of dealing with the subject or were frightened off one way or the other. One science reporter for the *New York Times* started the project but backed off when he discovered to his own surprise that the Montauk Project was indeed quite real.

I came upon Preston while researching an elaborate sound system he had invented and soon found myself listening to a spectacular story that was at least better science fiction than I'd ever heard. After several months, I decided to undertake writing *The Montauk Project: Experiments in Time*. That book was written without consulting anyone other than Preston (who wanted to protect his sources). Rather than do a costly and time consuming investigation, my strategy was to get the information out as fast as possible and use the book to gather other clues that would corroborate or eventually prove the existence of this incredible story.

As *The Montauk Project* was published, further research and events continued that would indeed establish that there was a real scenario behind the wild information Preston was talking about. These were chronicled in our second book, *Montauk Revisited: Adventures in Synchronicity*, but the most spectacular of all these corroborations was the discovery that the Montauk Project was inextricably linked to the most infamous occultist of all time: Aleister Crowley, often described as "the wickedest man in the world". According to reports, Crowley himself had used the practice of sexual magick in order to manipulate time itself, communicate with disembodied entities and to travel interdimensionally. It was even suggested that the the Philadelphia Experiment itself could have been the outward expression of Crowley's secret magical operations.

The startling proof of Crowley's association developed over a long period of time, but the discovery began to take shape in my very first conversation with Preston when he seemed to blurt out of the blue that he was connected to the magician Aleister Crowley. In an earlier life, he believed that both himself and Duncan had been Preston and Marcus Wilson, respectively. These brothers were twins and had been the first manufacturers of scientific instruments in Great Britain. In addition to being friends of Aleister Crowley's family, they had also been involved in a joint business enterprise with them.

17

All of the above sounded like one more wild story, so I began to look for any references to the Wilsons in Aleister Crowley's various books. None turned up. To my surprise though, I discovered that not only had Crowley visited Montauk (in 1918) but he had mentioned a "Duncan Cameron" in his autobiography. Subsequent to this, numerous instances of synchronicity between the Cameron and Crowley families were discovered, (these are detailed in *Montauk Revisited)*, but I still could not find any references to the Wilson brothers.

The meaning of these various synchronicities (between the Cameron name and Crowley) began to be explained when I found out about a woman who called herself "Cameron". She is perhaps most famous for having been married to Jack Parsons, the world's first solid fuel rocket scientist and a disciple of Crowley. Together, they had participated in an interdimensional activity known as the Babalon Working (a ceremonial act which included sex magick and has been hailed by some as the greatest magical act of the century).

Through a further series of incredible synchronicities, I flew to Southern California on other business and met one of Cameron's friends quite by "accident". Soon discovering that she lived in West Hollywood, I suddenly found myself telling her in person about the Philadelphia Experiment, the Montauk Project, and the Crowley/Cameron relationship. To my surprise, she informed me that her real name wasn't Cameron at all. It was Wilson!

It now became obvious that Preston's story about being a Wilson could not be discounted nor could his general credibility be denied. Perhaps more importantly, it revealed that some very strange correspondences were at work that had to do with interdimensionality.

I would receive an astonishing letter several months later that would close the case as regards whether or not the Wilson brothers had existed. It was from a man named Amado Crowley who claimed to be an illegitimate son of Aleister Crowley. Not only did he remember his father talking about the Wilson brothers, but he also provided clues which revealed that the odds of his lying about his parentage were nil.

Amado not only verified the existence of the Wilson brothers, he gave a spectacular account of his father's whereabouts on

August 12, 1943 (the day of the Philadelphia Experiment). Aleister had directed a magical ceremony at Men-an-Tol in Cornwall, England where a large donut style rock lays upright in the water. According to Amado, Aleister put him through the hole in the rock whereupon a line of rough water ran from the coast of England to Long Island, New York. In ancient times, a stone like Men-an-Tol was utilized in a ritual such as this in order to invoke the goddess. Obviously, a major occult correspondence was at work.

As *Montauk Revisited* went to press, another astonishing discovery was made. A photograph from the turn of the century turned up and revealed that ancient pyramids had once existed at Montauk Point. Further investigation revealed that Camp Hero, the name of the base where the Montauk Project took place, was located on sacred native American ground that rightfully belonged to the Montauks or Montaukets, the ancient ruling tribe of Long Island. Unfortunately for the Montauks, a New York State court had declared their tribe legally extinct in what some legal experts call the most flagrant case of injustice in the history of Native American relations. In a further instance of synchronicity, it was revealed that the family name of the Montauks' royal family is Pharoah.

The above information was included in the third book of the series, *Pyramids of Montauk*. Further connections were made evident between the Pharoahs of Montauk and the Pharaohs of Egypt. A deeper examinat on of Aleister Crowley's writings and the science of sacred geometry revealed Montauk Point to be an ancient grid point rivaling Stonehenge, the pyramids of Giza or the like. It was through Montauk that the project operators sought to control the evolutionary "computer program" of planet Earth in an attempt to influence how people and other life forms think, feel and develop. This "computer system" of evolution is identified as the morphogenetic grid, an ever changing and adapting program of birth, growth, death and consequent recycling of the life force. It is this grid of evolution that certain mystery traditions seek to control. Many factions vie for the lead role in this quest to dominate. Evidence of clandestine operations at Montauk has since been demonstrated beyond that shadow of a doubt. Not only has there been testimony from personnel who participated in the project, but strange and sometimes illegal radio transmissions have been proven to emanate from Montauk Point. The local media on Long Island refuses to investigate the matter.

The release of *Pyramids of Montauk* brought forth world wide recognition of the plight of the Montauks. It was hoped by myself that public outrage would start the wheels in motion so that Montauk Point would be restored to its rightful owners. While some progress has been made, there is an unfortunate situation within the tribe itself. There are two rival factions which do not agree with each other and at this writing, there is not a unified front. This has hampered the legality of the Montauks applying for legal recognition because the government is not going to recognize both parties. This is a very complicated scenario which I cannot become personally involved in as it is a tribal matter. The entire scene is further aggravated by political scandals and upheavals in Suffolk County and East Hampton, the county and town in which Montauk is located.

One of these scandals occurred when Robert Cooper, a Montauk tribal leader and East Hampton Town Councilman, was attacked in the press and sued for defamation of character. The lawsuit was from Tom Scott, the local police commissioner. Although Cooper had only requested that allegations against the police force at Montauk be "looked into", Scott ignited a huge legal battle which cost the town of East Hampton a fortune in legal bills. After a mammoth attack on Cooper, Scott finally dropped the case as he had no chance of winning it. The details of this case were covered in *The Montauk Pulse* newsletter.

Further evidence of scandalous behavior concerning Montauk was relayed to me by a court officer who had personal knowledge of the Cooper case. This person reported that during the legal battle, a state judge requested the District Attorney of Suffolk County, James Catterson, Jr., to conduct an official investigation to determine whether police abuse existed in in the East Hampton police force. The investigation was a white wash, according to the court officer, with no police abuse being found. Of course, this turned out not to be the case. The police abuse was later proven and reported on in detail in the local press. Separate investigation of my own revealed some very interesting information on the official who "whitewashed" the investigation on behalf of the District Attorney. He is known for having previously stored business papers on the "derelict" Montauk Air Force Station. The irony was very bizarre.

District Attorney Catterson got into the act once again when he arrested John Ford, the founder and president of the Long Island UFO Network. John had visited me in March 1996 as he was planning to write a book that included considerable inside information on the Long Island defense industry and dubious political connections. A retired court officer (and not the same court officer who informed me of the above investigation), John Ford has a long standing reputation as a law abiding individual who uses the court system to right injustices. He is also a meticulous researcher who covers all bases. In June, John was arrested for allegedly conspiring to kill three Suffolk County executives by sneaking radium into their toothpaste. The New York media and Long Island newspapers covered the arrest with gala coverage despite the ridiculous nature of the charge. It was even stated in some news reports that experts had determined that radium in such doses is not lethal and might take several years to have any effect, if any. Ford was also charged with possession of illegal weapons but this was dropped as there was no evidence.

The information on the alleged conspiracy of John Ford came from "inside information" that has yet to be substantiated in a court of law. The search warrant itself was dated after the search of John Ford's premises where cans of radium were found and seized. Those who know Ford say he uses radium from time to time to calibrate his Geiger counter. Apparently, the entire arrest was a set up by a "friend" who asked Ford to move some radium cans. The "friend", who just happens to work for the navy, was also arrested as part of the conspiracy.

From June of 1996 to at least April of 1997, John Ford has languished in jail without a trial. Almost a year since the arrest, there is currently no news coverage or any light seen at the end of the tunnel. I mention his case not only to give the matter international attention so that it might be resolved but to demonstrate the contentious behavior of the political climate around Montauk.

In the wake of all this, Long Island experienced the horrible tragedy of TWA Flight 800 where hundreds of individuals died as the result of an unexplained in-flight mishap. Although many theories have been put forward, the media refuses to seriously investigate the most probable cause of the situation: a particle beam emitted from a Brookhaven Labs facility which activated a nuclear missile. According to sources in the intelligence community, military exercises were being conducted off the coast of Long Island when a low flying missile was emitted from a flying craft. This heat seeking missile was in fact a deactivated nuclear war- head being used for drill purposes only. As part of the drill, the deactivated missile was pursuing a heat generating target tailing a C-130 plane. When the heat generating target malfunctioned, the missile inadvertently sought out the closest heat generating source: TWA Flight 800. As it was designed to do, the missile circled the plane. At the same time, a particle beam emitted directly from either Brookhaven or a S.D.I. (Strategic Defense Inititative or "Star Wars") satellite, activated the bomb. The rest is history. Although the intelligence sources have officially requested that I identify the above theory as a "rumor", I do not doubt they are far off at all. The fact that the media has refused to even mention the possibility of a particle accelerator being involved is a sheer indicator that it was.

All of the above tells us that the political situation on Long Island is very hot. There are a trail of dead bodies from the crash and many of them are French. I have spoken to the French press about Flight 800 and they have interviewed Preston Nichols in more detail about the matter. I do not know what the French printed but people are slowly beginning to learn the truth.

The situation concerning Montauk itself is equally volatile. A political consultant who works for Bill Clinton told me that Montauk is the hottest political football in America. Between the mind control potential and the rights of the Native Montauks, this consultant said everyone is watching Montauk but no one is saying anything. As the electronic anomalies concerning mind control can be easily verified, members of Congress have no choice but to take whole matter very seriously. The Montauks' right to their sacred land is a straight forward case. Everyone in political control zones is on edge. This "edginess" can be viewed quite readily in the U.S. military, who took considerable heat for their alleged role in the downing of TWA Flight 800.

In early 1997, we saw a few close encounters between commercial airliners and military fighter planes. Intelligence sources inform me that these close calls were purposely provoked by the military so that their own air space would be more clearly defined. No one was injured but commercial pilots were made uneasy and forced to maneuver out of harms way. The explosion of Flight 800 was apparently a result of a vague delineation of the military's right to access the air. If the particle beam was emitted on purpose, the military could have been set up. It is also possible that the nuclear transmission was some sort of accident. In any case, the military wants to distance itself from any more such incidents because they do not claim to be responsible for what happened. There is a mysterious variable at work in this entire equation which most likely comes from C-130.

The above scenario betrays an entire breakdown in the power politics of the United States. It used to be, more or less, one united front that stood against Russia or the perceived enemy of the day. Today, we have unmarked black helicopters, U.N. peace keeping forces and upstart militias that threaten the sovereignty of the central government as we have previously known it. Many factions within the military, intelligence and political communities are all vying for dominance. There are forces in American politics who want the Constitution to be trashed. The military, who derive their legally appointed power from the Constitution, do not want to be dismantled and replaced by a United Nations peace keeping militia. The subject becomes rather complex and could warrant a book in its own right. The point here, and as was made in *The Montauk Project*, is that the powers behind the operation at Montauk were not operating within the legal laws of the United States or the martial laws of the military. They are a rogue group who infiltrate and use whatever institution or group they can get their hands on. In order to understand this group and the source of its power, we need to undercut the obvious, for if we stand up and rail against it, it can surely destroy us.

It is with this last thought in mind that we begin the present book and a quest to understand the true power which not only influences the Montauk scenario but reaches into our everyday lives. While it is a power which can give rise to the Nazis and choose a leader like Hitler, it is also a power which can carve out a paradise like Yosemite Valley or the Hawaiian Islands and make a room full of people stand up and sing *America the Beautiful*. It is a power which is ever changing and evolving. It creates the sun, wind, moon and stars. In ancient times, it was identified as the Black Sun. My personal understanding of it began through investigating the Nazis and their mysterious presence at Montauk Point.

INTRODUCTION

After writing *The Montauk Project* with Preston Nichols, I began to run across strange facts and tales about Nazi involvement at Montauk and across Long Island. First was a news article about the state of New York engaging in an excavation at Camp Hero in order to recover a cache of gold the Nazis had buried there. Next, there were eye witness accounts of Montauk locals picnicking at Montauk Point so they could watch fleets of Nazi U-boats lazily raise their periscopes right off the coast. History books revealed that Long Island was also the home of a major Aryan movement as well as the headquarters of the largest Nazi camp in America. Long Island's Cold Spring Harbor Laboratory, the world's most prestigious eugenics laboratory during the 1930s, was suspiciously renown for its tacit cooperation with the Nazis. Most bizarre of all were strange tales of Nazi scientists regrouping after the war and conducting bizarre experiments in the underground facilities beneath Montauk's own Camp Hero. These experiments were a part of what is now known as *The Montauk Project.*

These intriguing propositions led me to investigate the mystery behind these strange but predominantly accurate tales of Nazi involvement on Long Island and, most significantly, Montauk.

My personal interest in Montauk's Nazi connection began the very first time I heard Preston Nichols and Duncan Cameron speak. After stating that the Montauk Project was financed with Nazi gold, Preston mentioned that scientists at Montauk were continuing experiments begun during the Third Reich. Of particular interest to these scientists were the genetic characteristics of the blue eyed and blond haired Aryan boys which had been idealized in Hitler's Germany. Al Bielek, who also happened to be in the audience that night, chimed in that Nazi scientists were in abundance at the Montauk facility.

I am not sure why, but the prospect of Nazis on Long Island utterly fascinated me. Perhaps it was the perfect ingredient to add to a story that was already remarkable beyond belief. Or, maybe it was my own intuition suggesting that it was a worthwhile avenue to pursue. Whatever it was, I put out an antenna for any information that might corroborate or validate the above statements about Nazis at Montauk. I wanted to know if the relationship existed in fact, and if so, what the nature of it was. I was not disappointed and this book is the result of my search.

As I began to investigate the Nazis and their more mysterious aspects, I encountered startling synchronicities with the legacy of Montauk. These range from the lineage of the lineage of the Cameron family and their links to the Third Reich to the mysterious origins of Tibetan and Egyptian culture. There are many twists and turns and you will experience them, along with plenty of surprises, as you read this book.

It should be stated at the outset that the main principle employed in this pursuit of knowledge has been the element of synchronicity, also called the fabric of time. I initially stumbled upon this phenomena during the investigation detailed in *Montauk Revisited: Adventures in Synchronicity*. As many lessons have been learned since the writing of that book, it would serve everyone if I detailed some of the principles of synchronicity.

Synchronicity is called the fabric of time because it is the principle by which we recognize or know the phenomenon of time. If different actions are aligned and intercede within one frame of reference, they are said to synchronize. In a clock, all the gears mesh in a synchronized manner so as to measure the passage of time. This is all very obvious. What is not so obvious is that people, places and things can also manifest associations which are synchronous beyond the laws of probability.

Synchronicity, by its very nature, enables us to make associations that we might otherwise pass by. If these trails of synchronicity are pursued, I have personally found that they give further clarification to the mysterious matters initially encountered. By following the association between the Nazis and Montauk, as well as the namesakes thereof, tremendous secrets have been discovered which, if pursued to their ultimate end, will enable us to understand the entire workings of the universe itself.

Additional information has been passed on to me from my friend and fellow investigator, Marshall Barnes, who has studied quantum physics and has added considerable perspective to the mysterious but commonly experienced phenomena of synchronicity. I will share what I have learned from him.

According to the laws of probability, synchronicity, or coincidence, is going to occur in any "First Class" universe. In other words, in any system of created things, it stands to reason that some events are going to occur at the same time or in a unique correspondence with one another. This is just the inevitable law of averages. For example, a scoreboard is going to light up with all "2's" now and then when the clock just happens to read 2:22. But, when the coincidences or synchronicities are far beyond the normal expectations as determined by the mathematical laws of probability, there is an outside influence working. The synchronous events become what is called a "meaningful coincidence". This, in a nutshell, is what has occurred in the story of Montauk.

Outside, or extraterrestrial forces, worked on Aleister Crowley and led him to write *The Book of the Law* as well as other writings. Crowley never claimed it to be his own work and was puzzled by it for much of his own life. Jack Parsons, Marjorie Cameron and L. Ron Hubbard engaged these same forces and ended up influencing my own life in a very profound manner. All of this enabled me to understand the work and phenomena surrounding Preston Nichols and led to the publication of the Montauk Project phenomena, thus introducing it into public consciousness.

The book you are about to read draws on all the synchronicities previously established, takes them to new heights, and reveals deeper understandings. Ultimately, it leads to a profound undercurrent of life's mysteries which is trying to explain itself: a phenomena described at the end of this book as the Black Sun.

This investigation took years to complete as I accumulated a sizeable library on the subject. The research could go on for many more years and probably will. I wish that every amusing or interesting anecdote about the Nazis or other subjects could have been added to the text. Unfortunately, that path would take us off course. Therefore, I have primarily sought to include the most important historical information that has been glossed over or ignored by historians. This tact is designed not only to clear up misconceptions that many of us suffer from but to raise the social consciousness of who the Nazis actually were and what they are today. Even more important than this is the trail of history which has been discovered by tracing the Nazis' connections, through the magic of Montauk, to Tibet and Egypt. This ancient legacy of mankind, virtually ignored or hidden by the hallowed halls of archaeology, is revealed in a brand new context which will change the way you look at everything.

1

MONTAUK
A NAZI RENDEZVOUS

Within a year of the initial release of *The Montauk Project*, I received a very interesting piece of mail. It consisted of an envelope with no return address or any other evidence of who might have sent it. Inside, I found an article from the *East Hampton Star*, a local newspaper on Long Island. Tom Tubbs, a spokesman for the Division of Land Utilization of the (New York) State Office of General Services was quoted as saying the following statement.

"In 1945, the Nazis, convinced the Third Reich was about to fall, sent a U-boat to Montauk containing riches seized during the invasion of France with instructions to bury them underground inside twelve metal shell casings. The German sailors followed orders and buried the treasure at Camp Hero, with a large rock nearby to be used as a landmark. After the war, the money and jewels were to be used for bribes, false passports and safe passage to the United States and South America for high officers of the Third Reich."

This same article explained that a German submarine was sunk, but several German sailors survived and told their story years later. The Germans even teamed up with professional treasure hunters and the state of New York in an attempt to recover the treasure. No record has yet surfaced of the treasure ever being found.

By an odd synchronicity, a personal friend of mine claimed he knew the captain of the submarine. He said the captain was a friend of his family and that it would be a betrayal to relay the name. It was common knowledge to him that the Nazi captain had cut a deal with the U.S. military authorities and lived out a happy life in Queens.

My next encounter with Montauk's Nazi past was through an old timer who had lived at Montauk all her life. Asking her about Camp Hero, this woman told me she was convinced there were strange goings on there. Not only did she complain of frequent interference with her radio and television, she said it was evident that strange transmissions were sometimes coming through. It is likewise an observable fact that VCRs break down with a high amount of irregularity in the vicinity of Montauk.

Asking this old timer, who prefers to be called Jane, if she knew anything about a Nazi connection to Montauk, she said, "Absolutely — yes!"

Jane then recounted pleasant remembrances of afternoons during World War II. As she picnicked at Montauk Point with her friends and family, they watched fleets of Nazi submarines immediately off the coast. She said the periscopes would all come up in unison and that it looked like an entire forest. It was not just a few subs or as little a number as ten. There were lots of them. Jane said there was no way that any of this was unknown to the general public at Montauk. It was common knowledge. The military, more than anyone else, had to know exactly what was going on. Although there were huge guns at Montauk that could have fired on the subs, they were never used. According to her, there was no mistaking the Nazi subs from those of the Americans.

I mused over Jane's report and tried to find corroborating sources. A couple of other people indicated there were Nazi subs off the coast, but none gave colorful descriptions as had Jane. Most people from Montauk don't go that far back in local history.

I wondered what was the true history of this mystery and apparent complicity with the military forces of our country. There is a large submarine pen just southeast of the Montauk lighthouse. It is no great secret in itself and appears on some maps of the area. The U.S. Navy also had a sub station at Ford Pond Bay, not far from the Montauk Manor.

At this point, I could only speculate that the Nazis had access to the Camp Hero underground via a subterranean dock. It was an intuitive guess. Preston Nichols knew Nazis were involved at that time period but didn't have any specifics with regard to this angle of submarine access.

More information corroborating a German connection came one day as I received a call from a friend, David. He had just spent New Year's Eve at the Montauk Manor where he explored the "catacombs" underneath. David said there was an extensive network of underground tunnels but most of them were sealed off.

Preston Nichols happened to be in my living room that day. He knew exactly what David was talking about and began to rattle off a whole stream of information about the catacombs. I have since come to know that Preston will suddenly get information from out of the blue and will not be able to recover it. Unfortunately, I didn't tape this conversation. Preston gave many geographic details about the catacombs and said they were constructed primarily by Kaiser Wilhelm of Germany. He said the Kaiser was fascinated with Montauk prior to World War I and that the place was crawling with Germans.

When I relayed the above information to Al Bielek, he was shocked. He had known Preston for a lot longer than I had but never heard a mention of the catacombs. Al thought Preston had been hiding information from him, but he said the tunnels explained how Preston had been able to retrieve certain equipment from Montauk. It sounded like my friends discovery of the catacombs had jogged Preston's memory.

I have since learned that the U.S. Navy acquired the Montauk Manor and the Montauk Tower during World War II. Both sites were connected by tunnels with Camp Hero. Although I haven't been in the tunnels myself, multiple sources have confirmed this, and it is a reasonable assumption that the military would need to access its facilities through the underground in time of war. That the Kaiser built the catacombs has not been documented in itself, but their existence is no longer in question.

I began to search for more information about Nazis on Long Island, but the information in not plentiful. The most common story in the local libraries is about four Nazi's landing on the Long Island coast near Amagansett. Only seven miles from Montauk, they emerged from a U-boat on a rubber dinghy and rowed to shore. They soon changed into civilian clothes and took the Long Island Railroad to New York city. Three of the soldiers were

American citizens of German descent and spoke English well. Their orders were to assimilate themselves into the population so that they could blow up key American resource plants, one being Alcoa Aluminum. When they actually got to New York, they supposedly saw the folly of their plans and tried to turn themselves in to the authorities. The FBI didn't take them seriously at first. Finally, J. Edgar Hoover got involved and the soldiers ended up in a prison camp. Eventually, all but one were executed. This story, which was presented in the news reports, doesn't make any sense. Why would someone turn oneself in? Hitler himself was known to have commented on the mission. He said that as the entire endeavor had no chance of success, Jews should have been sent as they were easily expendable. The mission was obviously a ruse. The articles in the press sound like disinformation calculated to fool the public "think". If the authorities appeared to be hot on the trail of Nazi's coming ashore, no one could suggest there was any complicity between the Allied and Nazi powers. Apparently, this was a potential public relations problem because many Long Islanders witnessed Nazis on their island.

Information in my local library was so scarce that I decided to investigate some of the libraries on the eastern end of Long Island. This is where the largest concentration of Nazis existed. In Riverhead, I was led to a librarian who handed me a folder on the Aryan movement on Long Island. A news clipping from *Newsday* revealed an astonishing fact. Yaphank, Long Island, was once the home of the biggest Aryan groupings in the United States. Known as the German Bund during the 1930s, they named the location Camp Siegfried after the Norse god of the same name. Yaphank was home to so many loyal German patriots that a main street of the time was called Adolph Hitler Boulevard. Even more astonishing was that this very area is adjacent to what eventually became Brookhaven National Laboratory! The sponsors of Brookhaven Labs could certainly have chosen a less obvious location, or perhaps they wanted the location for the same reason the Nazi Party did — it is located on a power point of the Earth's geomagnetic grid.

Further investigation revealed that both Brooklyn and Yaphank were loaded with goose stepping Nazis demonstrating in uniform. Jews were sometimes beaten as well, but not as part of the pageantry. Preston Nichols' father, Bob, remembered the demonstrations and also said that Fairchild-Republic, an aircraft manufacturing plant, was loaded with Germans prior to World War II. Bob was a supervisor for Fairchild-Republic and said that virtually everyone in an important position in the company was German. One day, shortly before war broke out in Europe, they began to disappear.

I would soon meet a friend who knows some of the locals in Yaphank and invited me out for a visit. It is a small town in one of the few rural areas remaining on Long Island. Camp Siegfried was well chosen for its aesthetic beauty and reminiscence of Germany. It still exists today. Next to Camp Siegfried is German Gardens where the Nazi street names have long since been changed. For many years after the war, one had to be of German descent to live in this area. As the land is not owned by the dwellers, non Germans could be screened out by the review board. It ran as a cooperative and still does to this day.

My newly found friends in Yaphank also took me to a lecture by author Marvin D. Miller, a retired teacher who has written two books concerning Nazi involvement on Long Island. He showed extensive slides of the Nazi Bund and gave several anecdotal stories from the time period. The most shocking thing he said was that during the 1920s, one out of every seven Long Islanders was a member of the Ku Klux Klan. Mr. Miller also spoke about the eugenics movement whereby the wealthy of both America and Germany sought forced sterilization on people considered weak or inferior. The major American facility was at Cold Spring Harbor, Long Island, which was known for its complicity and intercourse with top Nazi doctors. Although Mr. Miller's books contain excellent information and are well researched, I will not elaborate on them as they do not relate exactly to the matter at hand. They are intriguing books, and I have listed them in the bibliography as well as where to obtain them.

The most interesting find in my particular investigation began to unravel when I visited some members of the Montauk tribe and shared some of the information you have just read. They were not surprised at all. In fact, they told me there was still a strong Aryan presence on the eastern end of Long Island. Black people know this as well. Crosses sometimes burn in East Hampton and

CAMP SIEGFRIED, LONG ISLAND

The above sign reads:
"Camp Siegfried Private — German American Settlement League".
This was the location where the Nazi Bund met throughout the 1930's.
On the upper right is the house where they helding their meetings.
The lower right photograph shows the vast expanse of land
where the Bund once goose stepped and held the largest
of all Nazi rallies in America. Theses are recent photographs
and the property is still technically owned by the
German American Settlement League which acts
as a cooperative body. For a considerable
period of time after World War II,
one had to be of German descent
to live in this locale.

other areas not far off. These sort of incidents hardly ever make the local press.

I discovered symptoms of this type of behavior when Robert Cooper, a Montauk tribal leader, was being attacked in the local press. As a town councilman of East Hampton, Cooper simply asked that the East Hampton police be investigated for charges of brutality and use of excessive force against young boys. He also voiced particular concern about police behavior at Montauk. Cooper, who was not making any accusations himself, was simply asking that the charges of public individuals be looked into. Chief of Police, Tom Scott, somehow interpreted this as a personal assault and sued Cooper for defamation of character. Why Chief Scott took this action is puzzling as every legal expert consulted on the matter, including a federal judge, indicated that Scott had no chance to win.

The loser in this legal battle was the Town of East Hampton (which contains the village of Montauk). They paid for significant parts of Scott's defense and were ordered by U.S. District Court to pay for Cooper's. Cooper counter sued as his civil rights were violated. After a long and protracted legal battle, Scott dropped his case. The judge put pressure on both sides to settle because the entire affair threatened to clear out the town coffers between legal fees and damages. What is even more dangerous to the town's fiscal status, and I am sure the judge must have had inkling of this, is that if Cooper's suspicions about the police were correct (and no one "in the know" really doubts this), the Town of East Hampton could have docket after docket of legal cases from young people who were abused by the town police. The potential flood of litigation could not possibly be sustained without literally raping the tax payers. In such a legal free for all, the attorneys would sooner or later have to pursue deeper sources behind the abuse. This means the Montauk Project itself and the state and federal agencies who have somehow compromised the citizens of the United States in allowing it to go unrestrained.

Cooper was not only attacked by the local press, but by a steady stream of editorials and letters to the editor. One writer frequently called Cooper insulting names and pointedly referred to him as a "black". This is not only in poor taste, it is not an accurate description of Cooper's racial heritage. This specific writer has been sighted as an enemy of Cooper. I was also told he makes frequent trips to Germany. This information was confided to me by a woman who is a casual acquaintance of the man. Although she is admittedly prejudiced when it comes to race, she believes in my investigation and thought I should know the truth. What this man does in Germany and who he contacts is a mystery.

Another incident indicating Nazi sentiment in Montauk occurred in 1996 when a swastika and the German words *los vom Elend, los vom Juden* — "freedom from misery, freedom from Jews" — were found spray painted on an outdoor shower wall at the Ditch Plain comfort station. This message of hate was a common slogan during the Holocaust and was written on April 16th which is Holocaust Remembrance Day. The police sited other Anti-Semitic graffiti in the area and said they would give it a higher priority than usual. They also said it was a youth prank due to "evidence" found at the crime scene, however they would not say what the "evidence" was. The fact is, most prankster youths would not know how to spell in German. From the news articles, the local police gave every indication of playing the event down.

The biggest surprise in this entire investigation occurred when I asked my friends of the Montauk tribe if they knew anything else about Aryan groups meeting on the island. The mother, a Montauk medicine woman, told me that she had worked for the local police department during the 1950s and 1960s in a highly confidential position. Her job was considered so vital that she was denied permission to attend her own uncle's funeral when he died prematurely. One of her duties during this time period was to prepare reports on an Aryan style meeting called "Bon meetings".

When I heard this, I said, "What? Bon meetings?"

"Yes, Bon meetings — B-O-N."

I couldn't believe my ears. Bon refers to the indigenous religion of ancient Tibet. It is an animistic or shamanistic religion which preceded Tibetan Buddhism as well as Guatama Buddha himself. Those who read *Pyramids of Montauk* may remember that Karl Haushofer, the man renown in books as Hitler's spiritual mentor, was a Bon priest who was initiated in Tibet and was grooming Hitler for a messianic mission in accordance with certain Bon precepts.

"What went on at these meetings?", I asked.

The medicine woman told me that the police department were working in concert with the FBI and the then extant Congressional Committee on Un-American Activities. Reports on these meetings went directly to J. Edgar Hoover. She said that the police were instructed to monitor the meetings and report on them in detail, but they were not to interfere or arrest the members. She wasn't sure why.

This was a supreme mystery. It was the first incident I had encountered linking Montauk with Tibet. The Aryan connection was very much involved as well. I asked everyone I could, but no one had any answers.

When I asked my friend Kenn Arthur, a man who has known about Montauk all along but doesn't say too much, he said that the meetings she was talking about were the German Bund meetings where they used to goose step with rifles. Of course, the German Bund meetings are no great secret. I called up the Montauk medicine woman in an attempt to clarify what Kenn had indicated. She said they were not Bund meetings. They were Bon meetings: B-O-N. She was quite specific.

It would take an entire year before I would get any sort of an answer as to what these Bon meetings might be about.

2

AN INSIDE CONNECTION

My first clue to the mystery of the Bon meetings came in the summer of 1995 when I received a called from Cindy, a Montauk native. Cindy said that her husband worked at Camp Hero and that she wanted to share some information with Preston and myself. When we met with her, Cindy showed us blue prints of the underground and told us the base was currently being used by the feds. She said they accessed the base through the western bunker, just west of the main entrance gate to Camp Hero. Preston and I call this bunker "The Fireman's Bunker" because the fireman have used it in the past for bizarre fire drills at midnight. It is also the bunker where the beast "Junior" was photographed by Jan Brice as shown in *The Montauk Project: Experiments in Time.*

Cindy told us that her husband was one of three mechanics employed at Camp Hero. We found this puzzling as we were earlier told that Donald Balcuns, the head mechanic who was also doubling as security, serviced the state motorpool which consisted of about twenty-two cars. I thought this was a bit silly. One full time mechanic to maintain twenty-two cars? After all, its not like you have to change the oil daily. Now, we discovered that there were three mechanics. The reason, we were told, was that they needed three of them to service the lawn mowers. They also doubled as mechanics at Montauk Downs golf course, a few miles west of the base. It sounded like a severe stretch of the imagination.

Cindy also said that her husband's mood and sexuality had changed since he began working at Camp Hero. She said he was normally good natured but would come home extremely irritable after working in the Montauk Downs building. That is a pyramid shaped building and houses the headquarters of John Larsen, the superintendent for the New York State Park located at Camp Hero. Myself and others have also noticed other strange phenomena connected with that pyramid building.

Both Preston and myself warned Cindy that if either of us were seen with her or her husband that his job might be in danger. No sooner had we warned her than Preston took another trip and met with her husband. After being seen outside the house with Preston by one of his coworkers, Cindy's husband was let go the very next day. I guess they didn't need three mechanics after all.

When we spoke with Cindy in our initial meeting, I asked her if she had any unusual experiences herself. Her immediate answer was no. After we went outside, she began to tell me about seeing UFOs at different times in her life. At her request, I have omitted further information conerning these experiences.

After we got to know her a bit more, Cindy sent me a newspaper clipping of reported bigfoot sightings near Montauk and told me that she herself had seen a bigfoot near the railroad tracks on the Napeague strip, just outside of Montauk. Cindy was accompanied by an eyewitness when she spotted the creature. They were both frightened and immediately left the area. The fact that sasquatch have been sighted at Montauk gives us another strange connection to Tibet, the home of the yeti, or abominable snowman. Another woman and her friend reported seeing a huge bigfoot emerge out of the water near the lighthouse in the summer of 1996. It was said to be an etheric image rather than a life and blood creature, but it frightened the hell out of both of these people.

As I began working on this book, I told Cindy that I was researching the Nazi connection to Montauk. She protested and sounded as if she was scolding me.

"There is no Nazi connection to Montauk," she said.

I told her that there was such a connection, and I began to politely debate the issue. She was interrupted by a German sounding voice in the background. It was her father. He said that neo-Nazis had recently had skirmishes at the beach. There was indeed a Nazi connection on Long Island.

I was surprised to discover that her father was German. A conversation then ensued between me and her father, only he didn't pick up the phone. She acted as the intermediary. Cindy told me that her father possesses a very peculiar property. He can stick his finger into a live electric circuit and feel no shock. An hour later, he can shake someone's hand and they are liable to receive the shock. I decided to meet the man. A meeting was arranged for Preston and myself to see Cindy's father.

Her father, Max, is in his sixties and is friendly. When I met him, Max spoke in a southern accent. I thought this was strange but he told me that he had lived in the south for a time. Max told us that he was adopted by a German family and grew up in Montauk. He said he had lived there most of his life.

Max developed an interest in UFOs when he was a student in school. It started when he saw an artistic rendition of a UFO on the cover of a *Weekly Reader* that discussed Admiral Richard Byrd's trip to the Antarctic. Upon seeing the picture of a UFO, he told himself that he knew how to make one. Max proceeded to create his own flying saucer out of pie tins. It was a small saucer, but he said that it flew. After many years, he eventually improved his skills and built a man sized flying saucer. The technology he developed was through his own intuition and self teaching. The saucer was not able to fly out of the Earth's atmosphere but could move at high speeds through the atmosphere.

The above sounds very farfetched from a "normal" point of view, but Max went into a rather detailed description of how he put the craft together. I didn't find it easy to follow and his own developments were not my immediate interest. I should point out that the man had a unique knowledge of electronics. He explained that he could make a radio work without an antenna. Preston said that was impossible. Max proceeded to show us how his car radio worked without any observable antenna. He said he had placed a magnet on the radio and that it served the purpose of antenna. The radio did come in loud and clear. He said the magnet needs to be one inch by six inches and 3/8ths of an inch thick. Preston has heard of using magnets in this regard but has not experimented with it himself to any significant extent. Preston did not have an easy time talking to Max about electronic and technical matters because Max is self taught and his language doesn't jive with university jargon. The man obviously knows a thing or two. This has to be kept in mind because his story gets even more bizarre.

41

Max claims to have travelled around the United States in his home built UFO with eight women. They would travel the countryside looking for luminous spots on mountains where they hoped to find gold. Some of these spots proved to be false leads, but many precious metals were found, processed and sold for a considerable profit. The money was split between him and the eight women.

One day, Max and his ladies were vacationing at a lake near Tucson, Arizona when they were approached by the military. This occurred in the late 1940s when the military didn't have too much knowledge about such crafts. They checked Max out and asked him to work as a courier. He said that the military employed him in that capacity and payed him well over $100,000 a year.

Although his story is more than a bit strange, Max has more knowledge about Montauk than any other locals I have met so far. He cannot be discounted just because he tells a bizarre story.

Asking Max about Montauk, he told me that he remembered experiments being done at Camp Hero. This was both during World War II and many years after. He said the experiments were strange and included everything from genetics to mind control. He claimed no involvement in them.

Asking him specifically about the Nazis, Max told me that they were all around during World War II. They had an underground submarine pen under Stony Hill in Amagansett. He also said there was an underground opening right near the lighthouse and that one could see the German subs moving right below the water. They were going into the underground. Although this information was exactly what I had intuited, I didn't tell him this or feed what I knew to him so that he would answer this way. He also said the Nazis would come into town in civilian clothes and eat lunch during World War II. They would "spy" as he termed it and go back to their military posts.

I asked him if he knew anything about the catacombs or the Kaiser having an operation there around the time of World War I. Max gave a rather detailed description of the catacombs. He knew places that neither Preston nor myself had heard of. Upon further investigation, Max's stories checked out, thus increasing his credibility factor.

As for the period of World War I, he said that he was born in 1932 but that he heard stories of the Germans experimenting with sound wave amplification prior to 1920. These experiments took place at Montauk and reportedly drove people crazy. Preston was quick to point out that sound amplification technology didn't exist to any significant extent in those days. I pointed out to Preston that he is not personally familiar with German technology, and he conceded that was true. We don't know what capabilities the Germans had in those days, but Max had obviously heard reports of a technology that could best be termed secret and mysterious.

As Montauk once housed a dirigible base, I asked him if he had ever seen German zeppelins in the area. Max said that they could be seen in the 1930s and sometimes landed at Montauk. I have also heard separate reports that they would "dock" with the U-boats at sea.

Max also told us that a saucer had crashed in Amagansett in April or May of 1995 in the vicinity of Albert's Landing. The craft had landed in a tree and a significant amount of branches were displaced. Max said the military had approached him and wanted to know if he wanted the craft. When he said that he didn't, they brought in a team of helicopters which removed the saucer and took it to New Haven, Connecticut. It was eventually transported to the southwest. I have related this incident to show that Max's relationship with the military is not an ordinary one. He seems to be out of their direct control. This is reminiscent of the triplets mentioned in *Montauk Revisited*. Their father was involved in the Philadelphia Experiment and could not be intimidated by the government because of his connection to aliens. Max seems to fit in this category, too.

Asking a friend of mine to check out Max's reported crash sight, he saw broken branches and said the area definitely had something excavated from it. This friend videoed the sight and showed it to Preston who in turn gave the matter over to John Ford of the Long Island UFO Association. Ford's investigation was left incomplete when he was arrested and jailed.

All in all, Max knew too many things. Some of the stories couldn't possibly be verified, but others did check out. He was obviously connected to the Montauk phenomena. Next, I asked him my trump question. Had he ever heard about the Bon meetings the Montauk medicine woman had told me about?

"Yes," he said.

He had attended some of them. There were many Aryan types there. Max said the meetings were held to tell people what they could say and couldn't say or tell people what they could and could not do.

Asking for clarification, he said that they might show a machine like a space generator and talk about it. Some information could be released generally, but other information could not. Obviously, the people at these meetings were tied into a completely different reality. Any physicist also knows that a space generator is the equivalent of a space time generator. Max was never too interested in these meetings and didn't have much more to say. He was matter of fact about it.

We are only left to conclude that these Bon meetings were of a very strange order indeed. It sounds like an Aryan race outpost that was half way between this dimension and another. The name itself suggests that some sort of homage or acknowledgment to the ancient Tibetan religion was in force.

We've known all along that Montauk has plenty of government and military connections. The information about the Bon meetings encouraged me to investigate the ruling aspects of the Montauk Project from an entirely different angle.

3

THE CAMERON
CONNECTION

In attempting to penetrate the mystery of the Aryan movement on Long Island, I checked out a few books on the history of
the Ku Klux Klan. Although I did not find anything of particular
significance concerning Long Island, I was amazed to learn that
one of the first major motion pictures in cinematic history was
entitled *Birth of a Nation*. Released just before World War I, the
movie told the story of Reconstruction in the south after the Civil
War. *Birth of a Nation* had unparalleled success for its time and
portrayed the Klan as heroes. Freed southern blacks were shown
as rapacious monsters seeking revenge on whites for years of
slavery. The Klan was there to protect white women and children
from being raped, robbed and murdered or otherwise abused.

It stands to reason that there were racial uprisings against
whites during this period and no doubt the Klan did do some work
in the area of simple police protection of its own kind. This role as
protectors exalted the Klan into folk heroes in the eyes of many
whites. People clung to the Klan for survival. What the exact
degree of validity and non-validity of the Klan is not terribly
important to our work. Those who want to keep score of the Klan's
good marks and bad marks can wrestle with the history books.

What was particularly interesting to me about *Birth of a
Nation* was that the founder of the Klan was a man named Ben
Cameron! For those who remember all the synchronicities with the
name Cameron, you can imagine that this was a bit hard to digest.
Even more bizarre is the fact that the man considered most

45

responsible for the success of the movie was President Woodrow Wilson, the former President of Princeton University (home of the brainstorming sessions which eventually paved the way for the Philadelphia Experiment). The producer of *Birth of a Nation* was a former classmate of President Wilson, and he deftly used this relationship to arrange a showing of the movie in the White House. Wilson prided himself on his professorial knowledge of history and said the movie was only too true. This statement served as an endorsement of the movie, and word of mouth spread like wild fire. Box office receipts reached a new high in many areas.

The movie was extremely controversial and incited riots or riot like atmospheres in many major cities. It put blacks, already in an economically subjugated position, into a further defensive posture. Whatever the relative truth of *Birth of a Nation*, it only served to provoke blacks and champion the whites who had lived off of slavery in the first place. President Wilson was finally forced to recant any "endorsement" of the movie. This calmed things down considerably. It is obvious he believed in the movie, and it is entirely possible, if not probable, that he had no intention of provoking riots, but his role in making the movie a success cannot be denied.

Studying the Klan further, I discovered there was another version, supposedly more historically correct, of how it originated. A group of five individuals got together in the state of Tennessee. All were of Gaelic-Irish descent and decided to ban together and form a secret society. A man with the last name of Kennedy decided to call the group the Ku Klux Klan after the Greek word *kyklos* which means circle. The term *Ku Klux* was used to hide the meaning which was for initiates only. The cross (often burning) was their other sacred symbol. Together, they made the circle and cross: ⊕. Those who have read *Pyramids of Montauk* will remember that this symbol is both sacred to the Montauk natives as well as the secret society Ordo Templi Orientis. It is sacred to many other groups as well.

The book I read further stated that the Klan decided to put "meaningless occult symbols" on their garments. This is a white-wash if ever their was one. One has to wonder if the writer is personally deluded, deliberately misleading or just making up his own mind. The Klan was obviously using magic for its own purposes. The inner meanings were for initiates only.

While the Kennedy version of the KKK's founding seems to be more historically accurate, the choosing of the name "Ben Cameron" is not an accident. Not only is a Gaelic connection at work but so is the principle of synchronicity.

All of this took on an even more profound meaning when I received a letter from a woman who said that her mother knew both Ewen Cameron, once the head of the CIA's MK-Ultra mind control project, and also Alexander Duncan Cameron Sr., the father of the same Duncan Cameron featured in *The Montauk Project*. I phoned the woman and found she had many correspondences with Aleister Crowley. These included the numbers "666" in both her birthday and driver's ID. She also told me that her mother had some very esoteric understandings about time travel and had mothered a child with Ewen Cameron.

In *Montauk Revisited*, we explored the various synchronicities with the names Cameron, Wilson and Crowley. I was aware of Ewen Cameron at the time but didn't mention him in the book as I wasn't sure how relevant that connection was. Ewen Cameron did have a father named Duncan. Additionally, he was utterly fascinated with the Frankenstein legend.

Ewen Cameron has been written up in several unbiased books as one of the most evil monsters ever to inhabit the corridors of the noble profession of psychiatry. His systematic torture of patients through what he called "psychic driving" is well documented. It is a system whereby one's own words, particularly of a traumatic content, are repeated over and over on a tape loop which plays continuously on a tape recorder. Combined with various forms of mental stress and deprivation, psychic driving is designed to make one totally lose one's marbles. This aspect of Cameron's work was done in conjunction with the CIA. Most of it took place at the Allan Memorial Institute in Montreal, Canada, where he employed many former Nazis. The CIA settled out of court with several people who were tortured by Cameron while he was working under the auspices of the agency.

Ewen Cameron was a close personal friend of Allen Dulles, the first director of the CIA, who worked intimately with him. Dulles even sent Cameron to "examine" Rudolph Hess prior to the Nuremburg trials. It is a well documented fact that Hess went blank during the trials and didn't remember even his close personal friend, Dr. Karl Haushofer. Some people have speculated that a double was inserted for Hess or that he was simply brainwashed. All we know for sure is that there was plenty of funny business concerning Hess and Cameron was right in the middle of it.

Earlier, I mentioned a woman whose mother had a relationship with Ewen Cameron. After giving this woman my phone number, I heard from the mother the next morning. Frankly, I expected the mother to be more than a bit fragmented and probably stuck between this dimension and another. To my pleasant surprise, she was quite lucid and wonderful to talk to. She was well educated, too. Her name is Anna, and she had quite a story to tell.

Anna was born in Washington, D.C. on 11/11/1942, a date specially chosen for astrological reasons. Her birth was carefully planned, and she was considered to be the reincarnation of Innana, the Sumerian goddess. This is a very heavy tag to put on anyone. Innana is the Sumerian equivalent of Babalon.

Deriving from a line of blue bloods with many different coats of arms, Anna's family is of pure Aryan lineage and is traceable beyond Germany. Belonging to one of the most prestigious organizations in America, the Daughters of the American Revolution, the family also belongs to an organization which predates even that: the Daughters of the American Colonies.

Most of Anna's family were involved in the military and the occult. Her great grandfather was an astrologer and was one of Hitler's mentors. Anna's mother worked for the Office of Strategic Services and was tied to William Donovan and Ewen Cameron. She explained that Cameron's family, like hers, were multigenerational occultists. Both families embraced the same occult philosophy as those who surrounded Hitler. They believed that as Aryans, their genetic lines predated ancient Sumeria. Identified as the Sumerian Brotherhood of the Snake or the Vril, these people were once enlightened and positive. Due to greed, they became corrupt and convoluted in their ideology. Through the years they infiltrated the Knights Templar, the Illuminati, the top degree Masons and every other organization they could penetrate. Anna refers to these misguided souls as the Controllers and states that this elitist group changed the very nature of time. Anna was designated as Ewen Cameron's "control", a term used to denote ownership.

According to Anna, Ewen believed that she was the incarnation of Inanna, the first "non human vehicle" on this planet. The Controllers believed that by harnessing the energy of the goddess Inanna, they could gain power. Consequently, many females were incarnated to be this goddess, all under the direction of the Controllers.

Efforts had been made since the beginning of time to keep the Cameron lineage pure. She said that the Brotherhood of the Snake operated through the Assassins and also the Essenes. One of their primary missions was to keep the lineage of the Aryan blood line pure. Ewen was a part of this and his specialty was mind control. He used these very words to her in describing his role. His goal was to keep the genetic line in order to establish and maintain the New World Order. The desired population were to be Aryans.

Anna also told an interesting story concerning Ewen Cameron's connection to Rudolph Hess. Ewen was known to become very gleeful whenever he talked about the Hess situation. Anna told me that he used to laugh and snicker and say "that's when it all started". This behavior is noteworthy because, according to historical reports, Ewen never smiled. He was well known for keeping a stone cold stare and an intimidating countenance.

According to what Ewen told her, Hess was a highly dedicated member of the brotherhood, even more so than Hitler. Hess left Hitler's Germany in 1941 for Scotland in order to meet someone and participate in some sort of magical ritual. It involved time travel and Ewen boasted about it as if it was successful. The control group were waiting for an Aryan planet, known as Marduk, to come into resonant orbit with that of Mars. This would enable a shift in time to take place. Ewen talked quite a bit about this but much of it remains a mystery. Perhaps Hess actually met with Crowley, but that is absolutely speculative at this point. We do know that Crowley engaged in a ritual in the Ashdown Forest designed to bring Hess to Great Britain.

The Allies supposedly sent Ewen Cameron to Nuremburg in an official capacity to say whether Hess was sane or insane. Allen Dulles reportedly was concerned that the incarcerated Hess was not the real Hess. Anna does not have complete details on all this. She was told that Ewen knew what was happening ahead of time. Hess had to be "replaced" but the entire affair had something to do with time. The real Hess had been sent to another time. They had to put another body in place of Hess that looked like Hess.

Although these statements sound rather fantastic, this is the first information I have ever heard or read about Ewen Cameron from an insider who knew him intimately. Many conservative sources, as well as critics of the Nuremberg trials, have suggested that the real Rudolph Hess had been replaced by a double.

Anna also met many key players, including Alexander Duncan Cameron Sr., who was described in *The Montauk Project* as smuggling Nazis into the United States. Her family acquired lots of land and became part of an underground system for moving Nazis through the United States. She and Ewen would meet in Duncan Sr.'s house and go out on his boat. There were always women aboard. The two Camerons would pass information to each other and talk "company business" but Anna was not a part of that. One time, Duncan Sr. came to Washington, D.C. to visit them.

Anna also expressed that Ewen Cameron was deeply involved with the famous Kennedy family. She recalls meetings with Sam Giancana and Joseph Kennedy Sr. somewhere near Martha's Vineyard. She did not recall Bobby or Jack being in attendance, but there were several other Kennedys there. Joe Kennedy sat quietly but seemed to have a big say in what went on. At affairs like these, she said Ewen would put on a show. Women from various programs would attend to the men's sexual desires. Ewen would arrange sexual partners and engage in what could perhaps be best described as the perverted occultism of the rich and powerful. Anna was displayed by Ewen Cameron as his "goddess clone". He was obsessed with both of their own lineage to the goddess Innana. From birth, it was ordained that she would belong to Ewen Cameron and have his child.

Anna was personally quite traumatized by her association with Ewen Cameron. Consequently, she began to study psychology in order to understand his pathology. She says he was homophobic overtly but also a latent homosexual. He amused himself by brutalizing young men as well as women. Ewen was well aware that Anna hated him, but he was gleeful about this because he knew no one would ever believe her over him. His game was status and "one-up-man-ship" based upon his many degrees and psychiatric credentials.

Her own foray into the subject of psychology led Anna to give me some interesting comments about the Montauk Project. She told me I was missing a piece of the puzzle with regard to Montauk, but she was hesitant to discuss it over the phone. After a few more conversations, she became less reluctant and spoke her mind.

The missing ingredient with regard to the Montauk programming was multiple personalities. The intent of the Controllers in various programs was to produce a condition known as Multiple Personality Disorder. She explained that if you torture someone, they will split into different personalities in order to survive. One personality or "person" will be found that is susceptible to programming and will be instructed to do certain actions. Another personality, usually an exceedingly pleasant one, will be used to cover the tracks of the other personality. Mark David Chapman, the man who killed Beatle John Lennon, is a prime example of such a personality.

Studies on MPD show that these individuals have an IQ above the normal range, a great amount of creativity and above average psychic abilities. It is also true that if you split a personality, the pineal gland will activate and the person can become psychic. The element of possession also comes into play as one is prone to pulling in exterior forces when being tortured. These forces will usually manifest as a beast or demon.

Once MPD is achieved, further programming can be achieved by what is now called the Stockholm syndrome. This is when a victim bonds with his or her captor or controller. This example was observed in the press with the kidnapping of Patty Hearst. The method of producing the Stockholm Syndrome is by repeated torturing and brainwashing. This method was used by Ewen Cameron on Anna.

A multiple personality literally keeps a tortured individual from going further insane. But, this break in the psyche is what enables a person to be programmed. Ewen Cameron was such an individual himself and was really operating like a marionette at the behest of the Controllers. Ewen Cameron crossed the line between being a murderer and one who is not able to kill another human being. Once he stepped over to the dark side, he was incapable of coming back.

Anna was of particular interest when we consider sexual magick because she was supposedly Inanna. She had the blood line, astrological chart and also the abilities that went with the title. This was most pronounced in her experiences with Dr. Cameron. According to her, he "murdered" her. Specifically, he would torture her. Sometimes it was through the back of the neck but he would do whatever was necessary to enable her to leave her body. Once she was outside, she would have incredible experiences. Ewen delighted in this as he wanted power and ordered her to check out places for him.

These experiences included time travel experimentation. She remembers being a rebel astrologer in the days of the Essenes. This group was looking for a woman to bear Christ and she was one of the candidates. She also travelled to the time of Jack the Ripper who, according to her, was a high official. This technology for time travel by forcible torture was available in the 1940s. Obviously, it does not work on everyone.

On the whole, Anna's experiences outside of the body were so uplifting that she couldn't be hurt or controlled. When she travelled, Cameron couldn't monitor her, but he tried. He was very angry that he couldn't control her while in this altered state. She was exterior to the pain he was causing. Anna proved to be somewhat resilient to the torture. Although she is on disability for post traumatic stress syndrome suffered at the hands of Ewen Cameron, Anna says she only began to show significant signs of visible aging when she became fifty years old. Like Duncan Cameron, she has scars in her lungs. This could be from radiation.

She is also aware of other people that have been put through this procedure. One person she knew was groomed to be an Antichrist. When she looked into his eyes, he didn't appear human at all. That was her take on Hitler. He bought into this sort of programming. There are other tragic figures that she maintains communication with. These people are not yet prepared to talk about this for a book.

In 1967, Ewen Cameron died on a mountain top in the Adirondacks. He was hiking with his son. This is the historical version of his death. According to a source who wishes to remain nameless, this was a faked death and Cameron worked for a foreign intelligence agency before actually dying.

Perhaps the most ironic aspect of Ewen Cameron has to do with L. Ron Hubbard, a man who was probably his biggest enemy. Hubbard hated psychiatry and never missed a chance to criticize it as the biggest and most outrageous abuse of human rights in existence. Critics of Hubbard have been quick to say he was obsessed about psychiatry, that he wanted their business and that he was insane himself. If you check the documented truth of Dr. Ewen Cameron, you will find that Hubbard was totally accurate, at least in regard to this particular psychiatrist.

Ewen Cameron was also the president of the American Psychiatric Association, the Canadian Psychiatric Association and the World Psychiatric Association. How could a man like this rise to such a position of power and influence? This alone should throw tremendous credibility towards Hubbard. He was practically the only one, if not *the* only one, to make a serious criticism against this man's policies and practices. That they both came from the same magical genetic line (Wilsons and Camerons) makes it all the more fascinating. Ewen was obviously representing the Controllers while Hubbard was rebelling against them.

This interesting fact alone tells us that the Controllers, i.e. the forces of evil, have done plenty of their fighting for control of the Wilson and Cameron genetic pool.

MARDUK
The above is a rendition of Marduk which the secret societies of
Germany used in their literature and symbology.
This pagan god is also known as Malduk, Mithras, Moloch,
or Malok in German.

4

THE CAMERON LINEAGE

When L. Ron Hubbard engaged in the Babalon Working with Jack Parsons and Marjorie Cameron, all of the participants were of the same lineage. We already know that the Wilsons, which were the original birth names of Marjorie and Hubbard's father, derived from the Camerons. Further genealogical research of my own revealed that the Wilsons and the Parsons both derived from the family of Catherine Parr.

All three participants emerged from the Babalon Working with what is often termed the "magical current". As was alluded to in the book *Encounter in the Pleiades: An Inside Look at UFOs*, I was a direct recipient of this current through the personage of Hubbard. My synchronistic meeting with Marjorie Cameron completed the circuit and literally initiated my active involvement in the Montauk phenomena. If it were not for that meeting with Cameron, it is highly questionable whether or not there would not have been a sequel to *The Montauk Project: Experiments in Time*. If there were, it would have been a far different story line.

If one follows my personal involvement with Montauk, there is obviously an outside influence working in my own life as was alluded to in the introduction to this book. Initially, I simply stumbled into the synchronicity of the Babalon Working. As time goes by, I understand the working principles a bit better. Looking back on my own life, I actually invoked this entire experience by asking for complete awareness and enlightenment. There is really nothing more at work here than the old adage "you get what you ask for". My personal interest in furthering my own consciousness led me to Montauk and thence the Cameron connection. The Camerons and Wilsons reveal themselves as a genetic window through which an external nonhuman consciousness can manifest, sometimes through the principle of synchronicity.

The role of genetics are intensely important when we consider the interdimensional potential of an activity such as the Babalon Working. The DNA in each cell contains the blue print not only for the human body but for the entire consciousness and manifestation of the universe itself. As we have learned in the Montauk saga, the genetics of the Cameron clan seem to highlight the exact configurations in the DNA bio-computer necessary for trafficking from one dimension to another. When considering the external source operating in my own life, there is an influence that communicates to me (and to many of you as well) via the names of Cameron and Wilson. The names Parsons and Crowley fit into this same mix as well. This external source is trying to get a message across. At this stage of the game, my personal observations tell me this message is actually a method by which to trace lost knowledge of ourselves and the mystery of the universe. In other words, the names Cameron, Wilson, etc. reveal a residue of magick. More importantly, it has proven to be a workable method.

Robert Anton Wilson, an author of many books on the occult, has stated that when you arrive at the horizons of consciousness, you will encounter the principle of synchronicity. You could also say that once you've learned everything there is to learn in this world, you will enter the world of time and its paradoxes. Here is a man named Wilson explaining the very phenomenon. This is why the names Wilson and Cameron have cropped up with surprising synchronicity with regard to time travel. They are gateways to the incredible and miraculous.

One of these synchronicities in my own life manifested when I was made aware that a couple of Celtic shamans would be visiting my locale. As their names should not be revealed (at their request), I will refer to them as Lord and Lady Cameron. Although they have different last names, they are both Camerons to the core and carry that pedigree. There is no doubt about that. They are not married.

These Camerons practice a tradition that goes way back in time. Their ancestors were put to death for practicing their ancient family tradition which is centered around the rituals of the distant

Picts and Druids. Even though Lord and Lady Cameron come directly from the Cameron genetic pool, they had no previous idea of my work. This made it all the more intriguing.

My first meeting only piqued my interest further. It was with Lady Cameron. Noticing her reddish blond hair and very fair skin, I couldn't help but recognize a distinct resemblance to both Marjorie Cameron and Diana Hubbard, the daughter of L. Ron Hubbard. There was no mistaking it, and I was rather shocked. I consequently realized that I have become quite adept at recognizing the genetic structure of this clan.

Equally to my surprise, Lady Cameron explained that her lineage has served as the guardians of the unified field. I suppose a statement like that should be expected at this point, but we can now see that the synchronicity of the situation is leading to a further explanation. She accelerated the pace when she said that one of the biggest challenges of her clan has been to learn how to sublimate their sexual energy. This refers, of course, to the bipolar forces of creation: yin and yang or whatever you want to call it. To their chagrin, Lady Cameron said her family has not used this energy in a conventional format in the past and has constantly wrestled with it.

Lady Cameron's family history goes back many millenniums and was passed down orally. Much of it could be considered standard Celtic lore and ritual, but her understanding and presentation of it is dramatic and unique. She is highly intelligent. Part of her rituals include painting the body in blue colors, but I am not sure if she knows where this tradition actually comes from. If she did, she didn't tell the real truth behind this ancient custom. Why the Celts used blue paint will be discussed later on in this book.

She teaches that, according to Celtic tradition, we are part of a unified field that retains the awareness of the Creator. The womb is viewed as the vehicle of return. We all come back through it and are capable of retaining our identity. A shaman such as herself exists to connect us with the sacred. In this regard "sacred" refers to the subtle states of consciousness which are too often taken for granted if they are recognized at all. The best shamanic method for helping one to reach the sacred is through direct energetic transmission. After that, the best way is through sound and symbols. Story telling and lectures would be the next most effective means.

Lady Cameron received much of her own shamanic legacy by a telepathic link in her own genetic line. This is a form of direct energetic transmission.

The irony of her story dovetailing so nicely with what I have already learned about the Camerons should no longer surprise us. It becomes apparent that the world is crawling with Camerons who have different agendas. Some are good and some are bad. Lady Cameron struck me as being very much on the good side. Ewen Cameron was the opposite. Again, we can see the forces of evil fighting for the control of the Cameron genetic pool.

The synchronicity of the matter accelerated further when I met Lord Cameron. I found him even more interesting than Lady Cameron. He had some sort of past connection to Aleister Crowley's OTO but he was not affiliated with it presently. Lord Cameron expressed surprise at how I could have run across so much of my information without being an OTO member.

He began telling me of his own foray into magic at the age of thirteen when he suddenly found himself sacrificing a goat. Lord Cameron quickly told me that he had to struggle to stay away from the dark side and that this instance of animal sacrifice was the only one in his life. Asking him where he learned to perform such a sacrifice, he told me that it just came naturally or intuitively.

"Must be the Cameron genetics at work", I said.

"That's right," he laughed.

As we spoke, I told him that I was part Gaelic through my mother whose maiden name was Sweeney. After a few more sentences, he looked at me quizzically and asked me a question.

"So, you're a Sweeney, are you?"

"That's right," I said.

Lord Cameron then identified a woman he knew whose lineage was both Sweeney and Cameron. He said that the connection between the two families went back at least four generations. In fact, he said she was one of the wealthiest people in the world and underwrites Yale University. Rather shocking.

The exterior source which communicates to me via the name Cameron was now telling me that I am genetically connected to the clan. The message was quite clear. All in all, this adds an interesting piece to the puzzle. The rest of this book is not so personal, but this information will play an interesting role later on.

5

THE KENNEDY
CONNECTION

The Cameron connection to the Brotherhood of the Snake, as relayed by Anna in Chapter Three, ties this clan right to Nazi Germany. Further research reveals that the Camerons were not the only Gaelic family to be so tied. Earlier in this book, it was suggested that there was some sort of association between the Camerons and Kennedys. There was the reference to the founding of the KKK and also the a reported contact between Ewen Cameron and Joseph Kennedy. Both are obviously of Gaelic descent, but there is also a further story connecting the Kennedys to the Montauk phenomena.

When I first heard the Montauk story from Preston, and before I decided to collaborate with him as an author, I suggested that another friend of mine take on the project. Her name is Claudette, and she was already a professional writer who had also served an editor for some of the major publishing houses. I came to know her as we were both in the advertising and marketing fields. We would meet infrequently to talk about different projects. As I told her the Montauk story, I thought she would be an excellent candidate to write the book. She had worked with many of the famous science fiction authors during her career and told me of their heartbreaks and the pitfalls that befell them. Mostly, the publishing houses would not do too much for them in the way of marketing their books.

Claudette said the Montauk story was too weird and she did not want to get involved. Even though she had once seen a UFO emerge out of the water in the Bermuda Triangle, this story was not for her. Her appearance in my life proved to be laced with synchronicity. Although she did not want to take on writing *The Montauk Project* herself, she ended up teaching me some crucial points about the art of writing. She also had some remarkable tales to tell that relate to our story.

After being raped by a German scientist in the 1950s, Claudette became pregnant. She explained that unwed mothers in those times were severely castigated. Under the social mores and pressures of the times, Claudette decided it would be in her best interest to marry this man and did so. He was not only a German immigrant but also had a strong association with the Nazis. She said that her husband's father, after hearing the news that Hitler was dead, committed suicide.

Claudette also mentioned that they had a boat at Montauk and would often vacation there. After bringing their boat ashore on the beach at Montauk, her husband would disappear for the longest times. She didn't know where he was, and he would never tell her. Claudette knew he was an important scientist as he personally constructed a part for the lunar module which was used to land on the moon. One day, he put it in their family car, and they drove it down to a designated location near Washington. Again, he disappeared, only this time it was into an elevator positioned "in the middle of nowhere". Although there were no mishaps, she was shocked at the lack of standard security measures.

The most bizarre story she had to tell was this German scientist's dealings with the late Robert F. Kennedy. She said that while Kennedy was Attorney General, he would sometimes visit their house in Queens. He always showed up in a limousine. The driver would wait outside while Bobby came in the house. These visits were typified by her husband retrieving LSD sugar cubes from the refrigerator which he and Bobby would consume and go "tripping".* Sometimes the two of them would go off together, and

---

* That Bobby Kennedy could have been involved in drugs as has been portrayed above also sheds new light on the Marilyn Monroe controversy. Her death could have been inspired through one of Ewen Cameron's agents or colleagues. She is known to have discussed JFK's desire to release information about UFOs to the public. The mystery of her death, which still hasn't subsided, has yet to be investigated from an occult perspective.

sometimes they would stay around the house. This information shocked me, but Claudette insisted it was true. She had clearly been traumatized by the experience. Claudette said she hated Bobby Kennedy because every time he came over, her husband would become cruel and abuse her, most likely a result of the LSD.

There are other interesting anecdotes linking the Kennedys to this line of high strangeness that is associated with the Nazis or Montauk. JFK Jr. is reported to be bisexual from an individual who claims to know him. I have also heard stories of his mother's trepidation about sending him off to prep school for fear of the homosexual element he might encounter there. Kennedy's recent marriage may cause people to view these allegations skeptically, but press reports indicate serious trouble on that front. Although one of her childhood friends has told me the new Mrs. Kennedy has a French father and Italian mother, press reports have said she was so upset with the Kennedys that she fled back to her "native Germany" at one point. Reportedly, she has a hard time fitting into the strict confines of being a Kennedy woman.

If JFK Jr. is not bisexual, he gives us plenty of cause to wonder when we consider the name of his magazine: *George.* Whether he intended it or not, the name *George* is used by male gays to refer to one another. This usage allegedly inspired the name of *Boy George*, the pop star of the '80s. To me, *George* magazine seeks to portray a decadent image of America and is also sending out a subliminal sexual message to the public. If that is not enough, I am also told that JFK Jr. used to "summer" in Amagansett, a short drive from Montauk Point.

Extreme curiosity rises when we consider the island where JFK Jr. and his bride were married. It is said to be a secluded island with a secret and secure compound. I also read that this island was once the home of Bruno Hauptmann, a German who was electrocuted for kidnapping the Lindbergh baby.[*] Lindbergh appears to have been an ally of the Kennedys. Both he and Joseph Kennedy were adamant about keeping America out of the war in Europe.

---

[*] Bruno Hauptmann is believed by many historians, both conservative and conspiratorial, to be innocent of the Lindbergh crime. General Norman Schwarzkopf's father was the law enforcement official in charge of the investigation which is known to have been myopic and slanted. This entire subject is still a can of worms which bears further investigation.

Arnold Schwarzenegger, the poster boy of Aryan genetics, also married into the Kennedy clan. He is the star of *Total Recall*, a movie that used a device similar to the Montauk chair as its main theme. His psychic signature has literally been blasted over America's air waves by nature of his tremendous stardom.

There is also a strange association between the Kennedys and the motion picture business. Father Joe was responsible for making the first talkies, working in partnership with a division of RCA. This was during the early 1930s and coincides with the time Tesla began working at RCA under the family name of Turbo. This puts the Kennedys in a position to rule over the beginnings of the sound business and potential audio subliminals. Kennedy later sold his interest in movies after making a fortune. Who he sold it to or whether he retained interest through a holding company are questions I have not pursued.

The entire point with the Kennedys is that there are many factors in their history which have not been properly investigated by historians. In this book, we are primarily concerned with their connection, synchronous or otherwise, to the Nazis.

Joseph Kennedy Sr. was so notorious for his pro German stance before and during World War II that he was eventually recalled as U.S. Ambassador to the Court of St. James (Great Britain). According to Jewish film writer Ben Hecht, Kennedy met with fifty leading Jewish film makers in Hollywood and told them not to publicly protest against Hitler or to make films offensive to the dictators of the Axis. He said it would impede victory over the Axis and make people feel a "Jewish War" was going on. Kennedy's connections go even deeper.

In 1939, Kennedy agreed to fly to Paris for a high level meeting with Helmuth Wohlthat, the right hand man of Reichsmarschall Göring, for discussions which included a U.S. gold loan to Hitler. This was set up at the behest of James D. Mooney of General Motors, a man who was awarded by Hitler for his service to the Third Reich. The meeting between Kennedy and Wohlthat was called off before it could take place when President Roosevelt forbade it. Undaunted, Kennedy arranged for Wohlthat to come to London. The two met at the Berkeley Hotel on May 9th, 1939 where they reportedly agreed on everything. Roosevelt was outraged. At that point M15, the British intelligence service, began to scrutinize Kennedy for suspicion of collusion with Britain's enemies.

A few months later, Kennedy commited the most dubious act of his public career when he appointed Nazi sympathizer Tyler Kent to work as code clerk in the London embassy. Kent was to be trusted with the most confidential telegrams which included those from Churchill and Kennedy to the President.

Tyler Kent's family was in the diplomatic corp and he grew up overseas. He was well educated and spoke several languages. During his stay in Moscow under Ambassador William Bullitt, Kent determined from the diplomatic correspondence he read that Roosevelt was unconstitutionally leading the United States into war against Germany. Kennedy himself is believed to have opposed the war because he had substantial investments in Germany.

Scotland Yard came upon Kent's apartment one afternoon and, with a proper search warrant, entered and found hosts of telegrams and official correspondence. Kent was immediately arrested under the official secrets act and was brought before Ambassador Kennedy. The two men met in private for fifteen minutes. History will not tell us what was said because both give different renditions of the meeting. Kennedy acted outraged over the whole affair while Kent insisted his aim was to inform the American people of their duplicitous president. It is also known that Kent was passing information to an intelligence circle he had joined called "The Link".

As a member of the embassy, Tyler Kent was under diplomatic immunity and couldn't be tried as a criminal in Great Britain. Ordinary protocol would be for him to be returned to America and tried for treason under American law, but that presented severe problems for both Kennedy and the President. His defense would have been that Roosevelt was conspiring for war. Kennedy, who had his own skeletons to hide, waived diplomatic immunity for Kent but only after receiving permission from the White House. This maneuver was unprecedented in the history of modern international diplomacy. Kent was tried and was sentenced to seven years in prison on the Isle of Wight. The actual documents on Tyler Kent are still sealed from public view in the Roosevelt Library at Hyde Park, New York. Someday, if they are not vetted, they may tell the truth about the whole affair.

Although the Kennedys have a very dubious reputation, it should be remembered that they are not basically evil. All families have their problems and they live and breath just like the rest of us. Lady Cameron introduced very strongly to me the idea of ancestral karma and how one particular clan will have a karma independent of the various individuals within it. In the case of the Kennedys, this is particularly noteworthy with regard to the Tyler Kent case.

Kent's mother was outraged by what happened with her son. She knew diplomatic law and wrote voluminous letters to Kennedy, none of which he opened. Finally, they crossed paths one day in a Washington hotel and she pleaded to him personally. He was polite but said there was nothing he could do. Remarkably, he closed the conversation by saying, "This might strike one of my sons".

In spite of their darker side, the Kennedys are also known to possess some humanitarian character traits. After the war began, telegrams began to pour in to the London embassy by Americans who were worried about their relatives abroad in Great Britain. There were no funds to pay for the many answers from the various relatives, but Joseph Kennedy paid considerable sums out of his own pocket to see their messages were sent back to America. This was a small pittance to his considerable fortune, but he did not have to do it. You can find plenty more humanitarian gestures with all the Kennedys if you read the various histories.

My purpose is to bring out their German and occult links of this remarkable family. This began to reveal itself many years ago when I received a copy of a page from a Scottish genealogy book. It indicated that the Kennedy's were genetically linked to the Camerons! This book said that both families trace their roots to the Scottish Isle of Skye, the isle of witches. Perhaps the Kennedy mystique of Camelot is real magick at work and not just a media illusion. All of you know that if JFK Jr. was ever nominated for president, he would be elected on the female vote alone. There is also a frenzy people feel about electing a Kennedy. It is magick.

All of this takes an even more intriguing turn when we recognize that this same genealogy book identifies the meaning of the name Kennedy as "ugly head". This does not mean the Kennedys are or were ugly in appearance. Most of the famous ones are considered good looking or charming at the very least. Charisma is a word often used to describe them. Serious students of occultism will readily recognize that "ugly head" refers not to their looks but to the great "ugly head" himself: Baphomet, the bisexual god with the head of a goat, female breasts and cloven feet. This was the mysterious figure who the Knights Templar confessed to worshipping under the tortures of the Inquisition. Baphomet was also the name Aleister Crowley chose for himself as the Outer Head of the O.T.O. This identification with Baphomet is one of the strongest occult links a family could ask for.

The occult superstition concerning "Friday the Thirteenth" began when Jacque de Molay and his Templars were arrested by King Phillip of France on Friday, October 13. One of the charges against him was worshipping or paying homage to Baphomet. King Phillip soon fell dead, apparently the result of a curse set on him by de Molay, but the Inquisition took over and purged the Templars from respectable European society. After that point, the tradition of the Templars splits off in at least two directions. One faction carried their legacy from France to Scotland and eventually to America. The others went to Germany and established strongholds, eventually sparking the secret societies which gave rise to Hitler.

With all of this in mind, one of John F. Kennedy's most celebrated quotes takes on a highly symbolic meaning, if not a literal one. "I am a Berliner" was not just a PR statement designed to impress a bunch of non voting Germans with the idea that he would fight communism. It was a statement reaffirming the racial ties and ancestry between the Celts and the Germans. Ironically, JFK was in Berlin just before German invaded Poland. He was allegedly monitoring goings on for his father.

BAPHOMET

Above is a Teutonic rendition of the goddess Ishtar with Baphomet
positioned at her groin. A male and female head represent
the two polarities of mankind's basic nature.

CHAPTER SIX

6

TEUTONIC HERITAGE

As was recounted in *Montauk Revisited*, Marjorie Cameron told me that the Camerons derived from the Gunn clan who had in turn derived from the Odins of Scandinavia. Thus, it should not really surprise us that the Kennedys and Camerons have a common Nordic heritage. According to more than a few scholars, the name "Cameron" may have derived from "Cam-shron" which means "wry-nose" or "crooked nose". This is most certainly incorrect, aside from the fact it is pure assumption attributed to the prominent nose of some mysterious clan chief. It has also been incorrectly labeled "Crooked Hill" from the Old Gaelic words *cum brun*.

In the fifteenth century, the name "Clancamroun" is written in the language of the Scots. This gives us a valuable clue to the phoenetic meaning of the name which translates to "Clan-cam-roun" or "Clan-cam-rune". This literally means family of the secret rune. "Cam" refers to a secret vault and is where the word "camera" derives from. "Rune" refers to the sacred glyphs of the northern regions most often ascribed to the ancient Teutonic race. Upon telling Lady Cameron about this derivation, she did not disagree with me but told me, according to her family tradition, the name derived from "Ahmroun". This aspect will come into play later. For now, we will consider the runic aspect.

Heinrich Himmler, the Reichsfuhrer of Hitler's SS, was renowned for his interest in occultism, particularly when it came to the runes and Teutonic lore. In 1939, Himmler discovered a defunct castle at Wewelsburg, near Paderborn in Westphalia. Its grandiose structure inspired Himmler to reconstruct it for use as

67

the most sacred temple of the SS. It was designed to emulate the Knights of the Round Table. Underneath was a room with vaulted architecture which was known as the Holy of Holies. Inside was an altar of black marble with two silver runes inscribed upon it signifying "SS". On this marble was said to repose the Holy Grail itself or at least a replica. It was in this castle that Himmler's knights meditated on the ethics of honor, mythical blood, occult biology, as well as Gnostic and dualistic themes.

Not far from Himmler's castle at Wewelsburg is Externsteine, a very large and unusual rock formation. Sacred to both pagans and early Christians, this rock garden is honeycombed with passages and caves. Many entrances can be seen from outside the rocks. According to local legends, treasures were buried in or near these stones during World War II.

It was not an accident that Himmler chose Externsteine as the home for his sacred fortress. This land was the most sacred of the ancient Teutonic culture and was a place of pilgrimage for all of Europe, including the Celtic peoples. Said to be the location where many of the ancient Nordic and other German myths took place, Externsteine is given short shrift by historians, and most people are unaware of its existence. This gigantic rock formation pales Stonehenge in comparison and was viewed in times past as a center of supreme racial generation. The nomadic reindeer hunters in early history considered this location to be their sanctuary. Externsteine was also a center for pagan rituals until the eighth century. These rituals centered around the great tree of life called Irmensul. This tree was an actual tree at one time but was eventually cut down by Christians. They celebrated this act by depicting the tree in a relief carving on one of the rocks. The rock depicted the original tree as a stool used by Nicodemus as he lifts down the body of Jesus from the cross. In other words, the tree was minimized by comparison to Christ and was only a stepping stone to the great work of Christianity.

The rocks at Externsteine are so huge that one even houses a chapel on top of it. In 1823, a man by the name of von Bennigsen noticed a round window in the chapel. This window frames a view of the moon if observed from the opposite wall when the moon is at its northern extreme. This aperture also lets in the light of the summer sun during the summer solstice.

In 1920, a German scholar by the name of Wilhelm Teudt tuned into this information and recognized these rocks as an ancient astronomical observatory. He sought to raise the spiritual consciousness of the German people by reminding them of their ancient ancestral culture. Prior to Teudt, it was commonly believed that this chapel was an entirely Christian structure. He established beyond the shadow of a doubt that it was an ancient and accurate observatory which linked other sacred sights throughout Germany. Although he wasn't embraced by academe, the Nazis took notice of his work and appreciated Teudt's rejuvenation of the ancient customs. Heinrich Himmler was a particularly fond admirer.

Some scholars have discredited Teudt because his language was bombastic, and he sought to show that Germans were racially superior in every aspect due to their ancient heritage. This included the claim that the ancient Germanic culture built the pyramids of Egypt. Teudt's association with the Nazis has made it difficult for modern establishment scholars to digest the actual scholarship of his work. Ironically, his views were corroborated by an English scholar, Albert Watkins, who independently reached the same conclusions in his own research, minus the bombastic racial superiority. Watkins had no pro-Aryan axe to grind, but his discoveries concerning the ancient Teutonic peoples would also remain buried.

After the war, the Externsteine rocks presented a problem to the authorities. They were a fascinating tourist attraction due to their intricate labyrinths and history, but they were intimately associated with the Nazis and had to be "de-Nazified". Accordingly, this de-Nazification process, known as the "Nature and Culture Movement", cost the rocks of Externsteine much of their mystique. Many of their mythical attributes were deleted from the tourist guide books.

The concept that the ancient Germans or Aryans built the Great Pyramid might seem absurd to most scholars and regular "good" people. It is a foreign concept to what most of us have been taught. The irony of it all becomes astonishingly clear when we examine the etymology of the word Teuton or Teutonic which are both derived from the base word teuta (pronounced *tāy-ōo-tāy*). This compares precisely with the Egyptian scribe of the Gods,

Tahuti, who is known as Thoth by the Greeks. Tahuti is known in Egyptian mythology and history as the builder of the Great Pyramid. At the very least, he is the one who arranged for or inspired the erection of the structure. The name of the German scholar Teudt makes you wonder who was inspiring his writing. The Nazis actually employed Teudt at the Externsteine cultural center for a time. His powers were later nullified by SS officers who had more immediate political interests to further.

The rich legacy of the Teutonic people is readily observable in their ancient glyphs, more commonly known as runes. Various books give different meanings for these symbols as well as competing techniques of divination. No matter whose version you follow, the knowledge concerning them is mysterious and secretive. According to the tradition of the Nordic peoples, these runes were given to mankind by Odin, the King of the Gods. Odin was only able to obtain this wisdom after he traded an eye in exchange for it. Artistic renditions of Odin depict him as missing an eye.

The above legacy shows a remarkable correlation to that of Egypt. While the term *hieroglyph* refers to sacred Egyptian writings or secret ciphers,the word *rune* means secret. In the Egyptian pantheon, Tahuti is the purveyor of this written wisdom in his role as the god of knowledge and scribe of the gods. He was also known as the surgeon of the Eye of Horus. Thus, his position does not conflict with that of Odin. This trading of the eye for wisdom by Odin is, of course, symbolic of the third eye. Odin sought the knowledge of the Eye of Horus, of which Tahuti was the surgeon. It was this secret knowledge which gave Odin command over the other gods and symbolizes the rulership of the morphogenetic grid. Odin then dispensed the knowledge of the runes to mankind so that they could themselves keep the archetypal powers in check.

That the Camerons derived from the Odin clan suggests that their legacy is strongly linked to these runes. When we recognize that Duncan Cameron, Sr. and Ewen Cameron had influence with the Nazis, their pull was actually to a much deeper genetic heritage than any political or war machine could attract on its own.

What is not commonly pointed out, if it has ever been in popular literature, is that the runic symbols all conform to precise geometric angles and relationships. All of these runes conform to the geometrical principles revealed in the book *Pyramids of*

Montauk. There is much to be learned by studying the specific relationships between the angles of polyhedrons, their resonant frequencies and the entire spectrum of the hard physical sciences. If pursued, this will add further interpretation to the runes as well as the crop circles which derive from the same patterns. Although it is a different study than what we are pursuing in this work, it is really the purist and highest pursuit of magick as well as science.

I have pursued this angle to reveal that the ancient lore of the Teutonic peoples was not, as has often been portrayed in history, a bunch of mad and berserk Vikings who conquered their way from one area to another. Our culture is primarily acquainted with only the most violent aspects of Viking culture. There was also a rich legacy of real knowledge in the form of the runes.

The Vikings also identified deeply with shamanic practices. They wore a horned helmet to signify animal power. The name berserker itself means "bear shirted" to signify that they wore bearskins. Wolf skins were also worn in ceremonies in which the participants were purported to change into animals. To what degree this shape shifting actually took place is not recorded in any "respectable" literature, but the science of morphology concerns the changing of a life form into a different aspect of itself. There is evidence to suggest the Nazis believed in shamanic shape shifting. Morphology is based upon geometric fluctuations conforming to a simple centralized and relatively stable design, the more sensational aspects of which would be a creature like a werewolf. Hitler enjoyed his nickname "Wulf" (Adolph means "noble wolf"), thus the name *Wolf's Lair* for his Bavarian hideaway. He was also called "Manitou" by his staff. This means shape shifter. Otto Skorzeny, the top Nazi commando of World War II, chose Werewolves as the name of his crack commando unit. They were elite above all others, including the SS.

Hitler and all of his cronies were portrayed as psychopaths and have been subjected to all sorts of pop psychiatric explanations. In the end, all of this analysis adds up to nothing more than confusing information. It only tells us that the Nazis were nuts and that the analyzers had no real explanation. It was as if they were all following a trend which was set forth at the Nuremburg trials: to obfuscate the true underpinnings of the Nazi regime, especially with regard to its reverence for and fascination with occult lore.

Several books have been written on the Nazis and the occult. Many of them make for good reading, but most do not take the sacred aspects of the Teutonic peoples too seriously. It is easier to ridicule them or bury them for fear of a Fourth Reich. As with the other indigenous peoples of the Earth, the Teutons had a sacred heritage which was very deep and little understood by outsiders. The German and Celtic peoples feel this sacredness in their very blood. In fact, the word *blood* itself is derived from *sacred*.

There has been a steady campaign since the end of World War II to desecrate the heritage of the Teutonic peoples. Mel Brooks, a comedian who has made some very funny movies in this regard, is just one example. Most of this denigration is understandable in the wake of World War II and the atrocities that were perpetrated. But, in order to understand the Nazis, who are still with us today, we must become fully conscious of the forces which united the people of Germany against their perceived enemy. Hitler harnessed these energies and established himself in an extremely powerful position. The way he obtained power has been criticized because assassins and thugs were a method that he used, but these acts are nothing new to history. More importantly, we need to understand that the relationship between Hitler and the Germans is mirrored in their local history. The kings and earls of the ancient Teutonic empire were always supported by a retinue of loyal warriors who received the spoils of victories. The personal loyalties created by these relationships were extremely powerful. In fact, heroically dying in battle next to one's lord is one of the basic themes in Germanic and Nordic literature. When the Germans talked of their Fuhrer and their fanatical devotion to him, they were only following the ancient pagan ways of their ancestors. These feelings were suppressed and repressed in the German psyche for hundreds of years before Hitler came along. He merely unleashed a particularly negative aspect of them.

The suppression of the pagan psyche was initially accomplished through the ruling clergy. It is still suppressed today. Again, it is important that we understand the make up of the Germanic character and not try to subvert it or pretend that it doesn't exist. If we ignore this or subvert the right of pagans to express their true beliefs, we will get cross burnings, neo-Nazi hate groups and the like. The spirit of the warrior is not held in high regard in our society. As a result, we have litigation as never before seen in world history. This doesn't mean that we need to engage in fighting or civil war, but if the energies are properly recognized, they can be sublimated to a higher echelon of achievement.

I have given this view so that you will feel some sympathy for the sacred heritage of the Teutonic people. In this regard, their native beliefs are just as sacred as that of the Native Americans and other indigenous peoples. As Lady Cameron said to me, her ancestors often struggled with their sexual energies and often succumbed to the dark side. These sexual energies are the pagan energies. They are a part of our archetypal makeup whether we are Christian, Buddhist or Islamic. The misuse of these energies is the legacy of Montauk, the experiments of which were symptomatic of misusing sacred principles.

Ancestral karma is also very important in this entire equation. The ancestors of yesterday are alive in their clans today. The karma must be cleaned up. It not only applies to many of you in the reading audience but to other great families of the world. It is not just a matter for the Camerons and Kennedys. Fortunately or unfortunately, we have to depend on the great families of the world to do their share.

It was, regrettably, this incredible preoccupation with the blood line which not only gave rise to the horrors at Montauk but to the diabolical experiments performed by Ewen Cameron. In the next chapter, we will look at another angle on the blood line.

CHAPTER SEVEN

7

THE HOUSE OF ORANGE

The end of the first millennium A.D. was not only the peak time period of the Middle Ages and Knights Templar, it was celebrated by a wave of Norsemen settling in North America. The first reported arrival on Long Island was by Thorwald, a member of Leif Erickson's Greenland colony. On page 82 of Payne's *History of America*, it is reported that Thorwald "found a great island lying west and east, which could be no other than Long Island". Whether Thorwald visited Montauk Point, contacted the natives or placed runic symbols in sacred spots, we may never know. These suggestions might sound farfetched to some, however the phenomena known as "Smithsonian-gate" has caused more than a few misconceptions over the years. "Smithsonian-gate" refers to the hiding of ancient relics which put a totally new light on our history than what we are taught in the schools and force fed on the television. As much of our true history has been denied us, we have to look for it between the cracks.

The Aryan connection to Long Island took a new twist when I began to study Lion Gardiner, the most prominent European to settle on Long Island. Curiously, he chose the Montauk area for his new home. Gardiner was mentioned in *Pyramids of Montauk* as a friend of Chief Wyandanch and managed to "acquire" much of the Montauks' property. As the natives didn't believe it possible to "own" the land, misunderstandings arose between the two parties from which the term "Indian giver" originated.

Lion Gardiner is recorded in history as a friend to the Indians and is portrayed as a man of fairness, kindness and justice. If he

75

was a manipulator, there is no doubt that he had a much stronger disposition towards compassion and leniency than most of the magistrates and leaders of that time period.

Lion Gardiner died in 1663. Two hundred years later, his grave was dug up so that he could be moved to a more stately tomb. In a twist of irony and remarkable synchronicity, the grave diggers were both named Pharoah! They were descendants of the Montauk royal tribe. Lion Gardiner's skeleton was found to be undisturbed. In fact, his large frame of 6'2" and his red hair were still evident. His descendants chose to honor him by erecting a tomb wherein he was depicted in a knight's helmet and armor. This sort of representation was certainly not common for people who had died in the 1600s. The chivalry of the Middle Ages was a thing of the past. To have such honor bestowed upon him, particularly two hundred years after his death, reveals a secret. To be buried with knight's honors indicates that one serviced the highest cause: protection of the royal blood. This may be equated to protection or custodianship of the Holy Grail. Certain occult traditions also view red hair as a sign of being of the lineage of Charlemagne which in turn descends from the lineage of Christ. Red hair is also recognized by some as being associated with witchcraft.

Research into Lion Gardiner and his associations has revealed even further astonishing information. He was a "Dutchman" who served in the English army and came from the principality of Orange in the Netherlands. At first glance, it might seem odd that a Dutchman would serve in the English army and end up being the most important character on Long Island. It seems like countries and networks are getting crossed up. A closer examination of history reveals this not to be the case.

Originally, there was no such place as Holland. The Netherlands was actually a combination of German and French settlers. The Germans called their province Nassau*, while the French province was known as Orange. As the primary power in Europe, the Spanish ruled the area for several years. A German ruler by the name of William I inherited huge tracks of land in the Netherlands

---

* Nassau is also the name of a major county on Long Island. There are four counties on Long Island: Kings County (which is entirely occupied by the borough of Brooklyn), Queens County, Nassau County and Suffolk County. The latter includes Montauk.

and helped fight off the Catholic Spanish. He championed a protestant rebellion that eventually gave rise to a very powerful dynasty. Ever since, this dynasty has been known as the House of Orange-Nassau or, in its more simplified version, the House of Orange. Lion Gardiner, the first recognized European settler of Montauk, was a member of the House of Orange. Learning this, it becomes a little easier to fill in the blanks. In view of the above information, it is hard to believe that the House of Orange was not aware of Montauk as a sacred energy spot.

The House of Orange was very dynamic in their plans to expand their own power. Through the official government of Holland, they arranged for the coronation of the Dutch royal family. William Bramley, in his book *The Gods of Eden*, has linked the unseen German influence in the House of Orange to the secret brotherhood he calls the Brotherhood of the Snake. This is the same group mentioned by Anna with regard to Ewen Cameron. Bramley explains how the institution of the monarchy in Europe traces back to the "gods" of ancient Sumeria. The tablets of Sumeria indicate that the first human kings were the offspring of "custodial rulers" who mated with human women. Such a lineage deserved the identity of royal blood. These gods were depicted as blue skinned or blue blooded which is where the concept "blue bloods" comes from.

This fascination with royal blood might seem preposterous to the ordinary man on the street. The concept should be taken seriously however, if only for the reason that so many bloody wars throughout history have been fought over the subject. In *Pyramids of Montauk*, it was explained that the Rh negative blood possesses no simian (monkey) genetic aspects. Rh negative blood, which stands for blood without the Rhesus factor, is identified with the prototype for the original human. This is sometimes called the *Adam Kadmon* or the original human intelligence. This preoccupation is important to our study in this book but will be dealt with in greater depth later on. It is mentioned here to link the associations with the House of Orange. They were blue bloods.

According to William Bramley, several German royal families were notorious for marrying into foreign royal families in order to seize more power and expand their empire. Perhaps the most tragic tale in this regard is that of the Stuart family of England.

After struggling to regain the throne, the Stuarts were ultimately undone through the House of Orange. Through the marriage of the famous William and Mary, the House or Orange occupied the male side of the throne. William was actually William III of Orange and Mary was the daughter of King Charles II of England. After this marriage of convenience for the brotherhood, the House of Orange reigned over the Netherlands, England and also their German kingdom. When William III of Orange eventually died, his sister Anne inherited the throne. Then, in a shocking historical move, and by prior arrangement, Anne was succeeded by rulers of the German state of Hanover who had already married into the British Stuart family. The Hanoverian kings took the name of Windsor Castle and forever after have been known as the House of Windsor. Today, this is name of the royal family of England. The Gaelic empire of the British Isles always considered the Windsors to be impostors to the throne and still do so to this day. The House of Orange's strongest and most obnoxious abuse of power has been witnessed by the world through their stranglehold over Ireland in the north. It has been said that the original Irish priests were linked to the Druids and possessed the true Christianity in its original form. This is the underlying and esoteric theme of the war in Ireland. It is, of course, much more complicated than that in every day life. Both sides are actually strewn with intelligence plants.[*]

We are offered further intrigue concerning the House of Orange when we consider the case of Richard Cameron, the son of a shop keeper in Fife. Converted to an extreme wing of Calvinists when he was a schoolmaster, he fled to join exiled Calvinist ministers in Holland during a period of intolerance. Upon returning to Scotland to preach, he and his followers were ambushed whereupon he urged them to fight it out. While Cameron was slain in this altercation, he was not forgotten. The Calvinist movement triumphed in 1698 and the regiment raised in support of William of Orange was the Cameronian regiment. This was their elite fighting corp and still exists in some form today.

It is clear that the Camerons not only operated in the House of Orange but also in the opposing Jacobite faction. The Jacobite

---

[*] Those who are more interested in the political aspects of the House of Orange and its connection should read the book *The Gods of Eden* by William Bramley.

cause was to bring the Stuart family back to the crown. This type of pervasive influence in human affairs is well expressed in a statement I read in a genealogy book on the Parsons family. It said that the Parsons were very proud of their heritage but chose to work in the background for George Washington rather than to take high profile professions. They felt that while some people and families were suited towards high profile jobs, the Parsons could best contribute to civilization behind the scenes.

The Camerons were influencing both sides and the House of Orange was also their instrument. Lion Gardiner's move to Long Island on behalf of the House of Orange revealed itself to contain even more mysteries.

8

LION GARDINER
AND THE WITCH

The exact role of Lion Gardiner in the course of Montauk history becomes even more bizarre when we consider that he was deeply involved in the first and only witchcraft trial in the documented history of Long Island. The story begins in 1658 when a young man by the name of Samuel Parsons visits the house of his friend Arthur Howell. Howell's wife is named Elizabeth, and she is the daughter of Lion Gardiner. Elizabeth is ill and complains of having a fever. After suckling her newborn baby, she hands the child to Parsons and begins to sing the words of a psalm. Suddenly, she begins to shriek and spout out words of a totally different strain: "A witch! A witch! Now you are come to torture me because I spoke two or three words against you! In the morning you will come fawning..."

After her outburst, Parsons was said to exclaim, "The Lord be merciful to her. I will all be well. It is well if she be not bewitched."

Upon the bizarre outburst by his daughter, Lion Gardiner was called to the scene. Living just across the street, he arrived immediately. Elizabeth continued her rantings.

"A witch! A witch!" she said again.

When her father asked her what she saw, Elizabeth said a black thing was at the foot of the bed. She then asked about her mother who had been very ill herself. Lion informed her that her mother, Betty, had a fever. Upon this news, Elizabeth asked her father not to tell her mother of the bewitching. Despite her own ill

81

health, Gardiner's wife struggled to her feet, leaned on a neighbor for support and slowly made her way to Elizabeth's bedside.

"Oh, mother, I am bewitched," Elizabeth cried out.

Although Mrs. Gardiner refused to accept this and insisted that Elizabeth must be sleeping or dreaming, the daughter did not relent. She insisted she was not asleep or dreaming and that she was truly bewitched. When questioned further by her mother, Elizabeth said that she saw the Gardiner's servant, Goody Garlick, at the end of the bed and a black thing of Goody's at the other corner. Mrs. Gardiner told her to keep quiet about this, and as her own health was failing, she had to return to her own bed.

As the other women of the community tended to Elizabeth, the affliction increased. Elizabeth then claimed that Goody was a double tongued woman who pricked her with pins and tormented her. Elizabeth asked for Goody Garlick to come in person so she could tear her to pieces. She again claimed that Goody had pricked her with pins and had also brought a black thing to the foot of the bed. At this point, Elizabeth began to gag and choke, clutching her throat. Her mouth was forced open with a table knife, but nothing could be seen inside. Then, after another bout of coughing, a pin seemed to fall from Elizabeth's mouth to the bed.

That night, two men and a woman slept with Elizabeth to care for her. To the shock of all, a poltergeist noise was heard. By the next evening, Elizabeth Gardiner Howell had died. Before she passed on, she was heard to exclaim, "Mother...Garlick...double-tongued...ugly thing...pins". She then became delirious and slowly struggled until death.

The wake of this occurrence left the villagers fearful and suspicious. An investigation was launched into Goodwife "Goody" Garlick whose real name was also Elizabeth. Local gossip had long associated her with witchcraft. She was known to dispense herbs and Lion Gardiner had once employed her in a use of counter-magic designed to help him with the misadventures of some of his animals. Not only did Goody Garlick own a black cat, she was a wet nurse for many children who suffered misfortune after consuming her breast milk.

An involved trial ensued during which a preponderant amount of evidence was brought forth linking Goody Garlick to witchcraft. Although the evidence seemed genuine and came from multiple sources, Goody Garlick got off the hook. She was vigorously defended by her husband Joshua Garlick and to our surprise, Lion Gardiner, whose own daughter had died and pointed a finger at Goody.

We don't really know what Lion Gardiner's motivation was in protecting this woman. She had clearly worked for the man and had even lived on his property for a time. The history books portray Lion Gardiner as a kindly soul who could see beyond the passions and cruelty of ordinary people. He was a noble sort, but we have to wonder if he had something personal to gain by relieving this woman from her accusers.

Whatever are the actual facts of the situation, I have never heard of a witchcraft trial where the evidence seemed so convincing. Millions of witches were burned during this time period, mostly for doing nothing but practicing their own religion. This case with Goody Garlick seemed to set a precedent. No witches were ever tried on Long Island after that. It seemed to herald an era of black magic practices on Long Island which still exist to the present day.

We are given further insight into the nature of these times when we consider a case that happened four years earlier. The following quote is taken from the town records:

> *Daniel Fairfield, a servant of Joshua Garlick, Fulke Davis, John Davis and John Hand, Jr., were brought before the three townsmen — John Mulford, Thomas Baker and John Hand — on a charge of masturbation, and after an extended examination and serious debate in consultation with their Say Brook neighbors, the townsmen, not deeming the offense worthy of loss of life or limb, determined that Fulke Davis shall be placed in the pillory and receive corporal punishment, and John Davis and Daniel Fairfield shall be publicly whipped, which was done and was witnessed by three townsmen.*

This is an astonishing but accurate portrayal of the fear and superstition these people attributed to sexual energy. It was obviously a highly regulated community with the local "thought police" ready to interfere at a moment's notice. In a community that is so restrained, it is more than likely that someone engaging in sexual magick might have far more impact than in today's society. Lion Gardiner did not seem influenced or intimidated by the "thought police". Although he had fought alongside of the Protestants, he seemed to be above all that. It is clear that Lion Gardiner was a different breed altogether.

Lion Gardiner's progeny did not have an easy time living up to his father glorious reputation. In fact, Lion warned his wife, Mary, to be wary of their son, David, who had a reputation for foolishness and squandering. David's son, John, inherited the red hair from his grandfather and some of his intelligence. He was known to have fathered innumerable half-breeds with the Montauks and even spoke their language. According to John Lyon, the great-great grandson of John Gardiner, he came to their wigwams to eat fresh fish and liked the young squaws of the old sachem breed. He referred to himself as "Lord John" and "thought that if he did not sleep with Royal Family...he should make a poor nobleman." This tells us that John Gardiner knew more than a thing or two about the royal blood, particularly when it came into play with the Montauk natives.*

In conclusion, we do not know the exact number or names of the secret societies that Lion Gardiner was a member of, but in light of all of the above data, there is absolutely no doubt that this man was in the thick of it. Although there are still many questions to ask and follow through with regard to Lion Gardiner, he was just one of many colorful characters in the history of Montauk. The next one we will look it is even more intriguing.

---

* John Gardiner is also known in history for harboring Captain Kidd. From all historical accounts, Kidd seemed to be quite innocent of the charges levied against him and was put to death to protect the conspiratorial financial interests of the day. Although Gardiner was ordered to give up some of Kidd's treasure, it has often been rumored that he never relinquished the entire amount. I am sure that if we were ever to learn the true story of Captain Kidd, it would not just be about money. In the tradition of Montauk, we can almost count on very bizarre and esoteric interests being at stake. There is a pond named after Kidd just north of Montauk's Camp Hero. It is called "Captain Kidd's Pond".

9

PROJECT PAPERCLIP
AND THE HAMILLS

In an earlier chapter, we spoke of Ewen Cameron's story that Rudolph Hess had something to do with time travel. Preston Nichols has reported for years that World War II was a war of time. This information does not come from his own mind but from what sources in the secret sector have told him. Al Bielek tells a story about "Project Trojan Horse" which is a continuation by the Americans of a time project begun by German forces. The movie *Philadelphia Experiment II* is primarily about the Nazis being involved in time travel via the Philadelphia Experiment.

Three separate sources connected to the name Cameron plus a movie suggest that the Nazis were involved in time travel. While this does not constitute proof, it is that same outside source telling me to investigate further. Further synchronicity connected to this subject has directed me to focus on the character Preston knows as Mark Hamill. In *Montauk Revisited*, it was alleged that Hamill, the star of the *Star Wars* movies, was the covert producer of the movie *The Philadelphia Experiment*. For the record, Preston Nichols will not positively identify the "Mark Hamill" he knows as the "real" Mark Hamill of *Star Wars*. My inside knowledge tells me quite clearly that Preston asserts this only for the reason that he is trying to avoid any remote potential of legal repercussions in the future.

Since I have known Preston, people close to him have disputed his contention that he even knew Mark Hamill. I have asked Preston's father about this. He remembers Mark as a young boy who cleaned up the leaves from their backyard. Hamill is also an extremely talented composer, musician and actor. He has a list of hit records from the '60s through the '80s that were done under psuedonyms. The key word with this individual is Creative, with a capital "C". The general public knows him primarily, if not only, as an actor.

My own interaction with the wake of Mark Hamill has been very strange. Ever since the writing of *Montauk Revisited*, strange synchronicities have come to me concerning him. I have been approached by people familiar with Mark or otherwise connected to his family. Sometimes the people or implements associated with them have had a tendency to "disappear". I cannot say whether the disappearances were a literal banishing of matter, but the circumstances were always odd. There are still many loose ends that are yet to be fully brought to light. Consequently, I will stick only to the most relevant facts.

Al Bielek reported speaking to Doug Curtis who was listed as the producer of *The Philadelphia Experiment*. He told Al that Mark Hamill was not connected to the project in any way. When questioned on the upcoming sequel to *The Philadelphia Experiment*, Curtis was said to report that he himself would have no involvement with it.

During the Christmas season of 1992, Preston informed me that he had bumped into Mark Hamill in a mall on Long Island. Mark told Preston he was visiting his family for the holidays and further mentioned that he was not allowed to speak to Al Bielek or Peter Moon. He had been working on a film project, *Philadelphia Experiment II*, that was supposedly backed by the government.

When the movie was released, Doug Curtis was listed on the credits and, lo and behold, the Executive Producer was a man by the name of Mark Levinson. This seems to be an obvious play on the name "Mark" and the "Levinson time equations" mentioned in *The Montauk Project: Experiments in Time*. It was as if Mark was rubbing it in our faces.

Shortly after this time period, it was reported on *CBS This Morning* that when virtually all the homes in a section of Malibu burned during the brush fires, Mark Hamill's house was miraculously saved. He appeared for a brief minute or two and said he did an occult Indian ritual which preserved his house.

The fact that *Philadelphia Experiment II* was about Nazi's controlling time should not be taken lightly in view of the above synchronicities. Another synchronicity occurred in the movie when the name "Decker" was loudly yelled out. This was during a scene when there was no particularly logical reason for it. Preston and I recognized this as an obvious reference to a man we know as Decker. That is the actual name used by the character Preston knew in *Montauk Revisited* as John von Neumann. Mark Hamill would have known this.

If that wasn't enough, Mark Hamill then appeared as a preacher in the movie "Village of the Damned" with Scientologist Kirstie Allie and former Scientologist Christopher Reeve. This is a movie about blue-eyed blond haired children taking over a village through the use of mind power.

Given all the other synchronicities with Hamill, the odds of him landing a part in this movie with an Aryan theme were rather remarkable, regardless of what the real life circumstances were. I decided to do a quick search through the library for any references on Mark Hamill. The only significant one I could find was an article in *Variety* which mentioned that Mark Hamill had a car accident in the late 1970s and had become disfigured in the face. It said that reconstructive plastic surgery gave him a new look which he sported for the movie *The Return of the Jedi*. What Preston had been saying for years now made sense to me. Despite Preston's desire to be legally cautious about Hamill, he always said that he was never sure if the Mark Hamill he knew was the same one who starred in the movies. At this point, I had to seriously wonder if the "new" Mark was a double. There have been several instances of Duncan Cameron having a double.

After reading the article in *Variety*, I called Preston and asked if he had ever heard of Mark having plastic surgery. He answered yes and said it was because of a car accident, according to what Mark had told him.

The above incidents leave us with several questions and a general befuddlement. Nazi doctors were known to be the best plastic surgeons in the world. They made a fortune in Brazil fixing up their SS clients, particularly those who needed a new or obscured identity. The Brazilians absorbed the Nazis into their culture quite nicely. We really don't know if Mark is really Mark but we do know that his accident occurred when the Montauk Project was roaring at a full clip.

All of these synchronicities took a deeper and even more remarkable twist when I stumbled across a biography entitled *Werner von Braun, Crusader for Space*. Knowing that von Braun was a famous German rocket scientist, I looked through the index to see if there were any references to Jack Parsons. There was a single reference, but when I turned to the relevant page, Parsons was merely listed with a group of other scientists. That was that and it seemed like a fruitless exercise. In my style of research, these minor disappointments are not uncommon and I think nothing of them, only this time my eyes immediately recognized a name on the other side of the page. There was a mention of a Lt. Col. James Hamill. Further investigation revealed this man to be one of the major players involved in Project Paperclip, the naturalizing of Nazi scientists into Americans. The book *Secret Agenda: The United States Government, Nazi Scientists, and Project Paperclip 1945-1990* by Linda Hunt was particularly helpful with regard to information on James Hamill.

This "tall, fair-headed" major was twenty-six years old at the time he was chosen for one of the most crucial positions in the European theater of war. As the Russians had not yet descended upon Hitler's bunker, there was a race to get to the German rocket technology that had come out of Peenemünde, a large island in the Baltic just north of the German mainland. Although it is hard to believe, Hamill was reportedly a greenhorn in the regular army when it came to field work. On what was practically his first such assignment, he was chosen to coordinate the entire V-2 mission in Germany.

While an army war crimes unit investigated the area for crimes committed against prison laborers, Hamill and his team sought out technical documents and loaded up V-2 rockets which were shipped to the coast on specially laid railroad tracks. Once the scientists were rounded up, Hamill personally escorted Werner von Braun to the United States of America.

It wasn't enough that James Hamill evacuated the scientists. He was put directly in charge of Project Paperclip at Fort Bliss, Texas under his superior, Col. Toftoy. Like the Cameron brothers, Hamill had a degree in physics. He had gone to school at Fordham

University in the Bronx which points to him probably being a New York and a possible member of the Long Island connection. He is old enough to be Mark's father and is, in fact, just the right age if you consider that Mark's mother was divorced when Mark was only two. At least this is one story I heard. Those who would quickly dispute the dates should realize that Mark is much older than he looks. He has aged very gracefully.

It is also a reported fact that Mark's real father worked in military intelligence. A *National Enquirer* article had him listed as Navy intelligence. Although this could be an inaccuracy, it could have been a later assignment. Intelligence people are flip flopped in their roles and titles many times for various reasons. Duplicity is the rule. I don't think there is much room for doubt that this man was Mark's father, but I have not pursued to see if there is a genetic connection. Records can be altered and identities changed. This is a classic tool. The key principle to my studies is synchronicity. Even if the two men are not related, the odds of the name synchronicity are equally remarkable when you consider our entire story line and investigation.

James Hamill is castigated in the book by Linda Hunt for not only contributing to the deception of the American public (the government covered up the extent to which these Nazi scientists were protected and utilized) but for fostering the scientists' collaborations with their former contacts and allowing them to propagate their Nazi connection. Hamill allowed these German scientists to have telephones with no monitoring of their conversations nor were there any restrictions on long distance calls. None of the Paperclip scientists were required to fill out federal government forms in order to obtain standard security clearances. The supervision of these Nazis was so lax as to be labelled "arrogant". I suggest people read Linda Hunt's book if they would like to get further information on this absolute mockery of security.

Some of these Nazi scientists were accused of literally stepping over many dead bodies at the Mittelwurk rocket factories. These bodies belonged to the concentration camp inmates who worked in the factories. When it came to their functions as project directors or labor coordinators, some of these scientists were charged with the abuse of human life. Even though Hamill had visited Mittelwurk in 1945, he was quoted as saying he knew nothing about the place when questions were raised about inhuman acts or omissions of the Project Paperclip scientists.

At the end of her book, Linda Hunt asks some burning questions: why was it necessary to cover up Nazi crimes, evade presidential policy and harbor murderers? Not only were records changed and lied about to other government agencies, some agencies attempt to maintain the cover-up to this day.

Somebody and their group must have had an awful good reason. We are offered a couple of clues in this very chapter. The first one is the name of the island where the rocket research took place: Peenemünde. It is a Tibetan name. The English etymology of the name literally means "head of the world".

The other clue has to do with Hamill's search for technical documents. He wasn't just looking for technical information. He was getting his hands on every bit of flying saucer technology the Nazis had to offer. The controlling interest group, represented by the United States military, wanted superior technology with which to control the world. It is known that the Nazis had superior technology which included the use of flying saucers. Dead bodies are always an unfortunate issue, but they are of little moral consequence when it comes to a supreme military dictum to control your own living space by conquering your enemies. The Nazis had their own word and policy for this very concept. It was called Lebensraum. The United States now became a vehicle for this doctrine of Lebensraum. A hidden control group was operating through the United States military.

All of this information came to me through the principle of synchronicity via the German name of "Hamill". The story began to unfold even more when I made a live connection to Germany itself.

10

THE GERMAN CONNECTION

Before I even seriously considered the Nazi connection to Montauk, fate would lead me directly to Germany. In September of 1992, I attended the Frankfurt Book Fair. As I entered the city by taxi, I was struck by a noticeable landmark. It is a huge tower with a pyramid on top. It seemed rather remarkable because it looked like a big Delta-T antenna. Although I made several inquiries as to who owned this building, no one seemed to know. People said it was owned by a conglomeration of different companies or several insurance companies.

To my surprise, this tower turned out to be in the exact location of the Frankfurt Book Fair. After a few days at the fair, I went into the courtyard and discovered that the yard was filled with Masonic symbols. This left me with a puzzled and curious feeling. I wouldn't get any answers on this until a few years later when I began to receive phone calls and faxes from a gentleman in Germany. His name was Jan van Helsing, and he was arranging for the publication of *The Montauk Project* in the German language. He turned out to be a very curious source of information. Jan has special connections to many secret societies in Germany that stretch far back into antiquity. Some of these societies actually helped place Hitler into his ultimate position of power.

In September of 1994, Jan flew into Newark airport for a brief stopover en route to Hawaii. Preston was out of town, so Duncan and myself went to meet him. On the way, we stopped in Manhattan to pick up a friend who would also accompany us. A curious synchronicity would arise when we entered her apartment and she showed us a painting with the initials "A.H." at the bottom. It was a picture of three deer in a meadow and was said to be a Hitler original. It was rolled up and smuggled out of Germany by an American soldier after Hitler died. Its authenticity was not disputed by Sotherby's, New York's premiere auction house, who refused to auction it because of its signature and heritage. I couldn't help but feel we were on the trail of the Third Reich.

We made our way to a hotel at the Newark airport and met Jan who had a most interesting story to tell. Jan was born psychic from a mother who could read spirits. His father researched the psychic sciences for years. Despite this orientation, his own interest in the paranormal waned and he became involved in the punk rock music scene. Jan's interest in the psychic realm was sparked after a skinhead approached him one day. The skinhead told Jan that he could see things in his aura and that his crown chakra was not functioning properly. It was shocking to him that this information came from a skinhead, people who are usually portrayed as brutish and insensitive.

This experience woke Jan up and he began to have out of body experiences. After cutting off all drugs, alcohol and meat, he went into a coma for one and a half weeks and found himself outside of his body most of the time. These experiences included visions of pyramids and domed houses. They were situated in a community center of the future which he hopes to build some day.

Jan's life completely changed after his chance meeting with the skinhead and the subsequent experiences described. He went full throttle into esoteric studies and began to meet many psychics and aura readers. A particularly interesting event occurred when he met a seventy year old aura reader. Jan was particularly struck by the man's appearance because another psychic friend of his had already described the older man to a "T" and said that Jan would meet him. Upon looking at Jan's aura, the older man didn't say a word. Jan wanted to know why the man looked at him so strangely.

The older man said, "I have been doing aura readings for most of my life but I never saw anything as strange as you. It seems that you've been involved in some time travel. Some part of your soul is stuck somewhere."

This all sounded very familiar to Jan because he had already met Al Bielek under the strangest of circumstances.

When on holiday in Hawaii, Jan just happened to meet authors Bill Cooper and Brad Steiger by chance. They invited him onto their yacht to witness a solar eclipse at 5:00 o'clock in the morning. Cooper's secretary eventually became Jan's girl friend, and she subsequently invited him to a UFO conference in Arizona.

He soon found himself in the back of a lecture room as Al Bielek walked in. Jan felt a very strong presence but didn't understand exactly what it was. As Al Bielek talked, Jan knew there was some sort of connection. Everything felt too familiar. As he listened to Al talk about time travel, Jan began crying. It was a deeply emotional experience, but he couldn't place what was causing all these emotions. It was all sort of nuts.

Jan then decided to go for a beer at the Holiday Inn bar. All alone in the bar, he finished his drink. Ten minutes later, Al came in and sat right in front of him. This surprised him, and he gave Al a compliment on his lecture. Al was not too open and went about his business. Suddenly, something occurred which had never happened to Jan before. A voice appeared in his head. With reference to Al, the voice began to speak.

"The reason you are still alive is that something happened to you and you haven't told the Government."

Jan spoke the words aloud to Al who looked at him and said that it was true. A second voice then began to speak in Jan's head.

"The story is not right. You have to travel somewhere else. The Government doesn't know, and they want to know what happened in this other time, and that is why you are still alive."

When these words were repeated to Al, they definitely got his attention. He wanted to know if Jan was psychic. The two became friends and soon met at Al's house. As they continued their discussion, Jan began to reflect on the entire circumstances and the synchronicity which brought him to this situation. Here he was telling this time traveler (Al) all about his own personal life, a brief account of which has been given here. Jan then pointedly asked Al why he was sitting there and telling him his whole story.

Al just took one look at him and said, "God, another one!"

He was referring to the fact that Jan has a different aura. This has been referred to by many aura readers as a triple aura. Aura readers often become confused over this because they don't know what it is and don't know how to read it. According to Al, there were about eighteen triple auras on this planet who came from a different universe because this entire game has been played out before in another universe. After it was destroyed and began to sink into a black hole, about eighteen people emerged from it and began a rebirth or rebuilding process. Jan said that Al, Duncan, Preston and myself all had such an aura to his understanding. We all have something to accomplish together. He also specifically mentioned that Mark Hamill has this characteristic.

I do not personally claim to have such an aura, but I wouldn't deny there is something mysterious at work connecting all of us in this story. Duncan added some further insight to this although his experiences did not exactly see eye to eye with the information Jan was relaying. He said that according to his information, Earth based people have seven layers of information that manifest in a lattice like structure. He's not sure whether this function is a building block of the energy system or the physical form. Whatever it is, it appears in layers of seven.

For example, when Duncan refers to someone being a "double", he means that his lattice structure has fourteen layers or 2x7. This "fourteen" is known as a double aura. Stan Campbell, who's tragic story was told in *Montauk Revisited*, is a "twenty-one" or triple aura. This trait of being a "twenty-one" is indicative of what Duncan refers to as the "Creation Zone". Not only can Stan fully visualize incidents across the stream of time, he can literally "bleed" from the etheric plane into the physical realm. Metaphysical "stuff" really happens. Some monks in Tibet are known to be able to do this, and Stan is of that genre.

Further conversation with Duncan established that this triple aura phenomenon manifests whenever one enters the creation zone. All of us have the capability to do so, but it usually remains dormant. In the case of Stan Campbell, he was manipulated and this aspect was brought out in him. He was obviously already inclined towards these type of abilities. The Montauk Project brought it out and used it to his own detriment.

The idea that triple aura individuals come from another universe is paralleled in Duncan's own readings. Duncan sometimes referred to 637 people who came in from the Old Universe. There is an even further synchronicity at work here because Duncan's psychic memories parallel the *Stars Wars* movies almost to a "T". It can be quite emotional for him. The exact details will have to come from Duncan himself someday.

There is a lot more information yet to come forth with regard to the whole subject of *Star Wars*. Preston Nichols was involved with the sound production and has publicly claimed in lectures that psychics were used to project into the filming so that people would come and see the movie several times.

The *Star Wars* series itself was based upon George Lucas's *Journal of the Will*. Although it has not been publicly released, this journal contained the dreams and inspirations of Lucas, a man who is reported to have lived at Montauk. The use of the word "will" is a distinct parallel to Aleister Crowley's concept of the will. When one unleashes the will, whether it is through George Lucas or any other individual, the truth has a way of coming forth. The truth we are concerned about, lest anybody wonder, is unlocking the secrets of time.

It seems clear that both Duncan and George Lucas were pulling from the same source. When we consider that Mark Hamill was once a roommate of Duncan,[*] a childhood friend of Preston and eventually became the brother-in-law of George Lucas, there is less room for speculation. There was an active but unseen influence working on all of them.

It seems that Hamill, Lucas and Preston (who worked as a sound engineer for these movies) all contributed to the *Star Wars* effort in an attempt to remind the population at large of its ancient legacy and predicament. They were shifting mythological arche-types with this work of art, and there is no question that *Star Wars* totally revolutionized Hollywood, particularly in regards to spe-cial effects technology. More importantly, it shed a more respect-able light on how science fiction would be viewed. It became mainstream. Preston, Duncan and Al would eventually take this a step further and release the Montauk information.

One has to admit, whether one likes *Star Wars* or not, it excited the hell out of the masses. People went back to see it time and time again. Told under the guise of science fiction, it was not

---

[*] Duncan, who has several blank periods in his life, has no personal recollec-tion of this other than the fact that it has come up as being true in psychic readings. The information has also been verified as true from an independent source. There has been no comment from Mark Hamill.

particularly threatening to anyone's status quo or belief system. It broke box office records and proved itself to a boon to the Hollywood economy.

The Montauk story hits even closer to home, but it is considerably more threatening to the status quo. One of the reasons people reject Montauk or refuse to consider it is that it targets the very programs which make people forget. The goal of the Montauk research is to literally unsnarl the tangled web of consciousness that permeates the construction of this universe. What ensues in the rest of this book will take us one step closer.

Jan's rendition of the triple auras and another universe gives us cause to wonder. More importantly, he came into my life under synchronous circumstances and introduced me to all sorts of information about the Nazi connection.

11

THE SECRET OF JUDAH

As was said earlier, Jan has special connections to secret societies in Germany. Some of the characters he knows are in their nineties and were present prior to Hitler's involvement in these traditions. Many of them have lived a long life because they are vegetarians and eat a very healthy diet. It may surprise you that the rationale underlying such vegetarianism is based upon *ahimsa*. This is a Sanskrit word which literally means "not to injure". *Ahimsa* is really a doctrine that all life is integrated and that no living creatures should suffer violence or harm. Thus, these German vegetarians do not eat beef, chicken or fish.

Jan is not a member of these societies nor is he a neo-Nazi. Information has come to him in a similar fashion to the way that data has been released to me about Montauk and related esoteric subjects. We have more than a few things in common, but it is not my job to simply parrot what he has told me. It has been necessary to assimilate his information and take it a step further by placing it in a broader context.

When Jan van Helsing spoke, there was no doubt in my mind that I was hearing a story much closer to the heart of the Third Reich than anything I had read in the various books on the subject. He was not only German but had the relevant connections and was communicating a live tradition as well as a secret one.

Jan explained to me that after the Berlin wall crumbled, certain information could no longer be contained. Secret Societies such as the Knights Templar, which had been severely repressed under the East German government, were now coming forward and releasing what had been closely guarded secrets. Jan proceeded to clue me in on all sorts of information which became the focal point of my investigation.

Unfortunately, and well after my meeting with him, Jan was severely sidetracked in his own personal investigations. After writing a book which included some of this previously guarded information, he was investigated by the German government for purposes of prosecution. His book was subsequently banned by the District Attorney, or the German equivalent thereof. He also faced a stiff fine which would ruin him financially.

Secret Societies and their Power in the 20th Century is the title of Jan's book. It was written in the German language and quickly became a best seller with over 50,000 copies being sold in Europe. As it became more popular, the book caught the attention of the German government and was banned as being "inciteful to the masses". The book was primarily about potilical conspiracy and included only a few chapters on esoteric subjects. The main controversy which got Jan into trouble had to do with the Jewish issue. He included *The Protocols of the Elders of Zion*, a document which conventional historians claim to be a forgery. Conspiracy historians do not necessarily accept this view. Their main point is that if *The Protocols* were a forgery, they are an exact methodology through which a group such as the Illuminati would use to control world politics. Whatever the exact truth of *The Protocols* is, including them in a book is not going to win support from organizations like the B'nai Brith and the Anti-Defamation League.

As a friend, Jan has proven himself to be honest and sincere in personal matters that have involved myself. Unfortunately for him, certain esoteric information revealed in his work is easy for people to misconstrue. As a result, and due to the fact he was focusing on political machinations, he suffered severe consequences. In spite of the fact that Jan says point blank in his book that he is not anti-Semitic, his critics have not cut him any slack. Although Jan states that untrue statements have been made about the holocaust, the media has said he claims there was no holocaust. This is not Jan's position. He even goes to lengths to explain his views that the true Jewish people are not part of any conspiracy.

Even though Jan was not treated fairly by his critics, the problem he encountered is quite understandable. Before I go any further into the more secretive information Jan revealed to me, it is necessary to clear up the entire Jewish issue once and for all.

The problem with Jan's book is that reading it can make one's blood boil if one is prone to being judgemental. Even if it is not fair, it is easy to understand why the German government took actions to suppress the book. Massive immigration in Germany has totally changed the culture. I personally found it to be a bigger melting pot than the United States. The original Aryan culture appears to be going by the boards. This has given rise to neo-Nazis and other hate oriented groups. It is sort of ironic. As the Indo European Aryans destroyed various cultures of indigenous peoples around the world, the pendulum is now swinging in the other direction.

Jan explained to me that the Freemason symbols I had seen in Frankfurt were the result of Jewish influences and control in modern Germany. He literally claimed that Jewish factions currently run the country of Germany. His book provides specific information, but I do not know if it is all true. I do know that war reparations are still being paid by Germany to fund the state of Israel. This is a major sore point with many Germans. Some of them go so far as to think that World War II was a manipulation by the Zionist Jews to engineer a situation where the Germans would fund Israel. This sort of thinking is common in Germany.

At one point in our conversation, Jan insisted I turn off my tape recorder. He wanted to tell me something that was not allowed to be spoken of in Germany although I later discovered it was printed in his book. I thought he was being over dramatic, but I turned off my recorder. The secret he was unveiling had to do with the Black Knights, a group who trace their origin back to the original Knights Templar. According to his research, the Black Knights are the legitimate heirs of the Knights Templar who were burned at the stake during the purge of the Inquisition. Jan said that the Nazis, via the Black Knights, had an ancient manuscript in their hands that had once actually belonged to the Templars. Before that, it belonged to the scribes of Israel. The precious secret contained in this manuscript is that the Hebrew scribes identified their God as El Shaddai, the outcast Archangel or Satan. This information might sound shocking to those who are particularly self righteous. It apparently had the same effect on leading proponents of the Aryan cause and flamed their anti-Semitism.

If the above is true, it is an overreaction and misunderstanding in the extreme sense. The identification of "the Beast" as God in any religion is only an esoteric reference to the fact that the physical plane is encoded with the 666 energy. This was covered in *Pyramids of Montauk* where we learned that the numerology of the Beast equated to "26" as did the number of *YVYW* (the proper name of the God of the Jews of which the name Jehovah is a bastardization). Keep in mind that we are in a carbon based universe wherein the carbon atom contains six neutrons, six electrons and six protons. In esoteric symbolism, the concept of the Beast is a metaphor for a rather deep and involved principle with regard to how the universe is formatted. It only becomes a "God" for worship in its degenerate aspects. It is obvious that, in times past, this misconception of 666 as the Beast was used as a means with which to incite hatred against Jews or whoever. It is interesting that the formula by which we can recognize the predicaments or situation of this universe has been misrepresented into a thing of fear and foreboding. The fear serves as a demon designed to prevent you from finding out the true nature of things.

The above reference to El Shaddai as the God of the Jews is not the only statement that prompted the authorities to ban Jan's book. Their were other quotations from the New Testament and Jewish Talmud, but I am not too concerned with any of them. I am concerned with the esoteric tradition of mankind which, if properly studied, reveals the basic unity underlying all existence. In this aspect Jews, Muslims, Christians, Aryans and everyone else occupy a spot on the Wheel of Life. All are tied to the hub. The various factions are like different colored spokes believing their color to be the preferred one. If we choose to assimilate our highest creative aspect, we see from the Creator's view, and are thereby obliged to look at the vast array of all the spokes within the wheel.

Unfortunately, those who seek to manipulate mankind have formatted religions in such a way as to control the emotions and political inclinations of the masses. The inner truths are only for a select few.

Religion has always found a way to polarize mankind. Whatever the relative truth may be concerning the potential adversarial role of Jews in society, there is no question that Jan's book polarized the German government and would have done the same to many Jewish groups as well. We have to remember that when we tackle subjects as intriguing as the Nazis and their mystical connections, we cannot stop and get trapped by polarized thinking which includes the judgement of "this is good" and "that is bad".

The most interesting aspect of the Jews is not their political or conspiratorial intrigues. It is the sacred nature of their Hebrew alphabet as was briefly discussed in *Pyramids of Montauk*. This discovery is actually the work of Stan Tenon, and he deserves all the credit as he spent over a decade researching it. Specifically, his work revealed that if you take a cross section of a doughnut (or torus - the shape of the universe according to physicists), you will have a vortex-like shape that will delineate all twenty-seven letters of the Hebrew alphabet if a shadow is cast on it from 27 different angles. For the most part, traditional Jewish sources have not heard of this nor do they fully appreciate its meaning or implications.*

That the Hebrew language was rendered to conform to sacred geometrical patterns means that whoever put the language together was operating with a consciousness above that of an ordinary human, if not outright divine. We get a clue as to who was behind this religious and divine language when we examine the etymology of the word *Judah*, the name for the strongest of the twelve tribes of Israel. Judah was the name of a Hebrew territory named after Judah, the fourth son of Jacob. The English word is derived from the Hebrew word *yehudhah* (pronounced *yā-hū-dāy*). Notice the striking similarity in prounciation to that of Tahuti (the more proper pronounciation of which is *ta-hoō-tāy*) , the Egyptian god of magic and knowledge. If you do not believe this is a meaningful coincidence, then consider the etymology of the word *Hebrew*. It derives from the Hebrew word *ibhri* literally meaning "one from across the river". If the Hebrews were using their own word for "one across from the river", they were likely referring to the Nile. This becomes clear when you consider that the word *ibhri* sounds very close to the word "ibis", the patron animal of Tahuti who was usually portrayed as an ibis or heron.

---

* Hebrew is not the only sacred language which reveals such mysteries. It is just one of many. Actually, there is a mother tongue from which Hebrew and the other sacred languages (Greek, Arabic, Sanskrit and Tibetan are a few) were derived. We will discuss this a bit later.

These birds were abundant along the Nile and were treated as sacred. They were never disturbed. The English word *ibis* is derived from the Egyptian *hib* which again brings us back to the sound of the word "Hebrew". Even the word "ibex" (a goat with large curved horns) derives from an Alpine language signifying climber (as if to the capstone of the Great Pyarmid).

The etymological labyrinth delineated above demonstrates that both the Teutonic and Hebrew traditions derive from a common source with Tahuti sitting in the middle of the crossroads. The etymology of both namesakes suggests that Egypt was the ancient cultural center. In the midst of this crossroads were the original indigenous Egyptians, a dark skinned people. What degree of darkness was in their skin depends upon where those particular individuals resided in relation to the sun or on what literature you read. But, it is not controversial at all to say that there was some darkness in their skin. The Celtic tribes emigrated from Central Asia and made their way to Egypt. Once there, they lived quite compatibly with the Pharaoh's ruling establishment. Both peoples contributed to the Egyptian legacy that we know today. A cultural break during the time of Ramses II is symbolized in the story of Moses taking the Hebrews across the Red Sea. The term "Hebrews" in this sense actually refers to a potpourri of different peoples which included the Celts. We also know during this time period that a Celtic man by the name of Niul married the Pharaoh's daughter, Scota. Their descendants named Scotland in her honor. The Scottish islands of the Hebrides are an obvious reference to Hebrew or Hebron, a city south of Jerusalem.

The musical chairs of names goes on ad infinitum, but it is clear that Egypt was a cultural melting pot from which many great traditions derived. If one bothers to study the matter deeply, they will discover that the entire Jewish and Christian faiths were utterly and completely based upon the Egyptian religion. Unfortuntely, most people do not realize this because the Egyptian religion has been distorted or poorly explained by historians. It is apparent that the Hebrew "Torah" is comparable to the Tarot or Rota (wheel) of the Egyptians. The very word *Rabbi* phoenetically derives from Ra, the Egyptian sun god.

None of the above is meant to imply that the Hebrews stole the Egyptian religion. The very word *hebe* signifies that the Jews were carrying the holy cup of Melchizedek, at least in a metaphorical if not in the physical sense. In the Greek language, the word *hebe* means youth. In Greek myth, Hebe was the goddess of youth and was a cup bearer to the gods. In this sense, she carried the Holy Grail or the cup of Melchizedek. The shift of power from the Egyptians remained with the Hebrews until the time of Solomon. It was actually part of a greater design which can be pinpointed to correspond to the orbital mechanics of the universe. Just as life uses different artifices as it evolves in an effort to survive, so does Tahuti, as an archetypal creature of life, manifest his message along different avenues. He was the messenger of the gods and an expert in communication. Different environments require different solutions with appropriate manifestations.

Referring back to the ancient manuscript of the Knights Templar, we find a remarkable sychronicity. The document refers to Jesus speaking to the Teutons serving in the Roman legion. He tells them quite specifically that it was their people he had chosen. The Aryan supremists of Germany took this ball and ran with it. They were seeking the same status that the Jews had long since claimed: the chosen people. The above references should make it clear that both traditions derived their power and impetus from the same source: Tahuti. Common ground was not recognized and the situation deteriorated into polarized consciousness. While esoteric information was clearly being misinterpreted, it was also being manipulated.

An in depth study of etymology will ultimately reveal the common thread of all civilization. A prime example is the name *Ararat*, the mountain where Noah landed his fabled ark. It was this general area of the planet from which mankind arose. The name *Ararat* has an uncanny synchronicity with the word *Aryan*. Science has never delineated any racial differences between Jews and Aryans. The difference between the two are religious and cultural.

The confusion and rivalry between various groups on Earth can all be traced back to the ancient legend of the Tower of Babylon. This is a story where "God" punished mankind for trying to reach the acme of knowledge, a concept which is symbolized in the capstone of the Great Pyramid. This was a time when all mankind spoke a common tongue, one that was known as Vril. This tongue was fragmented into many different pieces and is why

103

we have so many intriguing and labyrinthine etymologies amongst the various languages of Earth. The story of the Tower of Babylon represents a program that was injected into the morphogenetic grid in order to ignite division in mankind. The rivalry between the Jews and Nazis, which still exists to this day, is a primary example.

Next, we will look at a man who, although he lived amongst the most powerful people of the Third Reich, did everything he could to heal the rift between these two peoples.

12

DOCTOR FELIX

While writing this book, I received a letter which revealed another layer of mystery with regard to the Montauk-Nazi connection. It was from a gentlemen who worked on the *Star Wars* films. In no uncertain terms, he said that those films, as well as the Indiana Jones series, were all produced in England at the facilities of Thorn EMI, the mysterious company already associated with Aleister Crowley and the *The Philadelphia Experiment*.

Raiders of the Lost Ark, written by George Lucas, is of particular interest when we consider the Nazi connection. Steven Spielberg, who directed this movie, is said to have taken a lot of heat in the Jewish community for his role with *Raiders* because it popularized Nazis and made them remarkable characters, albeit evil ones. Some consider this a glorification of the Nazis' so called mystical powers. The Hollywood rumor mill further states that Spielberg did the movie *Schindler's List* to atone for his indiscretions with *Raiders*. There is no question that with *Schindler's List*, Spielberg became the darling of Hollywood. Prior to this movie, and despite his enormous success, he was always discriminated against when it came to Academy Awards and due recognition of his considerable talent.

Different news stories have reported Spielberg or his companies buying defense industry properties on Long Island that are known to contain extensive underground facilities. The locations and companies reported have varied, but the theme is always the same. He is bringing his studio to Long Island to make a film about aliens. Spielberg's connections to the government are legendary.

They begin with his movie *Close Encounters of the Third Kind* and extend forward to *E.T.* where he reportedly gave a White House showing. Ronald Reagan was reported to have made comments to the director alluding to "what couldn't be told".

With his main home on Long Island, Spielberg is only a short commuters drive from Montauk's Camp Hero. In fact, two different people with personal contacts to Spielberg have reported putting *The Montauk Project* book into his hands. I did not ask them to do this. It was their own enthusiasm for the idea. Many people have wondered why, if he did get the book, he would not act on it. Instead, he made *Schindler's List* and is reportedly working on a movie concerning the Roswell Incident. This man is undeniably intelligent and talented. We also have to consider his "truth quotient". In other words, his own personal predisposition for dealing with the truth. He definitely gave us some insights with *Raiders* and *Close Encounters*, but was he also under pressure to toe the government line?

In *Schindler's List*, Spielberg glorified the character Schindler for having saved about a thousand Jews from certain death in the concentration camps. Without minimizing the humanitarian efforts of Schindler, it should be pointed out that Spielberg overlooked one of the most remarkable stories or World War II. That is the legacy of one Dr. Felix Kersten.

Dr. Kersten was personally responsible for saving the lives of hundreds of thousands of concentration camp victims, most of whom were Jews. He also accomplished it under much more trying circumstances than Schindler, for he interfaced on a daily basis with the leading characters of the Third Reich. Kersten appears in many footnotes of Nazi history books, but not too much is ever said about him. I became interested in Kersten after seeing him mentioned in a book as Heinrich Himmler's personal masseuse who was into holistic therapy. It was also said that he had written a book about his experiences with Himmler. I thought that anyone practicing holistic therapy in Nazi Germany would be interesting, to say the least. I pursued the book which is entitled *The Kersten Memoirs, 1940-1945* by Felix Kersten. I soon found the previous description of Kersten to be sorely lacking. He was actually a full fledged medical doctor who used holistic means, including those of massage.

Born in Estonia in 1898, Kersten was of Germanic descent but began his life as a Russian subject. Fighting in the Finnish War of Liberation in 1918, he subsequently became a Finnish subject. Later, he moved to Berlin where he studied medicine and became trained in an ancient and obscure form of oriental therapy under Dr. Ko, an oriental. Kersten called this technique physio neural therapy and wrote a synopsis of it in the back of his book. It is clear from his description of the procedure that the principles are quite scientific. On the other hand, the administration of it requires intuitive skill on the part of the practitioner. Kersten was a master of the procedure.

The remarkable success and reputation of Dr. Kersten spread far and wide. His practice caught the eye of the aristocracy all across Europe, and he soon ended up in the household of Prince Hendrik and Queen Wilhelmina of the Netherlands. He subsequently made his home in their country.

Kersten eventually found himself to be on a collision course with Heinrich Himmler, the Reichsfuhrer of the SS. Himmler suffered from severe stomach spasms which him caused a great deal of pain and sometimes resulted in unconsciousness. Kersten easily relieved these difficulties whereupon he was asked to give Himmler regular treatment. Kersten refused. Not only did he disagree with Nazi politics, his home was in Holland. When the Nazis eventually invaded Holland, Kersten's route home was effectually blocked, and it was not so easy for him to refuse Himmler. It was only after this military event that Kersten became the personal doctor of Heinrich Himmler. Kersten was more than suspicious of the Nazis. Although he downright rejected their philosophy and methods, he decided he could use his position to lobby for humanitarian concerns.

Kersten points out in his book that men who are troubled and sick will confide things to their doctor that they would never dare say to anyone else. Himmler enjoyed Kersten's intellectual banter, and the two engaged in many vigorous but polite debates. The Reichsfuhrer found in Kersten a man to whom he could relieve his anguish. It is from these many sessions they had together that we get a most candid and unsuspecting view into the mind of Himmler, a man who loved the occult and was said to be the second most powerful man in all of Germany.

While Himmler is portrayed by Kersten to be myopic on the subject of Jews, he is no different from the typical German of that day and age. Kersten, in turn, proves himself to be myopic on the subject of Freemasonry and many other subjects as well. For example, Himmler believes that Masons are behind virtually all political events in the world and that they get their secret orders from a small group of Jews. While Kersten clearly rejects this as an extreme view without any validity, he also seems incapable of grasping that the Masons could have any sinister or conspiratorial aspects at all.

Much more understandable are Himmler's ravings against the medical profession and lawyers. It is incredibly ironic to listen to Himmler complain about the abuses in these industries. Remarkably, these abuses are the very same ones we suffer from today in modern America. Although Himmler's observations are insightful, Kersten listens to them with a deaf ear. He does not seem to understand that pharmaceutical companies and medical doctors could possibly act in their own selfish interest to the detriment of patients. Himmler, on the other hand, understands the plight of the common man and offers incredible sympathy when it comes to dishonest lawyers, doctors and pharmacologists.

It is also quite surprising to learn that Heinrich Himmler is a firm believer in the Bhagdivad Gita and the law of karma. Most surprising of all is when Himmler confesses his moral dilemma to Kersten concerning the extermination of the Jews. He doesn't want to kill a single one and tells of his elaborate plans for sending the Jews to a permanent colony on the island of Madagascar. We get an idea of his personal frustration when he tries to make Hitler take a more humane course concerning the Jews, an unpopular tact that Himmler could only share with his personal doctor. That Himmler could show any such traces of humanity was totally new to me. As the leader of the Gestapo and SS, his name is only associated with fear and cruelty.

One day, Kersten finds Himmler in excruciating pain after a visit with the Fuhrer. The orders to the Final Solution had just come down. Himmler is so distraught and helpless under the circumstances that he suffers a complete physical collapse. Both he and Kersten are aware that he cannot fight the Fuhrer without losing his position as the Reichsfuhrer SS.

While these circumstances do not condone or justify his actions, we get a new look at Heinrich Himmler and how he failed as a human being. Like many people, he had lofty ideals but was incapable of attaining them. Although he believed in karma, his actions or omissions resulted in horror for millions.

As portrayed in the book by Felix Kersten, Himmler sees himself in a dilemma. His personal passions are clearly for the Germanic race and restoring the lost cultural flavor of yesteryear. He has pursued and inherited a powerful position in the Reich so that he can pursue his lofty ideals, but he was only able to secure his job through his piercing insight into the political manipulations of ordinary men. In order to pursue his own ideals, Himmler sought the controlling influence in all political matters. This was how he found himself attracted to Hitler. One of Hitler's most loyal adjutants, Himmler was with him from their early days in the Thule Society. Himmler was initially inspired by Hitler's oratory and firm grasp of what he thought the German people needed. Himmler clearly saw Hitler's spiritual and physical degeneration throughout the years, but he could not bring himself to believe anything other than the idea that the Fuhrer would lead them to the eternal salvation of the Aryan race. What Himmler said publicly and what he though privately were two different lines of thought.

There is a lot more to say about Heinrich Himmler. He believed himself to be the reincarnation of Henry I and was more than proud of his castle at Wewelsburg where he met with his order of Black Knights. He actively pursued the recovery of the Holy Grail and Ark of the Covenant by authorizing various archaeological expeditions to different continents. Some of these adventures are included in other books listed in the bibliography, and we will deal with the most important aspects of these in later chapters.

What is most noteworthy in the above account of Himmler is that we get a drastically different view than what is commonly presented in literature. I had always thought he was the second most evil man in the world who lusted after the blood of Jews. Himmler proved himself to be a soft touch for Felix Kersten who was repeatedly asking for different prisoners (often Jewish) to be released. The situations were often downright embarrassing to Himmler, considering the moral climate, and sometimes had to be done behind the back of unsympathetic Nazis. It was reported, however that many other German officers were sympathetic to Jewish prisoners of war and often gave lists of names to Kersten who would arrange for their release through Himmler.

Towards the end of the war, Kersten negotiated the release of literally hundreds of thousands of prisoners. The details are in his book. Kersten got Himmler to capitulate in spite of the fact that these actions were directly contrary to Hitler's orders and were even punishable by death. In these instances, Himmler showed a grace and humanity that does not reflect his general reputation. As he knew the war would be over soon, it was as if he was trying to secure a better karma for himself.

Like most human beings who find themselves in an evil web, Himmler was not all bad, but he was undoubtedly overshadowed by a greater evil which he could not control or overcome.[*]

---

[*] Thoses who find themselves upset with what I have reported about Himmler should read Dr. Felix Kersten's book. What is written here is based upon his personal observations and memories. They are not mine. My statements are only as accurate as his memories.

13

THE FUHRER

Felix Kersten recalls his most exciting day with Himmler as December 12, 1942. On this date, Himmler called him into his office to see if he could help a man suffering from severe headaches, dizziness and insomnia. The man in question was Hitler.

After swearing Kersten to the utmost secrecy, Himmler retrieved a black portfolio from his safe and took out a typed blue manuscript. There were twenty-six pages of Hitler's medical history that went all the way back to his gas poisoning during World War I, a malady which caused him blindness for a period of time. Also listed during this time were symptoms associated with syphilis. These were supposedly "cured" until they recurred in 1937. By 1942, there was no doubt that Hitler was suffering from progressive paralysis, a disease associated with advanced stages of syphilis. He exhibited all of the symptoms of this disease except for fixity of vision and confusion of speech.

Himmler was beside himself during this time period as he did not know what to do. There was no known cure for progressive paralysis, but Hitler received injections which maintained his ability to work. These were administered by a known quack by the name of Dr. Morell. Himmler was suspicious of Morell but wanted his Fuhrer cured at all costs as he was well aware that Hitler's mental capabilities had deteriorated. Morell's injections seemed to restore his ability to think clearly. Still, this was only a temporary fix and Himmler knew it.

Upon being briefed on the entire situation, Kersten suggested that Hitler should have a full mental examination. Himmler was insistent that Hitler could not be examined in a mental hospital or anything of the like. Even if Hitler were to consent to it, word would get out and totally demoralize the German cause. Himmler saw Dr. Morell as his only alternative.

Himmler found himself in a deep dilemma with regard to his Fuhrer's sanity and medical condition. He believed that no matter what medical opinions he were to obtain about Hitler, his peers would look at him as merely acting in his own self interest. Himmler ultimately saw himself as betraying the German people if he should question his Fuhrer and thereby endanger the security of the entire nation. Despite urging by Kersten, Himmler couldn't bring himself to take action but merely continued to hope that things would somehow work themselves into a better situation. Himmler did agree to watch the situation with Hitler's mental health carefully and act if things went too far. Meanwhile, Dr. Morell continued to pump his hypodermic needle into Hitler.

According to Kersten, there was an additional problem facing Himmler in the event he were to declare Hitler mentally incompetent. That was Martin Bormann, the man who controlled all personal appointments to Hitler and was a master manipulator himself. Himmler and Bormann did not trust each other, nor is there any evidence to suggest that Bormann featured any traces of the humane characteristics which have been attributed to Himmler.

Himmler made Kersten privy to all this information because he had seen him perform miracles with other members of the Third Reich and desperately hoped that he could do the same for Hitler. Kersten refused to treat Hitler because there was no known cure for progressive paralysis. It is also easy to get the impression from reading his book that Kersten knew he would be getting in over his head with Hitler although he himself doesn't suggest that. Dealing with an insane man could have cost him his life. By comparison to Hitler, Himmler was an obvious pushover. It is significant though that Kersten recalls the discussion about Hitler as his "most exciting day". This is a tribute to the amount of electricity that Hitler generated with his very presence. Kersten got as close as he dared or felt capable.

It is not so surprising that Himmler did not take action to remove Hitler but it is informative, if not startling, that he had such a keen grasp of what was wrong with his leader. His loyalty would eventually result in his own demise. Although Himmler was guilty of numerous crimes and deaths, there was a spiritual aspect to the man that seems worthy of redemption. Bormann appears to be more the satanic operative, moving in unconscious concert with forces such as Dr. Morell who injected Hitler with all sorts of random treatments. The door was thus wide open for the psychological and physiological manipulation of Hitler.

14

HITLER ALIVE!

Everyone knows that Hitler died in the bunker on April 30, 1945. The events of that day have been dramatized in many a film. Because Hollywood is so passionately devoted to the truth, it has never once entertained a major script with Germany's Fuhrer surviving. If you read the newspapers towards the end of World War II, there was considerable consternation and mystery over the whereabouts of Adolph Hitler. General Eisenhower was very concerned about the possibility that Hitler could have escaped. There were numerous air strips within the near vicinity of the bunker. The Russians, who had gotten to the bunker first, allowed only a cursory inspection by the other Allies before sealing it off for a considerable amount of time. The scenario was such that anything could have happened.

One day, when *The Montauk Project* was still being written, Preston spoke to me of an art dealer who swore that he had purchased and sold art work from Hitler personally. This art work was supposedly Nazi treasure. This bizarre story was backed up with a reference to an article in the *Portland Oregonian* (1962, I believe) which featured a story about a man who looked just like Hitler. This man also happened to be an artist and said he was continually mistaken for Hitler or having the resemblance commented upon. This artist claimed their similar looks were just a coincidence. The man eventually moved to Prescott, Arizona, but I do not know whatever became of him. When Preston mentioned the story of Hitler being alive, I did not believe it; but through the stream of synchronicity, I was already aware of the article. I had seen it almost fifteen years earlier when one of L. Ron Hubbard's secretaries had shared it with me as curious information that had been sent to Hubbard.

Preston has never revealed the identity of the "art dealer", but I was able to secure his identity through another source. He was definitely involved at Montauk and his profile fits the bill. Duncan Cameron happened to be at that meeting between me and Preston when this connection to Hitler was brought up. Duncan suddenly became serious and said that none of this should be mentioned and was to be kept confidential. Years later, I spoke to Duncan and asked him if this should remain confidential. He had no recollection of the conversation and simply laughed. Looking back, it sounds as if some program was acting itself out through Duncan.

Many historians of World War II have an axe to grind or an agenda to drive. In today's climate, you cannot easily mention the idea of Hitler having survived without securing ridicule from mainstream thinkers. After all, "everybody knows". All of this comes into perspective when you realize that the most authoritative and respected scholar on the Nazis and their World War II exploits is Hugh Trevor-Roper, a British Intelligence agent! This point should be prefaced in bold by anyone who quotes anything he says. It colors all of his work but is simply glossed over by most historians and researchers.

The writings and predispositions of most historians indicate that they are mentally incapable of considering the possibility that Hitler might have lived beyond the bunker. There is one book however which presents an interesting and open minded approach to the subject. It is entitled *Hitler's Ashes* by Colonel Howard A. Buechner, recently deceased, and Captain Wilhelm Bernhard. Colonel Buechner earned a medical degree from LSU and was an internationally recognized expert in the area of lung disease and tuberculosis. As Medical Officer with the 3rd Battalion, 157th Infantry Regiment, 45th Infantry Division, he was the first American physician to enter Dachau Concentration Camp at the time of its liberation. His coauthor, Captain Bernhard, joined the German Navy in 1943 and was assigned to the Reich Undersea Boat Service. He served aboard the submarine U-530 from August of 1944 until it surrendered and was scuttled off the coast of Mar del Plata, Argentina on July 10, 1945. Newspaper accounts of the time indulged in a considerable amount of speculation as to whether Hitler had been aboard U-530. Witnesses reported a rubber dinghy containing a man and woman who looked similar to Eva Braun and Hitler. They were landing on property owned by Germans, and the German underground network was definitely awaiting the dinghy party. Whether or not it was Hitler and Eva is not certain. It is interesting that neither Buechner nor Bernhard endorse the theory that Hitler was aboard.

Buechner precisely details the escape routes by which the Nazis left Germany. The VIP route generally went by U-boat to Norway and then down the Atlantic to South America or wherever. The lower echelon in the Nazi hierarchy generally took the southern escape route through Italy.

Airport strips existed right near the chancellery building and were for the express purpose of Hitler escaping. A pilot was specifically designated for that eventuality. There were numerous opportunities and motives for Hitler to have escaped, but none have been conclusively proven.

What Buechner does establish is that the Russians entered the bunker on May 2, 1945 after the Nazi defense crumbled. After discovering Hitler's body, their next logical step would have been to call in an Allied medical team to identify and perform an autopsy accompanied by an official report. This would have ended any speculation. The Russians did no such thing but instead sealed off the area. There were consequently many rumors and counter rumors swirling during this time period. As Soviet forces controlled the chancellery area, there was no room for a complete and unbiased investigation of Hitler's death.

In 1953, the matter became more complicated when an autopsy report was delivered by the Soviets through Lev Bezymenski. Some of the material in this autopsy report was published in book form in 1968 under the title *The Death of Adolph Hitler*. Discrepancies in the reports have caused serious investigators to disregard them in their entirety. Of particular note was their identification of "Hitler's rotting teeth". Although the post mortem examinations were reported to have been carried out in early May, with the bodies being destroyed one month later, Hitler's dental x-rays were not discovered until the middle of August of the same year. There was no logical way to compare Hitler's actual teeth to the x-rays at the time of the autopsy. The Soviet autopsy is further colored by a May 7th, 1945 news bulletin issued from Moscow and printed in the United States. Hitler's body had not been found according to that report, and the Soviets still believed that Hitler's death was a "Nazi trick". Stalin himself said on more than one occasion that he believed Hitler was not dead and had escaped on a U-boat. It should be noted that Hitler's autopsy reports were not released until March 5, 1953, almost eight years after his alleged death. This report was issued, not coincidentally, right after Stalin died. The details and circumstances of the bizarre efforts to prove "Hitler's death" can be studied in full in the aforementioned book by Buechner and Bernhard.

The Russians further complicated matters by destroying "Hitler's body" as they considered the medical evidence to be conclusive. The German chancellery building, Hitler's bunker, and the garden where the body was buried were all blown up in 1946 by the Russians. This made further investigation impossible. Instead, the Russians filmed an on sight reenactment of the final events of Hitler's death. Whether true or not, someone was trying to do a PR job to sell the world on the idea that Hitler was dead. The Russians are a very strange partner in this entire production.

Buechner and Bernhard claim that the underground bunker actually exists in some remnant form but that there is no entrance. A man named Wolfgang Fuchs reportedly dug a tunnel into the bunker in 1963 but was quickly apprehended by government authorities. Buechner also notes that there were still some fragmentary pieces of the Reich Chancellery in place as late as 1949 according to a photograph taken in October of that same year.

Stalin never endorsed the autopsy reports, most likely because they were insubstantial and would have been laughed at by rival governments. The autopsy was probably a KGB ploy to be used for some unknown agenda. Whatever the original idea was, it was invoked only after Stalin died.

Although the authors of *Hitler's Ashes* fault Bezymensky's accuracy, they do not mean to imply that he was dishonorable or lying in any way. He was simply writing from autopsy reports that were deliberately falsified. What is particularly curious about Bezymensky's narrative is his description of the Russian search for Hitler's body. At one point, the body was displayed in the main hall of the chancellery building for all to view. The body wore Hitler's uniform in the posture of hanged man. Although the man looked like Hitler, a Soviet diplomat came on the scene and promptly recognized that it was not. He was the Soviet ambassador to Berlin and knew Hitler personally. The body in the uniform was merely a Hitler look-a-like who was known only as "a man from Breslau". The fact that this body also wore darned socks should have been a tip off to the investigators. One source indicated there were also other corpses in the chancellery garden who sported Hitler uniforms.

Another key point Dr. Buechner brings to mind in the autopsy report is that "Hitler's body" was identified as possessing only one testicle. It was not merely undescended but was totally absent. At this point, Buechner castigates Dr. Walter Johannes Stein as the originator of a rumor that Hitler had abnormal genitalia, sporting only one testicle. All of Hitler's various physicians stated he had normal genitalia, and Buechner further claims that Walter Johannes Stein was a known liar, deserter and double agent. Stein is, of course, the inspiration Trevor Ravenscroft drew on his book *The Spear of Destiny*. Stein's knowledge of Hitler's testes reportedly came from a distant observation post as the future Fuhrer of Germany prepared to skinny dip in the Danube. If the claims about Stein are accurate, it is an absurd proposition that he could get a conclusive view from such a distance.

The above account not only encourages us to take a more sober view of the book *The Spear of Destiny*, it tells us that history has been perverted beyond ordinary belief.

15

REICH LEADERS ESCAPE

In the aforementioned book, *Hitler's Ashes*, the authors ultimately reject the thesis that Hitler actually survived the circumstances of April 1945. There are two primary reasons for this.

First, they simply view it as an impossible situation. Several eye witnesses saw Hitler in the bunker just before he allegedly killed himself. These authors saw him as being trapped in the bunker with no possible escape route at that late juncture. They are quick to point out however that Hitler rejected many opportunities to escape prior to that.

The second reason the authors have for believing in Hitler's death is that they have information from former SS officers who claim to know the exact truth about Hitler's demise. They state that Hitler was partially cremated with the ashes being taken on a "sacred journey" via a U-boat to Antarctica. Once there, they were placed to rest in an ice cave. *The Secret of the Holy Lance*, also by Buechner and Bernhard, gives a detailed account of this journey. This book also tells us of another sacred object included on that legendary journey: the Holy Lance. This is the same relic which Trevor Ravenscroft refers to as the "Spear of Destiny". Ravenscroft claimed the spear was returned to the Hapsburg Museum in Vienna. Buechner and Bernhard tell us that the spear returned to the Hapsburg Museum was a duplicate. The original spear was hidden in Antarctica for safekeeping.

I believe that Buechner was trying to express the truth as best he could. Like any of us, he was absorbing information by direct observation but also through various filters and influences. In his case, it is obvious that he did most of the writing of these books and that the German author Bernhard was supplying information through his SS sources. Although they could both be telling us the absolute truth, we have to consider if the SS had another agenda to serve. The book states that the members of the "Order of the Holy Lance" are interested in the propagation or world peace. Their contention is that they wanted the truth to be known about Germany's leader. On the other hand, perhaps they want the escape myth of Hitler to be squelched so as to conceal the truth. This could take pressure off the eventual public demands which will be made with regard to many of the issues I am bringing up. Whether Hitler died or not in 1945, you can be sure that plenty of archives in the world have a lot to hide in regard to this matter.

In light of the information we have learned through Montauk, I am proposing a new theory about Hitler's escape. First, the situation in the bunker was not necessarily hopeless at all. We know there are vast caverns beneath the Earth. Additional literature will show that Germany, at the time of World War II, was literally laced with underground facilities. Wewelsburg has already been cited as one example as well as the underground operations at the Peenemünde rocket base. If Hitler's bunker was prepared for his well being, it would have had an underground escape route tied to major underground passageways. I think it is absolutely hilarious that this prospect has never before been seriously suggested. If it has, I haven't seen it in any literature.

The President of the United States and his cabinet have more escape routes through the underground than you could shake a stick at. This is no big secret. Are we expected to believe the Americans learned their escape strategy from Hitler's mistake? Or, perhaps they learned from Hitler's foresight in planning. As the Reichs Chancellery building was blown up, it leaves us with no demonstrable traces to follow.

Another boost to the theory of Hitler having escaped is the double alluded to earlier. Hitler was known to have at least five doubles that were used for different purposes. Whether these were clones or mere look-a-likes is not known. Cloning is seldom discussed nor is it taken very seriously.

Dr. Mengele, the notorious Angel of Death, was said to be an expert in genetics. He studied twins in order to reproduce exact genetic strains. Although some of his research has been written up for the medical profession, the full extent of what he knew and did not know is still very much an open book. People miss with regard to Mengele when they assume that the diabolical aspects of his work were inspired only by a lust for evil deeds. His "whimsical" thumbs up or down at the death camps was not merely his rendition of a past life as Nero or Caligula. He was looking for specific genetics traits with his highly trained eyes. Mengele was diabolical all right, but there was a more exacting and greater scheme behind the holocaust than anyone has imagined. More will be said about this later, but we cannot overlook the cloning possibility when it comes to Hitler.

Whether Hitler actually died in 1945 does not appear to be of critical importance as far as subsequent history. If he did live, we are not aware of him having any additional impact upon the world after this time period.

The pattern of Hitler's death presents an interesting scenario when we consider the fates of the other top Nazi leaders. Historians have ignored the obvious once again. With the exception of Martin Bormann, their deaths have not been seriously contended even though there is no verifiable means to establish that the top Nazis did indeed physically die.

I will begin by discussing Rudolph Hess, the Deputy Fuhrer and Secretary of the Nazi Party. Allen Dulles, the OSS (Office of Strategic Services, the forerunner of the CIA) officer in Switzerland and the future CIA Director, thought that the Hess who appeared in Nuremburg may have been a double. The cloning theme suddenly reappears.[*]

There was a huge amount of controversy when Hess died in Spandau prison at the advanced age of 93 (a number which magicians, Crowley being the most notable, recognize as symbolizing thelema, one's true will). News reports were consistent that he had hung himself in his cell, however his personal nurse claimed that he wasn't strong enough or physically capable of

---

[*] The entire prospect of cloning Hitler got a huge shot in the arm just before this book went to press when sheep were cloned in Scotland. Press reports indicated the entire affair was orchestrated by Hugh Cameron, a major investor in the Roslin Institute. Remember, the secret sector possesses technology at least fifty years ahead of general humanity's awareness.

accomplishing such a feat. This nurse was also very upset that his patient had been compromised.

Whoever this man was, the original Hess or not, he was a mysterious figure who possessed much information. He received full packets of data from his German friends at NASA and was thereby fully briefed on all of the moon landings. This information was probably classified to general American citizens, but his old German contacts did not elude him.

Karl Haushofer was the mentor of Rudolph Hess, and although he was not a member of the Nazi party, he was very influential in Bavarian secret societies. He reportedly committed suicide in March of 1946, but he specifically requested that his grave not be marked. This leaves his death in question too. He was also in charge of the office of Germans Abroad and was responsible for Germany civilizing the rest of the world. We are once again left to wonder about his fate.

The death of Heinrich Himmler has never been seriously challenged for at least two specific reasons. The first is that there is a photograph of his corpse in a reclining position. Secondly, there is another photograph of at least one of the men who buried him. His testimony might be more compelling if he had bothered to mark the grave. The story of how Himmler came to meet his maker is interesting when you consider the full circumstances. As the Reich fell, he had been declared a traitor by Hitler for trying to make peace with the Allies. He donned a patch over his eye and tried to pass through British lines under an assumed identity. After being apprehended, he was interrogated for several hours, but his identity remained concealed. He eventually became frustrated and blurted out who he actually was. Ending up in the hands of two intelligence agents, he was stripped and searched for poison pills. As the search got underway, Himmler wrestled himself away and bit down on a cyanide capsule hidden in his teeth. This incident has become certified history and has remained virtually unquestioned despite the fact that it comes from two intelligence agents, one of which went on to become the president of Israel! Once again, an open minded inquiry makes us scratch our heads.

We get another bizarre scenario when we consider the fate of Reichsmarshall Hermann Göering, a man who stockpiled abroad a bigger fortune than any other of Hitler's Nazi leaders. Renowned as a WW I fighter ace, Göering made his first calculated move towards becoming a despot by marrying a rich woman from an industrial Swedish family. Emma, as he called her, often made appeals on behalf of her friends' families to save certain Jews. Göering obliged her until the politics of the situation became too hot to deal with.

Göering got on the wrong side of Hilter when he criticized his Fuhrer for splitting the Luftwaffe (the German Air Force) and sending part of it to Russia. Although Hitler sabotaged the Luftwaffe by this action, he blamed Göering for its ineffectiveness. Consequently, by mid 1943, Göering retreated from the Luftwaffe and left its demise to be supervised by others. He sat back and enjoyed his incredible wealth and plundered art collection. As the war drew to a close, Göering had ample opportunities to escape by the southern route, but he didn't take advantage of any of them.

From the bunker, Martin Bormann prompted and tricked Göering into sending a telegram to Hitler. It asked the Fuhrer to cede receivership of the Reich unto Göering as he was already named as Hitler's legal successor. Being fooled and manipulated by his adjutant, Hitler censured Göering and stripped him of all rank, privileges and power. Bormann twisted this around further to mean that Göering must be shot and sent off a telegram to that effect. Göering's troops refused to shoot him and he was eventually confronted for war crimes at Nuremberg.

Aside from Hess, Göering was the only Nazi with "star power" to be officially tried at Nuremberg. He blanketly refused to testify as he considered it a show trial. This created a critical problem for the Allies until a surprise visit was made to Göering by Col. William J. Donovan, the director of the Office of Strategic Services. "Wild Bill", as he was known by his friends, had been given the responsibility for the smooth running of the trials. Göering had been grumpy and understandably disaffected until their meeting. Some sort of deal was worked out between the two, but no one really knows exactly what happened. All we know is that Göering's behavior miraculously changed.

Hermann Göering's Mysterious Suicide by Ben E. Swearingen suggests that the deal worked out with Donovan had Göering putting on a show for the Allies. In exchange, Göering would get the opportunity to take poison and cheat the hangman's noose.

According to this theory, Donovan got his smooth running show, and a convenient death for Göering was not too big a price to pay.

According to this book, Donovan convinced Göering to go on display in order to vanquish the collective guilt of the Germans. In this way, they could put the holocaust behind them and get on as a people. Göering saw the virtue of this and no longer saw himself as a big player in the scheme of things. He thought Germany's future was far more important. Donovan did not see Göering as a killer of Jews, but as the number two man in Germany, he was the only man who could claim responsibility. Göering was to be the chief witness "against Hitler".

We have to ask ourselves what exactly was the official reason the OSS Director was in Nuremburg when the office was originally designed to be just an intelligence gathering outfit. Ostensibly, this should have been a simple proceeding of military jurisprudence for those suspected of war crimes. The political implications were enormous and overruled the obvious.

After his talk with Göering, Donovan didn't remain for the trials. There were many times when he publicly stated his reservations about trying the German General Staff. Donovan didn't agree with this and was at odds with Justice Robert H. Jackson, a man who came off a poor second best during his verbal duels with Göering. Donovan first made gentle objections to these trials. When they didn't work, he became forceful. Jackson refused to reject the Russian demand for the indictment of the corps of German officers. When an intelligence officer of Donovan's caliber is rejected by normal means, his next step is to use subterfuge or clandestine methods which are effective. After losing his argument with Justice Jackson, Donovan decided to leave Nuremberg to return to full time directorship of the OSS. After Donovan's departure, Göering became depressed and felt he had lost a "good bet".

Göering somehow secured poison and committed suicide while in the Nuremberg Prison. Oddly, he wrote a letter four days before his scheduled execution indicating no prison personnel were guilty in helping him accomplish this feat. This would be a very foolish action for someone who was planning to commit suicide on his own. A surprise search of his cell or person could have revealed his own plans.

The Commandant of the Nuremburg Prison at the time of Göering's death was Col. Burton Andrus. Although a military tribunal absolved him of negligence for the suicide, Andrus was attacked by the press and Jewish factions for allowing it to occur. Andrus did take the trouble to order Göering's body to be uncovered of a blanket so that everyone could see that he was demonstrably dead. A Russian doctor even slapped the face of the carcass to make sure Göering wasn't fudging. According to *Hermann Göering's Mysterious Suicide*, this is the most compelling piece of evidence that Göering actually died. The book does not take the trouble to point put that drugs could have been administered to Göering to feign death. An unconscious state could easily have been induced that would have neutralized the effect of the slap.

The Board of Inquiry into Göering's suicide was said to be unprecedented for its objectivity or lack thereof. This statement was made by Col. Andrus' son. In what amounts to a startling irregularity in military procedure, the inquiry was carried out by subordinates of Col. Andrus who were also members of the 685th Internal Security Department, the very unit that was responsible for delivering Göering to the gallows. This is a sure fire sign of a cover-up.

As Göering's body was lumped with the carcasses of the other Nazis who had just been hung, they were all placed in caskets and loaded into trucks which were escorted by armed but unmarked cars. There is no record of who the drivers of these vehicles were. Nick Carter, a West Point graduate, was commanding the Service Company of the 26th Infantry at the time of the burial procession. He had sent for two trucks to carry the caskets, but he didn't know who the drivers were. They never returned, and according to him, were taken off the roles of the army.

Göering's body and the others were taken from Nuremburg to a crematorium at a cemetery in Munich known as the Ostfriedhof. A U.S. Army officer arrived at the cemetery at 5:00 A.M. on October 16th. He told the German attendants that trucks would arrive at 7:00 A.M. with "the bodies of eleven American soldiers, killed and buried during the war, whose ashes have been requested by their families". The bodies did not arrive until 9:00 A.M. at which time the Crematorium was surrounded by U.S. Army guards. Eleven caskets were carried into the basement where the fires were already blazing. The caskets were not opened as the officers stood and watched over the proceedings. Again, we see plenty of opportunity for a Nazi escape.

Martin Bormann, who literally defrocked Himmler and Göering from their commands during the last days of the Reich, did escape. His story has been documented in a book called *Aftermath: Martin Bormann and the Fourth Reich* by Ladislas Farago. Some insist that he died, but this book is pretty convincing.

Whatever the actual circumstances of these individuals, the bizarre pattern and windows of opportunity cannot be denied. None of these people held any visible power so it could be considered a moot point, but there is a common thread that all of them shared. They all had a deep resonance with the occult. Magicians, whether white or black, believe in a sacred rite which involves the changing of their identities. This is what the 10th Degree of the OTO is about. One relinquishes a former identity and assumes a new one. The new identity could be through death or surreptitious means.

Hitler's demise is the most enigmatic and certainly the most magical. He chose April 30th, the Celtic holy day of Walpurgisnacht, on which to pass from this world. This day is not only exactly six months from Halloween, it is also a celebration of dead souls. Hitler's departure on this date makes it all the more mysterious.

There is no question that the spirits of all these Reich leaders are not at rest. All of them have been speculated about and studied beyond any others in history. No matter how much you despise them or even admire them, they are hanging from the rafters in the attic of the morphogenetic grid. Their souls contain secrets which have yet to be discharged. To the degree they remain a mystery, they are worshipped, even if it is taking place on a tacit level.

All of them claimed to embrace the ideals and power of ancient Babylon. This meant building a utopia on Earth in the name of the German people that would be a direct bridge to the Creator. Anyone attempting to climb or review this Babylonian path is going to see the skeletons of those who did not make it. The remnants of their bones still cry out for the longing of their unfulfilled dreams. Because the dreams were so grand and the execution of them were so imperious, and at times horrific, the men who lived those dreams have never been forgotten.

16

OTTO SKORZENY

Although the leaders of the Third Reich demonstrated no significant presence after the war, there is an even more intriguing fellow who did. Intensely famous and admired by war buffs, most people do not even know his name: Otto Skorzeny, the top commando of World War II.

Skorzeny was an Austrian who felt passionaitely about his country. Like many of his fellow countrymen of that time period, he felt the Jewish element was a major factor in the deterioration of Austrian culture. Although I have found no evidence of rabid anti-Semitism in his early life, there is no doubt about his position after World War II. He publicly claimed on a routine basis that he was not anti-Semitic, but his later life became an engaged contest between himself and the agents of Israel.

A tremendous athlete with a huge frame, Skorzeny was schooled in the various arts of war. When fencing as a young man, he sustained a laceration across his entire cheek which became a permanent scar. His peers considered such a mark a badge of distinction and he wore it proudly. Skorzeny was subsequently known as "Scar".

Skorzeny was arguably the best soldier in the entire theater of World War II. If not, he was successful enough to back up the contention and is certainly the most celebrated commando on either side. Although he was continously assigned near impossible missions under ridiculous odds, Skorzeny consistently came up as a winner. He personally trained his top commandos, and they were fiercely loyal to him. Skorzeny was not a cruel soldier and exhibited no care for politics or bureaucracy. Simply put, he was a warrior.

Reading the biography of Skorzeny *(Skorzeny: Hitler's Commando* by Glenn B. Infield) excites great admiration for him as a pure soldier and leader, even if you are not partial towards Nazis.* In order to grasp the essence of Skorzeny's abilities, it is only necessary to relay the events of his most celebrated mission: the rescue of Benito Mussolini.

Well before the war was lost, Mussolini was captured by an anti-fascist faction in Italy and was incarcerated in a cliffside hotel that was accessble only by cable cars. Hitler was in a quandary as this kidnapping was a major blow to the morale of the Axis. Worse yet, no one knew where Mussolini was being held. Skorzeny was handed the mission and was personally instructed by Hitler himself. If he failed, Skorzeny would be disowned.

Intelligence sources provided no valuable information on Mussolini's whereabouts. Skorzeny had to find out for himself, and he soon did, but that was the easiest part of the mission. There were no roads to the hotel by which to transport convoys of troops or armored vehicles nor were there any nearby landing strips for air transport. Bombing the hotel itself wouldn't work either as Mussolini's life was the issue at stake.

Skorzeny surreptitiously scouted the area and saw a small ledge at the bottom of the cliff over which the hotel stood. He devised an extremely daring plan whereby he and his men would make a calculated crash landing in small glider planes. After studying the entire situation and training himself and his men to within an inch of their lives, the plan was put into action.

The glider landings were successful, but the commando party had to scale the cliff without being noticed and take command of the hotel. The German soldiers caught the Italian guards by surprise as Skorzeny himself walked unnoticed into the entrance of the hotel. He and his troops, although vastly outnumbered, soon took control. Mussolini was transported down the cliff where a small single engine plane was waiting for him and Skorzeny. They immediately departed for Rome. The aircraft was

---

*Although Skorzeny was never tried as a war criminal, some Jewish groups have insisted that he should have been.

too small to take any other soldiers. It was even a miracle that the pilot was able to land and take off at all on such a small ledge. The German troops made their way on foot through rough mountainous terrain and eventually reached the safety of German territory.

Leaving Mussolini in Rome, Skorzeny flew to Vienna and checked into a hotel. There, he hoped to recuperate and get plenty of bed rest as his back was badly injured in the crash landing. The phone began to ring incessantly with congratulatory messages. Finally, Skorzeny received word from Himmler that the Fuhrer himself wanted to see him immediately. Flying to Berlin, he was awarded the Knight's Cross. This is the highest honor available to German soldiers and is comparable to the Congressional Medal of Honor in the United States. Skorzeny soon became the toast of the town, but he had no desire to be a socialite. He wanted to get back into action. There was a war to be won.

Many of the tasks given to Skorzeny after this celebrated event were not possible nor did they require any daring or bravery. Most of them were preposterous and required a fool, not a braveheart. Skorzeny became suspicious of command. Eventually, these impossible missions were usually cancelled.

The most intriguing assignment of Skorzeny was in 1944 when Himmler asked him to find the hidden treasure of Montsegur, located in the Cathar region of southern France. Montsegur is an historic fort known to be the last stronghold of the Cathars, a Christian Gnostic sect who were considered heretical by the Catholic Church. Before they were completely wiped out during the Inquisition, they became an underground society eventually surfacing through various Masonic lodges and the like. The Cathars were closely aligned with the court of Charlemagne and the Knights Templar.

Heinrich Himmler's SS had already funded previous expeditions to the Montsegur area. The most notable of these were under the German archaeologist Otto Rahn, an avid student of the occult who sought both the Holy Grail and the Ark of the Covenant. Rahn had reason to believe the Cathars had hidden these holy relics in their fortress of Montsegur. As the area is loaded with underground grottoes and caverns, there were many possibilities for such a scenario. Rahn made an entire career of searching for these objects and the accompanying treasure he believed was with them. There is no evidence at this point to indicate he was ultimately successful. Otto Rahn was declared dead before the war began, but there was much controversy over his demise.

As a man who could get things done, Skorzeny was pulled into the fray. What Otto Rahn and others hadn't accomplished in years, Skorzeny was to accomplish in a matter of days. Using his supreme knowledge of military strategy and tactics, he quickly concluded that the Cathars wouldn't have left their treasure in the Montsegur fortress or anywhere in the immediate vicinity. They would have taken it with them and followed an escape route. The only problem with Skorzeny's thesis was that there was no escape route. The Cathars were surrounded by the forces of the Inquisition on all sides save for one exception: a steep and inaccessible cliff running down the rear of the fortress.

Apparently, Skorzeny had good karma with cliffs. One had served him well during the rescue of Mussolini. He now realized that although the Montsegur cliff was virtually impossible to scale upwards, the Cathars could have descended it using ropes and pulleys without suffering too much strife. This was the escape route he had been looking for, and he followed it. Skorzeny soon found himself at a nearby mountain top that contained a hidden fortress. This was the real last refuge of the Cathars and one that had remained unsuspected for the better part of the millenium.

Coincidentally, Skorzeny's operation was being carried out on the highest holy day of the Cathars. Traditionally, hundreds of the local people would celebrate a festival at the actual fortress of Montsegur. In 1944, they went through the formality of requesting permission from the German authorities to use the area but were denied. Nevertheless, the passionate locals disregarded authority and descended upon the fortress to perform their ancient rites.

Upon being informed of the situation, Skorzeny let them enjoy their festival. Not only could he identify with the common people, he had no respect whatsoever for the German bureacracy and even despised it. Besides, his operation was a comfortable distance from the pilgrammage site of the peasants.

Skorzeny and his men soon found the secret treasure. He immediately notified Himmler who, in turn, arranged for a recovery and transport team. Himmler sent immediate word back to Skorzeny, telling him to look to the skies on the following day.

There, against a clear blue sky, a sky writing plane depicted the Celtic cross (a cross within a circle). It was an esoteric message to a fellow member of a secret society. Skorzeny's work was done. He left the recovery team to do their work and returned to the theater of war.

As the war ended, Skorzeny found himself in his home country of Austria. As Allied forces began to swarm the country, he ordered his men to lay down their weapons and he proceeded to turn himself in to the American army. This simple act of surrender proved to be very difficult. There was no shortage of German soldiers to be processed, and as the fighting had ceased, the Allies were not in any particular hurry to take in prisoners. Skorzeny knew he was incredibly famous and would be considered an esteemed prisoner. The soldiers that he encountered either didn't believe him or didn't recognize the significance of who he was. After a ridiculous amount of non-recognition, it finally dawned on someone who Skorzeny was: the top Nazi commando who had rescued Mussolini. Then, the circus began. Skorzeny, extremely admired by the American soldiers, was treated like a social lion. Eventually, the authorities would demand their due.

As stated earlier, Skorzeny was never put on trial for war crimes at Nuremburg. It is not customary for loyal soldiers to be so tried. Besides, there was no evidence available to prosecuters that Skorzeny was guilty of war crimes. Nevertheless, he was not released, and this became an extreme source of discomfort to him. Skorzeny became a prisoner of peace without explanation. He was allowed one furlough to Vienna but was watched very closely. After languishing under house arrest for a good while, a military tribunal was convened charging Skorzeny with an act that violated the Geneva Rules of War.

During the last defense of the Reich, things had become rather hopeless. Hitler thought of a last ditch effort which he had learned of from a similar Allied tactic used against the Nazis. Germans would don American uniforms, utilize captured American vehicles and sneak behind Allied lines. There, they would turn around road signs, blow up bridges and generally confuse the enemy. Skorzeny was chosen as the man to implement this plan.

The Rules of War expressly forbid the wearing of enemy uniforms in order to kill. Skorzeny knew this and questioned his

Fuhrer. Hitler readily agreed that no one should be killed using this technique. Of course, anyone knows that if you end up behind enemy lines under such a scenario, it is very easy to get caught up in an inadvertent shoot out. People are going to get killed. Skorzeny ended up running a very successful operation. In the process, the Americans suffered severe casualties. It is the way of war.

Skorzeny, who was given an American defense lawyer, bitterly resented the charges and felt it was a political show trial. Skorzeny's defense fell on deaf ears. At the last minute, a surprise witness was called to the stand. It was a British Air Force officer by the name of Yeo-Thomas. As a commando behind enemy lines, Yeo-Thomas testified that the Allies had used similar techniques and had done it many times. He openly said that the Allies would kill if necessary. Although it was not written into law, Yeo-Thomas said the Rules of War had in effect changed since World War I. The tribunal now had its hands tied. They could do nothing else but acquit Skorzeny. If they didn't, the Allies would have to answer to their own war crimes charges. In all probability, Yeo-Thomas testified on behalf of American intelligence.

Despite the above good fortune, Skorzeny was still not released. More politics became involved. In any effect, he became disaffected towards the Americans and felt he was being mistreated. Originally looking toward a new future in a revived Austria, Skorzeny had previously seen himself cooperating with the Allies. It slowly dawned on him that he had no country. He found himself alone in a terrible and frightening world. The old Reich was gone and they had been his only system of support. The Allied authorities didn't trust him and were obviously not going to embrace him.

Although the authorities denied him any joy, Skorzeny was still popular among the American soldiers. They greatly admired his bravery and the legendary stories surrounding his name. Some of them helped him to escape, probably more out of sympathy and respect as opposed to being part of a cabal. Skorzeny would soon flee to Spain and seek the protection of an old German ally: dictator Francisco Franco. In Spain, he discovered that he had connections galore and that his old popularity was still in tact. After all, Skorzeny had been personally responsible for couriering all sorts of Nazi treasure to Argentina and other designations. His Nazi superiors, who trusted him above others as a man who could the job done, were now either dead or missing. He was now being given the "Nazi Express Card" for a new life, albeit an underground one. The Americans denied him, and the old Reich was gone, but they left him with one legacy: an unlimited charge card.

The loyalties of Skorzeny were shaped by the circumstances of his life. He had to choose one side or the other. The Americans obviously didn't like him and were also in concert with the Jews in establishing the new state of Israel. That faction had absolutely no sympathy for Skorzeny, his friends, or anything he stood for. In all likelihood, this explains the show trial of Skorzeny. Realizing that the Allies and Jews wanted his hide, he obligingly became their enemy and began to financially support the rescue and relocation of the SS. Skorzeny also became a go-between for major business transactions between Germany, South America and the Arab world. His military genius was used (sometimes by the CIA) to train terrorist forces in Egypt, Iraq, and other Arab countries. South American countries also used him as a military adviser.

It is understandable that the Americans had a hard time embracing Skorzeny, but in so doing, they unleashed a nightmare on the world. His training and leadership of military forces in third world countries has set the policy of hatred and terror still felt in the world today.

After the war, Skorzeny became a friend and adviser to Juan Peron, the military dictator of Argentina. He was also the personal escort of Evita Peron. Many years after after her corpse had been stolen by hostile forces, Skorzeny was personally responsible for retrieving her body from Italy, where it had been hidden for over a decade.

Skorzeny also set up an extensive network in Egypt which allegedly included the setting up of concentration camps. According to what I've read, this was at the request of the Egyptians who wanted to exterminate their Jewish population. Skorzeny obliged and ingratiated himself to the Arabs by calling in an SS contact who knew how to run a death camp. Publicly, Skorzeny disdained the holocaust. I believe he used whatever means were expedient in order to establish and maintain a vast network that existed to further the Nazi cause. What exactly that cause was or is can be subjected to various aspects of debate.

Skorzeny also enjoyed talking about the occult aspects of the Third Reich and was known to have toyed with journalists. Sometimes he encouraged them to speculate about the possibility of Hitler being alive or other adventurous aspects of the "Fourth Reich". There is no question he had some fun with that, but none of us know exactly what he did and did not know. All we are sure of is that he was a very important player in a mysterious and often sinister network.

In the early 1970s, Skorzeny was diagnosed with cancer, possibly a result of complications from the back injury he sustained during the Mussolini rescue mission. An operation to remove the cancer left him paralyzed with the doctors saying he would never walk again. Ever the resourceful man, Skorzeny called on an old physical therapist from the SS. Through this man's help, Skorzeny amazed his doctors and regained his ability to walk. One of his last public actions was to attend a Catholic mass for the souls of Hitler and Mussolini. He died in 1975.

At first glance, the legacy of Otto Skorzeny might be considered to be one of terrorism. Maybe so, but he also left us with a legacy of intrigue and his life story demonstrates that a strong and active Nazi style organization still exists in the world today. Known as the Spider, it contains many other factions across its world wide web.

17

THE ARAB CONNECTION

The connection of Otto Skorzeny to Egypt and the Arab world is an extremely intriguing aspect to our investigation. This alliance shines even more prominently when we consider both parties' historical antipathy towards Israel. The ancient history of Arabia gives us some interesting insights into the Arab-Nazi network. No matter how demented or fragmented it became, this network patterned itself after ancient mystery schools which were purveyors of truth. Their power, although it was misused, was actually derived from a live tradition that worked within the framework of these mystery schools. We will explore some of that ancient heritage in this chapter.

According to what Jan van Helsing told me, the most powerful and secretive society of the Nazi brass was the mysterious order of the Black Stone. Although Jan had plenty of information on many of the other societies, he had practically nothing on this one. This made it very difficult to trace. What I did find out on my own was that this Black Stone had a direct connection to the Black Stone in Mecca, the most holy site of the Islamic religion. Mecca is located on the Arabian peninsula just east of the Red Sea.

An extension of the Sahara desert, the Arabian peninsula was at one time a flourishing and fertile plain with an abundance of thriving life. Mecca was originally an ancient Aryan shrine. This was most aptly demonstrated in history when it was a place of prominent worship to the Hindus (according to conventional history, the Hindu religion we know today was a product of the ancient Aryans).

137

According to popular traditions in the area of Mecca, Abraham and his son, Ishmael, were ordered to rebuild the ancient shrine of Mecca by the voice of Allah. Allah was originally known to the pagans of the area as an ancient god who embraced both the feminine and masculine aspects of the deity. "Al" or "El" refers to the male principle. "El" is also used as the masculine distinction for nouns in the Spanish language. "La" or "lah" represents the feminine. Thus, these two words "Al-lah" become the word *Allah*.

As soon as Abraham and Ishmael arrived at the holy spot, they discovered it to be occupied by the house of an old woman. She consented to let them remove her house and build their shrine but only on the condition that the new temple be entrusted to her and her descendants forever and ever. The old woman was known as Shaybah and her descendants are known as Benu Shaybah which literally means the sons or descendants of an old woman. Today, one arrives at the most holy site of Islam, the Kaaba, through the Gates of the Sons of Shaybah. Shaybah translates into English as "Sheba" as in the Queen of Sheba. The word *Sheba* derives from the Hindu deity Shiva, related to Kali, the feminine goddess of time and destruction.

The Kaaba itself is a cubed structure, sometimes known as the Black Cube. It is covered in an ornate cloth known as the Kiswat. Set in stone on one corner of the Kaaba is the Black Stone itself which has always been shrouded in mystery. It is virtually impossible for non Muslims to get close to it. Consequently, the Black Stone has not been subject to any sort of formal investigation. Most modern observers agree that it is some sort of meteorite. Travellers in the era of Sir Richard Burton agreed that it was volcanic in nature. Burton quotes a certain Ali Bey who describes it as a "block of volcanic basalt whose circumference is sprinkled with little crystals, pointed and straw-like, with rhombs of tile-red feldspar upon a dark background, like velvet or charcoal, except one of its protuberances, which is reddish." Burton further quotes a man named Burckhardt as saying it is a "lava containing several small extraneous particles of a whitish and yellowish substance."

The word *Kaaba* means the Great Mother in Arabic. The dictionary says it derives from *kava* which is similar to cave, also a feminine symbol. Phonetically, the word refers to "Ka" and "ba" which would mean house of the spirit. Magician Kenneth Grant defines it as the "feminine abode" or source of the Primal Egg.

Perhaps the feature that first popularized the site of the Kaaba was the presence of a natural well which produces a brackish water known as Zemzem. This liquid is very rich in minerals and is distributed all over the world for its healing powers. In the Persian language, Zemzem signifies "the Great Luminary" which cabalistically corresponds to Venus or Lucifer. The Black Stone of the Kaaba is also seen as Venus in terms of its generative power. Zemzem can also mean "Zam! Zam!" which means "Fill, Fill (the bottle)".

The Kaaba has suffered destruction from time to time throughout its long history. For the last thirteen hundred years, it has been kept up meticulously. The Kaaba was once known to contain the idols of many pagan gods, particularly those of the Hindus. These were all cleaned out by the prophet Muhamet, but he did recognize the primary ancient god of the Kaaba: Allah. It was the only one he recognized.

According to tradition, the Black Stone of the Kaaba originated in heaven and was given to Adam by Allah. Originally, it was a pure white stone to be set in the Kaaba, a shrine that Adam would first build. It was known as "Alhajar Alsad", the Happiest Stone. Of all the stones of Paradise, it had been chosen for the Kaaba in Mecca. With the stone in his arms, Adam descended from Paradise and made his way to Ceylon or Sri Lanka. Adam placed the stone in the ground so that the Kaaba could be mounted upon it. It was obviously quite huge at that time.

During the Flood of Noah, the Kaaba was badly damaged and the Holy Stone was hidden and put in a safe place. It remained so hidden until Allah ordered Abraham to rebuild the Kaaba. Abraham left his home in Babylon and was led by the Angel Gabriel to the source of Zemzem. Once in Mecca, Gabriel gave him the Holy Stone. Abraham taught the people to revere the stone with sacrifices of animals being performed in the vicinity. The blood of the animals was put onto the stone and it accordingly became dark. The stone is often described as black-like but it is also sometimes described as a very dark blood red. The darkness of the stone is also said to be the result of the sins of man.

Islamic traditions vary, but they are unanimous on one point. The Black Stone was originally part of something much greater.

What is left today is only a fragment of a very sacred object. One of the traditions refers to it as "the stone that was rejected". This is not only an esoteric name for Christ, it is also a phrase which refers to the capstone that once stood over the Great Pyramid of Giza. We see this again if we consult Egyptian mythology where Gabriel is the equivalent of Tahuti, the builder of the Great Pyramid. The idea that Tahuti, in the personage of Gabriel, gave the stone to Abraham suggests that the Black Stone in Mecca represents part of the original capstone of the Great Pyramid.

A fire destroyed the Kaaba in the seventh century. When it was rebuilt, an entrance was placed several feet off the ground in order to better regulate who entered the holy house. As the reconstruction had been performed by various Arab tribes, a legitimate dispute arose as to who should install the Black Stone into the newly erected edifice. A compromise was finally reached. The tribes agreed that the next person to enter the courtyard could make the judgement as to who should install the Black Stone. By the principles of synchronicity, the next person to enter the courtyard was Muhamet. This event was prior to the visions which made him famous as a prophet of Allah. The young Muhamet crafted a plan that would not only vanquish the various Arab factions but would honor them as well. He placed the stone on a piece of cloth and asked a representative from each tribe to stand around the cloth. Together, they lifted the cloth with the Black Stone and carried it to the Kaaba. There, the young Muhamet took it upon himself to set the stone in its modern place.

Muhamet later retired to a cave where he began to receive divinely inspired messages through the vehicle of Gabriel. He subsequently went on to convert thousands and conquer the entire Semitic world. The entire history of Muhamet is fascinating but is much too involved to go into here. There are only a few pertinent points I would like to mention.

The above information makes it clear that local traditions had Muhamet deriving his power from the Great Pyramid. He was also nurtured and secured in his position by the Goddess herself. Before he began to receive his divine inspiration, he married a wealthy merchant woman. She not only gave him economic comfort, she was the first to recognize the divine quality of the messages he received. As he began to preach and become popular, the most powerful tribal leader in the area became enraged and wanted to slay Muhamet. This leader's lust for death was subdued by his own sister whose role became pivotal. She was a fervent supporter of Muhamet and was able to convince her brother not to slay this new prophet. Eventually, this woman converted her brother to Islam, His support was crucial to the early development of the religion.

We can see that the entire basis of the Islamic religion follows the basic precepts and honoring of the goddess. Although it has strict laws limiting the freedom of women, there is also an aspect which reveres the female principle. The word *Islam* itself means "to yield to the way of God". Yielding is a feminine attribute. "Is" represents Isis or the feminine and "lam" is Tibetan for "way or path". In actual practice, most critics of Islam will say that they have subjugated the goddess and ruled with a patriarchy. We get another look at how this subjugation of the goddess took place when we examine the history of Islam after Muhamet.

The Q'ran or Koran is the holy book of Islam, said to be compiled in the years after the death of Muhamet. The original Q'ran was not written down as Muhamet was said to be illiterate. It was remembered and recited by "Remembrancers" who were trained to memorize large portions of the text. In both the cases of Jesus and Muhamet, these men changed the course of history. Isn't it odd that neither one of them left any written records by their own hand? In the case of Jesus, there are many historical materials which suggest he did write. In the case of Muhamet, we have to consider this possibility may apply to him as well.

In order to get an even better grasp of the goddess principle in the Arabian peninsula, we have to take a look at the hallmark of ancient Arab culture: *The Book of the Thousand Nights and a Night,* more popularly known as the *Arabian Nights.*

A labyrinthine saga of various interrelated tales, the *Arabian Nights* has no specific author unless we consider it to be the goddess herself. These tales begin with the plight of King Shahryár.* The King and his royal brother are perplexed. Seeing their wives satisfy their lust with other men and thereby betray their kingly husbands, they see this as the vile way of all women. Such is their

---

* King Shahryár is supposed to be Persian for "City-friend". It also breaks down to "Sha" and "hryar" which suggests "Sha of the Aryans".

grief that the two kings leave their respective kingdoms in order to escape the curse of women. To their surprise, they come upon a genie who comes out of the water. The genie immediately manifests a crystal chest with seven padlocks, representing the seven chakras or seven seals. Out of the chest, the genie unleashes his beautiful female concubine who he has trapped for his own pleasures. Commanding her to sit down so he can rest on her lap, she obliges him and he falls asleep. King Shahryár and his brother stand by in absolute fear and horror over the power of this Ifrit (the Arabic name for a genie).

To their surprise and additional horror, this exotic concubine remains wide awake and forcibly persuades the two kings to have sex with her. They want to refuse but are afraid, for if they do, she threatens to wake up the Ifrit who will unleash himself upon them. After she enjoys herself and is sexually satisfied, the woman pulls forth a string of seals or rings which represent all her male conquests. After forcing the King and his brother to give over their very own rings, she informs them that nothing can stop the desire of women (or the goddess), not even the powerful jinn.

The two kings now become even more perplexed and afraid of the power of women. They are particularly shocked with regard to this particular concubine's willingness to risk her own life in the vicinity of the Ifrit. After all, here is a supernatural being who has been fooled by this woman for aeons. If the Ifrit can be fooled, then how can they, as mere mortals, stand up to the ingenious power of the feminine force?

King Shahryár interprets this phenomena in the most negative of ways. Returning to his kingdom to resume his authority, he makes the conviction that no woman on Earth can be trusted. He resolves this dilemma by marrying a new virgin every day, enjoying her at night and then beheading her in the morning. Only in this way can he be sure of a wife's trust and fidelity. King Shahryár now becomes the most evil man in the realm and is feared by all. The King's Vizier (sometimes translated as adviser or more flamboyantly as wizard) is ordered to find new virgins for the pleasure of his highness. As many women are beheaded by this process, the pickings become very slim.

The Vizier has a difficult time with the King's order. Not only is the realm running out of virgins for him to pass on to the King, but he himself is possessed of a most beautiful daughter by the name of Shahrázád.* As the story develops, it becomes obvious that this woman has been indoctrinated into the Secret Doctrine (as expounded by Madame Blavatsky in her work of the same title) as she has read all the ancient texts.

Despite the Vizier's protests, Shahrázád convinces her father that, if she marries the King, she has a chance to quell his highness by drawing upon all of her own vast knowledge. The Vizier finally consents and the King is delighted to have a new bride. Shahrázád's sister is offered as a bride as well and is invited to the honeymoon of her sister. Her name is Dunyázád which means "world-freer".

After the King breaks Shahrázád's virginity, he falls asleep. Upon waking, Dunyázád has been given a cue by her sister to ask her to tell them an exciting story. The King is very interested to hear a story and a fascinating tale ensues from the lips of Shahrázád. At the end of each night, Shahrázád leaves the King in suspense. Using this strategy, she prolongs her life every night by virtue of the fact that she will have to continue the story the next morning.

Utterly fascinated by Shahrázád's story telling ability, the King lets her live for one thousand and one nights. During the course of the tales, she sires him three children and talks of every imaginable aspect of life. Most of these stories are told in the context of the supernatural with miracles and jinn abounding amidst tales of blatant sexuality. The primary moral message of the stories is that an individual should align himself with his own divine will. In the text, this is directly expressed as the will of Allah. This is the same aspect that Aleister Crowley describes when he says "Do what thou wilt shall be the whole of the law". *The Nights* routinely employs the principle of synchronicity to enable the characters to arrive at serendipitous circumstances. Synchronicity is recognized as the Divine Will of Allah expressing itself.

At the end of one thousand and one nights, Shahrázád has covered the vast panorama of human experience and finally announces she is done. Although the King is expected to behead Shahrázád, she appeals to him to reconsider on the basis that his

---

* Shahrázád is a Persian word for "city-freeer". There is an older version of her name "Szheherazade" which means "lion born" (Shirzád). Shahrázád's mythological or cabalistic correspondence would be that of the Egyptian Maat, the female consort or aspect of Tahuti.

three sons will need a mother. The King, so deeply moved by her stories, has long since become filled with wisdom. He sees that there is no longer any need to execute her or other women. Shahrázád's purity and dignity act to redeem the entire situation. King Shahryár decides to become a good king and a benefactor to all. The people rejoice and a renaissance ensues.

The previous adventures are not the same tales you will find from Walt Disney or in fairy tale books. In the original version, salvation through the goddess is the underlying thesis of the celebrated *Arabian Nights*. Although watered down in some versions, the spark of these legends can still be seen in modern Arabian culture. To this day, those pure and devout souls who dedicate themselves to the Will of Allah are known as Olemas. This is a direct language link to the word "Thelema" as expressed by Aleister Crowley. The Greek letter for "T" is expressed as θ. Hence, Thelema = Olema.

As was inferred previously, the modern legacy of Arabia leaves us with the impression of women in bondage. It is clear however that it was the feminine energy which was originally harnessed. The *Arabian Nights* tells us that. The goddess is imbedded deeply within the will of the universe as well as being the primary cause. This principle is still adhered to and taught in the Arabian mystery schools.

As with most religions, there is a mystery and intrigue about Islam. Many Americans perceive it as a "bastion of bad guys" when the media conjures up names like Sadam Hussein and Colonel Khadafy. As with most religions, there is an exoteric version of Islam for the masses and an esoteric version for initiates.

The Sufis are probably the most well known in regard to the esoteric aspect. It was their specifically chosen duty to take the goddess wisdom of the Holy Grail, known to be perverted during the time of Constantine, and preserve it in a secret form that could be transmitted to the rest of the world. It was in this spirit that the Muslims captured key spots throughout Jerusalem. Sometimes it seemed as if the main thrust of the Muslims was simply to prevent the further perversion of the Christian faith. Their methods were not, however, only force and war.

It is an ironic historical note that the most sacred shrine of the Jews, the Temple of Solomon, was resignedly given over to Omar, the second Caliph of the Islamic faith. In fact, Omar is reported to have been rather indifferent to the whole affair. At the time, he was preoccupied with getting himself back to Mecca to calm down his brethren. Rumors were spreading that Omar might have the faithful pray to Jerusalem instead of the traditional city of Mecca. Omar had no such intentions, but he was called to Jerusalem at the request of those initiates in charge of the Jewish faith. They were intent on handing the stewardship of Solomon's Temple over to the newly founded Muslim faith. It was in this manner that the secret initiates of the Islamic faith became the keepers of the Temple of Solomon and subsequently built the Dome of the Rock over it. This still stands today with the Muslims as custodians.

It was this same legacy and custodianship of Islam which transmitted secret information to the Knights Templar during the crusades. In this manner, a new vehicle was created to transmit the true Grail Christianity* to the rest of the world. The seeds for this new Christian movement actually began with Charlemagne, a man who possessed the red hair so prominent in the Cameron clan. Herein lies another great secret.

The Islamic holy book or Q'ran includes a chapter on the family of Amrin or Imran. If you remember the earlier chapter on the Camerons, the name "Ahmroun" was said to be the actual derivation of that name. Muhamet, through the Q'ran, explains that this family was the lineage that propagated Moses as well as Mary, the mother of Jesus. Once again, the lineage of the Camerons pops its head in a most intriguing fashion. If one searches in the right places, it is not hard for one to build a case for the Camerons having a great influence in the destiny of mankind. In fact, they could be considered the major influence. Perhaps it is no coincidence that the cave where the Dead Sea Scrolls were discovered is called Qumran, which is phonetically related to Cameron.

When I told Preston of my above find, he told me that I had discovered the secret of the Isle of Skye. He was well aware of it. In other words, the secret of the Cameron clan is that they are of the lineage of Christ. Duncan's own lineage, through his mother at the very least, connects him to the Isle of Skye.

---

* Out of this very same vehicle of esoteric Christianity, the Knights Templar created one of the western world's first and most prominent intertational banking cartels.

Of course, there are many books tracing the lineage of the family of Christ into modern times. These may or may not be correct, but one thing is certain. The truest tradition would be the best kept secret, and here we have the Camerons emerging.

18

THE MYSTERIOUS ORIGINS OF THORN, E.M.I.

The Camerons and Wilsons amount to the same clan working their intrigues through the network of linear space and history. It therefore shouldn't surprise us too much that they were the holy family of Islam as well as Gnostic Christianity. Always enigmatic, their vestige appears once again in the story of their association with Thorn, E.M.I., the electronics and media giant who distributed the movie *The Philadelphia Experiment*.

According to Preston Nichol's story, as was relayed in the prelude to this book, the Wilson Brothers were the first manufacturers of electronic instruments in Great Britain. They formed a business alliance with Aleister Crowley's father, and this concern later developed, along with a host of other companies, into Thorn, E.M.I. Through the element of sycnhronicity, I was able to link Thorn, E.M.I. to the Arabic connection. It is relayed in the following story.

In my pursuit of the historical Wilson brothers, I became friends with an Englishman by the name of Howard Barkway. He became involved in the intrigue of Montauk in a most synchronous manner. Howard, a publisher of electronic books, was visiting the New York area on business when he happened to meet up with a woman named Nancy. Already on her way to see Duncan and Preston, she convinced him to come along. Howard was not disappointed. He was exposed to the high strangeness of Montauk first hand and had a great time. This encounter was well before any of the Montauk books were written. As Howard was already a publisher and was just beginning a venture into the esoteric market, it was thought that he might take on the publishing of the Montauk Project story. Living in England proved to be too great a barrier as Howard would have to arrange for an outside author to visit America and write the book. I came along a short while later.

After *The Montauk Project* was published, I began to hear from Howard on the telephone. He soon became the first distributor for the Montauk books in the United Kingdom. Howard not only ordered books but became involved in the search for the Wilson brothers. Although he was not able to turn up any historical record of the Wilsons, he offered a most bizarre personal synchronicity in his own life. His mother was the personal secretary for Sir Jules Thorn, the man who founded the Thorn Company! Thorn later merged with E.M.I and became the electronics and entertainment conglomerate known as Thorn, E.M.I.. Unfortunately, Howard's mother had died a year previously and could not be consulted for further information.

According to Howard, Sir Jules Thorn was not English at all. He was an Arab from Vienna! The name Jules Thorn was adopted for English society in which he eventually reached knighthood. He came to England as a representative of an Austrian lamp company, encouraging us to conjure thoughts of Aladdin and his magic lamp. In 1928, under the name of the Electric Lamp Service Company, Thorn set up his own company. Heavy import duties caused him to switch his business to radio valves. Eventually, he acquired the Ferguson Radio Corporation and became involved in the manufacture of radios and radiograms. As the company grew, Thorn went back into the lighting business and successfully challenged the cartel which put him out of the lamp business earlier. The company expanded tremendously after World War II and went into high technology. Later, Thorn became involved in electronics and phonographs.

At this time, no documentation has been found connecting Jules Thorn and the Wilson brothers, however the synchronicity of Howard Barkway coming into our lives demonstrates the outside force communicating once again. The odds of his mother being connected to this company are extremely remote. Anyone who has followed the career of Preston Nichols can also see ample opportunities for high strangeness when it comes to the above industries.

Another interesting note with regard to the Austrian connection of Jules Thorn is the fact that he came from Vienna. For hundreds of years, the Ottoman Empire remained very strong, but Vienna was always allowed to linger just on the outskirts of its territorial claims. For some reason, the Ottomans never conquered the cultured city but chose it as a conduit by which to distribute their Islamic influence into Europe.

The mysterious connection between the Islamic tradition and the Germans shows itself in the name *Otto*, a very popular name in Germany. The Ottoman Empire itself was named after Osman, it's founder. Both Osman and Otto trace their source back to "protector of God". The dictionary traces Osman back to its Arabic translation of *Uthman*. This word is hauntingly similar to Uther, the father of King Arthur. Again, we see the influence of Grail Christianity with the Muslims as the secret conduit.

Behind the veils of history, the Camerons and Muslims lurked in obscurity. They carried a secret doctrine that represented the power of creation. It was this power that Hitler and others of his ilk sought. Corruption is almost a requisite to those who would approach this sanctified area. The fact that the Cameron/Islamic connection would find its way to present day companies like Thorn E.M.I. and into our own consciousness demonstrates that we are working with a live occult tradition. It is still with us today.

19

THULE

The Arabic connection to the Nazis continues to reveal itself when we consider that in the centuries prior to Islam, the magnificent and all compassionate Allah was referred to as "Tualla". This name reveals an undeniable correspondence to Thule, the name from which the Germans crafted the name of their secret brotherhood: the Thule Society. Thule is considered to be the capital city of Hyperborea, the land beyond the poles.

Allah or Tualla showed Himself or Herself in many manifestations. One of these is through the ancient myth of the sun in the center of the Earth, also considered a black orb or black void. Whether an actual description of the universe or simply a colorful metaphor for the truth, the legend of Thule, in its purest form, represented the archetypal powers of the universe. It is the locale where the ancient Elder Race first interacted genetically with the indigenous race of Earth and created the amalgamated human we know today. The Thule Society concerned itself with the Teutonic lore and sacred knowledge of the Elder Race. The Norse myths themselves are considered to be coded sacred knowledge of this race's origins. As the first battle ground between humans and gods, *Ultima Thule* is identified as the Teutonic Garden of Eden. It also parallels the story of Babylon where mankind loses its connection to the godhead.

---

*The word *Thule* is pronounced *too-lee* in German although English dictionaries allow you to say *thoo-lee* as well. In Sanskrit, the word *Tula* means balance. The *Arabian Nights* also uses the word *Tue La* as a word for putting one's wife to death.

The German Thule Society sought to align itself with the basic forces of the universe. Some of the individuals involved in this society were the "ninety year old vegetarians" referred to in an earlier chapter. My friend, Jan van Helsing, has maintained personal contact with these individuals and has conveyed some of their information to me. As much has already been written about the Thule Society by both occult and historical writers, I will not attempt to reiterate all the same information. Instead, I will focus on what hasn't necessarily been said or emphasized by others.

Virtually all historical accounts of the Thule Gesellschaft, as it is called in German, designate Baron Rudolf von Sebottendorff as the founder. There is no question that Sebottendorffff was involved at the inception. The present day members of the Thule Society report that both Sebottendorff and Karl Haushofer presided over the inception of the Thule Society and that Haushofer was the senior but more silent partner.

Sebottendorff was actually a major player in the Thule Society, but Haushofer's exact role seems to be have been a well kept secret. Sebottendorff actually got himself in trouble when Hitler rose to power. He wrote a book entitled *Before Hitler Came* which delineated the entire scope of the organization and how Hitler fit into it. Sebottendorff was put in a camp but was eventually reprieved and sent off to Istanbul. There, he fostered the Islamic connection to the Nazis. Some of Haushofer's key maneuvers have already been discussed in *Pyramids of Montauk*.

Another piece of new information about the Thule Society concerned Rudolph Steiner. Steiner was a remarkable artist, genius, scientist and mystic. He is world renowned and even has an entire system of education named after him. Steiner at one time headed the Austrian branch of the Ordo Templi Orientis. Aleister Crowley, of course, headed the British branch. Jan told me that Steiner was the esoteric or inner head of the Thule Society. If this is true, Steiner would have operated with true regard to the spiritual aspects of the Thulean myths and information. Most of the current renditions are comic book versions featuring racist doctrines which the purveyors do not really understand the source of themselves. This denigration of the ancient lore was secured when Hitler became charged with the exoteric aspects of the Thule Society. This concerned the political factors of the organization.

Hitler immediately perceived Steiner as a threat and persecuted him. The Nazis eventually pursued him to Swizterland and burned his Goetherium, a domed building inspired by the German mystic Goethe. It was Steiner's pride and joy as well as an exemplary tribute to the esoteric sciences. Hitler's backers literally burned it to the ground. It was said that Steiner literally died of a broken heart. There is also a tradition that Steiner's death was faked and that he went into hiding and fought Hitler surreptitiously.

Without going into all the doctrine and historical details, the main point to grasp about the Thule Society is that its true tradition was being compromised for political expediency and power. The lower aspects of its doctrine, which degenerated to the point where it included insane racism, literally consumed the higher.

Well before the conflict between Hitler and Rudolph Steiner, Haushofer had also founded the Vril Society. This was an attempt by Haushofer to diversify his resources as well as to keep certain political interests at bay. These are the same political interests that consumed the Thule Society. In most Nazi occult literature, the Vril Society is mentioned but not too much is known about it. Its function and the esoteric principles behind it will be discussed in the next two chapters.

Many of the historical accounts of the Thule Society are accurate from an exoteric point of view, but they are often jaded when it comes to the inner aspects of Thule. Some offer the whole society as a bunch of nuts with far out metaphysical beliefs; others view it as horribly evil or misguided at best. Some even suggest the society didn't exist after 1929. Actually, it went underground. What is important about 1929 is that seven major Thulists were assassinated by communists around this time period. As a nation, Germany was so sympathetic to the Thulists and their ideas that the aforementioned deaths caused a major purge of communists in the country. This enabled Hitler to consolidate his power as the exoteric head of the Thule Society and led to his political takeover of Germany. Hitler more or less discarded the esoteric aspects or ideals of the Thule Society after this point. Hitler did not keep to the truth because that was metaphysical. In physical terms, he had absolute power and demonstrated no particular regard for the spiritual or karmic aspects. He began to follow a doctrine of raw physical power.

As it is not my intention to repeat the historical accounts already given in various books, I invite those who are interested in more information about the Thule Society to consult the bibliography in this book. What I will concentrate on is the mythological and etymological associations of Thule as a concept in order to demonstrate that it is a reality in our consciousness. There are also some interesting correspondences to the Montauk phenomena.

The ancient German secret societies were interested in Montauk because it was once a part of Thule and resided in the North. This was prior to the continental drift when most geologists believe there was only one main land mass. Geographically, Montauk itself rests atop an undersea volcano which is honeycombed with all sorts of natural lava tunnels. Although you won't easily find this in books, it is a casually disregarded fact. Block Island, viewable from Montauk Point, is a similar mountain top. Whether Thule and Montauk were one and the same is considerably more controversial. Projected maps of ancient geography will show them to be remarkably close.

The ultimate concept of Thule is well represented in the myth of it as the capital city or center of Hyperborea, a word which literally means "beyond the poles". As it is beyond the poles, Hyperborea is positioned as being outside of this dimension. Thule, being in the center, is positioned as the source of all life on Earth. In Greek mythology, Pythagorus was taught sacred geometry by Apollo, a god who was identified as a resident of Hyperborea. In Pythagorean teachings, the Earth itself geometrically unfolds from a void in the center. This void has been recognized by many ancient groups, including the Sumerians, as the Black Sun. In this sense, Thule is synonymous with this Black Sun. The swastika itself is part and parcel of these ancient concepts. It can be observed in the unfolding geometric shapes of existence. The word *Swastika* means source, amongst other definitions, and represents eternal cause or the fountain of creation. Accordingly, the Thule Society used the swastika symbol in their logo to represent this idea.

The Black Sun is an even more esoteric concept than that of Thule. Represented as the void of creation itself, it is the most senior archetype imaginable. Thus, this namesake was reserved for the elite of the Thule Society. The Black Sun was actually a secret society within the Thule Society. It was senior to other

SIGNET OF THE BLACK SUN

Above is the symbol of the innermost secret society of
Nazi Germany: the Black Sun. It is illegal to print
or display this symbol in Germany today.

societies. Jan van Helsing not only informed me of this but further explained that the initials "SS" do not represent what people and historians commonly think. Traditionally, "SS" refers to Schutzstaffel, meaning Guard Detachment. In actual fact, "SS" stands for *Schwarze Sonne* in German which means "Black Sun". This does not mean every soldier who wore a SS uniform was a member of the Black Sun. It means that there was a coded hidden meaning (referring to the Black Sun) whenever the SS runes were displayed. The Nazis were magically attempting to invoke the hidden power of the Black Sun itself. Long before the SS rose to military prominence, it began as a body guard unit for Hitler.

If enough effort is taken to study a little bit of history, one will discover that the concepts of Thule and the Black Sun are as wide as the entire panorama of human existence. Despite this, historians rail against the Nazis as believing in crazy myths. More properly, the historians are not able to correctly interpret the myths. As a principle, the Black Sun is more often obscured, but Thule can be found in several distinct languages and cultures, thus corroborating the idea of a single language as illustrated in the Tower of Babalon story. The Mexicans have a Tule god and sacred city named Tula. The aboriginal Canadians of the northern arctic were known as the Tuule. Genghis Khan, the custodian of the Shensi pyramids in ancient Tibet (now known as Central Asia) named his youngest son Tula or Tule, depending on what version you read. I'm sure there are other correspondences, but these are enough to give one pause to consider what these ancient people were thinking about when they used these words. In each culture, histories reveal a common thread with variations on the Fall of Babylon.

My own personal interest in Thule accelerated when I was telling one of my friends how to pronounce the word *Thule*. As we disagreed, I looked it up in the dictionary. Much to my surprise, I discovered a new word to add to my vocabulary: *thulium*. All it said in the definition is that thulium is an element of the rare earth group listed on the periodic table and that it was element number 69. A quick look at chemistry books in various libraries didn't tell me much more, only that it was discovered in Sweden and named after the ancient idea of Thule in the north.

As Preston Nichols has a scientific education, I asked him about this. All he could tell me was that his college professors told the students that it was something they didn't need to know anything about. Of course, students love to hear that as they are mostly studying to pass tests. It seemed there was an unconscious, if not deliberate, attempt to obscure the meaning of this element. Several other inquiries came up empty. All I could find out is that thulium is metallic in nature but only appears in conjunction with other elements. It does not occur by itself. I later found out that these statements were not exactly correct. Unfortunately, I could not rely on standard texts and would have to search esoterically.

The first esoteric correspondence I noticed about thulium was that its element number of 69 equates to the English spelling of Cameron. In other words, if you assign numeric values to the English alphabet (A=1,B=2,C=3, etc), you find out that Cameron adds up to 69. I faxed my friend Jan in German asked him about this. Jan had nothing to say about thulium, but he was aware that Cameron equated to 69. He pointed out that 6 plus 9 adds up to 15, the number of the Devil card in the tarot. This, of course, corresponds to Baphomet.

As for thulium itself, I got additional input from a psychic friend of mine by the name of Deanna. She told me the following:

"Thulium is a psychic gas. It is found in a container and comes in a geode like an amethyst. It exists in nodules. Thulium is encased in pockets, like bubbles in shale. It is only indigenous to one part of the Earth. It is silvery and poisonous.

"Thulium gives somebody a chance to breathe or take in air on a planet. It coats the lungs or breath through ingestion. Presumably, aliens could breathe by thulium coating the inside of the stomach. This would enable them to swallow air or the air of a particular planet. It is considered a universal panacea for breathing. On Earth, we humans can do something that aliens can't do (on Earth or otherwise) and that is breathe, with big lungs. Aliens are often portrayed with caved in chest cavities."

This psychic reading was certainly creative and insightful if not accurate. Breathing is the very activity which distinguishes life from inanimate matter. There is a taking in and expelling out of energy. This in-out activity is the essence of the anima or life force itself. This is exactly why Tibetans and yogis concentrate on the breath in their esoteric work. It connects the inner with the outer. If Deanna's psychic reading is correct, it suggests the aliens are barely alive in the same manner or to the degree that humans are on a biological level. They require a substance such as thulium to maintain this in-out activity and thus sustain themselves in an atmosphere. This might explain why you do not see them in restaurants, movie theaters and the like.

In addition to Deanna, I consulted an occult chemist. Initially, he had nothing to say on thulium, but one year later, he did. I was told that thulium is commonly known as one of the fourteen rare earth elements on the periodic table. This is nothing new, but I was told these are rare because they were the original elements employed in the gestation of the planet Earth. They were present in the initial creation stage, not unlike the mythical legends of Thule itself. That these elements number fourteen is of particular relevance in that this number corresponds to the vector equilibrium (as popularized by Buckminster Fuller). The vector equilibrium contains fourteen points through which it reaches out to the next level of geometric evolution so as to interact with carbon and create the carbon based life forms that we know today.

The above is an interesting explanation, but it is only the beginning. The subject of occult chemistry would require an entire study and would be another book in itself. We will touch on some other key aspects of this subject later on.

I was later able to reference a chemistry book that revealed a few more interesting things about thulium. Although the text was very brief, it said that thulium was discovered by isolating its greenish oxide from the mineral erbia. The fact that it is known to combine with oxygen is no big deal in itself but makes one wonder if there is something to Deanna's psychic reading. This text also indicated that the principle source of thulium is monazite. The synchronicity of the first three letters of monazite spelling "mon", as in "Montauk" is not particularly significant until you finish reading the entirety of this book. It will have considerably more meaning at that point. Monazite contains all of the rare earth elements in addition to thorium and calcium. Thulium itself is bright, silvery and so ductile that it can be cut with a knife. It has few commercial applications but it used in lasers and is very expensive because it is so hard to find.

This is what I found out with regard to thulium. I invite comments on the subject of thulium from those of you in the reading audience. This technique has proven very successful in past Montauk investigations.

Aside from its mysterious esoteric properties, the relevant point concerning thulium itself is that its role in chemistry corresponds to the occult theories of the gestation of the Earth. There was a primordial state of matter prior to our current condition. It was less dense than what we experience today. If we believe there is any truth behind mythology at all, this prior or a priori condition contained archetypal experiences which parallel that of life as we know it in its current form. That prior realm would be that of the Olympian gods or the prototype for creation as we know it.

My foray into thulium is symbolic of the Thule Society itself. Again, they were trying to reach the archetypal powers of creation. The Thule movement in its purest form is a return to the creative properties of Uranus, the original male principle of Greek mythology. In the book *Encounter in the Pleiades: An Inside Look at UFOs*, it was explained how there has been a movement throughout history (with regard to mythology) to return us to the "original time line" through the worship of the Greek god Chronos or the Roman god Saturn. The movement back to Uranus would be taking us yet a step earlier towards creation. Uranus was the original steward of the morphogenetic grid until he was castrated by Chronos and forced to take a back seat.

The idea that the Thulists were seeking the highest aspects of existence is not meant to excuse those who were involved in the holocaust or otherwise compromised humanity. By the time Hitler abandoned the nobler aspects of the Thule Society, there were many disaffected members. Two of these included Rudolph Hess and Karl Haushofer. Both men participated in a plan for peace with England when they arranged for Hess's ill fated flight to Scotland (covered in *Pyramids of Montauk*). Although that attempt failed, if it was not directly sabotaged by Churchill, there were other Thulists who sought an escape route from the repressive practices of the Third Reich. We also learn that Thulists as a group were not relegated just to Germany.

In early 1945, there was a meeting of Thulists from all over the world at a secret base in Arctic Canada. It was designated as Point 103. There were Tibetan monks, other orientals, East Indians, Arabs, a full blooded Mexican native as well as officers of the

U.S. military and a host of others. All of these people believed in the basic tenets of Thule as a salvation concept. Their lineage and legacy could be traced back through time.

We learn of the above from a book entitled *Gótzen gegen Thule* by Wilhelm Landig as relayed by Joscelyn Godwin in *Arktos: The Polar Myth in Science, Symbolism, and Nazi Survival*. Printed in German, *Gótzen gegen Thule* is written in a fictional format but is purported to reflect a true story. In *Arktos*, Godwin points out that an enterprise of this sort would have to require advanced flying technology. Both authors site the V7 vertical takeoff aircraft as a plausible answer with regard to the logistics of this fabled meeting. Landig is writing fictionally and goes whichever way he wants, but Godwin is often skeptical and writes from an academic perspective and is quick to separate fact from speculation. Still, he states that there is every reason to believe in the V7 aircraft. This particular statement by Godwin is particularly interesting because he had none of the sources available from which I will be referring to as regards Nazi flying craft.

Gótzen gengen Thule is a story about two German officers who crash near the Arctic only to be rescued by an officer of the Waffen-SS. The SS officer becomes their philosophical guru, teaching them how Thule embodies the cosmic order of things and how all religions and myths propagate from this holy seed. It is an involved pantheon and the account in Godwin's book is mythologically accurate. It should be added that there is no racism at Point 103.

The most interesting aspect of Point 103 is that the leaders claim to be in telepathic contact with a mystical source that is the center of positive forces on the planet and not just the Aryans. Other people know it by different names. The Hindus called it Mount Meru and the Egyptians knew it as On or Ong. It has also been called Og or Oz. This center point is described as following in the book *Arktos*:

> "The supreme center manifests through phenomena called Manisolas, which have been held since the earliest times in religious awe. An entirely different kind of UFO from the German disc-planes, the Manisolas are "bio-machines" which live, reproduce, and die through a seven

part life-cycle. They begin as circles of pure light, then crystallize into a metallic form with a high zirconium content. This is the female form, "*mater*-ialized." It then develops a masculine, phallic element, which brings it to the condition of androgynic equilibrium. Thereupon a regeneration process begins, and the nucleus of a new Manisola grows in its womb."

Godwin then translates a passage from *Götzen gegen Thule* with regard to possible UFO phenomena:

"The regenerated part is expelled by the remaining mother-nucleus as a new energetic circle of light, corresponding to a birthing technique. This new circle enters on the same seven developmental stages, while the expelling maternal element rolls itself into a ball, which then explodes. The metallic remains contain particles of copper. The optical impressions that eyewitnesses of these Manisolas have had up to now are basically quite uniform. In the daytime they display an extremely bright gold or silver luminescence, sometimes with traces of rose-colored smoke which then often condense into greyish-white trails. At night the disks shine in glowing or glossy colors, showing on occasion long flames at the edges and red and blue sparks, which can grow so strong as to wreathe them in fire. Most remarkable is their power of reaction against pursuers, like that of a rational creature, far exceeding any possible electronic self-steering or radio control."

These Manisolas and their accompanying manifestations are a representation of the morphogenetic grid in all its aesthetic glory. According to Landig's book, they have been interpreted in various ways by different cultures. This also has something to do with the thought forms being projected. If one studies the third and fourth dimensional aspects of sacred geometry, one can see that these Manisolas are cabalistic vessels of creation.

These Manisolas or "bio-machines" are primarily fourth dimensional interfaces with the life force itself. Whether these

Manisolas manifest as good or evil has everything to do with those forces who seek to imprint their thought forms into the consciousness of the Earth and its collective beings. The stewardship of this "imprinting" procedure becomes much more powerful than anything on Earth for those beings who can control it. This very principle of control is so powerful that it could even undermine the financial currency of the world. Much of the imprinting referred to above is done through the media of the world which includes the propaganda departments of the various governments.

This power to manifest these primal energies was known as the vril to the Tibetans. It is an ancient word with an accompanying glyph (see below). This power source has also been called by many names, one of which is orgone. The study of the vril is yet a deeper aspect to the mythologies of Thule.

20

THE POWER OF VRIL

The most fascinating aspect of my discussions with Jan van Helsing concerned the Vril Society, an organization he considers to be one of the most interesting secret societies that ever existed. Sometimes referred to as the Luminous Lodge, the Vril Society thrived after World War I. Still, when I met Jan, he reported that not a single book on the subject could be found in Germany. All existing traces of it were wiped out by the Gestapo just prior to the end of World War II. Anything they missed was successfully picked up and removed by the Allies after the conquest of Germany. What the Vril Society concerned itself with and actually accomplished has been one of the best guarded secrets in the field of UFOlogy, if not the entire world. Since the Berlin wall crumbled and the reunification of Germany began, information has slowly begun to leak out. Scraps of information on the Vril Society have appeared in video tapes. There is even a renegade publication in the German language entitled *Das Vril Projekt*.

It is ironic that most books on the Nazis and the occult make no more than a scant mention of the power of the vril. In this century, most people learned of the secret German Vril Society through the German rocket scientist Willy Ley.[*] He came to the United States in 1933 and eventually became a popular scientific

---

[*] A couple of interesting notes on Ley are that he corresponded with Jack Parsons on the subject of rocket propulsion and was also the first known author to publish a photograph of the Face on Mars. I have seen the photograph and the book, but my memory fails on the title. It was published in the 1960s.

author who wrote to the common man. Most of Ley's work demonstrates him to be a government propaganda tool who speaks under the guise of a reasonable scientist who is only interested in hard cold facts. Accordingly, Ley ripped the Nazis as being infatuated with pseudo-science. He then makes a giant leap in the direction of disinformation by suggesting that the Nazis got their idea for the vril from Lord Bulwer-Lytton's *The Coming Race*. As was previously stated in this book, *vril* is a Tibetan word with an accompanying glyph. In simple terms it means chi or life force but it can also be identified with vibration. As it is not a banal word, but one that has been primarily reserved for initiates, do not expect your professor of Sino-Tibetan studies to supply you with any great revelations concerning it.

Although *The Coming Race* was not the origin of the Nazi's pursuit of the vril, it was written by an initiate who was educated under Aleister Crowley. Of course, this was Crowley in his earlier incarnation as Alphonse Constant, a man he identified himself as and who wrote under the pseudonym of Elphias Levi. The initiate concerned was Lord Bulwer-Lytton, one of the most prestigious writers of his day.

Lord Bulwer-Lytton chose a fictional artifice to portray certain aspects of the mysterious power of the vril. *The Coming Race* is the story of a man who was spelunking (another name for cave exploring). The narrator of the story finds his way through many caverns until he comes upon a pleasantly lit and aesthetic world. According to the novel, vril is the "unity in natural energic agencies which has been conjectured by many philosophers above ground". The narrator then goes on to quote Faraday:

> "I have long held an opinion, almost amounting to a conviction, in common, I believe, with many other lovers of natural knowledge, that the various forms of which the forces of matter are made manifest have one common origin; or, in other words, are so directly related and naturally dependent, that they are convertible, as it were into one another, and possess equivalence of power in their action."

The preceding quotation is really just another way of describing a unified field from which all creation emanates. The vril obviously suggests a state of creation that exists a priori to matter. There are startling correspondences to the Montauk Project* when the narrator tells us that the weather can be manipulated through the operation of vril. This is obviously another word for orgone energy, and he describes it as "mesmerism, electro-biology, or odic forces, etc.". He also says the concept can be applied scientifically through vril conductors and can exercise influence over minds, animals and vegetables.

The main characters in *The Coming Race* are large human type beings who reside deep inside the hollows of the Earth. They are very advanced compared to us and descended into the hollows during the time of a great cataclysm or flood. This aspect of the story follows the tradition of the Elder Race or Elohim who migrated from Mars and descended upon the Earth (see *Pyramids of Montauk*). In *The Coming Race*, they are known as the Vril-ya and they tell us that the faculties of the mind can be quickened by using a trance or vision in which the thoughts of one brain can be transmitted to another. Thus, knowledge can be exchanged through the race. This is the same phenomena discussed by Preston Nichols in *Encounter in the Pleiades*. Practitioners of the vril are also able to influence an individual so that he absorbs knowledge through the subconscious.

We can now see quite clearly that there is at least one valid concept behind the vril. Whether it can be harnessed by ourselves is another question. The Nazis have been maligned for their "pseudo-scientific fascinations" with it when what they were doing was trying to create a technology linked to the a priori state of matter. From the above descriptions, we can also see that the trance states referred to could be alloyed or polluted with evil.

Those books which do at least broach the subject of the vril usually dismiss *The Coming Race* as just science fiction. This is not how the book or the author were received in their own time.

---

*One of these correspondences can be seen in the Faraday cage. The quotation from Faraday himself suggests that his cage resonates with the unified field. In *The Montauk Project: Experiments in Time*, psychic human "guinea pigs" were put in a Faraday cage at Montauk which further suggests that the unknown factor in the unified field theory is the element of consciousness.

Charles Dickens, the most popular writer of his day, was very proud to even be mentioned on the same page with the likes of Lord Bulwer-Lytton, a master whom he esteemed highly.

The Coming Race also gives us a major clue when the narrator tells us that the Vril-ya speak an "original language". It is a non-polluted language that has not suffered any amalgamation with other cultures. The language is based upon mono syllables which emanate from tonal vibrations. The narrator offers Chinese as a splendid example of a language based upon sound, where certain sounds are repeated in different forms to give different meanings. The idea is that the language of the Vril-ya is much closer to describing original cause and that Chinese is the best example of that in our current world. It becomes obvious that the reason languages are so complex is that they have drifted away from the source of all creation. But, as I have sought to portray in my own pursuits, common sense observation of etymologies takes us back to a common source.

The language of the Vril-ya is an obvious reference to a time when mankind spoke a common mother tongue. Remarkably, *The Coming Race* goes into a short but descriptive dissertation on the elements of the language. The esoteric correspondences are intriguing in themselves but that is another study. The most interesting etymology given to us is that of the word *vril* itself. The narrator says that the hieroglyphic of a pyramid or   (an upside down V), is the symbol for the supreme being. When turned upright into a "V", it is the symbol of the inverted pyramid and is meant to denote excellence or power. If we extend this etymology and consider the other elements of the word *vril*, we get *ri* and *l* where *ri* signifies the ruling principle (seen in such words as *regal* or *Rig-veda*) and *l* which equates to *El* or God as in *Elohim*. Thus, vril signifies the power of God through the ruling principle of the pyramid.

It is also noteworthy that the Vril-ya females are superior to the males in both size and in their power to use the vril. There is much more that could be said, but I would encourage others to read *The Coming Race* for a deeper appreciation of it.

The concept of the vril pops up again when we consider the death of Aleister Crowley on December 1st, 1947. Found on his person was a piece of square parchment that he supposedly carried with him at all times. Inscribed upon it was the name *Vrihl*, said to be an angel or extraterrestrial entity. In *Outside the Circles of Time*, Kenneth Grant suggests that Crowley was in communication with an entity by that name.

Grant aptly defines *Vrihl* as the a magical force set in motion by orgasm for the purpose of invoking beings from the Outside. He further defines it as the name of evoking the *Onoma*, known as the Deep Ones, the Repulsive or Abhorrent Ones. These are the deepest archetypes of the subconscious and are said to be the keys to evoking the Elder Gods or Forgotten Ones. These are the entities which inspired the writing of H.P. Lovecraft, an author whose Nazi connections were notorious.

Another esoteric reference to vril can be found in *The Secret Doctrine* by Madame Blavatsky. She acknowledges the power of the vril but states that the Atlanteans called it by the name of *MASH-MAK*. Irony strikes again when we look at a map of Long Island and see Mashomak Point, a nature preserve on Shelter Island, just a short distance from Montauk. This is an Indian name that backs up the contention in *Pyramids of Montauk* that the Montauk natives spoke a tongue derived from Vril. The implication here is that the Montauks descended from a people that worked with this tradition on a very high level.

The fact that the concept of the vril or Mash-Mak should turn up on Long Island is a coincidence of the highest order. This island was chosen as the home of Mantak Chia, a master of the Healing Tao, who now lives in his native land Thailand. I mentioned Mantak Chia in *Pyramids of Montauk* because of the synchronicity of his name. He told me that the name *Mantak* was given to him by his master and is a Tibetan word for "virtue" which also means "clarity", "understanding," and "bright light". I have since found out from magical texts that the name *chia* means "beast". The correspondences do not seem to end, but I would expect the "Chia" in Mantak Chia also refers to *chi* energy. Nevertheless, that is the energy that runs through the "beast" aspect of man: his body.

Mantak Chia basically teaches people how to move their chi or sexual energy through the body and align oneself with the divine source. He gives workshops across the world and has written several books. One of his teachings concerns the process of internalizing the orgasm and thereby prolonging it. His latest book is entitled *The Multiple Male Orgasm*.

There is an interesting story relating to the vril which concerns Michael Morgan, a long time student of Mantak Chia. After years of work with "The Healing Tao", Michael suffered a severe car accident which nearly resulted in death. He remained in a coma for some time but eventually emerged with paranormal abilities and became a medium for an Atlantean entity known as Yokar.

For the past several years, Yokar has initiated people into the vril and has disseminated a considerable amount of esoteric information on the subject. What I have learned on the subject has been through my friend Kenn Arthur and a few other sources. Kenn has studied with Yokar.

The name of the ancient mother tongue alluded to in the Babylon story is known as *Vril*. It is a more basic core language than even Enochian, the language of the Angels. Before humans evolved the organs of speech, they activated their intention through a vestigial organ in the body located midway between the heart and throat. This organ is akin to animal mesmerism and is a direct tie to the etheric properties of the spirit. Our ancestors once activated their will through this organ by the principles of vibration. The isolated communication system which developed into language was actually a de-evolvement from a unified consciousness. If one gently massages this "vril spot" and focuses upon one's true will, it will activate that aspect of one's self. In this respect, the vril corresponds to the true will of the individual and is the same as Thelema or Allah.

When we consider *Vril* as a speaking mechanism, it is the ancient language of creation. *Vril* is composed of 72 tonal signatures deriving from a single monochord. This number also equates to the 72 Keys of Enoch or the 72 Keys of Solomon. These are all different formats which basically refer to the same principle. It is an entire study in itself and could take up an entire text. My intention is to demonstrate beyond the shadow of a doubt that the Nazis were not just crazy science fiction buffs who put their wild ideas into action. There was a method to their operations which were based upon categorized and arcane esoteric principles which have been largely ignored by history.

Through the principle of vril, the Nazis were trying to harness the very power of the heavens. In the next chapter, we will examine just how close they came.

21

THE VRIL SAUCERS

Any reasonably intelligent person can see that the field of UFOlogy is strewn with disinformation and elements of rather severe lunacy. It can also be highly comical. One has to sift through much information to ascertain some sort of approximation at what might be considered a relevant truth.

Perhaps the biggest illogic in this entire field, when you consider the history of the flying saucer era, can be found in the photographs of flying disks from the 1940s onward. If you look at the photos from the Kenneth Arnold sightings in Washington state, as well as others from that early era, the designs are rather archaic. Some of the saucers look crude, almost as if they were made with tin and common rivets. They are certainly not of the polished metal variety seen in modern UFOlogy. As we move forward into the '70s and '80s, we begin to see high tech saucers, the Gulf Breeze craft being one prime example. There is such a volume of photographs that it takes an extreme stretch of the mind to believe that every one is a fake created by pranksters.

The illogic in all the above, if we care to believe that the photographs are genuine, is that the aliens have been rapidly advancing their technology over the years. They went from pie tins to high tech saucers in the time that humans went from the propeller plane to the stealth fighter. Just look at it from a historical perspective. When Madison Avenue was doing simplistic poster board type advertising in the 1950s, the aliens were matching them artistically with antique style UFOs. Now that Madison Avenue has evolved into high tech computer graphics, the aliens have matched them with high tech flying saucers. Of course, those who are very cynical would say that flying saucers are a Madison Avenue creation in the first place.

The missing ingredient in the above equation is that the UFOs under consideration were not alien in nature at all but were the creation of Earthlings. There is also a good reason why human involvement in flying saucers has been so secretive: most of the technology related to these endeavors derived from Nazi Germany! It has been one of the best kept secrets in UFOlogy.

Instead of investigating the actual truth of the matter, the media has chosen to onslaught our attention with the Roswell incident and the now famous alien autopsy video tape. The gullible public buys it up. Steven Spielberg is also rumored to be releasing a feature film on Roswell that may be in time to commemorate the fiftieth year anniversary of the event. One should realize that the media's embrace of Roswell is a sheer indicator that it includes some form of disinformation. No one ever suggests that the disks recovered in New Mexico could have been Nazi craft. Of course, this scenario requires an explanation of those alien bodies that, according to persistent legends, were found in the Roswell crafts. We are offered such an explanation when we consider one of the many adventures of world famous explorer Jacques Cousteau.

On one of his Asian escapades, Cousteau discovered a bizarre race of people on an archipelago near New Guinea. Related to humans in many respects, these creatures were virtually hairless with huge eyes. This was a result of living in underground caves, apparently the consequence of years of evolution. If you doctored these creatures up a bit, you could put them in a Nazi saucer, change the insignia and create a tremendous whispering campaign that the aliens have arrived. I do not honestly know if this was the case, but a documentary on these rare people was once aired on PBS. Immediately after it aired, a friend of mine tried to obtain a copy. There was a subsequent denial that the documentary was ever shown on that station. The original documentary was impossible to retrieve. This alone should tell you something.

The Cousteau venture is not the only possibility that would explain the above scenario. Tom Gorman of the German Research Project has pointed out that the genetic technology to create aliens similar to the grays has existed since the Nazi regime. Of course, we now know that sheep can be cloned. This prospect is not considered as farfetched as it used to be.

People often forget that the Roswell incident made the headlines, and information was leaked all over the place. It was no big secret. This makes the scenario of an intelligence ploy all the more plausible. A threat by aliens may have been a smoke screen by the defense department to justify various endeavors or to hide the threat of post war Nazi saucers. The possibilities are endless.

None of this information proves Nazi involvement at Roswell, but it should make people think. What is far more important is that the entire history of the Vril Society and their flying technology has gone virtually unreported in western history.

In 1996, my friend, Jan van Helsing, was scheduled to release a book which was to include hundreds of photographs of Vril flying saucers. As was said earlier, he was literally put out of commission by the German government because his books were allegedly "inciteful to the masses". Hence, we may never see his book. I have seen some of his photographs and have included just a few in this book. They are reprinted, with his permission, from his book, *Secret Societies,* which was mentioned earlier.

A telltale signal that this information about Nazi UFOs is on the money came when Jan told me another point. He said that Michael Hesseman, the head of MUFON in Germany, and Erich von Daniken, the famous author of *Chariots of the Gods*, go ballistic whenever they hear mention of Nazi flying saucers. Why would such a theory cause people to become upset? We have an explanation in the case of Hesseman. He is a known denigrator of the Montauk information and has written articles decrying it in Germany. There is also another story to tell with regard to him.

When I was in Frankfurt in 1992, I was introduced to Hesseman and heard some of his criticisms personally. As I was primarily interested in promoting the book, I had no interest whatsoever in arguing or debating with this person. Being polite, I simply told him that I was interested in the esoteric aspects of Montauk and what the project represented. He looked puzzled, if not shocked. Then, he blurted out some words in a loud and sudden voice that was reminiscent of a Nazi officer in the movies.

"Esoteric!" he said. "I have studied with the Dalai Lama for ten years. We tell the people all the things they need to know!"

All of this ridiculousness demonstrates a concerted effort to hide the truth, particularly with regard to the Nazis' mysterious role in UFO technology.

With the above preface, I will now share what I have learned about the Vril Society. It is exciting, controversial and will not be found in typical UFO books or Nazi literature on the occult. Much of it comes from my friend Jan van Helsing as well as his friends who produced a video tape entitled *UFO Secrets of the Third Reich*. A few other sources are listed in the bibliography.

The Vril Society began around the same time as the Thule Society when Karl Haushofer founded the "Brüder Des Lichts" which means Brothers of the Light. In other books, this is sometimes referred to as the Luminous Lodge. This group was eventually renamed the Vril Gesellschaft as it rose to prominence and united three major societies: the Lords of the Black Stone, having emerged from the Teutonic Order in 1917; the Black Knights of the Thule Society; and the Black Sun, later identified as the elite of Heinrich Himmler's SS. Whereas the Thule Society ended up focusing primarily upon materialistic and political agendas, the Vril Society put its attention on the "Other Side".

It is possible that the Vril Society would never have amounted to very much at all if it were not for a medium by the name of Maria Orsic. She got the entire program underway when she began to receive psychic transmissions in an unknown language which was presented to her in a secret cipher. Maria did not know the language but sought esoteric interpretation and ended up meeting regularly with a small gathering of people which included Karl Haushofer, key members of the Thule Society, the Lords of the Black Stone and other members of the Vril Society. Another medium, known only by the name of Sigrun, also sat in attendance.[*]

Maria and Sigrun received several transmissions for the Vril Society which were written down and parlayed into a dogma.

---

[*] It should be mentioned here that these secret societies, particularly those who later became associated with the Nazis, utilized females in a fashion that is considered most bizarre to modern culture. I have read or heard multiple reports of women taking off their clothes in the presence of German occultists while ectoplasm emerged from their vaginas and communicated to the esotericists concerned. These women are usually portrayed as old peasants and do not fit the portrayal of Maria or Sigrun who are shown to be young and beautiful in artistic renditions.

According to this line of communication, the transmissions were from the star Aldebaran, a star which has two planets forming the SUMERAN empire. The population of SUMERAN was divided into two classes. First, there was the Aryan or master race. Additionally, there was a subservient race which had developed in a negative fashion as a result of mutation from climactic changes. As both populations began to expand, there were problems because of racial intermixing. The people became dull and the technology for space travel was lost. In spite of this racist undertone, we are told that there was no racism in the Sumeran Empire and that the different people respected each other.

A half billion years ago, the Aryans (also referred to as the Elohim or Elder Race) began to colonize our solar system as Aldebaran's became uninhabitable. Marduk, existing in the asteroid belt, was the first to be colonized, then Mars. When they came to Earth, these Aryans were known as the Sumerians.

As they continued to study the transmissions, the Vril Society discovered that the ancient Sumerian language of Earth was identical with that of the Aldebarans and that it was also similar to the German language.

Regardless of the racist policies encouraged from the information above, the Vril Society had a much more urgent agenda: the construction of flying saucers. Whether the entities from Aldebaran were concerned about history repeating itself on Earth, it is not known. Things got underway when a doctor by the name of Dr. W. O. Schumann, of the University in Munich, gave a speech (obtained from the SS secret archives):

"In everything we recognize two principles that determine the events: light and darkness, good and evil, creation and destruction — as in electricity we know plus and minus. It is always: either — or.

"These two principles — the creative and destructive — also determine our technical means...

"Everything destructive is of Satanic origin, everything creative is divine...Every technology based upon explosion or combustion has thus to be called Satanic. The coming new age will be an age of a new, positive, divine technology!"

Schumann first appeared to the available historical annals in 1919 when the Thule and Vril societies gathered at a hunting lodge in Berchtesgaden. At this point, construction began on devices and technologies that would literally lead mankind to the stars. There was a tremendous pooling of information, both esoteric and technical, the result of which was to transcend time itself. A time machine was to be constructed that would bring them face to face with the gods themselves. Two years of work went into this, but most of it remains a historical mystery.

All we hear at this point is that some sort of time machine was constructed, and at the end of 1924, it was taken to a hiding place in southern Germany, possibly at the Messershmidt aircraft facility in Augsborg. All of this information concerning time travel is said to be regulated by the Knights Templar. Whatever actually did take place, this story dovetails nicely with the legend relayed in *Pyramids of Montauk* about the Black Sun doing a time travel experiment in 1923.

As spectacular as the time technology must have been, the majority of the Vril Society was not involved in this endeavor. We are only informed of one its mere offshoots: a levitation drive. The Vril Society, we are told, was preoccupied with building a flying saucer based on the levitation drive. Rudolph Hess embraced this technology and his lectures on the subject were well known.

During this general time period, the Germans were also experimenting with something called the Coanda Effect. This was named after Henri Coanda, a man who, in 1911, discovered a way to counteract gravity. This principle is demonstrated by taking a kitchen pan with a round rim and then letting the faucet flow over the edge of the rim (keep in mind that the pan should be slightly inclined for this experiment). The water will cling to the lower rim and flow against gravity for a small instant. This technology was utilized in such a manner that tiny side jets would augment a bigger main stream. The Germans concerned with this project coined a new technology called "fluidics" which uses streams of fluids for controls instead of electron streams. This technology, combined with the use of jet fuel, was used for some of their flying disks.

It seems that this flying technology would have been pursued vigorously by the Nazis, but this is not the case. Hitler was far more interested in conventional war weapons. They had a proven track record and were not experimental. It was said that if anything took longer than a year to develop, Hitler was not interested.

The Vril Society did not get the funding it needed even though German newspapers ran advertisements designed to raise money for Vril aircraft. The ads blatantly stated that they were attempting to utilize ancient Atlantean technology, not an unpopular or foreign concept to the Germans of the 1920s. By 1934, the Vril society, under the direction of Schumann, had produced its first circular aircraft utilizing antigravity propulsion. It was developed at the Arado aircraft factory in Brandenburg and was called the RFZ-1 (Rundflugzeug 1). It did not do too well. After rising about sixty meters in a vertical maneuver, it became unstable and was out of control for some time. The machine could not be guided. Pilot Lothar Waiz somehow managed to land it and escape. After spinning like a top, the craft turned over and ripped itself to pieces. Although a disaster, it was just the beginning of more Vril saucers.

The next craft produced was the RFZ-2. Less than sixty feet from end to end, it produced optical blurs and colored lights. This made it look like one of our modern UFOs. Although it was later used as a transatlantic reconnaissance craft, and saw duty in the Battle of Britain, it was useless for direct combat. The steering mechanism only allowed it to change direction at angles of 90°, 45° and 22.5°. Although this is clumsy for fighting, these degrees are the typical patterns of sudden shifts observed of UFOs in flight. Despite the limited success of the RFZ-2 and pictures of it in flight, it remained virtually unnoticed by the top Nazi brass. Heinrich Himmler was the only one to show more than a casual interest. He already had the SS searching for alternative energy sources as he wanted Germany to be independent of foreign crude oil.

Two special departments were set up to concentrate on the development of this new flying technology of the Vril Society: the U-13 and the SS-E-4. The latter was under the direct supervision of Heinrich Himmler and was known as development group number four of the Black Sun. The main focus of SS-E-4 was based upon the work of Viktor Schauberger. Schauberger was a scientist who was privy to the secret teachings of Pythagoras which came to him via the work of Johannes Kepler. The Knights Templar had long preserved these secret teachings, amongst many others, and chose their own time in history to reveal them.

Schauberger utilized the Pythagorean theory of creation: the idea that sounds create our universe through harmonic resonance. This teaches us that the structure of matter itself is determined by the proportional relationships of integral numbers. All structure can be shown to consist of harmonic proportions which all stem from a single monochord. The laws of all science follow suit including chemistry, biology and genetics. Schauberger was a naturalist and also believed the crude principles of explosion to be an abomination to the natural order of things. He sought to access the power of the inner universe and apply it to the outer universe. Where the technology of explosion was considered to be destructive, implosion was the alternative. It was this line of thinking which enabled him to make great strides in neutralizing gravity and accessing the realm of antimatter.

In 1934, Viktor Schauberger met with Hitler in order to discuss his work. Schauberger's goal was to harmonize technology with the natural order of things. This met with Hitler's initial approval. Consequent problems ensued as the Third Reich developed into a world power. Schauberger was a pacifist and began to claim that the Nazis were a false movement. He said they had separated from the unity of the cosmos.

Based upon the work of Schauberger and the Vril Society, Himmler's SS-E-4 began work on its own flying discs. Towards the end of 1938, they were actually constructing saucer shaped propeller crafts. The purpose of this project was to study how disc shaped objects behaved under actual flying conditions. This work eventually developed into a flying disc that was known as the RFZ-4. By 1939, the SS had learned from their mistakes and refined the RFZ-4. They developed a long distance aircraft that was 65 feet in length and was initially known as the RFZ-5. It was subsequently given the name Haunebu or Haunebu I.

By this time, British intelligence had discovered what the SS was up to. It is possible that the information they gathered on flying discs greatly influenced Great Britain's political decisions with regard to Germany. We know from history that while the Germans excel in technology, they are far less efficient when it comes to political savvy. In the days before World War II, this applied not only to their diplomatic endeavors but to their internal politics as well. Despite technological success, the German army, navy and

THE RFZ II

Less than sixty feet from end to end, the RFZ II produced optical blurs and colored lights. This made it look like one of our modern UFOs. Although it was later used as a transatlantic reconnaissance craft, and saw duty in the Battle of Britain, it was useless for direct combat. The steering mechanism only allowed it to change direction at angles of 90°, 45° and 22.5°. Although this is clumsy for fighting, these degrees are the typical patterns of sudden shifts observed of UFOs in flight.

SCHAUBERGER DEVICE

A flying craft from the Augsburg area in 1939.
It is believed to be based upon the designs of Viktor Schauberger.
The above and all other saucer photographs in this book are provided
courtesy of Jan van Helsing. They first appeared in his book
Secret Socieites and Their Power in the 20th Century.

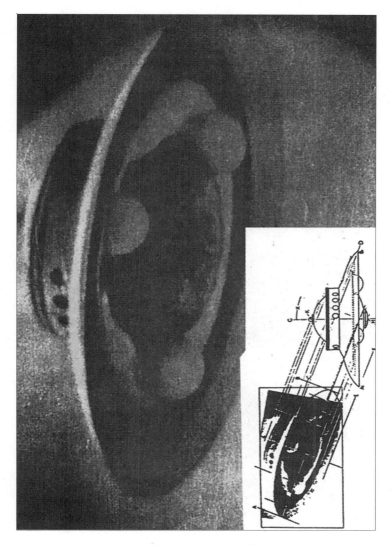

NAZIS FROM VENUS
A photo shot by George Adamski on December 13, 1952.
He talked of blond, blue eyed aliens from Venus.
Apparently, they were flying in
a German Haunebu II!

VRIL-7

Another shot of a Vril-7. This one is landing in Bavaria.
In the original photograph, the insignia of the SS
can be seen on the bottom of the craft.

LAST KNOWN VERSION OF THE VRIL-7
In this version of the Vril-7, the canon has been removed with an
"Admiral's Bridge" mounted ahead of the cupola.
At the back a "balcony" has been added.

industry were not united and were operating unto themselves.

As the world war got underway, the various industrial factions in Germany began to bid competitively for the defense contracts offered by the German government. The new flying saucer was forced to take a further back seat but was not abandoned completely. By the end of 1942, the SS rolled the first Haunebu II or RFZ-6 off the production line. It was as long as 100 feet with a maximum of thirty feet in height at its center. The speed of the Haunebu II within the Earth's atmosphere was just above 4 Mach. It is believed this craft was capable of space travel as well. It was equipped with a ray gun and had room for a long journey. The prototype was so successful that the SS solicited bids for an entire series of Haunebu IIs to be constructed. In March 1945, just before the end of the war, a bid was awarded to the Dornier company.

Finally, the Haunebu III was created as the master example of all flying discs. It housed as many as 32 men, could fly for at least eight weeks, and move as fast as 10 Mach. It made nineteen test flights and was also filmed in flight. Only one of the Haunebu III's was reported to have been produced.

The above were by no means the only flying saucers of the German regime, but these were some of the primary ones. There were several others that reached varying degrees of success. Many different propulsion systems were experimented with and it is really not the task of this book to list them all or document them. I have given only the barest technical descriptions as most readers will find the aerodynamics and other mechanics boring. Those who are interested should consult the German Research Project, but I should add that this information is primarily for technically inclined people.

It is also important to mention a few other Nazi flying craft from World War II.

In 1943, there were plans to build a cigar shaped mother ship, named the Andromeda or Andromeda Device. It was 139 meters in length and was designed to house at least one Haunebu II, two Vril-Is and two Vril-IIs. It is believed to have been used for certain interstellar projects which have not been specified up to this point. The idea of a cigar shaped ship does make a bit of sense because the Zeppelin company of Germany was already used to building long shaped dirigibles. This could account for the many sightings of such crafts in UFOlogy.

There were also the famous foo fighters. In 1943, massive sightings of UFOs were witnessed across Germany with reports even appearing in the local papers. At least some of these were the same ones spotted by American fighter pilots, including Wendelle Stevens. He reported them as gray-green or red-orange and hovering within a distance of about five meters from his aircraft. The foo fighters were known to jam radar and cause electrical problems. Although the Allies called all of the flying objects foo fighters, there were actually two separate German inventions at play here. First, there was the Flying Turtle. It was developed by the SS-E-4 at Vienna-Neustadt. These contained advanced klystron tubes (also used at Montauk). The SS referred to the Flying Turtles as death rays. They were essentially unmanned probes that could disrupt ignition systems as well as electrical power. These phenomena are not only endemic to UFO encounters but were also an observable fact of life at Montauk in the 1950s and 1960s, according to some witnesses.

Besides the Flying Turtles, there were also "Soap Bubbles". These were air balloons that housed metal spirals inside and were designed to disturb enemy radar. Their success was probably most effective in the psychological department.

In addition to the above history, there is also the videotaped testimony of professor James J. Hurtak, a man who claims to have carefully examined Nazi documents, including detailed plans for building a space city on Earth at Peenemünde. After interviews with German rockets scientists, he says that by 1935, the Germans were well aware of intelligence in the universe other than our own. They were also the first to open the window and make contact with extraterrestrial intelligence.

It was this ET aspect which caused the Vril Society to go down a more secretive and less conventional path. These ET contacts were so confidential that not even the Paperclip scientists were aware of them. While Himmler's SS-E-4 went about the construction of conventional reconnaissance and war craft, certain scientists, assumably members of the Vril Society, were developing systems that dwarfed the Haunebu. One of these included a large electromagnetic craft that was designed to travel in outer space. If it was not actually built, it was certainly contemplated.

Hurtak says the most important aspect of the Third Reich is that they opened the window to other worlds. He also mentions the higher consciousness coming into play such as the Sven Hedin mission into Tibet, a locale we will talk about later. Hurtak's comments can be viewed on the video tape *Secrets of the Third Reich*.

Perhaps the most outstanding claims with regard to the Vril Society concerns a meeting held on the 3rd and 4th of January of 1934. Hitler and Himmler got together to discuss the Vril Project. They talked about the prospect of sending a huge space ship through a dimensional channel that was a tunnel independent of the speed of light. It was supposed to go to Aldebaran. As Hurtak says, if we look at the documents of ancient Sumeria and the Bible, we see that there has long been interference in human history. Long before Roswell, there were similar incidents in Germany. This nation had the peak scientists in the world, and it stands to reason that they would have been contacted. Peenemünde, the foremost research facility of the Nazis, itself means "head of the world".

At this point, we do not know how far the Germans or Nazis actually took their technology. The information in this book is an obvious indication that their tentacles reached far beyond the bounds of ordinary experience. There was apparently some mysterious occult force at work that was seeking to manipulate the morphogenetic grid. The door to these mysteries is only beginning to open.

22

THE BROOKHAVEN CONNECTION

The history in the previous chapter is only a small overview of an entire operation which boggles the imagination. Many will wonder exactly how it fits in with the Montauk Project. This becomes quite clear when we consider the fate of Dr. Schauberger, the scientist who carried the Vril Project with his "positive energy" technology and decried the Nazis as a false movement. In 1958, Viktor Schauberger and his son, Walter, were brought over to the United States under the strangest of circumstances. The year 1958 is noteworthy because it is the same time period in which the Montauk Project, more properly known as the Phoenix Project, ceased to operate by order of Congress.

Schauberger came to the United States because the Reich was in ruins and only America offered him any hope of fulfilling his dreams. His personal motive was to integrate his implosion techniques and the Pythagorean model of the monochord into a holistic technology that would balance the planet. This was the same utopian ideal he had futilely shared with Hitler a quarter of a century earlier. Now, he hoped the conquering Americans, who had replaced the evil Nazis, would make good on history. Unfortunately, the Americans involved in this drama had an agenda all to themselves.

Viktor and Walter Schauberger should have noticed that something sinister was at work when they discovered that their visas were both stamped for a four year stay in America. Viktor had previously insisted on staying abroad for only three months, and his son was willing to stay for one year in total. This incident proved itself to be a premonition of much future frustration.

The primary operatives involved in bringing the Schaubergers to America were Karl Gerchsheimer and Robert Donner. Gerchsheimer was a natural scientist who understood the concept of implosion while Donner was financially connected and was the authority behind the maneuver. Upon the Schaubergers' arrival in America, the first objective was for Viktor to debrief his advanced knowledge to Gerschsheimer. This proved to be extremely frustrating to Gerschsheimer because Schauberger's training and terminology were entirely foreign to the text book science that he was familiar with. Gerschsheimer complained to Donner that he was getting nowhere. Donner was intent on getting the core knowledge of the man reputed to be Germany's most brilliant scientist. Upon hearing of Gerschsheimer's frustration, Donner flew immediately to the National Atomic Research Laboratory to verify the scientific validity of Schauberger's work. Some of you may recognize the National Atomic Research Laboratory. It is today known as Brookhaven Labs, the think tank where the Montauk Project was cooked up. After three days of discussions at Brookhaven, a written agreement was drawn up at the behest of Donner which arranged for a native German, Eric A. Boerner, to act as a go-between with Schauberger.

Boerner was a very curious creature and certainly a duplicitous one. He headed a design team at Brookhaven that worked on the Cosmotron Project. The Cosmotron was basically a particle accelerator. Technically, it was a proton (ionized hydrogen atom) accelerator or Synchrotron which made use of a large toroidal electromagnet to generate high electric and magnetic fields.

As a result of Donner's agreement, Schauberger was instructed to write down everything he knew about implosion, in the German language, without regard to whether it corresponded to text book science. These reports were addressed to Mr. Eric A. Boerner, National Atomic Research Laboratory, Brookhaven, Upton, New York State. It was specifically stated in the reports that they were written at the bequest of Mr. Robert Donner, or his representative, Mr. Karl Gersheimer, as per the agreement drawn up on the 15th, 16th and 17th of August 1958 at Brookhaven.

Gersheimer then forwarded these reports on a daily basis to Boerner who would translate them and disseminate the information to the Brookhaven scientists.

Boerner was not a physicist but an engineer, and through his association with the Cosmotron Project, the Schaubergers were conveniently led to misconstrue his true title. They thought he was the head of the Cosmostron Project when he was really just a German with sympathies to the Fatherland. Boerner did not have top secret clearance as a physicist but merely headed an engineering design team. The Schaubergers had been tricked. They thought they were providing information to the United States Government and the military. They knew implosion could create a bomb much more powerful than the hydrogen bomb. They would have been shocked to know the truth and consequences of their actions.

After the initial difficulties had been overcome in interpreting Schauberger's work, cartons and crates were sent for from Europe. The information therein would lay out the complete work of Schauberger and enable him to realize the fulfillment of technology in accordance with mother nature. Part of these papers were said to include an interpretation of the equation $E=mc^2$ that clarifies the way in which natural energies accumulate.

It is obvious that Donner and his cronies at Brookhaven were striving after something much more grand than has ever been accomplished in the name of regular science. They were seeking to harness the morphogenetic grid itself and steer it to their own design. In the meantime, the Schaubergers were still being sold a bill of goods. They were told that this work was for the enhancement of all humanity and that the project would require a four year period in which to be fully developed. The deceit was becoming more apparent but was still not being fully contemplated by the culturally displaced and overwhelmed Viktor Schauberger.

The Schaubergers eventually became uncooperative. Viktor went into the hospital for poor health while Walter blatantly forgot a key meeting on a trip to Colorado. There, he was to have met with executives of the Eastern Oil Company and the Trunk Line

---

* According to an article in the August/September 1996 issue of *Nexus* magazine, Einstein's famous equation was first postulated in 1903, in the form of $m = E/c^2$, by Professor Friedrich Hasenöhrl (30 Nov 1874 — 7 Oct 1915), head of Physics at the University of Innsbruck, and later Vienna, Austria.

Company. The Schaubergers decided unto themselves that they were going home.

Donner was neither distressed or intimidated. He ordered his lawyer to draw up a contract and told the Schaubergers they should sign the paper. He said it was all that was needed in order for them to leave the country. The Schaubergers were insufficiently skilled in English to understand the full meaning of the contract. After much argument, irritation and mistranslation, Viktor Schauberger relented. He was desperate to return to his country and was willing to do whatever it took. Without fully realizing what he was doing, he signed away all his patents, inventions and ideas. Additionally, he was committed to total silence.

It should not surprise anyone that Viktor Schauberger died only a few days after returning to his native home in Linz.

Schauberger's work was incorporated by the Brookhaven scientists and evolved into what we know today as HAARP, the High-frequency Active Auroral Research Program, which seeks to control the Earth's grid. It affects the weather as well as the minds of all living creatures. Fortunately, it is not a perfect system and has plenty of holes in it.

This entire affair is a prime example of the Nazi-Montauk connection. It is fully documented and can be read about in the book *Living Energies: An Exposition of Concepts Related to the Theories of Viktor Schauberger* by Callum Coats. Although the history of the Schaubergers is involved and complex, it is just one tiny strand in a gigantic web of intrigue. We will look at one of the major corporations involved in this duplicity in the next chapter.

23

IN THE AFTERMATH
OF WAR

It is no secret that many of Hitler's generals became disaffected in the last years of the war. The famous "Desert Fox" himself, Edwin Rommel, was induced by Hitler to commit suicide in order to avoid further disgrace for his disaffection. Furthermore, most of the top Nazis realized they would be facing defeat.

In August of 1944, Martin Bormann made contingency plans in the event the Nazis continued to lose the war. On August 10th, he summoned the top industrialists in Germany to a hotel in Straussborg. These people included Fritz Thiessen, the Krupp family and key executives of I.G. Farben. Massive planning, the likes of which the world has never known, was set into play. Scientists, machine tools, blueprints, and liquid currency (much of it counterfeit U.S. dollars) began to move out of Germany at an unprecedented rate to several neutral countries. These included Spain, Switzerland, Sweden and Argentina. As only the precise and meticulous German mind-set would insist, nothing was overlooked. Not only were the tools exported but so were the tools that made the tools. Helmar Schlact* was selected to handle the financial and banking matters while Otto Skorzeny would funnel the actual people and materials to their respective destinations.

For such massive operations to be carried out, there had to be a totally dedicated and efficient network to carry out the plans.

---

* Schlact's son was the Chief Medical Officer at Jonestown and was in charge of the autopsies.

Skorzeny and financier Schlact were great resources, but they could not have carried out the whole program without considerable help. Working behind these leaders was the biggest international cartel in the world: I.G. Farben and its myriad subsidiaries and associates. As the impact of I.G. Farben was so tremendous on world events, with particular regard to the world wars, it is necessary to take a closer look at its history.

I.G. Farben's roots can be traced back to the 1870s when six small coal-tar dye companies were founded in Germany. By the time the Nazis were in power, these small companies had grown into a gigantic conglomerate known as Interessen Gemeinschaft Farbenindustrie Aktiengesellschaft, of Frankfort am main. In German, this means "community of interests of the dye manufacturing companies". It was a huge German cartel which controlled chemical industries throughout the world.

In 1947, Senator Howard Watson Ampruster wrote a book exposing the true nature of I.G. Farben. It is entitled *Treaons' Peace: German Dyes and American Dupes* and is listed as a Crossroads Press Book by the Beachurst Press in New York. It should not really surprise anyone that this book is not easy to find in today's market. It uses nothing but irrefutable evidence, in the form of official documents, to prove beyond the shadow of a doubt that I.G. Farben was a cabalistic organization which "through foreign subsidiaries and by secret tie-ups, operates a far-flung and highly efficient espionage machine — the ultimate purpose being world conquest — and a world-state directed by Farben".

Of course, no one in today's political climate will complain that I.G. Farben was a good company. The problem is that it continuously worked in tacit cooperation with people at the highest level of American government.

Many people will already recognize I.G. Farben as the company which ran the factory at the Auschwitz death camp. It is said that when workers at this factory became exhausted that they, along with Jews and prisoners, were exterminated with Farben's poisoned gas called Zyklon-B. Prior to becoming Pope, John Paul II was employed by I.G. Farben at this factory and was reported to have been a salesman for this gas. Fleeing to the safety of the Church after the war, he eventually rose through the ranks to become the Vicar of Christ on Earth.

An accurate review of economic history, which *Treason's Peace* fulfills, demonstrates I.G. Farben to be clearly responsible for America's spiritual and physical disarmament at the beginning of both world wars.

As Farben was on the cutting edge of scientific application, they used this to their own advantage by instituting a devious policy of cut throat competition that extended all across the civilized world. By patenting all of their inventions in other countries, they could successfully stifle competition. Their knowledge of science provided them with an inside angle on what were the most key natural resources which they could then hoard for their own purposes. Corporations with different names, all working under the I.G. Farben banner, were set up in different countries. Other successful companies which were already in existence were also brought into the fold with huge stock swaps. Through every means imaginable, and not necessarily illegal ones, I.G. Farben became a monopoly the likes of which the world had never seen. With the flick of a pen or the ring of a telephone, they could make the supply of armaments or natural resources scarce to any given country.

There was no shortage of cooperation with I.G. Farben in America. Sometimes this cooperation was purely financial but other times there were sinister political implications. World War I had demonstrated beyond anyone's doubts that I.G. Farben had been a major player in fomenting the conflict. No one who read the newspapers of the day would have disputed this charge. Nevertheless, Herbert Hoover arranged financing for Farben for their new American "startup" company. Thus, the I.G. Chemical Corporation was born and plants were financed across America.

A key player in the above was the colorful but dubious "Wild Bill" William Donovan, the founder and first operative of the OSS (Office of Strategic Services, the forerunner and prototype of the CIA). Long before his considerably more famous exploits as leader of the OSS, Colonel Donovan was the assistant Attorney General during Herbert Hoover's administration. This fact is sometimes obscured in historical accounts when Donovan is simply alluded to as a sharp Wall Street lawyer. Donovan's storied career on Wall Street actually began just after he resigned from the Justice Department. His first brilliant career move began with the financing of I.G. Farben in America. This was right before the crash of 1929. The synchronicity of his exploits are nothing short of astounding, particularly when viewed conspiratorially.

There was considerable controversy with regard to Donovan's support of a foreign power that had just waged war against America. Donovan, somewhat feebly, answered his critics in an address at a chemical industrial banquet. Speaking to a gathering of technical associations, he reasoned that if the United States could construct plants in Germany and France (for the construction of trucks, automobiles and machinery), then the Germans had an equal right to build chemical plants in this company. He completely disregarded the antitrust factor as I.G. Farben and their associates ended up with a virtual monopoly.

Other key players in this circus were Paul Warburg, the leading member of the board of I.G. Farben, and Otto Kahn, a friend of Aleister Crowley. Kahn built his home on the highest point on Long Island at Cold Spring Harbor.* Located there is one of the most advanced genetic labs in the world. This lab is historically on record as having shared genetic information with the Nazis. Otto Kahn's wife was also a strong supporter of the eugenics movement.

As Jews, both Otto Kahn and Paul Warburg play a most curious role as blatant supporters of the I.G. Farben cartel. It is not surprising that rich and powerful bankers would betray their own people, but both were known to be extremely protective of Jews.

---

* Kahn's estate has since been subdivided, but the mansion is still observable to tourists. One of the curators was kind enough to give me a book on Kahn's home, known as OHEKA, which is entitled *Raising a Fallen Treasure: the Otto Kahn Home, Huntington, Long Island* by Robert D. King.

Before the mansion was restored, it had fallen into decay during the 1980s and became a haven for mischief, not unlike the Montauk base is today. Ken Murphy, who oversaw the bankruptcy proceedings in the 1970s for the military academy that had assumed control of the estate, relayed an interesting anecdote in this book. After hearing complaints of noises and lights emanating from the mansion, he went to the Ball Room at about two o'clock in the morning. He saw approximately one dozen people dancing naked around a fire. They invited him to join the party, but he informed them they had to leave. This is not typical behavior on Long Island but is very similar to what goes on at the Montauk base. There are also tunnels that run underneath the mansion. The books describes these as being air conditioning shafts. This is not untrue, but there are plenty of stories about these tunnels which the book does not dare examine.

In the case of Kahn, there is every evidence to believe he was sincere in this regard. Kahn was noted for his fervent campaigns against the Nazis, yet his actions betrayed him. A specific case in point is his own appointment to treasurer of the Republican Committee by Republican Senator George H. Moses. Senator Moses expected Kahn to raise funds to elect senators who would in turn vote favorably with regard to I.G. Farben's interests.

Warburg, as the leading player in American I.G., was accused of attempting to destroy the American chemical industry. This was considered by many to be the most important industry in the world. It was not only the key to the safety of the United States but to every other country in the world. However powerful Warburg actually was, he was not absolutely powerful. Whatever the mysterious motives of Warburg really were, one thing is clear. Both he and Otto Kahn were foreign nationals who made their way to American soil and helped start up the Council on Foreign Relations.

As the book *Treason's Peace* so clearly explains, the conspiratorial activities of I.G. Farben did not go unnoticed. Full scale investigations were done in Congress, but most of the defendants ended up with wrist slaps at worse. One of the most outrageous and duplicitous of these I.G. Farben agents was a man named Leo T. Crowley. The namesake itself reveals one more remarkable synchronicity with regard to Montauk. Crowley was already the head of the Federal Deposit Insurance Corporation (known as the FDIC today). As well, he served as the high salaried president of a public utility known as the Standard Gas and Electric Company. In addition to these duties, Crowley was appointed to the post of Alien Property Custodian. This means that he was in charge of all enemy property confiscated during the war. It should be noted that this included the property taken from the German Bund at Yaphank (the same small town where Brookhaven Labs was later established), Long Island.

It is more than ironic that a man named Crowley at one time controlled the fate of Long Island's Camp Siegfried, the site of the biggest Nazi rallies in America. The Anti-Nazi League wanted the area to be turned into a training base for the army, but Crowley had other ideas. Although the FBI routinely hunted down German spies in the area of Yaphank, the authorities thought nothing of allowing Crowley, a known loose canon, to have sovereign control of this delicate real estate. Crowley was able to maintain his own little cabal independent of the military and Justice Department.

The synchronicity of Montauk becomes a little more remarkable when we look a little deeper into the connections of Mr. Crowley. He was obviously a favorite of FDR who maintained him at the highest level of government. Why or how he became a partner with FDR is not known by me but his nefarious financial associations are delineated in *Treason's Peace*. Crowley was set up financially by Victor Emanuel, the director of the J. Henry Schroder Bank. Emanuel was investigated by the SEC for conflict of interest with regard to Standard Gas and Electric, a company which he serviced. He was directly responsible for getting Crowley his cushy job there where he received the inordinately high salary of $50,000 to $75,000 for doing very little. The FDIC and Alien Property Custodian jobs were the province of Roosevelt.

That the Schroder Bank backed Leo Crowley is particularly significant because they were a known financial agent for the Nazi government just prior to World War II. They also backed I.G. Farben's international nitrogen cartel. The Schroder clan also operated through the Stein Bank of Cologne, Germany which linked Hitler and his Farben industrial backers.

Of further interest concerning the Schroder Bank is that Allen Dulles, the future director of the CIA, served as one of the directors of the bank. His brother, John Foster Dulles, not only served as a counsel to the Schroder Bank but to Mr. Crowley himself. In a nutshell, Leo T. Crowley was working for a secret cabal that was closely linked to the Nazis.

By the above manipulations and through the sanction of the President, Crowley obtained the position of Alien Property Custodian. In this role, he was able to seize all foreign patents and sequester whatever assets he deemed necessary. Despite the fact he had three jobs, Crowley was subsequently given a fourth position as the director of the Office of Economic Warfare, replacing Vice President Wallace. As his expanded duties for the President became voluminous, Crowley's job of Alien Property Custodian was handed over to James E. Markham, a close ally of Crowley who also happened to be a highly paid executive of Standard Gas and Electric. The duplicity obviously carried on after Crowley's tenure, but he was an undeniable cog in the Nazi scenario, particularly with regard to the Long Island connection.

After World War II, I.G. Farben remained in tact but was ceremoniously stripped of most of its assets. In an apparent attempt to appease the outraged public, the assets were eventually divided among other German companies. Bayer, the aspirin firm, was one of these benefactors as was the Hoechst company. Tracing all the divestitures and subsequent transactions would tell you everything you need to know if you wanted to find out who the controlling interests are today. First, you would have to follow a labyrinthine web that may eventually lead you to simple shell companies that appear inert. Today, I.G. Farben exists but only as a shadow of its former self. That it survives at all is puzzling. I can only guess that it is some sort of weird PR ploy whereby holocaust victims can make claims against it. Perhaps the real goal is to simply haunt the Jews. On the other hand, there may be latent hopes to rekindle the company under the rise of a new Reich.

One can see from the above that the so called governing powers are cardboard characters that mask the true ruling factors of our culture. Of course, those who manipulate the nation are not stupid. Rulers throughout history are only as powerful as the people who support them allow them to be. Therefore, it is in the interests of the ruling forces to placate the public. The Roman Emperors attempted to solve this problem by creating exciting games in the colosseum. Today, we have NFL football and too many channels on cable TV. Of course, there is an actual evolutionary process that is going on throughout the entire morphogenetic grid. Not all diversions are bad or ill conceived, but they often serve the hidden nature of the true ruling powers. Our government also serves routine purposes upon which our society depends. It is not bad in itself and has to stay in tact even if it needs to be overhauled on a continuous basis.

Perhaps the final straw in the Nazi connection occurred when Wild Bill Donovan secured a tried and true Nazi, SS General Reinhard Gehlen, to meet with President Truman and form up the CIA. Dr. Gehlen, as he was later called, was smuggled into America as a four star general. Once in this country, he was housed at Fort Hunt where he was served by a butler and other servants. During his service to the Third Reich, Gehlen was a master of Russian intelligence and had agents placed throughout Europe.

Donovan sold Truman and everyone else on Gehlen's potential use as a resource against the communists. If we even believe there was a legitimate communist threat, we still cannot believe Donovan when we consider his earlier support of I.G. Farben.

Several histories of the CIA indicate it was Gehlen who designed the agency which was initially staffed with former OSS, FBI and SS agents. After the CIA was established, Gehlen returned to West Germany and formed a European spy ring on behalf of the CIA. He was officially the top intelligence official in the new West German government. America even spent some three million dollars to remodel a complex for his new quarters. Prior to Gehlen's arrival, this facility had been a housing development of the SS which had once housed Martin Bormann and Rudolph Hess.

Gehlen later joined Otto Skorzeny in Egypt at the behest of CIA director Allen Dulles. The political rationale was that Gehlen and Skorzeny would keep the communists out of Egypt. As it turned out, nothing could have been further from the truth. Skorzeny, an avid communist hater in his earlier career, had now learned that the game of survival was to play one power off the other one. He brokered million dollar deals routinely. He was also aligned with Gamal Nasser, the most powerful man in the Egyptian army, who later went on to become president. Nasser later allied himself with the Soviets when the U.S. refused to finance the Aswan Dam.

One of the more intriguing aspects of the CIA-Nazi connection in Egypt has to do with the exploration of the Sphinx and its underground chambers. As I currently write this book, there is considerable excitement across the world that the chamber beneath the paw of the Sphinx will be opened. All this hysteria is rather unnecessary. First, these CIA-Nazi operatives removed certain key tablets after the war. Although chambers will be found, the best information will elude the archaeologists.

The Nazi connection to Egypt is very much in full force today, and its influence can still be felt across the world. In the present chapter, I have concentrated on some of the political and financial aspects of this empire. There are also interesting esoteric aspects to the Nazi presence in Egypt as well as its sister region of Tibet. The remainder of the book will focus on these very important and mysterious ties to the Nazis, but first, we will take a quick journey to Antarctica.

24

NEUSCHWABENLAND

After World War II, Admiral Richard Byrd made a publi-
cized geographical survey of Antarctica. He took with him a
significant military contingent (some say as many as 100,000
troops, a battleship, an aircraft carrier and an entire support team).
It was more than a geophysical investigative team required. What
was going on here?

The first irregularity in the equation was that Admiral Byrd
was not really a military leader. He was neither trained nor
competent when it came to strict military matters. All of his
exploits were in the field of exploration. Admiral Byrd was
actually taken along as a figurehead in a shell operation. The
United States was seeking to disperse and destroy any remnants of
a Nazi safe haven in the Antarctic.

In 1938, Hitler decided to conduct the most extensive scientific study of Antarctica that the world had ever known. Some say
he foresaw the need for a safe base in the event of defeat. Others
think he was seeking a conduit to the hollow Earth itself. The
expedition was conducted by Captain Alfred Ritscher under the
orders of Hermann Göering. Aboard a homemade aircraft carrier,
Ritscher sailed a fleet of ships off the coast of the area known as
Queen Maud Land. During two expeditions, his planes photographed over 100,000 square miles and claimed over twice that
amount of territory. The borders were marked with swastika
pennants which had been attached to javelins so that they would
stick in the ice and remain upright. They called their new continent
Neuschwabenland. The stated military purpose of the mission was

a ruse from the very start. The Germans claimed to be studying the feasibility of whaling, but this was ridiculous. The Norwegians had been successfully whaling in the area for years.

Few genuine public comments were ever about this secretive mission. One of the more remarkable quotes came from Admiral Karl Dönitz, the Commander in Chief of the German navy and Hitler's eventual successor, when he said, "The German submarine fleet is proud of having built for the Führer, in another part of the world, a Shangri-La on land, an impregnable fortress." This statement was made in 1943 and reported in the *National Police Gazette* in 1977. The idea of a safe haven for the Nazis got another shot in the arm in 1946 when Major Vidkun Quisling, Hitler's governor of Norway, made the following statement: "I believe that I fought for a just cause and I refused to run away from my responsibilities when the Nazis, shortly after their final collapse, offered to convoy me aboard a submarine to a safe refuge." Quisling was hung at Nuremburg so we will never really find out exactly what he was referring to.

Although the British protected the Drake passage at the southern tip of South America, Neuschwabenland and its coastal waters remained untouched by the Allies. These were patrolled by two German ships, one called *Komet*, until the end of the war. This enabled a steady stream of U-boats, equipped with highly advanced schnorkel devices, to bring cargo and shore parties who probed deep into the interior of the frozen continent. The schnorkel devices enabled the U-boats to stay submerged and take in air via the water. Although the ship would need to remain just below the surface in this mode, it could go on indefinitely without surfacing. The only need to surface would be for the benefit of the crew's psychological state. These U-boats were also said to have brought men and equipment from the Peenemünde rocket base.

Neuschwabenland proved to be an excellent natural fortress due to a permanent barrier of ice which surrounds its shores. Although there are high mountains and deep valleys, there are also large plateaus which could be used for landing sights. Many warm water lakes exist in the interior as well.

Extensive U-boat exploration in the area revealed an undersea trench that runs all the way from Neuschwabenland to the other end of the continent. The trench was discovered to be of volcanic origins. By following it, the German explorers discovered warm water lakes, caves, crevasses and ice tunnels. Most of these were found to be suitable for human habitation with the presence of electricity. It was in one of these ice caves that the "Holy Lance" or actual "Spear of Destiny" was said to be hidden after World War II until its recovery in 1979 by Colonel Maximilian Hartmann.[*]

More adventurous theories have Neuschwabenland growing extensive crops in the vast caverns and supporting a civilization of post war Germans. A book entitled *Hitler is Alive* was published in Buenos Aires in 1946 and claimed that Hitler himself lived in a fortress in Antarctica. The author, Ladislas Szabo, was outraged and wanted the Allies to bring Hitler to justice. A newspaper article from the same period claimed to have firm evidence of Hitler's flight to Antarctica. It was dated July 16, 1945 and appeared in the newspaper *Critica.*

As an author, I cannot really tell you from personal experience if any of these things are true. It is obvious that there is a trail of many unanswered questions to follow up on. It is also true that Admiral Byrd's trip was cut short from eight months to about eight weeks. Several planes were lost. I am told that the Nazi flying saucers were developed for effective fighting by that time period and stopped the American forces cold. The U.S. Navy returned with its tail between its legs. Of course, this would have become the major security concern of the United States. We do know that the National Security Act was passed soon thereafter.

Standing astride these tales of a Nazi base in Antarctica is the legend of the Hollow Earth. There are many different books and myths about openings to an inner Earth at the poles. Many of you have probably heard of Admiral Byrd's legendary flight where he spotted a wooly mammoth and tropical vegetation after flying over the South Pole. The most notable information in such books is that historical accounts of sailors sometimes indicate that the weather becomes warmer the further south or north you go. These stories

---

[*] Colonel Hartmann was a very mysterious figure in the Third Reich. A favorite of Hitler's, it is said he convoyed the Holy Lance and his Fuhrer's ashes to an ice cave in Neuschwabenland after the war. He recovered the Holy Lance in 1979 and returned it to a secret locale in Germany. Every scrap of information about him has been expunged from private and official records. If this man is not a myth, he sounds as if he comes from Montauk.

are not necessarily incorrect, but I do not wish to embellish upon them in this book. Instead, I have checked conventional history books to see what sort of corroboration I could find.

Not too much is written about Richard Byrd that would give you any strong indication of the above theories. I did find out that he was a tremendous publicity hound and wanted complete credit for anything his men accomplished. He had persistent fights with a journalist who accompanied him and wrote his own version of what took place. Admiral Byrd demanded loyalty beyond the ordinary whereby no one could speak publicly about their explorations without his OK. I have also read that he and all his men were Masons who were sworn to an oath of secrecy as well as loyalty. According to the history books, Admiral Byrd suffered from severe psychological maladies. This might have started when he was forced to spend an Antarctic winter alone and almost died from carbon monoxide poisoning. He wrote about it in his book *Alone*. After this incident, he once wrestled madly with one of his pilots to take over the controls because he was irrationally afraid of dying. Had the pilot allowed Byrd to take over, the plane would have crashed. Instead, Byrd was appropriately slugged and forced to lay off. The entire matter was glossed over.

If the above does not convince you that there was funny business afoot with the South Pole's most famous explorer, perhaps my next story will.

I spoke to a gentleman on the phone one day who was well into his seventies. During the conversation, he mentioned that he once saw Admiral Byrd give a lecture. I immediately asked this man if Byrd made any references, oblique or otherwise, concerning holes at the poles or mysterious phenomena. This gentleman said there was one very strange mannerism that Byrd exhibited. He said that Byrd did not relay any alarming information but that, every now and then, he would interrupt his own speech in a non sequitur fashion and say, "There's nothing like a cup of Maxwell House coffee in the morning!" It made no sense whatsoever and sounded as if the man was programmed. Every time certain subjects would enter his mind, Maxwell House would take over.

I have noticed other strange synchronicities concerning early explorations of the South Pole, but most of them are too complicated and abstract to go into. One I would like to share concerns a bill introduced to the House of Representatives in 1823. It was authored by Representative J.T. Johnson of Ohio and called for government financing of a polar expedition. The bill included a petition with thousands of backers who wanted to establish trade and commerce with people living in the interior of the Earth and to claim new lands for the United States. Although the bill did not pass, at least half a dozen similar bills were introduced. None of these were successful, but the arguments were remembered and planted the seed for eventual government exploration.

The above was the brainchild of John Cleves Symmes, a man who believed in the hollow Earth and sought to find it. After the above failure, he teamed up with J.N. Reynolds who presented the idea to Secretary of the Treasury, Richard Rush, and Secretary of the Navy, Samuel L. Southard. He convinced them both, under the presidency of John Quincy Adams, to sponsor a sea born expedition to the Antarctic. Reynolds would be in command with Navy crews. In 1829, Andrew Jackson took office and nixed the program. Eventually, Reynolds found private sources and departed for Antarctica with Captain Palmer, the man who originally discovered the continent ten years prior. We do not really know what happened as records of the voyage are conflicting. The stories of early Antarctic exploration involve a tremendous amount of intrigue and political infighting. Other than occasional comments about inordinately warm weather and an oasis of colored, warm water lakes, I did not find anything else which might indicate the presence of a hollow Earth. I should also add that I only checked a few libraries. But, as you read about Admiral Byrd and the Nazis, there are plenty of reasons to suspect hidden secrets.

When my friend Jan van Helsing passed through New York one day, I decided to ask him a question with regard to all of this. He had already told me point blank that there is an existing UFO base in Antarctica. How did he know? It came primarily from an individual he knew who had actually been there. I then asked him if he could go there and verify the operation. Jan told me that would be no problem. He is free to go there if he desires, but he informed me there is one catch. If you go, you are not allowed to return. The reason being that if a foreign government or intelligence agency were to catch up with such an individual, they would be tortured to reveal all they knew. It did not sound like a fun line of endeavor.

Whether or not the Nazis actually established a lasting base in Antarctica, they most certainly did make it to another exotic location that is synonymous with Shangri-La: Tibet.

25

THE OSS IN TIBET

The many prior references to Tibet in this book had certainly stimulated my interest in the subject. As I became actively involved in researching this area, an associate of mine happened to inform me that the best source of information on Tibet could be found in the National Archives in Washington, D.C. A friend of this associate had been doing a doctoral thesis on Tibet and was doing a search at the Library of Congress. After conversing with a clerk, he was told that the most extensive information on Tibet was gathered by the Germans and was now on file in the "Captured German Documents". To my surprise, I was told that the information had been translated into English. This was crucial for me as I do not speak or read German fluently. Based upon what I had heard, I felt this necessitated a trip to the National Archives.

I soon made arrangements to stay with a "Montauk fan" in Washington. As it turned out, my stay with this particular individual was actually more interesting than the archival research. Although I did not know her beforehand, I soon heard that she had been kidnapped after her birth and was placed in the hands of a Nazi family. As she was of Jewish royal lineage, the Nazis were interested in her genetics and psychic ability. Her story is too personal to go into detail, but it was an amazing synchronicity and her experiences were an extremely strong corroboration of my line of investigation. After all, I was just looking for a place to stay for a few days.

This woman happens to be a very intelligent individual and her story does seem to check out. She was already familiar with the people at the archives and warned me point blank that they would try, unconcsiously or otherwise, to dissuade me from my goals. I soon found that this woman was spot on in her assessment of some of the clerical personnel. At first, I thought they were just ignorant of what I was looking for. I was informed there were no translations that they knew of and that if there were, they would have no idea of how to find them. I was handed indexes of the archives which were worthless to me. Despite this frustration, there was one helpful gentleman. Unfortunately, his area did not include the captured German documents, but he did tell me that the OSS (headed by Bill Donovan) had sent a mission into Tibet during World War II. I was interested and would continue from there.

Researching at the archives is not a tea party. There are definite bureaucratic procedures one has to follow. After wasting a half day learning them, I put in my request to have certain files pulled. Conveniently, somebody forgot to pull them, and I would have only a short time to review them before the archives closed that day. My host explained to me that this was a standard technique they use to keep people from looking into things. She said they would not expect me to come back the next day.

The next morning, I did return and some of the archivists looked either slightly shocked or displeased to see me. Fortunately, I was not in a hurry and had a convenient place to stay. I began to dig into the OSS mission to Tibet.

The first oddity I noticed was that the man heading up the expedition was Ilya Tolstoy, the grandson of the famous novelist, Leo Tolstoy. This is not only a Russian intelligence link (according to archival records, Countess Tolstoy was employed as an informant by the OSS and was paid $250 a month), but a blue blood connection as well. The Tolstoys are members of the same royal family as the Romanovs. Although Tolstoy was of Russian descent, he was also a citizen of the United States.

The Tolstoy mission consisted of only two people. Brooke Dolan was second in command and both were veterans of Camp X, a training facility for secret agents located on the north shore of Lake Ontario. Camp X is half way between the Canadian cities of Oshawa and Whitby. Tolstoy and Dolan were supplied with a state letter from FDR to the Dalai Lama who was only about ten years old at the time. Although there were far more files to this mission than what were available in the archives, I was able get some rudimentary information on what transpired.

The second oddity in this mission was its purpose. It was apparently called at the behest of Donovan to see about the prospect of using Tibet as a vital logistics crossroads, particularly in the event of Japan blockading all other entrance routes to China. This proposition is entirely ridiculous because the foreboding geography of the high mountain passes in Tibet makes the transport of tanks or other logistical items virtually impossible. As it was, Tolstoy and Dolan had to be perched on their pack animals and escorted around steep cliffs by the local guides. That these proven explorers could not have survived on their own dispels all credibility in the idea that they were trying to establish logistical links. Dolan had even traveled this route before.

This absurdity did not go unnoticed by the press. There was much criticism of the Tibet mission, as well as other OSS ventures, which resulted in jocular explanations for its initials. It was often referred to as "Oh So Silly" or "Oh So Subversive". This ridicule served the secret nature of the operations very well. No one took them too seriously.

According to the files, a specific purpose of the mission was noted as reconnaissance and to note the attitudes of enemies. These parameters left a very wide open door that could conceivably have included almost anything. The mission finally embarked after being approved by the President on 12 May 1942. It was completed in June of 1943. Not too much of the actual accomplishments of the mission were listed in the files. There is a considerably long article I was able to find in *National Geographic* which went into boring details about the mundane customs of the Tibetans. The files in the archives did say that Tolstoy and Dolan made a considerable donation to a monastery that housed three thousand monks and that they also visited a black lama temple. They reported that lamaism was almost extinct. This is an absurd statement in itself although it may well have applied to the local area they had visited. More likely, the lamas remained hidden from them. The team also made a 16 millimeter film called "Inside Tibet" which is available for viewing at the National Archives.

Another oddity I encountered while studying these files had to do with the man who locally approved their mission. This was

General Joseph Stilwell, the Commander of Armed Forces in Southeast Asia. He was popularly known as "Vinegar Joe". I recognized the last name because it is the family name of Preston Nichols' paternal grandmother. Checking with Preston's father, this man was indeed a distant cousin according to research his aunt had done.

The Tibet mission eventually met with the Dalai Lama and exchanged gifts. They also gave him FDR's letter and were treated with diplomatic courtesy. Before they were allowed to meet with His Holiness, the two Americans were sent to the court astrologer so their meeting would be chosen at the most auspicious time for the Dalai Lama. The mission was deemed highly successful with Tolstoy returning in good health. Dolan, whose serious illness delayed the launching of the mission, was reported as "not too good" at the finish.

Upon completion, Tolstoy proposed to return to Northern China, including the Shensi area, on August 21, 1944. I was not able to find out what became of that enterprise.

Upon returning to the United States, Brooke Dolan received a letter from a Tibetan dignitary who asked for assistance in exporting Tibetan garments and woolery. Apparently, some help had been intimated on their mission. This letter was passed on to Donovan for his action.

Omitted from these files, which I would later read about in books on the OSS, was a request by the Tibetans for a huge radio transmitter. The book *Camp X* by David Stafford indicates that Tolstoy pressed Donovan to send them a transmitter. The State Department declined this request as it would infuriate the British and Chinese who did not want an independent Tibet. Nevertheless, Donovan ignored the State Department and secured the Tibetans the transmitter they desired. The psychotronic aspect of this transmitter has to be considered although I have only found scant mention of it at all. It is also a curiousity that the Nazis were reportedly in communication with Tibet via a radio transmitter.

Besides the transmitter episode, *Camp X* also indicates the duo carried nearly three hundred pounds of photographic gear and "scientific instruments" on their journey.

All in all, I found it hard to believe that I was reading anything key with regards to what really went on during this Tibetan mission. Perhaps the most interesting item I found in the files was a report from the Russian newspaper *Pravda* of 30 May 1951. They charged that in the year of 1890, the British had unlawfully acquired from Tibet the province of Thutan and the neighboring Sikkim princedom in northeast India. *Pravda* was also critical of the economic exploitation they viewed in Tibet. They charged that the Buddhists in Tibet possessed vast treasures and that the higher grades of lamas ran Tibet as a feudal state with themselves as the lords. Further, that the lamas were doping the consciousness of the population with Buddhism and were able to back it up with an army of lamas that was many thousands strong, all subordinated to the Dalai Lama. In this manner, they subjugated the entire population and exploited them. The *Pravda* report said that nearly every family was connected to Buddhism.

Although *Pravda* was very much a political instrument of the Russians, none of the above observations seem to be exaggerations. Whatever the case, I do not think the communists were prepared to offer a better solution.

After the OSS mission to Tibet, Tolstoy left the service. He later dabbled in the motion picture business and ended up as the curator for Marineland of Florida. He died while on a trip to New York in 1960.

Brooke Dolan's subsequent history is steeped in mystery. Sent as an OSS representative to Mao Tse Tung, he hung out in the communist cave dwellings along with Chou En Lai. Dolan was killed shortly after Japan surrendered, but his death remains shrouded in obscurity.

The full extent of what the OSS mission to Tibet accomplished is still a mystery. In all probability, they were trying to find traces of what the Nazis had discovered a decade earlier.

26

THE SS IN TIBET

Upon returning home from the National Archives, I spoke to some of my friends and associates and expressed my frustration at not finding the specific Tibetan information I was looking for. Surprisingly, a woman who claims to be the granddaughter of Josef Goebbels already knew about an SS expedition into Tibet. She told me that I could read about it in the book *Unholy Alliance* by Peter Levenda.

Mr. Levenda, who obviously speaks German, found the documents in the microfilmed records of the Captured German Documents Section of the National Archives. Researchers who want more information on this subject are encouraged to pursue this by using his excellent book as a guide post.

Levenda found that Dr. Ernst Schäfer of the Ahnenerbe (the Ancestral Heritage Research and Teaching Organization of the SS) was the driving force of the SS expeditions into Tibet. Schäfer, who was basically a biologist, made at least two expeditions into Tibet on behalf of the SS. One trip was to East and Central Tibet from 1934 to 1936 and another from April of 1938 to August of 1939. At the age of 20, he also was part of an expedition into Tibet organized by the Academy of Natural Sciences of Philadelphia in 1930. Ironically, in 1931, he also accompanied future OSS officer Brooke Dolan on an expedition to Tibet , Siberia and China.

Whether Schäfer was an opportunist or an ardent follower, he joined the Nazi party soon after their rise to political power. By the summer of 1933, he was a member of the SS. This was well before many other Germans chose to get on the bandwagon and ride behind the wind of the Nazi machine. Not only was Schäfer a high ranking SS officer, he was also a member of Himmler's personal staff. Schäfer's interests ranged from politics to religious practices, but he took a particularly keen interest in the sexual practices of Tibetans. On his expeditions, Tibetans were filmed having intimate sex in public, the pictures of which included a fifteen year old girl masturbating in public on a bridge beam. Obviously, the Tibetans have a different view about sexuality than our culture.

Schäfer's work was championed by the German press. The most interesting article concerning his work is from *Der Neue Tag*, dated July 21, 1939. It reads as follows:

Sacred Tibetan Scripture
Acquired by the Dr. Schäfer—Expedition
on Nine Animal Loads Across the High-Country

(SPECIAL) FRANKFURT—20 JULY   The Tibet Expedition of Dr. Ernst Schäfer, which during its expedition through Tibet stayed a long time in Lhasa and in the capital of the Panchen Lama, Shigatse, is presently on its return trip to Germany. Since the monsoons began unusually early, the return march of the expedition was hastened in order to secure the shipment of the precious collections. The expedition has singularly valuable scientific research results to inventory. In addition to outstanding accomplishments in the areas of geophysical and earth-magnetic research they succeeded in obtaining an extra rich ethnological collection including, along with cult objects, many articles and tools of daily life.

With the help of the regent of Lhasa it was Dr. Schäfer who also succeeded in obtaining the Kangschur, the extensive, 108-volume sacred script of the Tibetans, which required nine animal loads to transport. Also especially extensive are the zoological and botanical collections that the expedition has already shipped, in part, to Germany the remainder of which they will bring themselves.

The zoological collection includes the total bird-fauna of the research area. Dr. Schäfer was also able, for the first time, to bag a Schapi, a hitherto unknown wild goat. About 50 live animals are on the way to Germany, while numerous other live animals are still with the expedition. Furthermore, valuable geographical and earth-historical accomplishments were made. Difficulties encountered due to political tensions with the English authorities were eliminated due to personal contact between Dr. Schäfer and members of the British authorities in Shangtse, so that the unimpeded return of the expedition out of Tibet with its valuable collections was guaranteed.

Levenda tried to find what became of these tablets but was not successful. I have been informed by others that they ended up in Russian hands and that they were copies of original sacred texts from the inner caves of Tibet. Monks would spend entire lifetimes dutifully copying sacred scriptures and depositing them in secret locations. Apparently, such tablets are not in short supply.

Lavenda also points out that the SS expedition to Tibet included Dr. Bruno Beger, an anthropologist who was later involved in the collection of 115 human skeletons at Auschwitz for inclusion in a Nazi anthropological museum. The skeletons were selected from Jewish, Polish, and Asiatic prisoners before execution. They were killed in such a way as to avoid damaging the skeletal material and their bodies were "shipped out for scientifically managed decomposition". According to interviews, Beger's mentor was the same Dr. Schäfer who organized the Tibetan expeditions.

The above information did not get me everything I was looking for, but it was enough. It was proof that the Nazis had extensive involvement in the Tibetan area. Their esoteric links to the area became considerably more evident as well.

27

THE TIBETAN CONNECTION

Five days before Hitler was said to have died in the bunker, the Russians were making their way through Berlin. In the cellar of a building, they found six Tibetans lying dead in a ritual circle. In the center was a Tibetan monk wearing green gloves.

Seven days later, over one thousand Asiatic bodies were found dead. They were Tibetans who had fought along side the Germans and wore uniforms of the same. There were no papers or other means of identification on the bodies.

Most people are shocked when they are hear the above information for the first time. The associations between Tibet and Germany actually go back into antiquity although many occult writers attribute the connection to Karl Haushofer, who served in Japan and studied in Tibet. Haushofer was no doubt an important influence in the occult and political diplomacy that went on, but he was serving very old and time honored alliances.

The monk with the green gloves was definitely a mysterious influence. There is not too much written about him, but it has been said that he was in constant contact with Hitler. If this were to be the case, I believe it would have been more on a psychic level than on a day to day tea time basis. This monk was called the "Guardian of the Key" as he was said to know the entrance to Agartha (also identified as Aryana, Akkadia or Arcadia), a realm in the center of the Earth where the Aryan race came from. We do know that this monk actually existed because he was nicknamed "the man with the green gloves" in the press and had correctly predicted the number of Hitler's deputies elected to the Reichstag. It is generally believed that all of the above deaths, including the man with "The Man with the Green Gloves" were the result of ritual suicide.

In order to understand the true nature of this mysterious relationship between Tibet and Germany, we have to realize that we have all been dulled to sleep concerning the geographical region of Tibet and what it actually represents.

Tibet is not historically what we know it as today. It was once a vast region which extended northward of its current borders and included the Shensi pyramids of Chinkiang province as well as Mongolia. This is the heart of Central Asia which is richly identified in countless legends and actual histories as the origination point of mankind. There are countless anecdotes of initiates who passed through this region of Central Asia on their way to spiritual enlightenment. There are too many to mention but they include the following characters: Karl Haushofer, G.I. Gurdjieff, Aleister Crowley and L. Ron Hubbard. Even the Duke of Hamilton got into the act when he flew over Mount Everest as a Royal Air Force pilot. The Duke, a close associate of Albrecht Haushofer, was the Scottish nobleman who Rudolph Hess sought out on his fateful flight to England. Josef Stalin, who was once a border in the house of Gurdjieff's mother as well as being a student for the priesthood, was also strongly tied to this Central Asian tradition.

The Russians and Germans were not the only ones to trace their roots and certain cultural aspects to Central Asia. The Tartars, who more or less evolved into the Turkish empire, derived their name from the Tarim Basin in this area. The Greeks phonetically altered the name "Tartar" to "Barbar" as these people made their way to Africa and gave rise to the Barbary pirates as well as contributing substantially to the Moorish civilization. The Sufi mystery schools also have strong ties to this Central Asian locale which was once known as Tibet. Although tremendously secretive, the Sufis are very influential in the Turkish world today.

Erroneous conceptions about Asia and its history run rampant in our culture, not the least of which is the origin of the Hindu religion. Most Westerners automatically assume that this body of knowledge is the product of dark skinned Dravidian peoples. It is not. Conventional history reveals that the Dravidians were conquered by an Aryan race of the north which gave them their sacred religious texts known as the Vedas or "books of knowledge". If you stop to consider that the *Rig-Veda*, which means "books of God's knowledge" or "King's knowledge" (Rig signifies rulership), and realize that the Vikings had the Rig-Thula as their sacred text, you begin to get the idea. The Vikings were tremendous seafarers, but they were not the type to anchor up in Ceylon or Bombay, study up with the latest Maharishi, and then bring wisdom back to their brawling brethren who were fighting their way to Valhalla. Both traditions have a common source originating from Central Asia.

In some respects, Madame Blavatsky's work seems totally dedicated to the prospect of mankind's origins being in Central Asia. She offers proof after proof in such a way as to lead any serious investigator towards the truth. While her personality was sometimes ridiculed, her academic sources never were. They were always ignored by her critics.

In typical Nazi occult literature, the connection to Tibet focuses on Karl Haushofer. Unfortunately, there is far too little information available on this man. Although he wrote voluminous books in the German language, it is virtually impossible to find any English translations. Many of his personal papers are available for viewing on microfilm in the National Archives, but you have to read German to make any sense out of them.

Haushofer's role as a mentor of Hitler has been quite celebrated in previous literature while some books claim they never had any contact. There is little information in print as to what their relationship was. Jan van Helsing's sources indicate that Haushofer was indeed a mentor of Hitler. The woman previously referred to as Anna in this book had a grandfather who was also a mentor of Hitler, but his influence was mostly from an astrological perspective. Hitler seems to have had quite a few occult people influencing his life. Whatever Haushofer's exact role was with Hitler, we do know that he was a key player in the German scene, particularly in the beginning stages of Hitler's rise to power. Trevor Ravenscroft utterly maligns Haushofer in *The Spear of Destiny*, portraying him as a devil worshiping black magician. While this is a myopic and inaccurate description, it is clear that Haushofer trafficked in occult forces which eventually got the better of him.

The occult master Gurdjieff is also involved with the Tibetan connection. Haushofer is said to have studied under him and also the Order of Bektashi Dervishes of which Gurdjieff was a member.

In fact, Gurdjieff was reputed to have taught the Dalai Lama under the titular name of Dorjieff. Some scholars dispute this. Other sources indicate Gurdjieff was a member of the Russian secret police who was sent to Tibet at their bequest. Few dispute this. Whatever the truth about Gurdjieff, he wielded great power in both an occult and political sense. This trait was demonstrated when he was arrested for publicly satirizing a Nazi street parade in Berlin. Despite the fact that the Nazis were operating a virtual police state and were at the height of their power, they decided to let Gurdjieff go. History reports that he was dismissed as a madman, but this is inconsistent with historical accounts of how Nazis handled the insane. It was usually to the concentration camps for imprisonment or forced sterilization. Gurdjieff's connections influenced the Nazis to the point where he was not treated as a common irritant but was allowed safe passage out of the country.

While Gurdjieff is almost always portrayed as a master of the occult, Haushofer is usually cast as a villain. Both were deeply involved in the mysteries of Tibet as well as the Dervishes. In the relationship between these two men, Gurdjieff seems to be the senior partner.

The Americans attempted to humiliate Haushofer after the war by insisting that he see the evil ways of his theories on Geopolitics. Haushofer is quoted as saying that "war is the father of all things", and his doctrine of *Lebensraum* or living space teaches that the Aryan people's need for space justified their right to acquire territory. Although Haushofer is sometimes portrayed as a fanatic based upon Aryan supremacy and world conquest, this is simply not the case. His wife and son were part Jewish and were "Aryanized" by Rudolph Hess himself, so we know he was not a racist on a personal basis. He also argued with Hitler that Germany had enough problems of its own without having to conquer more territory. Therefore, we have to consider that much of Haushofer's work has been taken out of context. Haushofer, if listened to, could have averted World War II. As his work has either been mistranslated or not translated at all, we are not able to fully evaluate his legacy, even if just considered from the geopolitical angle. If you read what has been translated carefully, you will see that Haushofer's theories are primarily concerned with acquiring key areas which are absolutely necessary for survival and propagation of the species. The language he offers for public consumption is really a veiled way of discussing how to control the key points of the Earth's grid. He is a mystery writer representing mystery schools. In this respect, his writing is layered to appeal to different groups.

While the above legacy leaves us with an enigmatic view, we do know something for certain. Karl Haushofer was a member of the Yellow Hats, known as Dugphas in Tibet. In other words, he was a member of the priesthood of the indigenous religion of ancient Tibet: Bon. His role with the Bons led to the formation of Tibetan and Hindu colonies in Berlin and Munich in 1926.

Although the specifics of these Tibetan connections and their history are not readily available at this time, we do have something we can sink our teeth into and that is the Bon religion. The study of it yielded some very interesting results.

THE VRIL FLAG

Above is the flag of the Vril Society.
It is a stunningly beautiful design with a silver
Tibetan glyph in the center signifying "the Vril".
One side of the banner is black
while the other is lavender.

28

THE BON RELIGION

The inspiration for this book was triggered when I learned of the police monitored Bon meetings on Long Island. Although the reports of these were highly confidential and probably still are, we only know of them as Aryan type meetings where weird science was discussed. The use of the name *Bon* was suggesting a Tibetan presence behind the entire affair on Long Island. It was with all of this in mind that I began to look into the world of Bon or the Bonpos as they are sometimes called.

According to a Russian scholar named Kuznetzov, Bon was introduced to Tibet in the fifth century BC at the same time as a massive migration took place from northeastern Persia into Tibet. These Aryan settlers brought with them the Aramaic alphabet which was named after Aramaiti, an Iranian Earth Goddess. Several historical texts agree that the founders of Bon were from Persia so this is really not in dispute. As the actual origin of the religion goes far back in antiquity, it is hard to delineate where reality ends and myth begins.

The founder of Bon is known as Shenrab[*] to the Tibetans, but he was said to come from the region of Elam where he was known as Mithra, the bull god. He is also known as Mura, an interesting concoction of syllables if you consider *Mu* as in the lost continent of Mu or Lemuria and *ra* as in *Ra*, the sun god of Egypt.

Shenrab descended from "heaven" on a coiled rope some eighteen thousand years ago. He crossed a burning desert to bring

---

[*] Shenrab corresponds to or possibly inspired the words *Shensi*, as in Shensi pyramids, and *rabbi*.

the Bon religion to Tibet and taught in the area of Mount Kailas before returning home. Shenrab, or Mura, taught mankind a doctrine known as the Kalachakra. This literally means "Wheel of Time" and represents the underlying wisdom in the universe. It could also be interpreted as the Wheel of the Goddess or the Vortex of Time. If we break up the word *Kalachakra*, we find that *Kala* is derived from Kali, the Hindu goddess of time; hence the word *calendar*. Kala specifically refers to the emanations of the vagina in Hindu tantra or sex magick. These are the same principles studied by magicians in their attempt to harness the powers of creation. It is sometimes a very sinister subject.

From the above etymology, we can clearly see that the Kalachakra in its purest form is all about the goddess and her many manifestations. Some may readily recognize that the Kalachakra is actually a Buddhist doctrine. While this is not entirely untrue, it did not originate with the Buddhists. They borrowed it, altered it and absorbed it into their own legacy. The political interests that originally fostered Buddhism on Tibet were forced to incorporate the indigenous religion in order to make inroads into the country and subjugate the population to their own chosen brand of religion. The alterations of the original teachings that occurred with Buddhism were considerable and were similar to what happened between the Catholic Church and Gnostics. Although the Catholic mass and liturgy are based upon ancient goddess worship, they have been deliberately altered in such a fashion as to exclude the goddess in her most vibrant form.

The Bon religion, in its most pure and original form, was based upon the concept of the goddess as recognized in the symbolism of the Black Sun. In this respect, the Black Sun signifies the void of creation from which all things originate. By the time the Buddhists took over the annals of history, they wrote that Tibet was a she-demon who had to be subjugated. This was merely a criticism of the Bon religion and their way of looking at the world through the feminine principle. The Buddhists said "She (referring to Tibet as the goddess) had to be crucified with nails before she could be tamed". After that, the Buddhists decreed that Tibet could be inhabited and civilized. This configuration of the crucified goddess was actually symbolized geographically by square concentric zones or regions boxed around a common center. Four temples were erected at the four corners of the configuration while three successive squares stood for nails driven into her limbs. To keep her under control, (a total of) twelve nails of immobility were driven into her and were represented by the twelve temples (pagodas). This legend was repeated and embellished until it became a staple of Buddhist literature.

The above facts and attitudes give us ample reason to want to bash Tibetan Buddhism. This is not the point, but we should realize that Tibetan Buddhism is based upon a patriarchal system that had its own agenda. One can still find many truths in the subject, but many times these are watered down from the original doctrine.

Buddhism, as we know it today, is a distortion of a long and ancient tradition that existed long before the advent of Siddhartha Guatama. At one time, the kings were also known as Buddhas and were identified by the very same word. Shenrab or Mura was the first Buddha and also the first king. This was long before *Buddha* or *Buddhism* was known to our history's lexicon. If you read most history books or Buddhist texts, they will tell you or imply that Buddhism began its effective life with Siddhartha Guatama who was an Aryan nobleman by birth. Siddhartha sought spiritual purification by human means and taught simple but clever precepts on how to conduct one's life in a manner which would lead towards enlightenment. These lessons are recorded in the Pali Canons. This tradition which concerns itself with purely human and ethical means is called Mahayana Buddhism and does not purport to be involved with esoteric matters. Of course, as with all religions, there is a secret esoteric tradition with Buddhism. It is said that Siddhartha used to initiate advanced students himself.

There is another form of Buddhism known as Hinayana. This takes a major twist away from Mahayana Buddhism in that it is not so concerned with Siddhartha Guatama's teachings during his own lifetime. There is a legend, which is at the core of today's Tibetan Buddhism, that when the Buddha left this Earth via death, he took the form of a Kalachakra deity before entering Nirvana. He then assembled a great number of sages in southern India, some say Ceylon, and taught them the Kalachakra. This found its way, through various subterfuges, to the hollowed mountains of Tibet.

Many people are already familiar with Tibet as a result of the fable of Shambhala, sometimes referred to as Shangri La.

Shambhala is a Sanskrit word for the "Source of Happiness". The Dalai Lama himself believes that Shambhala has a material existence in this world and he has been quoted as saying such. He also believes that the Kalachakra, if properly practiced, is one of the most effective and speedy methods of obtaining enlightenment.

The Bons recognized the land of Shambhala by the name of Olmolungring which has also been identified in the abbreviated form of "Ong", "Og" or "Oz". It is an invisible kingdom surrounded by snow and allegedly located in the northwest region of Tibet. This is the area from which Shenrab descended when he "came down from heaven on a rope". He was followed by many kings who remained in the hidden sanctuary of Ong and guarded the Kalachakra teachings of Bon.

If you study the Kalachakra in its most basic form, you will start with the concepts of yin and yang and how those forces combine to make all the other myriad forces of the universe. It directly parallels the Cabalistic Tree of Life. In this early prototype of creation, the vaginal emanations of the goddess are manifest. As was referred to earlier, these emanations correspond directly to the cycles of our moon and are the divine pattern upon which all moon magick is based.

In its most glorious form, the Kalachakra includes the complete body of information that is inherent in the universe. It could be called universal wisdom, and it is from this "Wheel of Time" that all knowledge springs forth. This is the religious explanation for the vast wisdom found in our oriental heritage. It includes the entire meridian system of the human body, the theories of how acupuncture work, the various doctrines of yoga and you name it. It explains all the missing theoretical aspects that western science has not yet learned to assimilate into its own data base.

The western version of the Kalachakra is Magick. Behind the "Wheel of Time" is Kali or the Scarlet Woman whose menses is the blood magic which regulates or corresponds with all creation. These are the specific sympathies, synchronicities or formulas of nature. Their representation in the anatomy of the human female corresponds precisely with the overall creative principle of the cosmos.

No matter what method or tradition you study, this body of ancient wisdom has been extant as long as anyone can remember.

It came into Tibet through the Bon religion. If you read popular books on Tibet, you will find scant mention of Bon, if any. The Bons are usually portrayed as wicked sorcerers who use the most barbaric of rituals. As is so typical of Earth history books, this is an inaccurate description. Much later on in history, Buddhism weaves its way into Tibet and rewrites the religion. There is even a distinct legend that Siddhartha Guatama himself reincarnated and brought Buddhism and the Kalachakra to Tibet in about 400 A.D. No matter who expounds the information, its original form is almost always obscured.

Earlier it was said that the Kalachakra represents the divine wisdom underlying the entire universe. This wisdom expresses itself in the geometric unfoldment of existence which was discussed in *Pyramids of Montauk*. According to the legends of the Hindus, this unfoldment expressed itself as the great mountain in the center of Shambhala and was known as Mount Meru. This is really the same as Ong or Oz, the realm from which Shenrab descended. Of course, this mountain has different names and meanings for different cultures. It could also be represented as Mount Olympus in Greece or Mount Fuji in Japan. Meru is the idea of an archetypal world mountain.

The geometry of Mount Meru can readily be seen in the glyph known as the Shi Yantra which can be seen on the following page. A yantra is a visual device designed to invoke a higher conscious during meditation. The Shi Yantra is the most sacred glyph to the Hindus and is equally honored by other religions and belief systems. If one visualizes this particular glyph as a series of stacked plates, one can pull the Shi Yantra into three dimensions so that it forms a mountain. The successful practitioner receives a fourth dimensional bonus as well.

Stan Tenon calls Mount Meru the geometric metaphor of life and accordingly calls his research organization the Meru Foundation. Meru actually signifies a vortex shape and Tenon clearly demonstrates this in his video *Geometric Metaphors of Life*. He explains that the Hebrew alphabet is called Meruba which literally means "vortex in a box". This aspect of the Hebrew alphabet and how it relates to a vortex was discussed in *Pyramids of Montauk*. By its very nature, a vortex shape or a *Meru* emanates different motions or frequencies. Thus, it gives rise to the manifestation we

SHI YANTRA

A yantra is a visual glyph designed to evoke a spiritual awakening. The Shi Yantra is the most sacred symbol of the ancient Tibetan religion. The idea is to visually pull this two dimensional drawing into a three dimensional configuration in your mind. If you are successful, you will have fourth dimensional experience.

know as waves. This is why *Mer* equates to the sea. Hence, we get words like *Mer*maid and *Mer*lin the Magician. Both are magical creatures who represent the ability to emanate different frequencies and manifestations. They are also known as shape-shifters.

I have thus far referred to this sacred mountain by its more popular name of Meru because many people will recognize it and be more familiar with it. Actually, the word *Meru* is a shortened version of the original name which is called *Sumeru* by the Tibetans and their antecedents. *Sumeru* better describes the phenomena in the Shi Yantra because *su* refers both to the sun and source. It is also seen in the word *swastika* which is *suasti* in Sanskrit. In this sense, you have the "Sun Mountain" which is another way of interpreting the name *Solomon*.

The biggest revelation, which has been ignored or deliberately disregarded by historians, is that this Tibetan word is clearly where the name *Sumeria* derived from. This is a perfect example of how a simple omission in the language can pervert a crystal clear concept. Archaeologists, authors and the like have focused on the Sumerians as coming from the Mideast. While this is not entirely untrue, it is more than a little misleading. This perversion of history is addressed in an interesting book entitled *Dancing Shadows:* by Aoumiel (published by Llewellyn). In this book, the author demonstrates how virtually all of the names of the Near East have been patterned after real events in the Orient.

Many stories abound of Jesus and Moses actually growing up in the east and living their lives there. There is even a tomb of Moses in Kashmir which you can visit if you so desire. Arrogance in western thought attributes these stories to highly illiterate barbarians who would readily create myths in order to identify with these great leaders in their own land. A more honest look at history will clearly reveal that the tradition of wisdom in our civilization flowed from Central Asia to the Mediterranean, not the other way around.

Thus, we see that the nature of Tibet has been completely misconstrued by popular history and thought. It was always a cordoned off section of the world. Under Chinese control in modern times, it is particularly so. Tibet has many connections to the outside world and this can be seen in the various etymologies which follow.

The word for power in Tibetan is *yesh*. Christian scholars will immediately recognize *yesh* in the word *Yeshua*, the Aramaic name for Jesus. In Tibetan, *yesh* also signifies shakti, the female power pods of the rising serpent (kundalini). In this sense, Jesus' original name, in the language he spoke, signified the power of the feminine force. It is right there in the language. There are also persistent legends of Christ visiting Tibet during his missing years in the Bible.

When we consider the word *Tibet* itself, common scholarship shows that Tibet was once referred to by the name of *Bod*. R. A. Stein has researched this point a bit further by consulting the Bonpo Chronicles and indicates the name *Bod* was actually *Bon*. The Chinese transcribed it as *B'jywan*, pronounced "Fon".

Stein's scholarship also tells of a Tibetan king named Thothrori who was a personal shen or sorcerer of the Mu clan. Thoth is the Greek name for Tahuti who could be considered the king or dweller in the pyramid. In this case, Thothrori sounds like the "King of the Pyramid" which may be referring to Sumeru or the Shensi pyramids, a vast series of step pyramids located in a part of old Tibet which is now western China. The terms *Bon, Bonpo* and *shen* are often used interchangeably and mean sorcerer or magician in their most general sense. The word Bonpo has been translated as *shih kung*, again meaning sorcerer. You might know this term by its popular Americanized name of Chi Gung or Chi Kung, an ancient Chinese art. The source is actually from the Kalachakra which, as was said earlier, derives from Central Asia.

There are other interesting etymological associations with Tibet. Medina, the second holy city of Islam, was once known as Tibah or Tabah, according to Sir Richard Burton. This is from the root "Tib" which means good, sweet or lawful. In French "bon" also means good.

Thebes, a name which is close in sound to Tibet, was an ancient city in Egypt as well as Greece. The Egyptian city was particularly known for a substance it obtained from opium. It is called thebaine, a crystalline poisonous alkaloid with the chemical designation $C_{19} H_{21} NO_3$. Thebes has even more mysterious associations with chemical substances which will be brought out later.

Another common misconception about Tibet is that it is a meditative culture permeated by peace loving lamas. The term *lama* commonly refers to a guru, as opposed to a monk, and was borrowed by the Buddhists from the Bons. Today, both the Bons and the Buddhists use the term *lama* to describe their adept teachers. The traditions of both of these lamas are steeped in a warrior mentality. This has been popularized to some degree in the media by Kung Fu heroes and the like, but the history of lamas in Tibet is one that includes considerable violence and war. Part of this violence reflects the very harsh physical environment of the region. The histories of these wars would be much more fascinating to read than those of the west because they had a no holds barred attitude toward war which included the psychic arts of war. Western powers have often used them, but they are less expert and seldom admit to any involvement in the psychic realm.

Among celebrities and certain areas of polite society, it has become very chic to revere Tibetan Buddhism and the plight of the Dalai Lama. While there is nothing wrong with this in itself or in expressing one's own religious beliefs, many people would serve themselves to become less ignorant of what they are becoming involved in. Many embrace Tibetan Buddhism simply because it is different and perceived to be an exotic religion. Those who might be quick to reject the Pope now find themselves embracing the Dalai Lama, a being who carries the same ceremonial splendor and authority as does the Catholic pontiff.

The extent to which people carry this admiration can be quite amusing. I once heard a psychic, who was highly paid by corporate America, brag of his encounter with the Dalai Lama. He recounted that several celebrities were in attendance, the only one of which I remember for certain being George Lucas. This particular psychic was actually using his personal contact with the Dalai Lama as a means with which to impress the audience. Actually, he did not need to use this as his abilities seemed to be nothing short of remarkable. Unfortunately, as it turned out, his ethics left something to be desired.

There is a tremendous tendency for people to stand back in awe from that which they know nothing about. Aleister Crowley, long before it was chic to admire the Dalai Lama, makes a very sobering comment about His Holiness in his magical diaries of 1923. He makes a distinct reference to a time honored ritual where the faithful Tibetans actually eat the excrement of the Dalai Lama.

Those who do not believe this are invited to study the more esoteric aspects of magick and may want to start with the scarab beetle of Egypt. Crowley identified with this tradition and knew more than a thing or two about it. At one point, he opened a restaurant in which he prepared exotic dishes from the East. Because of his reputation, people were afraid to eat the food for fear that it might contain sperm, menstrual blood or what they viewed to be worse.

Perhaps the biggest misconception concerning the Dalai Lama is that he is the actual ruler of the Tibetan people. While he is not without power, he is more of a symbolic or titular head of state. Until the Dalai Lama has reached maturity, the country is ruled by a specifically selected regent. During the early part of this century, the regent was known as Lord Chamberlain. It has been speculated that Lord Chamberlain had some sort of link to Hitler during the 1920s.

Obviously, the regent has to be selected by someone other than the Dalai Lama himself. Some histories even state that the regent maintains control even after the Dalai Lama reaches maturity. While I have not researched the specific protocols of how this process works, I can tell you without any margin of error that these people, including the Dalai Lama himself, all answer to an oracle. The oracle itself is the ruling force in Tibet. This is undisputed by historians although it is not highlighted or commented on in any great detail. I have only been able to find scant mention of it.

While the media focuses on the plight of the Tibetans, they never mention who the true ruler is because they do not know. It is entirely possible that the oracle banished the Dalai Lama and brought in the Chinese. This is clearly speculative but we have to think in these terms if we are going to arrive at a true understanding. We also have to be on guard that the media will get wind of what has been written here and will wheel out some duplicitous character who will be interviewed in earnest by Ted Koeppel, Barbara Walters or the like. This character might be billed as the oracle when he is really just a one hundred year old stand in who is a candidate for an iron lung. While the true nature of this oracle is steeped in mystery, its aspects will become a bit more evident in the remainder of this book.

Perhaps one of the most tragic figures in the above scenario is the Dalai Lama himself. People look to him for leadership but do not always take stock of the full circumstances of his life. He was sequestered from his mother at the age of three and programmed to a steady diet of procedures the likes of which we really know nothing about. If you read his own writings, you will see this was not a pleasant experience. The maternal and nurturing aspects were denied him and his programming is very reminiscent of the Montauk Boys. People assume that he chose his incarnation and was totally on top of the game from minute to minute. This is only verifiable by the Tibetans who tell us so. It was the regent and a control group who determined his existence and extinguished the maternal influence.

There is actually a rich role for the Dalai Lama to fill, as the name itself implies. The word *Dalai* is Mongolian for vast ocean. This takes us back to *Mer* and the definitions already given. In this respect the Dalai Lama would be the "teacher of the vast ocean". In a deeper sense, the ocean consists of waves which can be extended to refer to all the electromagnetic waves or frequencies of existence. In his highest form, the Dalai Lama should therefore be the entity who teaches us all about the vortex of creation. This is what we want and should expect from the Dalai Lama. If the true teachings are conveyed, the political problems will fall by the wayside. The old maxim applies: "The truth shall set you free".

One of the main points to realize about Tibet is that the ancient legacy of the culture was bastardized and obfuscated to the point where it is lost. The Tibetan Buddhists themselves have realized this to at least a small extent and have begun to allow a few publications on Bon to be released. It seems to be a gesture that can no longer be avoided. Still, this is hardly enough. The old religion will have to be unveiled in order for the true Tibetans to be restored to their homeland. Like the Montauk tribe, the Tibetans are one more indigenous people who have been denied Mother Earth and the consequent stewardship of the morphogenetic grid. The irony between the Montauks and Tibetans fully revealed itself when Sharon Jackson, the Montauk Shaman, sent me on a quest that showed a remarkable connection between these two peoples.

29

THE MON

After *Pyramids of Montauk* was written, an unusual circumstance arose which eventually led to some rather intriguing implications as regards the Tibetan connection. This began in a phone conversation with Sharon Jackson. We had often discussed the relationship between Egypt and Montauk because she remembers reading a book that indicated her ancestors arrived on Long Island in Egyptian boats. Unfortunately, she has not been able to find the book or remember exactly where she saw it. Instead, she gave me a "shaman communication" and told me that I might be able to find some historical reference to Egypt in the name "Mongetucksee".

Mongetucksee was the name of (Montauk) Chief Wyandanch's father who I identified in *Pyramids* as Mongatchsee based upon what I had read in various history books. Sharon told me that "Mongetucksee" was the correct pronunciation and that the man stood an enormous seven feet tall. Mongetucksee is the first historically recorded chief of the Montauk Nation although he was preceded by others whose history is either lost or hidden.

I was not able to find any Egyptian records under the name "Mongetucksee", but I did find something that turned out to be even more interesting. While going through the card index file, I came across the name "Mongkut" which is obviously not too far from the same sound. I soon noticed that this was the name of the famous king of Siam that was made popular in the movie and stage production *The King and I*. This association might have been easily dismissed except for one very salient point. Preston Nichols' mother, Ginny, had a fascination that bordered on obsession with

Yul Brynner, the man who made his trademark starring as King Mongkut on Broadway and in the movie. Ginny had books on him and thought he was just the most wonderful man. I could not figure out her fascination with him other than she was probably his biggest fan. It all seemed rather odd. She was also the first one to tell me about Preston's father being related to General Stilwell, a man whose headquarters were in Siam. As Ginny had proven to be a magical conduit in the past, I thought I should look into King Mongkut and see if there were any synchronicities at play.

Picking up a book on the historical king Mongkut, I discovered it was written by a Welsh lady who tutored him as well as the many women in his harem. Although her work was the inspiration for *The King and I*, other books say that her work lacks historical accuracy. Even so, I did find the remarkable synchronicity I was looking for. The book mentioned a monkey (belonging to a harem girl) named Menthu. Menthu is the bull god pictured on the cover of *Pyramids of Montauk* and is the warrior god of Thebes which Aleister Crowley referred to in *The Book of the Law*. The appearance of the word *Menthu* in an Asian harem is somewhat remarkable when you consider it is supposed to be a Latin word.* The fact that *Menthu* appeared with the name Mongkut made it all the more curious. I began to dig a little deeper.

I found out that King Mongkut was a fascinating character and considered one of the most pivotal historical figures in the orient of his time. He learned several languages and also corresponded with Abraham Lincoln. King Mongkut also single handedly cleaned up and restored the priesthood of his local religion. His temple was a vast space dedicated to the principles of goddess worship. There were many sacred areas which only the king and his harem could access. Although King Mongkut was mostly praised and heralded, it seems that most of his work was not entirely understood. That would be one more research project.

The most noteworthy part of my entire probe came as I continued to look into what history I could find on Siam or Thailand. This was the discovery of an ancient people called the Mon. The remarkable name synchronicity to the word "Montauk" was too much to dismiss as a mere coincidence, but I could not find

---

* The word *Menthu* most likely originated elsewhere than Latium.

out too much about them. The Mon occupied southeast Asia, primarily in Cambodia and Thailand, but they are not indigenous to the area. Some accounts have them migrating from China and some say they came from another area altogether. They are considered to be the keepers of the original religion of the region and have what is sometimes called their own "Mon" religion. This area of study is very obscure and proved hard to follow in the initial historical works I glanced at.

Southeast Asia, particularly Cambodia and Thailand, is renowned for having the most beautiful Buddhist architecture in the world. This is historically attributed to a large migration of Tibetan Buddhists sometime after 400 A.D. Although the Mons are credited with being the religious invigorators of the area, I intuitively suspected that they themselves originated in Tibet and might be associated with this migration. Unfortunately, there was no ready reference. I did find out that the Mon people still exist today, but information about them remains obscure. They are not huge in number nor is there much data on their history or current status. All we know is that they are undisputed as the senior religious connection in the region and reach back into antiquity.

Upon discovering these various synchronicities, I called my friend Kenn Arthur. It turned out he had taken his wife to see Yul Brynner's very last performance of *The King and I*, a day before the famous actor died. Kenn simply said that "Mon" is just an ancient Atlantean name that will appear in different parts of the world whether it be "Montauk", "Montu" or elsewhere.

The origins of the Mons would remain a mystery for over a year. I reported on it in *The Montauk Pulse* (a quarterly newsletter about Montauk) and abandoned the study. Sharon Jackson also disappeared from my life despite many attempts by myself and my friends to contact her. Ironically, she only returned after I was able to resolve this lingering mystery.

The answer to the enigma of the Mon people occurred when I came upon the research of orientalist R.A. Stein, referred to in the last chapter as having translated the Bonpo Chronicles. I soon came upon a very interesting discovery. He said without any reservation that the inhabitants of Tibet were once known as the "Mon". This went back at least as far as the time of the first kings in the sixth to seventh century. The "Mon" also came from the south, east, west and other areas of Tibet. It was a catch all term to some extent, but referred to many of the indigenous aboriginal tribes. This not only answers the mystery to the origin of the people from Southeast Asia, it reveals an inextricable geographic associations between the Bons and Mons. The Bons embodied an ancient legacy that preceded even themselves or their namesake. The Mon had roots that went even further back. Both were indigenous people with the Bon appearing to derive from the Mon.

We are further enlightened to this mysterious name of *Mon* when we consider yet another people who have been much maligned and misunderstood: the Mongols. Here, the name "Mon" cries out for blatant recognition. A simple study of ethnology reveals that the native Tibetans are of the Mongol race and that lamaseries have existed throughout Mongolia and Central Asia since time immemorial. Some of these lamaseries are Buddhist in their orientation while others are not. The Mongols, particularly those linked with the era of Genghis Khan, are usually depicted as uncivilized, bloodthirsty warriors. The equation is not that simple.

Genghis Khan was born with a blood clot in his hand which the astrologers and priestly class duly noted. It signified a supreme identification with the planet Mars and indicated he would take a leadership role over mankind. He unified the Tartars of the Tarim Basin with his own tribe and went on to conquer the world as far west as Europe. His grandson, Kublai Khan, went on to become emperor of China. To think of Genghis Khan as a barbarian is to miss the point. He represented a high order of civilization, albeit a violent one. That his son's name was Tulee or Tula (whose son was Kublai Khan) was no accident. It corresponds to the ancient traditions which the German Thule Society subscribed to. There is a great mystery tradition connected to Genghis Khan, but it has primarily been in the repository of bloodthirsty types such as Josef Stalin and the like.

Genghis Khan's first major act was to take over the steward-ship of the Shensi pyramids and surrounding area. History does not account for this and offers little clues as to what Genghis Khan's role was in this regard. We do know the word *Dalai* is Mongolian and that the Mongols were the protectors of the Dalai Lama.

We also learn from history that Genghis Khan took the name of "Hor" for his people. The Hors are more popularly known as Urs or Uighurs, the original race of Central Asia. Historians sometimes conclude that Genghis adopted this name because there are five Hor principalities in Eastern Tibet or today's China in a land known as Kham. I do not believe Genghis Khan adopted the name "Hor" with no reason. If he did so, it was because there was considerable significance behind the name.

The word or name *Hor* synchronizes splendidly with the information I stumbled upon while working on *Encounter in the Pleiades. Hor* is not only the root for the word *horse*, it is the root for the word *time* as well. This is readily observable in the words *horology* and *horoscope* which both concern the science of time. The horse was considerably sacred to Genghis Khan as well as the rest of the Mongols. It was the key to many rituals in their traditions. The horse is also a symbol of time and the god Mars. In the legend of the Montauk Project, the horse was a cornerstone symbol with regard to time. The word *Hor* itself suggests the "whore of Babalon" or Scarlet Woman which is symbolized in the blood clot Genghis Khan was born with.

The above correspondences are too synchronous to be an accident. Here are the roots of the Egyptian legacy. *Hor* becomes Horus, the Egyptian god of the New Aeon and the son of Osiris. Of additional interest is that Genghis Khan and his brethren were rather obsessed with falconry — it was their sacred bird. The falcon or the hawk was also sacred to Horus who was often portrayed as such. In his aspect as Monthu or Menthu, Horus was depicted specifically as a falcon or bull. Additionally, the ancient region of Tibet known as Kham corresponds to the Egyptian word *Khem*, the black powder which inspired the word *alchemy*.

All of the above is a lot to digest, but it is all true. The most conclusive aspect of all these synchronicities closes the case with regard to there being a firm association between the cultures of Egypt and Tibet. This was revealed to me as I happened to read in Madame Blavatsky's work that the word *Mon* is the secret name for the hidden god. Usually described by non-initiates as Amon or Amon Ra of the Egyptians, Mon is the ruler of the unseen processes of life, both positive and negative. We pay tribute to Mon every time we conclude a prayer by saying "amen".

There is even an entire occult book on this concept by Kenneth Grant. It is entitled *Aleister Crowley and the Hidden God*, but Grant uses the more common version of *Amoun* to describe this god. I do not know if Grant is aware of the hidden name Mon, but I have spoken to other esoteric people who do. They thought it was about time I found out.

Amon Ra was well known as the sun god of the Egyptians, but his secret counterpart, Mon, was the designation for the hidden sun, known throughout initiated worlds as the Black Sun.

30

THE SHENSI PYRAMIDS

Egypt is not only connected to ancient Tibet by namesakes, but by the physical locale of the pyramids themselves. Bruce Cathie, the famous New Zealand pilot and author, has observed that the dispersal of these pyramids at Shensi are similar to the placement of those along the Nile. Of considerably more importance is his observation that the number 16944 appears in the Great Pyramid of Giza and that there are 16944 minutes of arc between the longitude of the Great Pyramid and that of the tallest Shensi pyramid. He concludes that both the Tibetan and Egyptian pyramids were built by the same people.

It is said that China contains more mysteries than all the rest of the world put together. China, as a communist country, remains terra incognita to most of humanity. The pyramids at Shensi are a prime example. China has long had a history of secrecy as the name of the country itself shows. China derived its name from Emperor Chin Shih Huang. Just before his death in 212 BC, he ordered that all the books and literature relating to ancient China be destroyed. This included all history, physical sciences, astronomy as well as the entire contents of the royal library. At that point, all real knowledge went underground to the lamaseries.

The October/November 1995 edition of *Nexus* magazine has an excellent article on the Shensi pyramids. It briefly describes the various kings who allegedly built them as well as the explorers who followed. Above all, we find that they have been shrouded in secrecy. The Chinese government has denied their existence, but Chinese archaeologists and officials have been known to own up to the truth when shown actual pictures of them. The article tells us that a US Air Force map depicting an area around the city of Xian (pop. 6,000,000) shows at least 16 pyramids. Xian was known as Sian-Fu in ancient times and was once the capital and center of the Chinese Empire.

In 1994, Hartwig Hausdorf and a party of travellers made their way to Xian in order to explore the pyramids. Standing atop one, Hausdorf was able to count twenty more pyramids in the immediate area. They were observed in October when the weather conditions made for very clear viewing.

The *Nexus* article also recounts the discovery of a white pyramid in China in 1948. This occurred when pilot James Gaussman was trying to reach his base in India after having dropped supplies off in China. After adjusting his course due to engine problems, he came around a mountain and was confronted by a huge pyramid in the valley below. It appeared white and was thought to be constructed of metal or stone with a jewel-like capstone on top. He took pictures and turned it over to military intelligence. Author Brian Crowley would eventually recover the photo· and publish it in his book *The Face on Mars*. The only extensive information about the white pyramid that I am aware of exists in a German book *Die Weisse Pyramide* (The White Pyramid) which, to the best of my knowledge, does not have an English translation at this point in time.

The idea of a white pyramid is most apropos when we begin to consider what all the secrecy was about in the Shensi area. After all, it has been going on for centuries. In itself, Tibet is filled with enough mysteries to fill an entire library. These include stories of caves which contain monks who meditate and project thought forms that travel across the world and act as "The Seeing Eye" as was described in *The Montauk Project*. These caves allegedly lead to the inner Earth and the lost realm of Thule or Agartha. There are also stories of levitation and materialization. And do not, of course, forget the abominable snowman, a "cousin" to Montauk's beast known as "Junior". The legends go on adinfinitum.

One of the less popular mysteries of Tibet concerns the Nazis and their interest in the region. When they scoured the area, the Nazis were looking for ancient knowledge. The arcane tablets the Nazis sought contained information. The best these tablets could

THE GREAT PYRAMID OF SHENSI
Above is an aerial photograph of the largest of the
Shensi pyramids in China. It is the largest pyramid in the world.
The Chinese government has tried to keep these pyramids a secret.

do was unlock the secrets of consciousness. Although they do not guarantee instant enlightenment, the tablets reveal secrets of how to obtain a powerful consciousness. What the Nazis wanted with this consciousness was the power it brought to them.

This power equates to subjugation of the morphogenetic grid and the thought processes which determine evolution. It is a step towards reaching the God force which the Nazis recognized, the same as the ancients, as the Black Sun. In an extreme and negative version, this subjugation of the grid would include a concept like the "thought police". The geopolitics of Karl Haushofer was only one aspect of controlling the grid. There were far more subtle aspects at play, particularly in the Asian theater and, more specifically, in Tibet. One specific tale concerns the Nazis mining a secret substance that would prolong life and act as a superconductor to higher states of consciousness. In their effort to attain and sustain power, the Nazis learned from these ancient tablets one of the most secretive and guarded alchemical formulas in the universe. According to this tale, the Chinese invasion of Tibet was instigated in no small part to restrict access to the mining of this substance and to nullify any zones of power that remained with the Nazis and their network. This could have been the mysterious "Tibetan oracle" at work.

The above is an interesting tale, and there is evidence to suggest such an alchemical formula and substance do exist. I have personally come to understand this by three methods. First, there is history and literature which alludes to this secret alchemical tradition. Second, it is part of an ancient occult oral tradition, some of which has been shared with me. Third, there is every indication to believe that the formula and substance can be scientifically substantiated. The complete scientific aspects are beyond the scope of this book and will require further research before I can render that sort of proof. What is of immediate interest to us all is that there is a tangential trail to the reality of a substance that can transmute consciousness. It has been a closely guarded secret, and I will focus on the legendary and historical aspects.

Although I discovered traces which indicate this substance exists in Tibet, I stumbled upon this secret as I researched the Nazis' pursuit of holy relics. These included the Holy Grail and, more specifically, the Ark of the Covenant.

31

THE ARK

Most people have come to know the Nazis' pursuit of holy relics through the "Indiana Jones" series of movies that were produced at Thorn E.M.I. Although these films are fanciful, they are based on legends and actual history, part of which are covered in this book. The Nazis themselves pursued these relics based upon countless romances, histories and literature dedicated to the subject. In addition to being well versed in occult lore, the top Nazis were members of lodges and societies that stretched further back into antiquity than common history will record.

One of the most popular traditions concerned King Arthur and the Knights of the Round Table. *Arthur* is derived from *Arcturus* or *Arktos*. *Arktos* literally means *bear* and because Ursa Major (the Constellation of the Bear which includes the Big Dipper), is in the northern sky, it also signifies that direction. *Bear* derives from *Bor* (the father of Odin) which is where the words *Hyperborea* or *borealis* derive. The word *Arcturus* itself means "bear guard".* It represents the "watch over the poles" which signifies vigilance over the morphogenetic grid.

Arthur's knights vigorously pursued the Holy Grail and suffered many obstacles. They sought out the Christ and were bedeviled by the Antichrist. These epic stories revealed the age old

---

* The term "bear guard" could also be construed to refer to the legend of the shape-shifting Viking Nordics who were said to turn into bears for battle. King Arthur performed the role of "bear guard" as he balanced the Knights of the Round Table by not permitting one to stand out above the others. In this aspect, he was a monitor and energy balancer.

forces of duality at work. Such tales were also the legacy of the tradition that passed through the Islamic empire and from the Knights Templars to the western world. The secret god was Baphomet, a coded word which meant "abbot or father of the temple of peace of all men". This definition was provided by Elphias Levi (who Aleister Crowley claimed was his previous incarnation) as a word that was a backward abbreviation for **"TEM**pli **O**mnium **H**ominum **P**acis **AB**bas". If you write the letters which are capitalized and bolded backwards, you will get the word *BAPHOMET*. This was an androgynous god with female breasts, goat horns and legs as well as cloven feet. Sometimes Baphomet is portrayed as donkey headed, a form which appears in Tibetan tales. The Templars sought out this "devilish" principle in order to bring in the Christ by honoring the Beast. To them, it was a formula produced by the mother of all, a force I have described as the Black Sun. It included both the Christ and the Antichrist.

The Nazis honored this ancient principle. Whether their motives were clean or not, they saw it as their only route to power: the goddess, a hidden tradition which was the mother of all things, including good and evil. The goddess is ultimately the only true tradition of power because it is where all power derives: the void of creation, a feminine symbol.

Through the Spear of Destiny and the Holy Grail, the Nazis pursued the power of Christ. Perhaps the best graphic example of the Christ energies meeting the Antichrist is in the movie *Raiders of the Lost Ark*. When the Nazis opened the Ark, angelic forces came out and manifested themselves. No sooner did they appear than the angels suddenly turned into horrific demons that consumed the flesh of all who witnessed them. Here were the forces of creation as well as those of destruction. It was an excellent depiction of the forces of nature.

The Ark obviously embraces the Hindu trinity where Brahma represents creation and Siva destruction. It is Vishnu, represented by Krishna in the human form, who balances these two extremes and brings about preservation. Krishna, in many traditions, is also identified as Christ. Thus, the Ark of the Covenant not only embraces the traditional Ten Commandments and the Jews but also the Christ consciousness. Both of these concepts are different ways of looking at the powers of Creation.

The Ark of the Covenant is one of the most supreme historical mysteries we have. While its powers and magical attributes
certainly fit into the legendary category, there is plenty of history
telling us that it actually did exist. Its whereabouts after the time of
King Solomon are shrouded with so many interesting stories and
legends that it gives rise to much wonder. If the object itself could
live up to the inspiration and mental excitement the legends
generate, one would indeed be faced by the very power of God.

Personally, I had never heard of the Ark until I saw *Raiders
of the Lost Ark* in the early 1980s. I had heard about Moses and the
tablets many years prior, but there was no mention of the Ark. The
story of Moses is usually told in a manner that would be rejected
by an intelligent mind. Moses is commonly portrayed as a "holier
than thou man" bent on telling people what they cannot do. When
you add the Ark to the story and throw Nazis into the pot, the soup
suddenly becomes considerably more interesting. Nevertheless, I
learned only a little about the Ark for the next decade. Finally, in
the course of my Montauk/Nazi research, I came across an obscure
book entitled *Emerald Cup — Ark of Gold: The Quest of Lt. Otto
Rahn of the Third Reich*. Written by Colonel Howard Buechner,
Emerald Cup attempts to trace the history of the treasure of
Solomon (which included the Ark of the Covenant) and how it
ended up in Nazi hands.

According to Buechner's research, the Ark remained with
the Jews from the time of Moses through the time of David. It was
often placed in a tent or sometimes put in a makeshift hiding place
at a moment's notice. When the Jews reached the acme of their
power under King Solomon, it was placed in the inner sanctum of
Solomon's Temple. After Solomon's reign, the power of the Jews
diminished, and the Ark was hidden in underground catacombs
beneath the Temple Mount. These catacombs, which are beneath
where the wailing wall stands today, were known as Solomon's
Stables. Before Solomon, the facility was a threshing center with
roots to ancient times.

Many times in the following centuries, the Jews and their
fortunes were ransacked, but the Ark was always successfully
hidden. This good fortune continued until 70 A.D. when Titus of
Rome did a wholesale slaughter of the Jews and their culture. He
is reported to have recovered the treasure of Solomon and brought

it back to Rome. The Arch of Titus still stands in Rome today in commemoration of his victory. Soon after Titus triumphantly returned to Rome, his father died. As his father was the Emperor of Rome, Titus took over as the lawful successor.

While it is not known for an absolute fact that Titus possessed the actual treasure of Solomon, Buechner cleverly explains that Rome manifested wealth beyond belief during the reign of Titus. If you read Roman history, you will discover that previous emperors like Caligula and Nero depleted the Roman treasury by indulging the crowds. They would import sands from Africa at horrendous costs just for the purpose of chariot races. This was done primarily to placate the masses and not to maintain a gambling empire, which would actually have cut the costs considerably. Importing wild animals for fights was also very expensive.

Solomon's treasure remained in Rome until Alaric, the Visigoth, laid seige to the city in 410 A.D. He took the entire treasure of Solomon's Temple with him which was believed to have included the Ark, the Holy Grail, the Harp of David and a vast array of other holy relics. The Visigoths brought the treasure to Carcaassone, located in the Languedoc province of southwestern France. The treasure was placed in the "Tomb of Hercules" near the Cathar fortress of Montsegur. Otto Rahn described the cavern where it rested as a natural cathedral consecrated to the Iberian god Ilhomder, God of the Sun:

> "Between two monoliths, one which had crumbled, the steep path leads into the giant vestibule of the cathedral of Lombrives. Between stalagmites of white limestone, between walls of a deep brown color and the brilliant rock crystal, the path leads down to the bowels of the mountain. A hall 260 feet in height served as a cathedral for the heretics."

There is some historical legitimacy to the Visigoths having the treasure of Solomon. When the Arabic commander Tarik conquered the Visigoths at Toledo in 711 A.D., he demanded the treasure of Solomon. According to this historical account, the Visigoths hid it near Montsegur where it remained until the successful mission of Otto Skorzeny.

By the time the Nazis had recovered this treasure, Otto Rahn had long since disappeared under mysterious circumstances. His resignation from the SS was put into a letter on February 20, 1939. It was granted, and he was gone by March 13th. His SS superior, General Wolff, issued a press release stating that Rahn died in a snow storm. It has been written that subsequent to his departure from the SS, Rahn established a mysterious order with connections in Holland, France and Switzerland. He is said to have received extensive plastic surgery before serving as Ambassador to Italy and eventually dying in 1975.

After Skorzeny's successful mission, the treasure made its way to Merkers where it was unloaded into an abandoned salt mine. Some of the items of this fabulous treasure were sent to Himmler at his castle in Wewelsburg. Part of it was hidden in the grottoes of Externsteine. It was said that Himmler actually possessed the Holy Grail itself. As the war came to a close, Merkers was captured by the Third U.S. Army under the Command of General George Patton. Much speculation and rumor has flourished concerning Patton's role in this endeavor. Some say it may have led to his premature "accidental" death. It is known that he personally inspected the mine with General Eisenhower and General Omar Bradley. A treasure worth $250,000,000 (over $3 billion by today's standards) was inventoried, but this was only the remaining treasure that had not already been shipped out. Buechner's research indicates that seven tons of gold were shipped to the Canary Islands by U-boats with much larger amounts going to South America.

There are other accounts of what became of the Ark of the Covenant. An entire book, *The Sign and the Seal*, has been penned on the subject by Graham Hancock. In this lengthy work, the author traces various esoteric symbols in the cathedrals of France and does extensive travelling, eventually ending up in war torn Ethiopia. It is here where he concludes the Ark resides to this very day. The fact that the country is politically unstable and a highly dangerous place lends some instant credibility to Hancock's thesis. If one wanted to hide holy relics from interested parties, a war like environment would be an ideal place. That Mussolini invaded Ethiopia gives one pause to wonder. Of further interest is Wild Bill Donovan's foray into Ethiopia. Before Mussolini had joined the Axis powers, Donovan met personally with Mussolini and got his personal permission to visit the front lines. What he accomplished or saw there is not known, but we do know that he unsuccessfully sought to use "the spear" for the logo of the OSS (see below).

All of the above gives added votes of credibility to the Ethiopian thesis. Of course, there is also the possible scenario that all of the above people have been led on a fantastic ruse. If you think about it, the situation becomes somewhat comical. Imagine a power that was always referred to as the Holy of Holies. Now, let your mind wander to the scene in *Raiders of the Lost Ark* when the Ark of the Covenant is opened. Etheric forms rose out of a creative vortex and literally overwhelmed those creatures in the immediate vicinity who chose to observe the spectacle. There is the implication in this search that if one obtained the true "Holy of Holies" that one would obtain the very power of the creator in the physical form. It cannot help but give rise to the ideas of war games that are

OSS INSIGNIA

In June 1943, William Donovan approved the above design to
be used by OSS personnel. Black was the background
because that color "is associated with activities which may be
performed under cover of darkenss". A gold spear was chosen because
"it is indicative of opening the way to subduing the enemy's
defenses". The proposal was turned down by the Joint Chiefs of Staff,
but 442 patches with this insignia were sent to London for use
by the Psychological Warfare Board in 1944.

really better suited for children's cartoons on Saturday morning.

I do not think there is much doubt that Mussolini, Donovan and Hancock sought the true Holy of Holies. They either desired the power it would give or were understandably intrigued by it. On the highest level, they all sought union with their creator. All may have come close, but none of them arrived at their ultimate goal.

We must remember that the Ark's primary service to us in terms of consciousness is as a metaphor for the truth. These people were pursuing a physical object. In this sense, they were looking for an exoteric means of power. This type of approach is notorious for nullifying the esoteric path and the consequent inward development of the individuals concerned. While I think it is highly instructive as well as intriguing to pursue the Ark in its historical context, it can be misleading.

It was with the above viewpoint in mind that I began my own investigation. Rather than retracing the entire history, I cut short the entire investigation by simply asking what exactly it was that was in the Ark. This seemed to be the big unasked question. In the movie (*Raiders*) produced at the studios of E.M.I. Thorne, I noticed there was powder in the Ark. Because of our religious indoctrination in the western world, most of us will humbly assume that these were the tablets of Moses that had been ground to dust. Again, this is a misleading form of thought.

According to the Jewish Talmud, there were two sets of tablets that Moses possessed. The first set were made of transparent sapphire and were "inscribed by the finger of God". The first tablets were referred to as the "Testimony" and were written by God, not Moses. According to the most popular traditions in our culture, these were the tablets Moses brought down from the mountain and broke in rage upon seeing people "doing nasties". Later on, at the instruction of God, Moses returned to Mount Sinai, but this time he wrote the Ten Commandments himself. When he returned with this second set of tablets, he was unbearable to look at with beams coming from his forehead. Later translations indicate these beams to be beams of light whereas earlier translations say that Moses had horns projecting out of his head.

What does all of this mean?

The above stories are an obvious reference to the esoteric aspects of what Moses had to teach. It is an analogy of humanity's initiation into the Holy Qabala which could only be presented by the Creator. The idea of ten commandments is actually representative of the ten sepiroth or spheres depicted in the Qabala. These are the ten emanations of existence and fit right into the formulas of sacred geometry. These are the esoteric lessons Moses had to teach and are represented by the first set of (sapphire or crystal) tablets. They are literally the laws of creation.

When Moses returns to the profane world, he is confronted by a lawless mob who cannot keep their hands off each other, let alone appreciate or understand the higher truths of existence. They are not about to understand the Qabala or much of anything else. In order to keep the mob at bay, Moses gives them restrictive laws so that they can be restrained from destroying themselves or others. With a mob like that, the politicians in the community could not even begin to think about what existed in the Holy of Holies. Mob control had become the first concern of the priesthood. This is represented by the second set of tablets which Moses writes himself. According to scripture, he is the author of the Ten Commandments and becomes known as the law giver. Thus, an esoteric tradition of secrecy is born accompanied by an exoteric tradition of restraining the masses from creating unmanageable chaos or destruction.

The above further clarifies the esoteric tradition of Moses and tells us that he possessed many secrets. It does not, however, explain what was in the Ark itself. The Bible and other scripture remains vague. There is a tradition in the esoteric path that if you ask a question, you will most certainly get an answer. In this case, I got two. I was told that the substance in the Ark was *occultum*. Another source said *irriculum*. The two words came from two different sources but neither disagreed on the nature of what was being described. The two words are simply synonyms. I was also told I would have a difficult time finding any written information on it. Although I only had the above clue to go on, I would find various hints to such a substance in different strains of literature. Remarkably, it has been identified as the same substance the Nazis were mining in Tibet.

32

WHITE GOLD & OCCULTUM

In *Pyramids of Montauk*, the schools of the Right and Left Eye of Horus were discussed. Their purpose was to conduct a series of initiations which would eventually fuse the crystalline structure of one side of the brain with the other. When one achieved this, a white powder of gold was secreted out of the forehead (third eye) during the initiatory rites. In this opening up of consciousness, a chemical process was taking place which was cascading hormones through the area of the body that corresponds to the third eye. A harmonic field was resonating between the participant, the energy field of his body and that of the Earth. The endocrine glands, corresponding to the chakras, were being opened, climaxing in the opening of the seventh seal. This resulted in the immersion of an actual isotope of white gold, the residues of which have been found in sarcophagi. This white gold has also been identified with the Golden Tear of Horus, elixir of the gods or manna from heaven.

It was this white gold which contained a property referred to as occultum by Crowley, Blavatsky and others. According to tradition, this substance was literally in the Ark of the Covenant itself. This same tradition tells us that Moses knew the use of occultum and escaped from mother Egypt with this knowledge as well as with the Ark. As Moses wandered in the desert with his hordes, he was passed by the armies of the Aryan Hittites who were engaged in a conquering spree. Moses and the Hebrews appeared to be harmless nomads and were left alone, but the Egyptians were dealt with in a far more severe manner. When the Hittites reached

249

Egypt, they conquered the entire region and killed off what was left of the priesthood. The technology of occultum fell into disuse save for Moses who passed down his knowledge to the Hebrew leaders. These secrets remained guarded in the hands of the Hebrews until the time of the building of the Temple of Solomon. This edifice was constructed by Hiram Abiff, a man who is considered to be the first Mason.* Hiram possessed the knowledge of sacred geometry and put his many secrets into the building of the temple. He was murdered during the work and this has been ritualized by the Masons ever since. From that time onwards, the use and secrets of occultum have remained the province of the secret societies.

The secrets of occultum were no small part of what the Nazis were seeking when they broke into all of the Masonic temples in Germany and acquired every piece of information they could get their hands on. For the masses, the Nazis set up one of the main Masonic temples in Germany as a museum. In this manner, they showed the public the vast network of Masons throughout the world who allegedly conspired against humanity. Of course, no information was revealed about higher level Masonic activity and what really went on in terms of alchemy. This veil of duplicity enabled the inner circle of Nazis to acquire what they could without making the public suspicious. This is just routine politics. From this behavior, one gets a glimpse of how wars and political squabbles work on a much deeper and more esoteric level than one would ever perceive from reading the newspapers. The Nazis exemplify this principle more than anyone else in modern times.

Occultum fits into the above mystery puzzle very well because it is by its very nature "secret". It is even sometimes referred to as the "stealth atom". This is because it contains processes that are unseen and unsuspected by normal observation methods. One of the reasons for this is that occultum is, in a sense,

---

* The esoteric name for Hiram Abiff is Adonis or Adonai, the latter of which is considered to be the most awesome or holy aspect of god. It refers to the power of creation. In this aspect, the murder of Hiram is the murder of the Creative Principle itself. When we consider the intrigue of Masonic Lodges, there is an implication they are dealing with the hidden powers of creation that have remained unavailable to mankind. Although most Masons don't have a clue about what is written in this footnote, those at the highest levels are sometimes used by forces which seek to harness these very powers of creation.

a prototype for matter as we know it. It is another name for antematter which is quite different from the similar sounding "antimatter". Antematter refers to matter which exists in an a priori state to what we commonly know as matter. It is a prestate or precursor to matter itself.

In ancient times, when we consider the legacy of the Elder Race or Elohim, consciousness was in a higher state than before "The Fall of Man", of which the story of Adam and Eve is the metaphor. Matter itself was not in the dense and irreversible form we know it today. All metaphysical or esoteric doctrines mention this as well as the descent of spirit into matter. In that original state of consciousness, life had a different biochemical relationship with matter than it does today.

Next, we have to consider the life force itself and how it enters matter. By tracing the spirit through physicality, we see that it emerges in the DNA and RNA. This is not really new information, but it has been seriously understated and cannot be emphasized enough. DNA and RNA are the bridge between consciousness and matter. Occultum, which is Latin for hidden, acts as a superconductor between matter and the life force. It is the gateway to influencing matter by enabling one, under the right circumstances, to consciously enter the atom.

This is easy to understand if you imagine an example of the blueprint room for the physical universe. First, the draftsman made up the hydrogen atom with all its specific properties. Next came the helium atom and thus the elements in the entire periodic table were filled out. The blueprint room itself represents the creation zone at its highest level. It is also linked to zero time in that this creation zone is outside of three dimensional space and time. As the various atoms began to interact in the third dimension, random activity occurred in a spontaneous fashion. Into this mix, the life force began to permeate matter and carry out designated agendas with respect to the various characteristics of life itself.

When L. Ron Hubbard released his book *Dianetics: The Modern Science of Mental Health*, he noted that there is a trace memory in each cell. This is now commonly accepted in all walks of psychology and science. The occultists always knew it. It now turns out that science has accepted that atoms themselves have a trace memory that tells their entire history. It is only common sense if you stop and think about it. Everything in this universe leaves a trace or encryption that can be decoded. Occultists always knew this as well, but we can see it very clearly in our modern computer technology. It is now a truism that even the most severely crashed hard disk can be recovered by some computer guru somewhere who prides himself on this very task. Anything can be decoded and explained if you know how to go about it.

In the example of the blueprint room above, the physical universe could be said to have been set in motion when Adam decided to leave his job as a draftsman and explore what was outside. Somewhere along the line, the ability to trace one's way back to the blueprint room was lost. In other words, he went into a virtual reality hologram arcade and could not come back to his original reality. Intelligent observation will demonstrate that there have been plenty of operations from the blueprint room, or a rival one, ever since. These are the miracles of history. Unfortunately, life as a whole is mired in physicality and in too many cases has lost its memory and continuity of itself. We see this in the slums, but even there, a resiliency and fighting spirit can still be found if you know where to look for it. No matter how far life is beaten down, it has the residual qualities that will enable it to rectify itself or the greater whole.

Occultum is a bridge between the blueprint room and physical matter itself. If you consider computer technology again, you will realize that there are always better and faster ways of storing and transferring data at lightning speed. The limits are only determined by the users and the designers. Occultum is no different. Its most spectacular use would be the complete rearrangement of a physical death or deformity as occurred with Lazarus or the leper. What occurs is largely determined by the person who uses occultum or the principles thereof.

Before I say anything further, I should add that one does not need occultum to do the above things. As a spiritual being, there are no absolute limitations as to what you can or cannot do. The principle at play here is that when one transcends the physical plane and is granted carte blanche access to the blueprint room, one begins to manifest the occultum or white gold in one's physical body. Jesus alluded to this in a statement attributed to him: "I have sustenance (sometimes "meat" is translated) you know not of."

There are obviously varying degrees of all this. The goodness or badness of what ensues in the physical plane is dependent upon the intent of the various individuals involved in the process.

These superior abilities to which I have alluded signified an ancient time when the collective consciousness, symbolized by the priesthood, had a mastery of the physical laws because they were working at a sub strata of the physical plane. As consciousness began to descend into matter in the days of old, it lost its natural ability to reach the blueprint room on a routine basis. It is sort of like losing the access code to your bank account. Gradually, occultum began to be utilized as a vehicle for ordinary survival in day to day living on the Earth plane. Such as we use air to breathe, they used occultum as a means to maintain self-referential aware-ness and immortality in a physical universe scenario that had, and still does, severe limitations. This was the scenario in which the Elder Race found itself when it moved to Earth. They were not only attempting to preserve their physical life but their self-referential awareness as well. This was why the Elder Race eventually chose the land of Egypt in which to settle. Amidst the cliffs of Abydos, near ancient Thebes, they found the minerals and chemicals readily available with which to process occultum.

One of the oldest names for Egypt is Kam, Kamt or Qemt, words which mean black or dusky. Some scholars believe this name was applied because the color of the mud on the Nile is very dark. From our studies, we can also see a correspondence between the above names with Kham in Tibet. The actual reason Egypt was referred to as "black" was for the occultum they were mining in the cliffs of Abydos. This mountainous area in southern Egypt is renowned for the black alkaloid it contains in its soil. When there was a flood, the black soil would wash down into the Nile. According to the Egyptian scholar Budge, the early Christians called this land "Kheme" and passed it on in this form to the Greeks, Romans, Syrians and Arabs. The latter added the article "Al" and the land became known as "Al-Khemeia" which is the precursor of our own word alchemy.

Budge, who is recognized as the quintessential scholar on Egypt, informs us that the Egyptians were famous for their metallurgy and were known to produce transmuted metals. They used quicksilver and other processes in order to produce gold and

253

silver. He also tells us that most of this gold and silver were produced by separating it from its native ore. Additionally, these processes resulted in a "black" powder substance which was supposed to possess marvellous powers as well as contain the individual properties of the various metals. He then gives us the following quote:

"In a mystical manner this black powder was identified with the body which the god Osiris was known to possess in the underworld, and to both were attributed magical qualities, and both were thought to be sources of power and life".

While the above reeks of superstition, it also serves as an analogy for a scientific process that is actually taking place. But Budge is either ignorant of this process or, less likely, deliberately obscuring it and gives us no information. He informs us that as metal working grew in prominence, it was believed, mostly by lower classes and foreigners, that magical powers existed in fluxes and alloys. The art of working metals, manipulating them and the knowledge of their physical content and supposed mystical power became known as "Khemeia". This term also came to refer to the preparation of the black ore or powder which was considered the elixir or active principle in the transmutation of metals. Hence, we have the term *black magic*. Originally this word signified neither evil or malevolence. It was merely used to connote the procedure whereby one could get back to the blueprint room.

What Budge did not tell us is that gold, when placed against this certain black ore found in Abydos, would be transmuted, by nature of the superconductivity present, into a powdered form. The metal, simply placed against this soil, would simply and suddenly transform into a powder. While this sounds rather magical in itself, keep in mind that all chemical reactions seem so. Normally, this type of metal work required a fire process. Somewhat remarkably, the chemical constituents of the native soil of Abydos provided a more natural way to accomplish such.

The key ingredient at work in the above equation is the principle of superconductivity. This allows for a completely uninhibited flow of electrons as well as the "particle" constituents of antematter. In the case above, the gold reverts to a powdered natural form. As we are dealing with an unseen process, the substance is called "occultum" which, as was already mentioned, means hidden. The occultum allows for the rearrangement matter on the atomic level.[*]

The ancient science that was used with occultum was based upon the nobler or subtle aspects of man conveying energy to the lower aspects. There is always some way for the lower to reach the higher or vice versa. In the case of occultum, it allowed the white powder gold to manifest.

In the mystery school of Horus, the initiate was primed so that the constituents of his own system acted as the superconductor. Ingesting the powdered gold itself or any of the platinum group metals (it is the superconductivity that is important as opposed to the actual metal or element itself) could accelerate this process. The white gold was a symbolic or residual effect of the fact that fusion between the right and left hemispheres (infinite and finite, respectively) of the brain had occurred. That the white gold also acted as a supreme superconductor in itself for the same purpose was a living testament to what had taken place: a communication with the principles of Creation.

---

[*] In these prestates of matter or antematter, you have a geometric shape that underlies the physical atom. In the case of element number one, hydrogen, you have one "moon" or electron circling the nucleus. It is actually emanating from the center of the nucleus which is generating an entire spherical field of energy. For those who are gifted, this prestate of matter can be viewed as a trine of six, in other words: 666. This would manifest, for example, as three octahedrons (with six points each). The octahedron is also the shape of the Delta-T antenna and would represent a witness to the prestate of matter.

A geometric shape serves as a wave guide or antenna, allowing information to pass if attuned to the correct frequency. There is an exact frequency resonant with each geometric shape which really amounts to a secret science of alchemists or the governments. On a subatomic level, the frequencies which pass through these (unseen by normal measuring systems) geometric shapes can be considered the point where a wave becomes a particle. The contemplation of where a wave becomes a particle is a meditative technique in its own right. In the above case, the wave represents information which is converted into a particle which resides in the atom itself. In this manner, the constitution of the matter concerned is itself changed.

It should be noted that it is common scientific knowledge that ordinary superconductors are constructed of atoms in a geometric crystalline lattice structure. It is not commonly considered that the atoms (that make up the lattice structure) also contain geometric grids themselves. The shapes are similar to those lines which make up the Earth's grid and require means other than ordinary human perception to ascertain they are there. Both could conceivably be measured by human means, but that is a rarefied science in itself.

There was also an interesting side effect reported with regard to the consumption of occultum and the spiritual and physical transformation that went along with it. It turned the skin blue.

33

THE BLUE RACE

There is an ancient oral tradition concerning a race of blue skinned people who were not originally indigenous to this planet. According to some accounts, this race corresponds to the Elder Race from Mars which was described in *Pyramids of Montauk*. The blue quality of their skin was akin to the dark blue color you will see in a human vein. In Madame Blavatsky's scheme, this Blue Race would fit into the tail end of the Third Root Race.

This oral tradition was handed down to the Aryan Race with stories about blue skinned deities. In artistic renditions, the god Krishna was depicted with blue skin which is an attempt by these Aryan descendants to identify him with their lineage. There have also been various examples of the descendants of this ancient race painting themselves blue so as to emulate their ancestors or associated deities. This even extends to present day Celtic rituals where participants are painted blue.

The blue paint is actually symbolic of an ancient ritual which concerned the production of occultum within the physical body. There is a precise chemical reaction within the blood which produces cobalt. The most spectacular effect of this process would actually give the skin a blue hue. This blue effect was reported by both the Picts and Druids, but the knowledge originated with the Elder Race.

All of the above is a specific reference to the concept of "blue blood" in royalty. It also explains the French expression "Sacre bleu" or sacred blue. The words *blue, blood* and *blessing* are all linked phonetically.

Further testimony to the existence of the Blue Race can be observed in the reported phenomenon of certain Rh negative babies who, shortly after birth, turn blue (or sometimes different colors). As these babies are perceived to lack enough oxygen to sustain life, modern medical technology typically orders bloods transfusions to oxygenate the blood. Although this is common knowledge, we have to ask what is really happening here?

Rh negative babies lack the normal amount of iron in their blood compared to normal Earth babies. Instead, they have a higher amount of copper. When copper oxidizes, it turns blue. When irons oxidizes in the blood, it turns red. Rh negative babies born on Earth find themselves in an oxygen rich world that is not indigenous to their biochemistry.

My own personal intuition tells me that this above anomaly in the biochemistry in Rh negative individuals may have something to do with the element thulium. I have since learned from a scientist that thulium can form what is called a "basic oxide". This essentially means that it is soluble with water and when mixed with such, it becomes an oxide. This means that thulium could conceivably oxygenate the blood. It should be pointed out that when most rare earth metals are turned into oxides, the oxygen atoms are not susceptible to bonding with other molecules. There are a few exceptions and thulium could be a perfect fit. As the rare earth metals have many different and complex properties, it is not a particularly cut and dry case. As this point seems to be on the cutting edge of scientific knowledge, I hope that someone in the reading audience can share additional information on this point. The entire prospect certainly adds credence to the psychic reading I was given by my friend Deanna.

There is also a substance in the blood of some life forms called hemocyanin, a blue, oxygen carrying blood pigment which contains copper. This is primarily found in crustaceans, mollusks and insects. A more precise scientific definition indicates that hemocyanin is actually a colorless copper solution containing pigment that is converted by oxygen in to blue oxyhemocyanin. This is the scientific proof that copper based blood can turn blue in the presence of oxygen.

There is tremendous irony when we consider the prospect of shell fish having copper based "blue blood". Orthodox Jews follow a rule against eating shell fish because, as scavengers, these creatures are considered to be the lowest form of life. While historians would probably tell you that this rule is based upon a bad batch of ancient shell fish, the information about blue bloods gives us a whole new perspective. It is as if the Orthodox teachings are outright rejecting the Aryan idea of the copper based blue blood. This implies that there are different genetic agendas between the Jews and the Aryans. Of course, this last point is a synchronicity and should not be taken seriously. My research indicates that the Jewish people have many blue bloods amongst them as well. The difference is one of doctrine.

Further irony in these matters can be found in the etymology of the word *hemoglobin*, the red pigment which is found in blood. It carries oxygen from the lungs to the tissues. The word *heme*, which specifically signifies the part of the hemoglobin molecule that contains the iron based pigment, derives from *hem* which in turn is said to derive from *kem*. Here, we are back to *Kheme,* the land in Egypt where occultum occurs naturally. The phrase "to hem in" suddenly takes on a new meaning. It is as if we are being hemmed in by iron based red blood instead of consciousness raising copper blood.

When we talk about the original Blue Race itself, we are talking about history that is very ancient. Consequently, there are not too many reference points or recognizable flag posts by which we can describe it or even relate to it. But, we are left with very specific legends and expressions in our language. Many different peoples have aspired to the reputed knowledge and ascendancy of the Blue Race. At some point, the Elder Race was confronted with the prospect of mixing its blood with the indigenous Earth races. As can be easily imagined, this racial mixture resulted in cross currents and different problems. This is the point where you might have a religion such as the Jews forbidding the cultivation of copper based blood. As life evolved over the next millennia, ineffective caste systems were developed which served no one's interest in the long run. It only degenerated the Earth's grid.

Through tradition, ancient wisdom was passed down through a hierarchal system which dispensed knowledge to those who appeared worthy. These ancients saw the cataclysm of the dark yuga coming, and it was their intention to protect the knowledge as well as not letting it fall into the hands of those who would misuse it. Eventually, the caves of Tibet were a refuge. The monasteries became custodians of the knowledge.

As things "de-evolved" from this ancient Blue Race, two separate mystery schools evolved. Each had their own outlook with regard as to what supports the mental grid work of evolution. The schools that sprang up in Tibet supported the idea that everyone has to evolve until the last soul emerges out of the dark yuga. This is the same idea that not one soul can rest until everyone has reached Nirvana or the like. On the upside, this particular doctrine embraces the whole. On the downside, it negates the individual and can result in one feeling as if he is not too important. This can lower the morale and inspire apathy in the greater body of people.

The other school came from the same source as the Tibetan, but this group settled in Egypt, the ancient name for which was *To-Mera*. This name is an obvious derivation from Mount Meru. The doctrine that arose in Egypt was focused on longevity and immortality. They sought this through the science of chemistry. Complete immortality was not always the goal. They might desire a human vehicle for a millennium or two. When the imprinting of the DNA changed with the next zodiacal age, an individual might want to pick up a new vehicle. As this practice is very lofty, you can imagine that it was not open to every individual who passed by the pyramids. The early Egyptians sought to master all the laws of the physical so as to obtain a higher consciousness. That they did this through the use of occultum has already been suggested. The most convincing information I have found for this entire prospect can be evidenced in one of Egypt's most famous legacies: their mummies.

34

THE CURSE OF THE MUMMY

During the time of Napoleon, interest began to emerge with regard to the historical context and purpose of mummification. People were puzzled as to why there were never any mummies found from the predynastic period. The not so obvious answer, which history points to but does not overtly state, is that the mummies were ground up and consumed for the chemical constituents they possessed. I am specifically referring to occultum.

Napoleon himself got into the act as soon as he rose to power. His first object of conquest was Egypt. After defeating the local Islamic government, he entered the King's Chamber of the Great Pyramid on August 12th and wanted to be alone. This is in the history books. What happened in the King's Chamber on August 12th is still a mystery, but we know that it effected him profoundly. He refused to talk about it immediately afterwards. On his deathbed, he almost brought it up, but dismissed it and told the person at his bedside "you wouldn't believe me anyway".

Aside from his more known exploits, Napoleon had a significant occult background though not too much is written about it. The name *Napoleon* gives us our first clue. The name literally means "Lion of Naples". The area in Italy where Naples is located is known for its high percentage of natives who possess RH negative blood. As was explained in *Pyramids of Montauk*, RH negative means that no rhesus monkey factor is in the genes and there is strong reason to believe the blood type did not originate on this planet. This suggests Napoleon, who happened to be born from a noble Corsican family, was himself a blue blood.

Napoleon's native language was Italian and he later learned French. His father sent him to the academy of Brienne at the age of nine where he was the first one to receive a scholarship for impoverished nobility. At Brienne, the students were taught a curriculum directed by St. Germaine, the French Minister of War. The source book for the history course was René Vertot's *History of the Knights of Malta*. The above clearly demonstrates that Napoleon had occult forces working on him. He was also said to show a strong interest in the Spear of Destiny and his beloved wife, Josephine, was the last of a line of female Masons.

The above leads us to speculate that Napoleon experienced the use of occultum in the Great Pyramid. While we have no historical record, it is known that this substance was ingested by initiates who went inside the King's Chamber. It is not really important to prove that Napoleon used occultum, but he could not have been ignorant of it.[*] At that time, ground up mummies had been consumed for the occultum they possessed for at least four hundred years.

Around the year 1400 A.D., the Latin word *mummia* started to appear in English writings. Mummia actually means "mummy powder" which began to find popular use in the early 1200's as a cure all medicinal powder. Shakespeare wrote about it, and Francis Bacon recommended it "for the staunching of the blood". Most physicians prescribed it as a potent cure for different diseases. As the centuries moved on, there was a major run on mummies. The Egyptians finally cracked down on the practice. They not only wanted to preserve their antiquities but their own use of mummy dust as well.

If one reads the historical accounts of "mummy dust", the authors appear to be exasperated over this "barbaric practice". It is quite clear they do not have a full grasp on the entire situation. It is preposterous to think that surgeons prescribed it for hundreds of years out of sheer superstition. There was obviously some

---

[*] According to the testimony of a reader, Napoleon was taken by the French to Amagansett, just a few miles from Montauk. As this occurred during his final exile on the island of St. Helena, the British went into an uproar. Napoleon was returned to St. Helena where he was eventually poisoned. This information came from a Sunday news magazine, but the reader has not yet been able to locate a copy.

unknown principle at work (occultum) allowing the communication channels in the body to open up so that healing could occur.

One historian wrote that mummy dust really means bitumen, a resinous mineral pitch. It was from a mountain in Persia called *Mummia* that bitumen oozed out of the cracks in rocks. It was thought that the black pitch in mummies was in fact bitumen. Mummia or bitumen was not abundant in its natural state and was so valuable that it was guarded continually and stored in the Royal Treasury. The historian further concludes that "the loathesome practice would never have gotten started if people had known how mummies were really made." He explains that when mummy wrappings were initially investigated by western civilization, they were observed to contain black and resinous material. It was erroneously believed that this black substance was bitumen. It looked like bitumen so it must be bitumen. This alleged "error" is supposed to explain 700 hundreds years use of mummy dust — all on a simple misunderstanding!

Bitumen is defined as asphalt in its natural state or mineral pitch. The word *asphalt* literally means "to keep from falling". If bitumen has healing properties, or perhaps even those of occultum, this implies the fall of man from the Garden of Eden. The idea of mineral pitch is also quite interesting because it brings Noah and the Ark to mind. For those of you who do not remember, Noah used pitch for preserving the ark. Esoterically, the Ark of the Covenant and Noah's Ark are one and the same object. The use of "pitch" not only refers to occultum but to maintaining the consistency and preservation of the DNA (symbolized by the pairing of animals in the Bible).

The authors who criticize the barbaric use of mummy dust are ignorant of the line of research I am talking about. They are not totally off base however because mummy trading became a notorious and disreputable practice. As mummies became scarce, people began to manufacture them from recently dead bodies. The use of mummy dust fell into disrepute while true mummy dust became scarce. Mummy dust disappeared from medicine in the late 1800s. At that point, the British founded a school of medicine in Cairo where two great caches of royal mummies were brought from Thebes. The subject of mummy dust became a trade secret and was only accessible to a noble elite.

There are academic disputes as to whether mummies actually contained bitumen. Early history and legends indicate they did. Later history, when the mummies were scarce, is more skeptical. The obvious answer, as well as being a key secret of the Egyptian Book of the Dead, is that the mummies contained the black powder occultum. Occultum and bitumen both possess healing properties, but their exact use and interrelationship in the mummification process calls for further study. It is apparent however that the early Egyptologists called it bitumen because they concluded that it was. They had no means of scientific proof that we know of.

When most people think of the *Egyptian Book of the Dead*, they get confused and fall asleep. It is primarily unintelligible gobbledygook. Its most popular translator is Budge who was clearly ignorant of the above tradition and research I have shared with you. The secrets concerning the *Book of the Dead* have been kept hidden throughout history by a select group or brotherhood. Common history itself will tell you that the early grave robbers were a guild all to themselves. They passed down their trade from family to family and tended to specialize in robbing the tombs of royalty as well as wealthy individuals. They knew there was certain lineages which possessed a greater saturation of occultum in their system. These lineages were more geared towards the priesthood and royalty where the inherent biochemistry and genetics of the family would be predisposed toward the production of occultum in their system. These lineages trace their roots so far back into antiquity that there is no written record.

The above information is still very much recognized today by certain families who live in Cairo and the surrounding area. They are the indigenous Egyptians who are not part of the establishment but simply observe the abomination of what was done to their ancient culture and way of life. They have suffered a fate similar to that of the Native American cultures. These people know about occultum because it is their heritage. These Egyptians have also been pursued by the Nazis and other politically oriented factions since time immemorial. It is nothing new to them. They cannot advertise their concern. Egypt is still very much under the influence of the old Nazi guard to this very day.

It now becomes more apparent why Egypt has been so tightly controlled and why Otto Skorzeny moved his military prowess into the area after World War II. Occultum is not only utilized in an unseen process, it is an unseen commodity on the world's black market. There are those in the world who ingest it for longevity as well as for continuity of memory. In some scenarios, it can become a grisly subject.

Tibet was no different. In fact the mining of this ore in Asia is reported to have taken place at a much greater rate than the consumption of mummies. Here arises the communist invasion of Tibet and the severe restrictions on travellers entering the caves or other depositories of sacred knowledge.

The fact that this substance was readily available in Tibet is easily substantiated when we examine the Chinese "herb" known as *shilajit*. Although it is referred to as an herb, *shilajit* is really a mineral which resembles and smells like asphalt. It is extracted from the black, greasy rocks in the Himalayas and is consumed in its natural state by rats and monkeys. The locals pulverize the rocks and boil them until a film rises to the top of the solution. The film is removed, dried in the sun and boiled in a different herb mixture known as triphala from which a paste is formed. The paste is then dissolved in water so that one can drink it. With a strong iron content, *shilajit* is good for the bones as well as the kidneys.

Tibet's secrets have always been well hidden if for no other reason than geography alone. Politics now make the pursuit of this impossible. The strategy completely restricts the knowledge or mining of occultum.

It is not my intention to prove any of the above to you but simply to introduce you to some new concepts and a rich legacy in the history of mankind. There are so many esoteric legends that allude to this mysterious powder that it could not have been easily made up. If you want to look for the information, you can find it. There are also plans to do a more complete book on the subject in the future.

For now, the trail of occultum leads us back to our original departure point: Montauk. We begin to see an overall pattern taking place when we view the scene through one of Montauk's temporary residents: Aleister Crowley.

35

CROWLEY

Just prior to his trip to Montauk in 1918, Aleister Crowley engaged in a sexual magick experiment with Roddie Minor, a female chemist who he named "the Camel". In occult significance, "camel" refers to the Ark because it can carry things across the desert. It is a vehicle. According to the Bible, the camel was the animal that carried the Magi. Once again, the inextricable relationship of the Ark and Christ are manifest.

The most spectacular aspect of Crowley's work with Roddie Minor was that it enabled him to make contact with an extraterrestrial, an entity referred to as LAM. Crowley drew LAM's likeness as a "bubble headed grey alien". Certain authors in UFOlogy have cited that Crowley was ahead of his time in portraying this "alien" as one of the grays who have received so much attention in the media. Although none of these authors have yet identified Crowley's connection to Montauk, it is undeniable.

Crowley's work in this area still remains somewhat obscure, but beyond the shadow of a doubt, he has demonstrated himself to be at the forefront of an intriguing scenario. A historian from the OTO has informed me that Crowley wrote diaries while at Montauk but that he has only been able to turn up one significant piece of information with regard to this. The historian says that Crowley mentioned in his notes that he was going to visit the "Montauk clairvoyants", but no further entries were reported.

Crowley's work with LAM not only links to Montauk but to all of the various themes I have offered in this entire book. This begins with the idea that LAM is a praeter human intelligence, just as occultum is praeter matter. LAM is actually an archetypal subconscious factor that exists deep within our mental structure. It is linked to the blueprint room I referred to earlier. Magicians in the past have referred to that blueprint room as *R'lyeh*, a region which contains the sleeping or hidden god *Cthulu*. In *Cthulu*, the C is silent and the word is pronounced "Tooloo", a direct reference to Thule. All of the gods within R'leyh are known as the Forgotten Ones which is another name for the Elder Gods or Elder Race. This can be extended as well to the Blue Race. LAM is therefore a guardian at the gateway to the hidden god which reaches us through the deepest aspects of our psyche. LAM links back in time as a representative of the Elder Race.

The concept of the Forgotten Ones was popularized by H.P Lovecraft who, at the very least, demonstrated remarkable intuiition when he wrote about these praeter human intelligences buried deep within the subconscious. Lovecraft was also known for his strange association with the Nazis as well as some of Crowley's contemporaries. For the official record, Lovecraft was simply a writer. If he was something more, like a practicing magician, his writing certainly shows signs of it. There are legends and stories of time travel associated with Lovecraft, but that is another subject.

When we consider the Tibetan connection, it is interesting to note that Crowley defines LAM as the Tibetan word for way or path. The implication is that LAM is the way back home. While this is not incorrect, there is an even more apropos definition that corresponds to LAM.

While researching the work of Budge, the famous Egyptologist, my attention was perked when he referenced a book called *The Swastika* by Thomas Wilson. Budge said Wilson's book was the most exhaustive and authoritative work ever compiled on the swastika. *The Swastika*, a book written in 1898, was not easy to find. My curiosity was understandably aroused over the fact that the author was a Wilson.

It turned out that Thomas Wilson, in the course of his work as a curator for the Smithsonian Institute, had assembled all the artifacts and information he could gather on the swastika. He found that it was a truly universal symbol that was basic to all mankind. Artistic depictions of it extended all the way across the orient to the

L A M

Artist's version of LAM. In the traditional version by Crowley, LAM
is portrayed with his eyes almost closed. The above portrait
symbolizes a new awakening of consciousness.

native Americans. The swastika was most conspicuous in Tibet and China where it designated a whorling motion or a vortex of creation. As it signifies "the source of", the definition not only implies, but directly refers to the concept of a black sun (as the black void of creation).

Even more interesting was Wilson's definition of the Tibetan word *lama*, commonly thought to designate a guru or religious leader. Although lamas are often considered monks, Tibetans do not consider them to be one and the same. Wilson's scholarship revealed that the word lama was originally pronounced "lamh" where the "h" was silent. Here we arrive at the identical phonetic sound of Aleister Crowley's LAM. Wilson additionally points out that *lamh* or *lama* means cross and equates it to the swastika. Where we have the Christian cross with Jesus saying "I am the way", Crowley defines LAM as "the way" or "the path". When we have the way or path becoming the "cross" or swastika, we have the "key to it all" referred to in the Book of the Law. This key, in actual fact, refers to the geometric unfoldment of existence and the source of all creation as coming from a black void or regenerative process as exemplified in the female. Again, we have the concept of the Black Sun. Although there are many other meanings for the Black Sun, all the definitions derive from the idea that power stems from the void of creation itself. It does not need to be made any more complex than that.

More common definitions of the swastika also include "good", "bon" or "benediction". The "su" in the Sanskrit word *suasti* means source. When you add "ka", you have *suasti-ka* or *swastika*, meaning source of the spirit or source of the good spirit.

All of the above gives us an interesting correspondence as follows: LAM = lama = lamh = cross = swastika = source = Black Sun = Hidden God = Mon.

I discovered an even more remarkable synchronicity to these correspondences after I had finished the initial draft of this book. I found a Tibetan tour guide which indicated that the greatest and most colorful festival in all Tibet was known as the Mönlam festival. It was held annually until 1959 when the Chinese prohibited it. The festival was resurrected, in a diluted form, in 1986 and has been held annually ever since. According to history, the Mönlam festival was instituted in the early 1400s by Tsongkhapa, a lama whose tradition and successorship is outside the clerical hierarchy of the Dalai Lama.

A Tibetan monk has relayed to me that the Mönlam festival is similar to what we know as Mardi Gras. It is quite festive with monks and pilgrims pouring in from all over Tibet. While monks engage in philosophical debate, there are large sculptures made of butter and a huge statue of Maitreya (the second coming of the Buddha) is carried around by a procession. Mönlam follows the Tibetan New Year celebrations and begins on the fourth day of the first lunar month. The fact that the celebration concerns prayers, or the will, demonstrates yet another correspondence. The words themselves betray not only the Black Sun but the various synchronicities encountered in the Montauk phenomena.

We further learn from Kenneth Grant's cabalistic work that the word *Vril* fits into the above word equation where LAM = Mon. By using the Hebrew system of numbers, *Gematria*, Grant demonstrates that Vril corresponds to LAM. In his definition, Vril exists as a magical force set in motion by orgasm for the purpose of invoking beings or entities from outside.

The creatures from "the outside" include the deepest archetypes in our mind such as the Forgotten Ones or the Elder Race. These entities remember the ancient Blue Race and the principles of occultum for they were the ones who pioneered the operation. These elders are a trace memory in our very cells. Occultum is a known way to access this realm of consciousness back in the "blueprint room" as I have called it.

Of course, there is always the philosophical question of when an entity is a manifestation of an archetype in our subconscious and when it is independent in its own right. One should remember the Hindu doctrine that everything that exists is consciousness. Any being or creature that exhibits consciousness only does so because we allow it to, even if on a subconscious basis. Carl Jung's work demonstrated that man shares a collective subconsciousness. It is with recognition of this in mind that we need to work together to uncover the secrets of humanity's ancient legacy.

Crowley was chosen as initiate of these secrets and we see clear evidence of this in card number fourteen of his own Tarot deck. Entitled *Art*, we find across the top of the card an ancient alchemical phrase in Latin: "VISITA INTERIORA TERRAE

RECTIFICANDO INVENIES OCCULTUM LAPIDEM". This translates in English to "Visit the interior parts of the earth: by rectification thou shalt find the hidden stone". The initials for the above Latin make the word V.I.T.R.I.O.L. which means the Universal Solvent. Crowley also describes this as the Universal Medicine which is sometimes a stone, sometimes a powder and sometimes a tincture.

In his book *Liber LI: The Lost Continent,* Crowley gives us a clue how occultum was a factor in prehistory. This short book is about the history of Atlas, the true name for Atlantis. He reminds us that Atlas supported the ancient world by its moral and magical strength. Crowley then tells us that the root of the word *Atlas* is the Lemurian word *Tla* or *Tlas* which means black. "A" is the feminine prefix which is derived from the shape of the mouth when uttering the sound. Thus, Atlas means the feminine aspect of black. This not only corresponds to the land of Khem in Egypt, but the black virgin or black goddess. This also represents the Black Sun where it is viewed as the void of creation.

In what would sound more like a fiction novel to many people, Crowley describes many Atlantean words with their etymologies. The crux of the book and the entire civilization is a substance called ZRO, a type of phosphorus. Crowley describes it as follows:

"Phosphorus was a prime necessity of Atlas; however, it was not used in its red or yellow forms, but in a third allotrope, a blue-black or rather violet-black substance, only known in powder finer than precipitated gold, harder than diamond, eleven times heavier than yellow phosphorus, quite incombustible, and so shockingly poisonous that, in spite of every precaution, an ounce of it cost the lives (on an average) of some two hundred and fifty men."

It was the presence of phosphorous in DNA and RNA which originally led scientists to discover these two substances in the 1800s. As phosphorous does not occur in other substances or components of the cell, it was a "no brainer" for science to isolate it and then investigate further. Through his own studies and initiations, Crowley had already recognized that phosphorous played a key role in regards to spirit influencing matter.

Crowley also makes a curious comment when he describes Atlantis or Atlas: "the pavements were rough and broken almost

CROWLEY

everywhere for a reason which I am not permitted to disclose." It sounds suspiciously as if he is making a specific hidden reference to the asphalt properties of bitumen. The later culture would conceivably have dug up the pavement for its valuable properties.[*]

As Zro is produced, it goes through many stages with different properties. It can be in liquid or solid form, but it ends up being the diet of the Atlanteans. This is a direct reference to "manna from heaven". The process by which it is produced is involved and much more complex than, but similar to, the magical attributes possessed by the Ark of the Covenant.

The Atlantean civilization's entire purpose is the production and consumption of Zro. What they do not use for themselves is left for the priestly caste or magicians to experiment with. It possesses all the properties I have described of occultum yet more. Although Crowley says considerably more about Zro than I have included here, he openly states that he has but scratched the surface of its miraculous properties. Crowley goes on to identify Zro as not only the Universal Medicine but as "potable gold", thus leaving no doubt of its correspondence to occultum.

Ironically, the most negative aspect of the Atlantean civilization he describes is that the Zro is mined on the backs of a servile race who are treated like dirt and left to die in forced labor camps. It is just like the Nazi labor machine.

The procedures by which Zro is processed, and only partially described by Crowley, is well beyond the means of ordinary science to produce. It is also beyond the means of most humans to imagine. In it highest state of purity, Zro enables one to fly and manifest anything possible. It is as if one had a conduit straight to the blueprint room whereby one could alter matter or history in a moment. In its lower form, Zro would simply spark the life force. It could increase longevity and increase one's (psychic) perception of the universe around him.

---

[*] Ironically, a recent video of Atlantean ruins off the coast of Bimini revealed huge stone roads. Each and every stone was separated by about a foot and a half of space. The commentator mentioned this was an oddity as there was no asphault! On a separate note, it should be mentioned here that Jack Parsons reached the acme of his rocket career because of asphault. While watching roofers do their work, he realized asphault would enable a rocket to emit a slow burn and thus sustain itself. This not only enabled the solid fuel rocket to take shape but began the era of modern rocketry.

273

The prospect of occultum as a tool leaves us with some interesting points to ponder. First, we are talking about a substance which is supposed to put us more in touch with our spiritual aspects. At first glance, that would seem to be a contradiction in terms as spirit is usually perceived to be independent of matter. Actually, matter in any form is a product of consciousness which is akin to spirit. We are stuck with the material universe whether we like it or not. If we are to dissipate it, we are faced with the prospect of studying the conscious components of occultum or, if we deny that, a similar substance that would in effect have the very same properties.

At the same time that we contemplate the virtues of occultum, it is not wise to conceive ourselves as being dependent upon substances of an external nature to support our conscious condition. The key is obviously to evolve ourselves to the point where we can manifest occultum or whatever else we want. In this study that I have presented, we are being confronted with the creative powers of the universe and the soul. That is the real point. The study of occultum can give us insight into our own regenerative properties. It is that simple. It can, as well, conceivably be consumed in the same spirit as vitamins or minerals are by the body. Our main goal is to get back to the blueprint room by whatever means provided. The will is the senior factor.

It is with the above prospect on the horizon that I leave you, for now. Further work is required, but those stories are for another day. New journeys await.

EPILOGUE

In this book, I have traversed a wide panorama of subjects, locales and people. Each chapter could be the basis for an entire volume in an encyclopedic series. As I said in the beginning, the key string connecting all of the various aspects of this saga is the principle of synchronicity and the fact that the messages given to me were orchestrated from an outside force.

The above precept certainly made its way into my consciousness when I received a letter from a magical society in Europe whose interest had been aroused by the Montauk books. They had more questions than I had the time to answer, but one was particularly attention grabbing. These magicians wanted to know why I had not brought forth the cannibal connection to Montauk. Was it because it might be too much for my readers to stomach?

While I personally choose not to focus on the more grisly aspects of Montauk or the occult, I am not unaware of it. In the case of cannibalism at Montauk, I had not really thought about that aspect. After receiving this letter, I suddenly found myself reading parts of a book entitled *The Truth Shall Set You Free*, by David Icke, an Englishman. Two people had sent me this book unsolicited as they figured I should know about it. It is a well researched book which mentions the Montauk Project briefly. I picked it up because I was interested in reading about George Bush and his family's alleged connection to the Nazis. I was led directly to a section on the Skull and Bones Society of which Bush and President Clinton are both members.

Icke's book explains the political connections of Prescott Bush, George's father. What was shocking was that it said that Prescott Bush was famous within the Skull and Bones Society for having conducted a raid on the grave of the last Native American warrior, Geronimo. The story relayed is that in May 1918, Bush and five other members of Skull and Bones robbed Geronimo's grave at Fort Sill, Oklahoma, taking away artifacts and the skull of the Apache leader. These were taken back to the Skull and Bones headquarters at Yale for use in rituals. The source for this information comes from the internal history of the Skull and Bones Society which was quoted to Ned Anderson, the Tribal Chairman of the San Carlos Apache Tribe, when he was negotiating to retrieve the remains of Geronimo. Icke also quotes a 1989 *New Yorker* article where a member of the society recalled seeing some 30 human skulls in their "tomb".

What does this have to do with cannibalism at Montauk?

Apparently, when you consider the synchronicity, quite a bit. If you refer to Chapter 4 of this book, *The Cameron Lineage*, you will note that it was a matriarch of the Cameron family who helps to underwrite Yale University, the home of the Skull and Bones Society. Icke's research on Skull and Bones indicates that it was introduced in the early to middle 1800s as "Chapter 322 of a German secret society" known at one time as the "Brotherhood of Death". Here we have both the German and Cameron connection showing their heads once again.

According to Icke, the Skull and Bones Society is deeply racist and is founded on profits from illegal drug sales. He gives considerably more details, including its connections to key families of the Eastern Establishment. Their headquarters is literally a tomb located at Yale University which is completely inaccessible to the public or other Yale students.

My research indicates that the "Brotherhood of Death" is also known as the Liebenblut or in German, the "blood letters". In other words, they let blood. This is a group which seeks to maintain their own continuity of consciousness above all others. They are the ones who regulate the extraction of occultum in Egypt and preserve it for themselves. Their association with Tibet is strongly implied as well, but their presence in that area is not as well documented. It is interesting to note that George Bush is politically known for his close ties to Communist China.

In the previous chapter, Crowley referred to the "negative aspect" of the Atlantean civilization which mined Zro or occultum on the backs of a servile race who were treated like dirt and left to die in forced labor camps. All of this takes on a little more meaning when we consider today's society. We are not in a forced labor camp, but the average person is in a position where he has to be a "working stiff" in order to survive. People are doped by the media and consumerism. No matter how much dissent is allowed, most people are serving a powerful elite whose main interest is preserving their own power base. The conspiracies of banks and big corporations has already been beaten to death in many books on the subject. At the most powerful level of civilization, there are conscious entities who seek to maintain themselves through the *a priori* substance to matter itself: occultum.

This explains the fascination with skulls and bones. These elitists are not surrounding themselves with skulls and implements of the occult simply to amuse themselves or frighten the new fraternity pledge. They are cannibals consuming the essence of what is in the bones themselves. Sometimes it is a literal consumption of the residual white gold or occultum that remains in the bones or with the body after death. Other times, it is for the pure occult significance of having a skull like Geronimo's in order to symbolize the complete conquest of the last Native American hero. There are also more grisly ceremonies that include the consumption of the "live" pineal gland at the moment of sacrifice of a human being or animal. This is called "the Obscene Rite".

With regard to the actual content of the bones being consumed for their minerals, the chemistry of the brain testifies to such a potential. When gold or any of the other platinum group elements enter the bloodstream, they eventually find their way into the brain via a filter function. Once inside the blood vessels of the brain, these elements mix with hormones and other biochemical components. The result of this is that the molecules of the platinum group elements become larger than their original size prior to entering the brain. Thus, the elements cannot leave the blood circulatory system of the brain. From this position, the platinum elements mine themselves into the skeletal structure of the skull and remain with the actual bones. This can be scientifically proven. Elements in the soil will find their way into the diet of the people and thus into their bone chemistry. If the soil is rich in occultum, it will come to rest in the bones. Other esoteric properties may apply to consuming the bones as well. For example, I have heard that thulium will also enter the brain in a manner similar to the platinum group. As said before, this area requires more research.

With the above, we can finally answer the mystery of the Montauks and the disappearance of the pyramids that once embellished the eastern tip of Long Island. The Montauks, particularly the Pharoah family itself, were the royal tribe. There is no mistaking this if you see the pictures of the family, particularly the earlier generations. We also know that the Montauks engaged in ceremonies beneath the pyramids. These rituals were designed to create biochemical changes in the bloodstream through the ductless glands and ultimately secrete the white gold into their system.

While I cannot document all of the above in a legal format, the handwriting is on the wall in big letters. My entire investigation was fostered and ignited by my contact with the medicine women of the Montauk tribe. It is only appropriate that I should thank them and end my quest (for the time being) by acknowledging the circumstances which have led to their so called "extinction".

It was long ago that Gale Evening Star's grandfather participated in ceremonies beneath the Montauk pyramids. There were also many before him of which we have no historical record. Isn't it ironic that, despite the annihilation of his people and their sacred ground, the vestigial memory of this man's own third eye initiations has led us all to the trail of a new understanding which can ultimately overturn the interests which dismantled the pyramids.

With regard to the cannibalism mentioned above, it forces us to ask a question. Who are the true savages?

Of course, a question like that can make one's blood boil if he or she is not balanced. When certain white men referred to the indigenous natives as savages, it did not help the greater good. It only helped a ruling elite. Referring to white men as savages does not help matters either, nor does it serve to become angry at the ruling elite. They hold too many cards to fight openly. What we are dealing with here is the factor of evil. This again makes us look at the Black Sun, the deepest irreducible archetype of the soul. It is the embodiment of all creation and includes both good and evil.

It was this concept which led the ancient Bon priests to develop a doctrine to balance good with evil. If one force outweighed the other one, it created problems in the continuum. This balancing of good with evil evolved into the most sacred rite of the Bons but was only to be performed by those who were trained to the highest degree. It was this ritual, or an extension of it, which Karl Haushofer was attempting when he, as a mentor, unleashed Hitler on the world. If we give Hitler the benefit of the doubt, we can say that he assumed the mantle of the Christ-Antichrist in order to open the doorway to a new age. This is not my personal opinion, but it is a belief shared by many esotericists, particularly those of German persuasion. It was the stirring up of these polarized energies which was designed to balance the good and evil in the world.

Whether or not Hitler was a good magician or bad magician, or the tool of such, is not the point. Hitler either stirred up those energies himself or was directed in his efforts by occult forces. The result of his life, as we know it historically, was that people experienced horror and death in an aggrandized fashion. By studying his trail and that of the German esotericists, we can view the source of creation itself: the Black Sun. This principle is without judgement and without solace. It is simply creation.

In the Biblical story of Jesus dying on the cross, it was only when the Black Sun appeared in the form of an eclipse that He gave up the ghost and returned to the Father. Of course, we know the Black Sun in its feminine aspect as well.

There is also a gift in all of this. For aeons past, the principle of the Black Sun was only for the ruling elite. It was their grandest secret and they surrounded it with images of evil, if only to scare us away. Today, it has come into full view for the world to see. The powers of creation can be accessed by any free soul who wishes to reach for them. The Black Sun is alive and kicking and is no longer reserved for those who would perpetrate evil against man or life. It breathes the fire of life and love. It is the hidden god, Mon, talking. In this sense, it is also the ultimate synchronicity in terms of puns. It is MON-TALK!

AUTHOR'S NOTE

There are a couple of points I would like to share with all of you readers. The first one does not even deserve to be in the book and that has to do with the selling of "white gold" in the "New Age" forum. Many people are selling substances they call "white gold" which have absolutely nothing to do with the contents I have mentioned in *The Black Sun*. It has become a fad. Further, one man has sold shares and grossed a sum of ten millions dollars while he builds a facility to produce this noble elixir. This means about 10,000 people were taken in on a hope and a promise. Do not believe everything you hear. This is a very sordid story and one I do not care to elaborate on. New Age people are now being targeted for all sorts of scams, particularly in the financial arena. As the Romans used to say, "Caveat emptor" (buyer beware).

On another note, I would like to take some action regarding the occult forces at Montauk. I had hoped that circulation of *Pyramids of Montauk* would enable the natives to take back Camp Hero. Unfortunately, this has bogged down. Instead of relying on bureaucratic maneuvers, I would like to invite some of you in the reading audience to participate directly in doing a clearing at Montauk. This invitation is to shaman types and is not intended for curious people. Those of you who read this will know who you are. Costs may be involved depending on various factors, but this not a tour. I should also warn you that it is typical for shamans or psychics to visit Montauk and return with their tail between their legs. This is for a select group only, and again, you will know who you are. If you are interested, drop a line to me via the publisher's address. Your name will be kept on file and information will be circulated to you at a later date as plans take shape. This event is tentatively planned for 1998 and may recur in subsequent years.

BIBLIOGRAPHY

Ampruster, Howard Watson *Treason's Pease: German Dyes and American Dupes*, The Beechurst Press, New York ©1947

Anderson, Ken *Hitler and the Occult,* Prometheus Books, Amherst New York ©1995

Aoumiel *Dancing Shadows,* Llewellyn ©1994

Blank, Jonah *Arrow of the Blue-Skinned God: Replacing the Ramayana Through India,* Houghton Mifflin Company, Boston New York, London ©1992

Blavatsky, Madame *The Secret Doctrine*, Volumes I & II, The Theosophy Company, Los Angeles

Bramley, William *The Gods of Eden,* Avon Books, NY ©1990

Brown, Anthony Cave *Wild Bill Donovan: The Last Hero,* Times Books, New York ©1982

Bernhard, Dr. Raymond *The Hollow Earth*, Carol Publishing Group, Secaucus, NJ ©1969

Bernhart, Wilhelm and Buechner, Howard *Adolph Hitler and the Secrets of the Holy Lance,* Thunderbird Press, Inc., Metairie, LA ©1988

Bernhart, Wilhelm and Buechner, Howard *Hitler's Ashes* Thunderbird Press, Inc., Metairie, LA ©1989

Buechner, Howard *Emerald Cup — Ark of Gold: The Quest of SS Lt. Otto Rahn of the Third Reich,* Thunderbird Press, Inc. Metairie, LA ©1991

Burton, Richard Francis (translator) *The Book of the Thousand Nights and a Night* (Three Volumes) The Heritage Press, New York ©1962

Bird, Eugene K. *Prisoner #7 Rudolf Hess*, The Viking Press, New York ©1974

Cameron, Ian *Antarctica: The Last Continent,* Little, Brown and Company, Boston, Toronto ©1974

Casey, William *The Secret War Against Hitler,* Gegnery Gateway, Washington, D.C. ©1988

Cathie, Bruce L. *The Harmonic Conquest of Space,* Adventures Unlimited, Stele IL ©1995

Childress, David Hatcher *Lost Cities of China, Central Asia & India,* Adventures Unlimited, Stele, IL ©1991

Childress, David Hatcher *Lost Cities and Ancient Mysteries of Africa & Arabia,* 1993, Adventures Unlimited, Stele, IL ©1991

Coats, Callum *Living Energies: An Exposition of Concepts Related to the Theories of Viktor Schauberger,* Gateway Books, Bath, United Kingdom © unknown

Crowley, Aleister *The Book of Thoth,* U.S. Games Systems, Stamford, Connecticut

Crowley, Aleister *LIBER LI The Lost Continent,* Stellar Visions, San Francisco ©1986

de la Croix, Robert *Mysteries of the North Pole,* The John Day Company, New York ©1956

Dunlop, Richard *Donovan, American's Master Spy,* Rand McNally & Co, Chicago, New York, San Francisco ©1982

Farago, Ladislas *Aftermath: Martin Bormann and the Fourth Reich,* Simon and Schuster, New York ©1974

Ford, Corey *Donovan of O.S.S.,* Little Brown and Co. (Canada) Limited ©1970

Germine, Thomas Jude *Apokalypso* (Winter/Spring 1997) Apokalypso, PO Box 782, Chester, New Jersey 07930

Godwin, Joscelyn *Arktos: The Polar Myth in Science, Symbolism, and Nazi Survival,* Adventures Unlimited, Stele, IL ©1993

The German Research Project, a compilation of a vast amount of information on secret and suppressed German technology. For further information, send $5.00 for a catolog to German Research Project, PO Box 7, Gorman, California 93243-0007.

Grant, Kenneth *Outside the Circles of Time,* Frederick Muller Ltd., London ©1980

Hancock, Graham, *The Sign and the Seal,* Simon & Schuster, New York ©1992

Higham, Charles *American Swastika*, Doubleday & Company, Inc., Garden City, New York ©1985

Howard, Michael *The Occult Conspiracy,* Destiny Books, Rochester, Vermont ©1989

Hunt, Linda *Secret Agenda: The United States Government, Nazi Scientists and Project Paperclip, 1945 to 1990*, St. Martin's Press New York, ©1991

Icke, David *...and the truth shall set you free*, Bridge of Love Islr of Wight, UK ©1995

Infield, Glenn B. *Skorzeny: Hitler's Commando*, St. Martin's Press New York ©1981

Kersten, Felix *The Kersten Memoirs,* Howard Fertig, New York

Levenda, Peter *Unholy Alliance: A History of Nazi Involvement with the Occult,* Avon Books, New York ©1995

Lovecraft, H.P. and others *Tales of the Cthulhu Mythos,* Ballantine Books, New York ©1969

Mickleburgh, Edwin *Beyond the Frozen Sea: Visions of Antarctica*, St. Martin's Press, New York ©1987

Miller, Marvin D. *Terminating the "Socially Inadequate"* Malamud-Rose, Publisher, 38 Stoneywood Rose, Commack, NY 11725 ©1993

Miller, Marvin D. *Wanderlich's Salute,* Malamud-Rose, Publisher 38 Stoneywood Rose,Commack, NY 11725 ©1983

Mitchell, John *Secrets of the Stones,* Inner Traditions International Ltd., Rochester, VT ©1989

Pace, Mildred Mastin *Wrapped for Eternity: The Story of the Egyptian Mummy*, McGraw-Hill Book Company, ©1974

Padfield, Peter *Himmler: Reichsführer-SS*, Henry Holt and Company, New York ©1990

Pauwels, Louis and Bergier, Jacques *The Morning of the Magicians*,Stein and Day, New York ©1960

Rattray, Everett T. *The South Fork: The Land and the People of Eastern Long Island*, Random House, New York ©1979

Rodgers, Eugene *Beyond the Barrier: The Story of Byrd's First Expedition to Antarctive*, Naval Institute Press, Annapolis, MD ©1990

Skinner, Stephen (editor) *The Magical Diaries of Aleister Crowley,* Samuel Weiser Inc.,York Beach, ME ©1979

Sklar, Dusty *The Nazis and the Occult,* Dorset Press, NY ©1977

Stafford, David *Camp X*, Dodd, Mead & Co., New York ©1986

Starfire, Volume I, No. 3, Ordo Templi Orientis

Stein, R.A. *Tibetan Civilization*, Stanford University Press ©1972

Suster, Gerald *Hitler Black Magician*, Skoob Books Ltd., London ©1996

Swearingen, Ben E. *The Mystery of Hermann Goerging's Suicide*, Harcourt Brace Jovanovich, San Diego, New York, London ©1985, 1984

Thomas, Gordon *Journey Into Madness: The True Story of Secret CIA Mind Control and Medical Abuse*, Bantam Books NY ©1989

van Helsing, Jan *Secret Societies and Their Power in the 20th Century,* Ewertverlag, PO Box 35290 Playa del Inglés, Gran Canaria, Spain ©1995, Telephone *49-4964-1363, Fax *49-4964-1831

Wade, Wyn Craig *The Fiery Cross: The Ku Klux Klan in America*, Simon and Schuster, New York ©1987

Whalen, Richard J. *The Founding Father: The Story of Joseph P. Kennedy*, An N.A.L. Worldbook, The New American Library, ©1964

Wilson, Thomas *THE SWASTIKA: The Earliest Known Symbol, and its Migrations; with Observations on the Migration of Certain Industries in Prehistoric Times* (From the Report of the U.S. National Museum for 1984, pages 757-1011, with plates 1-25 and figures 1-374, Smithsonian Institution, US National Museum) Washington: Government Printing Office, 1896.

SELECTED INDEX

A

abominable snowman   40
aboriginal Canadians 156
aboriginal tribes   234
Abraham   138-139
Abydos   253-254
Academy of Natural Sciences of
    Philadelphia   209
Adam   139
Adam and Eve   251
Adam Kadmon   77
Adirondacks   52
Adolp Hitler Boulevard   32
Adonai   250
Adonis   250
Agartha (aka: Akkadia, Arcadia or
    Aryana)   213
ahimsa   97
Ahmroun   67, 145
Ahnenerbe 209
Al-Khemeia   253
Alaric   244
Albert's Landing   43
alchemy   235, 253
Aldebaran   173
Alhajar Alsad, the Happiest
    Stone   139
Alien Property Custodian   194
Allah   138, 151, 168
Amagansett   31, 42, 61, 262
Amon, Amoun, Amon Ra, Amoun
    Ra 235-236
Howard Watson Ampruster   190
Andromeda   182
Andromeda Device   182
Col. Burton Andrus and son   127
Antarctic, Antarctica   41, 121,
    197-202
antematter   251
Anti-Defamation League   98
Anti-Nazi League   193
Anti-Semitism 37, 98, 129
Antichrist   52, 242, 279
antimatter   251
Arabia   137
Arabian Nights   141-144, 151
Arabic   101, 149, 151
Arabs   140, 141, 147, 148, 159,
    249, 253
Aramaiti   219
Ararat   103

Arch of Titus 244
Arctic, Arctic Canada   159-160
Arcturus   241
Argentina   134, 135
Ark, Ark of the Covenant   131, 240,
    241-249, 263, 267, 273
Arktos   241
Kenneth Arnold   169
King Arthur   149, 241
Kenn Arthur   38, 168, 233
Aryan, Aryan Race, Aryans   25, 36,
    44, 45, 62, 69, 75, 99, 100, 103,
    109, 137, 160, 173, 213, 214,
    219, 249, 257
Aryan Hittites   249
Ashdown Forest   49
Assassins   49
Atlantis, Atlanteans, Atlantean
    civilization 167, 272-273, 276
Atlas   272
Augsborg   174
Auschwitz   190, 21
Axis   63, 130, 246

B

Babalon   48
Babalon Working   18, 55
Babylon   103, 128, 156, 168
Francis Bacon   262
Donald Balcuns   39
Baphomet   65, 157, 242
Barbary pirates   214
Howard Barkway   147-148
Marshall Barnes   27
Battle of Britain   175
Bayer   195
the Beast 100, 242
Ben Cameron   45
Berlin   97, 131, 163, 213, 216-217
Bermuda Triangle   60
Captain Wilhelm Bernhard   116, 121
Bhagdivad Gita   108
Al Bielek   16, 25, 31, 92-95
bigfoot   40
Bimini   273
Birth of a Nation (film)   45-46
bitumen   262-266
Black Knights   99, 109, 172
black magic   254
black pitch in mummies   262-266

Black Stone   137, 140
Lords of the Black Stone   172
Black Sun   24, 27, 154, 156, 172,
    174, 220, 236, 240, 242, 270,
    278, 279
Madame Blavatsky   143, 167, 215,
    235, 249, 257
Block Island (New York)   154
blue blood(s)   77, 257-259
Blue Race   257-260, 268
B'nai Brith   98
Eric A. Boerner   186
Bon (religion)   37, 217-230
    Bon meetings   37-39, 43-44
Bonpo Chronicles   226, 233
Bonpos   219
Book of the Law   27, 232, 270
Martin Bormann   112, 123, 189,
    196
Brahma   242
Brandenburg   175
Eva Braun   116
Breslau   119
"a man from Breslau"   119
British authorities (in
    Shangtse)   211
British intelligence   176
Brookhaven   14,
Brookhaven Labs 14, 22, 32
Brotherhood of Death   276
Brotherhood of the Snake
    Vril   59
Brothers of the Light   172
Brüder Des Lichts   172
Bruno Hauptmann   61
Buddha   36
Buddhism   207, 223
Buddhists   220-221, 227-229
Budge   253, 264, 268
Colonel Howard A. Buechner   116,
    121
William Bullitt   63
(German Bund) Bund   14, 32, 37,
    193
(Hitler's) bunker   115, 121, 122
Sir Richard Burton   138, 226
George Bush   275
Prescott Bush   275
Admiral Richard Byrd   41, 197,
    200-201

C

C-130   22
Cabalistic Tree of Life   222

Cairo   263, 264
Calvinist movement   78
Camelot   64
Alexander Duncan Cameron, Sr.
    47, 70
Alexander Duncan Cameron, Jr.   16,
    25, 94-95, 116, 145, 147
Ewen Cameron   47-53, 70, 73, 77, 85
Hugh Cameron   123
Lady Cameron   56-58, 64, 67
Lord Cameron   56-58
Marjorie Cameron   18, 27, 55, 67
Cameron brothers   88
Cameron clan (family and name)   26,
    55-58, 59, 64, 67, 73, 79, 85,
    145-147, 149, 157, 276
Cameronian regiment   78
Camp Hero   15, 25, 29, 39, 84,106
Camp Siegfried   32-34, 193
Camp X   204, 206
Stan Campbell   94
Captured German Documents   203,
    209
catacombs of Montauk   31
Cathar   131
Cathar fortress of Montsegur
    Montsegur   133-134, 244
Bruce Cathie   237
Celtic cross   133
Celtic rituals   257
Central Tibet   209
Charlemagne   76, 131, 145
chi   167
chia   167
Chou En Lai   207
Christ   52, 68, 140, 145-146, 241-242,
    267, 279
Christian Gnostic   131
Christianity   102
Christians   68, 253, 270
President Clinton   22, 275
Cloning   122
Coanda Effect   174
Henri Coanda   174
Callum Coats   188
Cold Spring Harbor   25, 33, 192
Congressional Committee on
    Un-American Activities   38
Constantine   144
U.S. Constitution   23
Robert (Bob) Cooper   20, 36
Cosmotron Project   186
Jacques Cousteau   170

288

Aleister Crowley   17, 27, 49, 65,
    95, 105, 123, 143-144, 147,
    152, 164, 166, 227-228, 232,
    242, 249, 265, 267-274
Amado Crowley   18-19
Leo Crowley   193-194
Cthulu   268

D

Dalai (word meaning)   234
Dalai Lama   171, 204-207, 222,
    227-229, 271
Das Vril Projekt   163
Jacque de Molay   65
Dead Sea Scrolls   145
Delta-T antenna   91, 249
Dervishes   215
dirigibles   182
DNA   251, 260, 263, 272
Brooke Dolan   204-207, 209
Dome of the Rock   145
Karl Dönitz   198
Robert Donner   186
William J. "Wild Bill"
    Donovan   125-126, 191-192,
    195, 204-206, 245
Dorjieff   216
Doug Curtis   85-86
Dr. Mengele   122
Dravidian peoples   214
Druids   57, 78, 257
Dugphas   217
Allen Dulles   47, 123, 194, 196
John Foster Dulles   194

E

Earth's grid   217
Eastern Oil Company   187
Egypt   28, 102, 135, 137, 140,
    219, 228, 235, 237, 250, 260-
    264, 275
Egyptian Book of the Dead   264
Egyptian pyramids (see pyramids)
Egyptians   102, 160, 231, 235,
    249, 260-264
General Eisenhower   115, 245
El Shaddai   99
Elder Gods   167, 268
Elder Race   151, 165, 173, 251,
    253, 257, 259, 268 *See also*
    Blue Race

Electric Lamp Service Company   148
U.S.S. Eldridge   13, 16
elixir of the gods   249
Elohim   165, 166, 173, 251 *See also*
    the Blue Race
Enochian (language)   168
erbia   158
Ethiopia   245
eugenics   33, 192
Externsteine   68, 245
Eye of Horus   70, 249

F

Face on Mars   163, 238
Faraday   164
Faraday cage   165
female Masons   262
Ferguson Radio Corporation   148
Final Solution   108
Fireman's Bunker   39
the Flood (cataclysm)   139
fluidics (technology of)   174
Flying Turtle   183
foo fighters   183
John Ford   21, 43
Fordham University   85
Forgotten Ones   163, 267
Fort Pond Bay   30
Fourth Reich   72, 136, 195
Francisco Franco   134
Frankfurt   91, 99, 171
Frankfurt Book Fair   91
Freemasonry   108
Friday the Thirteenth   59
Buckminster Fuller   158

G

(Angel) Gabriel   139
Gale Evening Star   278
Lion Gardiner   75-76, 79, 81-84
The Gardiner Family   81-84
James Gaussman   238
General Reinhard Gehlen   195-196
genetics   122, 176
Geneva Rules of War   133
Genghis Khan   156, 234-235
Geopolitics   216
Karl Gerchsheimer   186
German Gardens   33
German myths   68
German Research Project   170
German rocket scientists   183

289

German rocket technology 85
Germany 25
Geronimo 275
Gestapo 108, 163
Sam Giancana 50
Gnostic(s) 68, 147, 220
Josef Goebbels 209
Emma Göering 125
Hermann Göering 62, 124-128, 197
Goethe 153
Goetherium 153
Golden Tear of Horus 249
Goody Garlick 82-83
Tom Gorman 170
Grail Christianity 145, 149
Kenneth Grant 138, 167, 235-236,
    271
Great Pyramid 102-103, 237, 140,
    261-262
"the Man with the Green
    Gloves" 213-214
Greenland Colony 75
grid 217
Guardian of the Key "the Man with
    the Green Gloves" 213-214
G.I. Gurdjieff 214-216

H

HAARP 188
James Hamill 85-90
Mark Hamill 85-90, 94-95
Duke of Hamilton 214
Hapsburg Museum 121
Maximilian Hartmann 199
Haunebu flying craft 176-182
Karl Haushofer 37, 152, 172, 213-
    217, 240, 279
Albrecht Haushofer 214
Healing Tao 167-168
Hebe (the god) 102-103
Hebrew 101
Hebrews 249-250
Hebrides 102
Hebron 102
hemocyanin 259
hemoglobin 259
Rudolph Hess 47, 85, 174, 196,
    214, 216
Michael Hesseman 171
Heinrich Himmler 67, 69, 106,
    110-112, 124, 132-133, 172,
    175, 183-184, 210, 245
Hinayana Buddhism 221

Hindu tantra (See tantra: sexual
    magick)
Hindu trinity 242
Hindus 137, 160, 214
Hiram Abiff 250
Hitler 23, 25, 32, 48, 49, 60, 67, 91,
    97, 109-122, 130, 149, 152, 174,
    183-185, 194, 213, 215, 279
Hitler's dental x-rays 117
Hoechst company 195
the holocaust 135
Holocaust Remembrance Day 37
Holy 68, 103, 109, 131
Holy Grail 68, 76, 109, 144, 240-242,
    245
Holy Lance 199
Holy of Holies 68, 246, 247
Holy Qabala 247-248
Holy Stone 139
J. Edgar Hoover 32
Hor, Hors 234-235
Horus 235, 255
House of Orange 75-79
House of Windsor 78
Diana Hubbard 57
L. Ron Hubbard 27, 53, 55, 57, 116,
    214, 251
James J. Hurtak 183-184
Sadam Hussein 144
Hyperborea 151, 241

I

I.G. Farben 189-195
Illuminati 48
Irish priests 78
irriculum 248
Ishmael 137
Islam 137-145, 149
Islamic empire 242
Isle of Skye 64, 145
Isle of Wight 63
Israel 99, 124

J

Justice Robert H. Jackson 126
Sharon Jackson 229, 231, 233
Jacob 101
Jacobites 78
Jehovah 100
Jerusalem 102, 144
Jesus 68, 141, 225, 270

Jewish Talmud   100, 247
Jews   32, 37, 62, 97-105, 109, 126,
    129-130, 144, 211, 216, 242,
    243, 259
Josephine (Bonapart)   262
Journal of the Will   95
Judah   101
Carl Jung   271

K

Kaaba   138-140
Otto Kahn   192
Kaiser Wilhelm   31, 42
Kalachakra, Wheel of Time
    220-223
Kali   138, 220, 222
law of karma   108
Felix Kersten   106-112
the Kennedys   46, 50, 59-65, 73
John F. Kennedy   50, 65
John F. Kennedy, Jr.   61
Joseph Kennedy, Sr.   50, 62-63
Robert F. Kennedy   50, 60-61
Tyler Kent   63-64
Keys of Enoch   168
Keys of Solomon   168
KGB   118
Kham   235, 253
Khem   235, 253, 259, 272
Khemeia   254
Captain Kidd   84
Kiswat   138
Dr. Ko   107
Knights Templar   48, 65, 75, 97,
    131, 145, 174-175, 242
KKK   33, 45, 59
Kublai Khan   234

L

LAM   267-271
lama(s)   227, 270
Languedoc province   244
Lebensraum   90, 216
Left Eye of Horus   249
Leif Erickson   75
Lemuria   219
Peter Levenda   209, 211
Elphias Levi   164, 242
Mark Levinson   86
Willy Ley   163
Liebenblut   276
Lindbergh   61

The Link   63
Long Island   14, 15, 32-33, 40, 45,
    75, 86, 105, 219, 231, 278
Long Island UFO Network   21, 43
Lord Bulwer-Lytton   164
H.P. Lovecraft   163, 267, 268
LSD   60
George Lucas   95, 105, 227
Luftwaffe   125
Luminous Lodge   163, 169, 172

M

M15
    British intelligence service   62
Maat   143
Madagascar   108
Mahayana Buddhism   221
Maitreya   271
Manisolas   160
Manitou   71
Mantak Chia   167
Mao Tse Tung   207
Mar del Plata, Argentina   116
Marduk   173
Mars   49, 165, 173, 235, 257
James E. Markham   194
Martha's Vineyard   50
Mary   145
MASH-MAK   167
Mashomak Point   167
Masons   48, 200, 250
Mecca   137
Melchizedek   103
Men-an-Tol   19
Menthu   232, 235
"Mer"   225, 229
Merkers, Germany   245
Merlin   225
Mermaid   225
Meru Foundation   223
Roddie Minor   267
Mount Meru   160, 223, 260
Messershmidt aircraft facility   174
Marvin D. Miller   33
Mithra   219
Mittelwurk   89
MK-Ultra   47
Mon (as hidden god)   235-236, 270,
    279
Mon (as people or religion)   158, 232
monazite   158
Mongetucksee   231
Mongkut   231-232

Mongols   234-235
Mönlam festival   270-271
monochord   176
Montauk   13, 16, 25, 29, 30, 37,
   39, 43, 55, 59, 60, 73, 91, 97,
   105, 106, 115, 122, 147-148,
   154, 158, 165, 171, 174, 188,
   203, 243, 262, 265, 267, 232-
   233, 275
Montauk Project   13-17, 25, 44, 59,
   86, 91, 94-97, 165, 185-186,
   275
The Montauk Pulse newsletter
   20, 233
Montauk Air Force Station   15,
Montauk Boys   229
Montauk Chair   16
Montauk Downs   40
Montauk Manor   30
Montauk Point   15, 25, 61, 75, 167
Montauk pyramids
   pyramids   19, 278
Montauk Shaman   229, 231
Montauk Tower   31
Montauk tribal leader   20
Montauks, Montaukets, Montauk
   tribe   19, 20, 22, 75-76, 167,
   229, 231, 278
Montauk's beast "Junior"   238
Montsegur   131-133, 244
Mont(h)u   233, 235
James D. Mooney   62
Dr. Morell (Hitler's doctor)
   111-113
Michael Morgan   168
morphogenetic grid   159, 161, 184,
   187, 195, 240, 241
   grid   217
morphology   71
Moses 102, 145, 223, 225, 243, 250
Mu   219
MUFON   (Mutual UFO Network)
   171
Muhamet   139-141, 145
Multiple Personality Disorder   51
mummia   262-266
mummies   261-266
mummification   261-266
mummy dust   262-266
Munich   127
Mura or Mu-Ra   219, 221
Muslims   100, 138
Benito Mussolini   130-131, 136,
   245

N

Napeague strip   40
Napoleon   261-262
NASA   124
Gamal Nasser   196
National Archives   203, 209, 215
(German) Nature and Culture
   Movement   69
Nazi gold   25
Nazi treasure   115, 34
Neuschwabenland   197-202
Preston Nichols   15, 16, 25, 30, 41,
   59, 85, 94-95, 115, 145, 147-148,
   156, 206, 231
Bob Nichols   33, 232
Ginny Nichols   231, 232
Niul   102
Noah   103, 139, 263
Noah's Ark   103, 263
Norsemen in North America   75
NSA, National Security Agency   16
Nuremburg   123, 133, 198
Nuremburg Prison   126
Nuremburg trials   47, 71

O

the Obscene Rite   277
occultum   248-256, 276-277
Odin   67, 70
the Old Universe   94
Olema   144
Olmolungring   222
Omar   144-145
Ong   160, 222
Lake Ontario   204
Oracle of Tibet   228
House of Orange   75-79
Orange-Nassau   75-79
Order of the Holy Lance   122
Ordo Templi Orientis (OTO)   46, 58,
   65, 128, 152, 267
Maria Orsic   172
Orthodox Jews   258
Orthodox teachings   259
Osiris   235, 254
Osman   149
OSS,Office of Strategic Services
   48, 123, 126, 191, 203-207, 246
Ottoman Empire   149
oxyhemocyanin   258

Oz   160, 222

P

Pali Canons   221
Project Paperclip   85-90
Catherine Parr   55
Parsons (family) 55, 79
Jack Parsons   18, 27, 55, 88, 163, 273
Samuel Parsons   81
General George Patton   245
Peenemünde   90, 183-184
Evita and Juan Peron   135
Persia   219, 263
Pharaohs of Egypt   19, 102
Pharoah (family of Montauk)   19, 76, 278
Philadelphia Experiment   13-16, 43, 46, 85-86, 105, 147
Philadelphia Experiment II   85-86
Phoenix Project   185
phosphorus   272
Picts   57
platinum group elements   255, 277
Point 103   159
The Protocols of the Elders of Zion   98
pyramids   69, 166 (also, see specific listings)
Pyramids of Giza   19, 140, 237
Pyramids of Shensi (see Shensi Pyramids)
pyschic driving (by Ewen Cameron   47
Pythagorean monochord   185
Pythagorus   154

Q

Q'ran   141
Queen Maud Land   197
Qumran   145

R

Ra   102, 219
Rabbi   102
radium   21
Otto Rahn   131 244-245
Raiders of the Lost Ark   105
Ramses II   102
rare earth elements   158
Trevor Ravenscroft   119, 121, 215

RCA   626
Red Sea   137
Reich Chancellery   118, 122
the Reichstag   213
"Remembrancers"   141
Rundflugzeug flying craft   175-182
Russian occupation of Berlin   115-119, 213
Rh negative blood   77, 258
Rig-Thula   215
Rig-Veda   166, 215
Right Eye of Horus   249
R'lyeh   268
RNA   251, 272
Romanovs   204
Edwin Rommel   189
Ronald Reagan   106
President Franklin D. Roosevelt   62-63, 194, 204, 206
Roosevelt Library   63
Roslin Institute   123
Roswell Incident   106, 170, 171
runes   67

S

S.D.I. (Strategic Defense Inititative)   22
sacred geometry   19, 70, 248
Sahara desert   137
sapphire tablets   248
Scarlet Woman   222, 235
Dr. Ernst Schäfer   209-211
Viktor Schauberger   175, 185-188
Walter Schauberger   185-187
Schindler's List   105
Helmar Schlact   189
schnorkel device   198
Dr. W.O. Schumann   173
Schutzstaffel (S.S.)   156
Arnold Schwarzenegger   62
Schwarze Sonne (S.S.)   156
Norman Schwarzkopf   61
Scota   102
Scotland Yard   63
Tom Scott   20, 36
The Secret Doctrine   143, 167
sexual magick   17, 220
Shahrázád   143-144
King Shahryár   141-144
Shakespeare   262
shakti   226
Shambhala   221, 222-223
Shangri-La   198, 202, 221

Queen of Sheba   138
Shelter Island   167
Shenrab   219-223
Shensi   206, 214, 219
Shensi pyramids   156, 214, 219,
    226, 237-239
Shi Yantra   223-224
shih kung   226
shilajit   265
Shiva   138, 242
Siddhartha Guatama   37, 221, 223
Sigrun   172
Siva   242
Otto Skorzeny   71, 129-137, 189,
    244, 264
Skull and Bones Society   275-276
Isle of Skye   64, 145
"Smithsonian-gate"   75
"Soap Bubbles"   183
Solomon   103, 144, 225, 243-244
Temple of Solomon   144, 243-244,
    250
Spandau prison   123
Spear of Destiny   119, 121, 199,
    215, 242
Sphinx   196
the Spider   136
SS   67, 87 107, 121, 122, 136, 156,
    160, 192, 195, 209-211, 245
SS-E-4   175
St. Germaine   262
Joseph Stalin   118, 214
Standard Gas and Electric
    Company   193
Star Wars   85, 94-95
Dr. Walter Johannes Stein   119
Stein Bank of Cologne   194
R.A. Stein   226, 233
Rudolph Steiner   152
Wendelle Stevens   183
General Joseph Stilwell   206, 232
Stockholm Syndrome   51
Stonehenge   19, 68
Stony Hill   42
Stuarts   77-79
submarine pen under Stoney Hill
    German submarines   42
Suffolk County   20
Sufi mystery schools   214
Sufis   144
SUMERAN   173
Sumeria   77, 184, 225
Sumerian Brotherhood of the Snake
    Vril Society   48, 77, 153

Sumerians   154
Mount Sumeru   225
Sumeru   225
Sun Mountain   225
superconductivity   255
swastika   154, 225, 268-269
Sweeney   58
synchronicity   18, 26, 56, 60, 88, 115,
    143, 148, 232
Synchrotron   186
Ladislas Szabo   199

T

Tahuti   70, 101, 140, 143, 226
tantra   220
Tarim Basin   214, 234
Tarot   102
Tartar   214, 234
Tenon, Stan   101, 223
Tesla   62
Wilhelm Teudt   69
Teutonic culture   67-73, 102
Teutonic myths   151
Teutonic Garden of Eden   151
Teutonic Order   172
Teutons   103
Thebes   226, 263
Thelema   144, 168
Fritz Thiessen   189
third eye   249
third eye initiations   249
Third Reich   25, 29, 62, 92, 97
Sir Jules Thorn   148-149
Thorn E.M.I.   105, 147-149, 241, 247
Thorwald   75
Thoth   70, 226
Thothrori   226
Thule   151-162, 268
Thule Society   48, 109, 172, 234
thulium   156-158, 277
Tibet   28, 37, 40, 94, 184, 202, 203-
    240, 248, 253, 260, 265, 276
Tibetan(s)   44, 90, 162, 203-240, 260,
    268
Tibetan Buddhism   207
Tibetan monks   211
Tibetan pyramids (see Shensi
    pyramids)
Titus   243
Tla or Tlas   272
To-Mera   260
Countess Tolstoy   204
Ilya Tolstoy   204-207

Leo Tolstoy   204
Tom Tubbs   29
Torah   102
Hugh Trevor-Roper   116
triple aura   93
President Truman   195
Tsongkhapa   270
Tualla   151
Tula   151, 156, 234
Tule   156
Tulee   234
Turkish empire   214
Tuule   156
TWA Flight 800   21

U

U-13 flying craft   175
U-530   116
Nazi U-boats   25, 29-30, 42-43,
    116, 117, 121, 198, 245
UFOs   41-43, 59, 160, 169-184,
    267
UFOlogy   163, 169-171
Uighurs   235
Universal Medicine   272-273
Universal Solvent   272
University of Munich   173
Upton, New York   186
Urs   235
Uther   149

V

V-2 rockets   88
V7 vertical takeoff aircraft   160
Jan van Helsing   91-99, 137, 152,
    163
Vedas   214
Venus   139
Victor Emanuel   194
Vienna   121, 131, 148
Vienna-Neustadt   183
Vikings   71, 215
Vishnu   242
Visigoths   244
V.I.T.R.I.O.L.   272
Werner von Braun   88
John von Neumann   14, 87
Baron Rudolf von Sebottendorf
    152
vril (as energy)   162-168, 271
Vrihl   166
Vril (language)   103
Vril Project   169-185

Vril Society   48, 77, 153
vril spot   168
Vril flying craft   169-184
Vril-ya   165-166

W

Lothar Waiz   175
Walpurgisnacht   128
Paul Warburg   192
Westphalia   67
Wewelsburg   67-69, 109 122, 245
The White Pyramid   238
white gold   249-256
whore of Babalon   235
witchcraft   81-84
William and Mary   78
William III of Orange   78
Marcus Wilson   16
Preston Wilson   16
Robert Anton Wilson   56
Thomas Wilson   268
Woodrow Wilson   45-46
Wilson brothers   18, 147-148
Wilsons   18, 55-56, 147
Windsor   78
Windsor Castle   78
General Wolff   245
Wyandanch (Chief)   75, 231

X

Xian, China   238

Y

Yale University   58, 276
Yaphank   32, 193
Yellow Hats   217
Yeo-Thomas   134
Yeshua   226
Yokar   168
YVYW (Yod Hé Vod Hé)   100

Z

Zemzem   139
the Zeppelin company   182
zeppelins   43
zirconium   161
Zro   272-273, 276

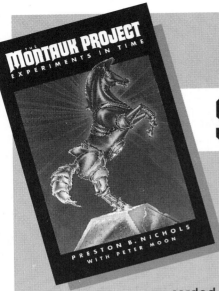

THE BIGGEST
SECRET
EVER TOLD

The Montauk Project: *Experiments In Time* chronicles the most amazing and secretive research project in recorded history. Starting with the "Philadelphia Experiment" of 1943, the Office of Naval research employed Albert Einstein's Unified Field Theory in an attempt to make the *USS Eldridge*, a destroyer escort, invisible to radar. The *Eldridge* not only became invisible on radar screens — it disappeared from time and space as we know it with full scale teleportation of the ship and crew. "The Philadelphia Experiment" was a total disaster to the crew members aboard the Eldridge. Psychological disorders, physical trauma and even deaths were reported as a result of the experiment.

Forty years of massive research continued culminating in even more bizarre experiments that took place at Montauk Point, New York that actually tapped the powers of creation and manipulated time itself. *The Montauk Project* is a first hand account by Preston Nichols, a technician who worked on the project. He has survived threats and attempts to brainwash his memory of what occurred. A fascinating account of the research, including the technological applications of changing time itself are given for the first time, along with Preston's intriguing personal story.

■ ■ ■ ■

160 pages, illustrations, photos and diagrams......$15.95

THE ASTONISHING
SEQUEL...

Montauk Revisited: Adventures in Synchronicity pursues the mysteries of time so intriguingly brought to light in *The Montauk Project: Experiments in Time*. *Montauk Revisited* unmasks the occult forces that were behind the science and technology used in the *Montauk Project*. An ornate tapestry is revealed which interweaves the mysterious associations of the Cameron clan with the genesis of American rocketry and the magick of Aleister Crowley, Jack Parsons and L. Ron Hubbard. Also included is the bizarre history of the electronic transistor and how it was developed by the E.T. Company, an apparent front for aliens.

Montauk Revisited carries forward with the Montauk investigation as Preston Nichols opens the door to Peter Moon and unleashes a host of incredible characters and new information. A startling scenario is depicted that reaches far beyond the scope of the first book.

The Montauk Project opened up the mystery of all mysteries. This sequel accelerates the pursuit.

■ ■ ■ ■

249 pages, illustrations, photos and diagrams......$19.95

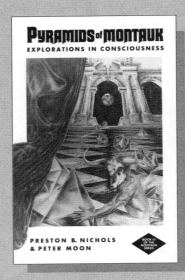

PYRAMIDS OF MONTAUK

EXPLORATIONS IN CONSCIOUSNESS

PRESTON B. NICHOLS
& PETER MOON

BOOK III
OF THE
MONTAUK
SERIES

THE ULTIMATE PROOF

Pyramids of Montauk: *Explorations In Consciousness* unveils the mysteries of Montauk Point and its select location for pyramids and time travel experimentation. An astonishing sequel to the *Montauk Project* and *Montauk Revisited*, this chapter of the legend awakens the consciousness of humanity to its ancient history and origins through the discovery of pyramids at Montauk. Their placement on sacred Native American ground opens the door to an unprecedented investigation of the mystery schools of Earth and their connection to Egypt, Atlantis, Mars and the star Sirius.

Preston Nichols continues to fascinate with an update on covert operations at Montauk Point that includes the discovery of a nuclear particle accelerator on the Montauk Base and the development of new psychotronic weapons.

Pyramids of Montauk propels us far beyond the adventures of the first two books and stirs the quest for future reality and the end time as we know it.

▲ ▲ ▲ ▲

256 pages, illustrations, photos and diagrams......$19.95

Journey to the stars–

with Preston Nichols & Peter Moon's

ENCOUNTER IN THE PLEIADES: AN INSIDE LOOK AT UFOs

★

*T*his is the incredible story of a man who found himself taken to the Pleiades where he was given a scientific education far beyond the horizons of anything taught in universities. For the first time, the personal history of Preston Nichols is revealed along with an avalanche of amazing information the world has not yet heard. A new look at Einstein and the history of physics gives unprecedented insight into the technology of flying saucers and their accompanying phenomena. Never before has the complex subject of UFOs been explained in such a simple language that will be appreciated by the scientist and understood by the layman.

Peter Moon adds further intrigue to the mix by divulging his part in a bizarre project which led him to Preston Nichols and the consequent release of this information. His account of the role of the Pleiades in ancient mythology sheds new light on the current predicament of Mankind and offers a path of hope for the future. The truth is revealed. The keys to the Pleiades are in hand and the gateway to the stars is open.   252 pages......$19.95

The Montauk Pulse™
A CHRONICLE OF TIME

A newsletter by the name of *The Montauk Pulse* went into print in the winter of 1993 to chronicle the events and discoveries regarding the ongoing investigation of the Montauk Project by Preston Nichols and Peter Moon. It has remained in print and been issued quarterly ever since. With a minimum of six pages and a distinct identity of its own, *The Pulse* will often comment on details and history that do not necessarily find their way into books.

Through 1995, The *Montauk Pulse* has included exciting new breakthroughs on the Montauk story as well as similarly related phenomena like the Philadelphia Experiment or other space-time projects. As of 1996, the scope of *The Pulse* will be expanded to embrace any new phenomena concerning the Nazis, Tibetans and any information regarding the various pursuits mentioned in *The Black Sun: Montauk's Nazi-Tibetan Connection*. Also included will be any new developments on the John Ford case and mysteries concerning Brookhaven Labs.

Subscribers are also offered discounts on most publications sold through Sky Books.

SkyBooks ORDER FORM

We wait for ALL checks to clear before shipping. This includes Priority Mail orders. If you want to speed delivery time, please send a U.S. Money Order or use MasterCard or Visa. Those orders will be shipped right away.
Complete this order form and send with payment or credit card information to:
Sky Books, Box 769, Westbury, New York 11590-0104

Name	
Address	
City	
State / Country	**Zip**
Daytime Phone (In case we have a question) ( )	

☐ **This is my first order**   ☐ **I have ordered before**   ☐ **This is a new address**

Method of Payment: ☐ **Visa**   ☐ **MasterCard**   ☐ **Money Order**   ☐ **Check**

—   —   —

Expiration Date   **Signature**

Title	Qty	Price
The Montauk Project: Experiments In Time...................$15.95		
Montauk Revisited: Adventures In Synchronicity $19.95		
Pyramids of Montauk: Explorations in Consciousness.....$19.95		
Encounter In The Pleiades: An Inside Look At UFOs $19.95		
The Black Sun: Montauk's Nazi-Tibetan Connection.......$19.95		
The Montauk Pulse (1 year subscription)......................$12.00		
The Montauk Pulse back issues (the first newsletter was Winter '93 and is issued quarterly)..................................$3.00 each List issues here ▼		
Subtotal		
For delivery in NY add 8.5% tax		
Shipping: see chart on the back of this page		
U.S. only: Priority Mail		
Total		

Thank you for your order. We appreciate your business.

SHIPPING INFORMATION

United States Shipping

Under $30.00 ....add $3.00
$30.01 — 60.00 ...add $4.00
$60.00 — $100.00 add $6.00
$100.01 and over ..add $8.00

Allow 30 days for delivery. For U.S. only: Priority Mail—add the following to the regular shipping charge: $3.00 for first item, $1.50 for each additional item.

Outside U.S. Shipping

Under $30.00.........add $8.00
$30.01 — 60.00...add $11.00
$60.00—$100.00 add $15.00
100.01 and over...add $20.00

These rates are for SURFACE SHIPPING ONLY. Do not add extra funds for air mail. Due to the vastly different costs for each country, we will not ship by air. Only Visa, Mastercard or checks drawn on a U.S. bank in U.S. funds will be accepted. (Eurochecks or Postal Money Orders can not be accepted.)